I0714715

Ancient Allies

LEGENDS OF LAIRHEIM

BOOK 2

Also By Tora Moon

Legends of Lairheim (Science-Fantasy)

Ancient Enemies (Book 1)
Ancient Allies (Book 2)
The Scourge Incursion (Book 3)
Exile's Vengeance (Book 4)
Redemption - A Novel

The Sentinel Witches (Urban Fantasy)

Crossroads to Destiny (Book 1)
Descent Into Darkness (Book 2)
Well of Sorrows (Book 3)

Indie Author Guides

Business & Accounting for Authors
Business Plans for Authors (forthcoming)

To get an up-to-date listing of all my books or to purchase visit
ToraMoon.com

LEGENDS OF LAIRHEIM

ANCIENT ALLIES

BOOK 2

TORA MOON

Lunar Alchemy Publishing

Ancient Allies, Legends of Lairheim Book 2
© 2016 by Tora Moon; 1st Edition
© 2024 by Tora Moon; 2nd Edition

All rights reserved. No part of this publication may be reproduced, distributed or transmitted in any form or by any electronic or mechanical means, including information storage and retrieval systems, without prior written permission by the author, except for the use of brief quotations in a book review.

Lunar Alchemy Publishing Company
ToraMoon.com

Publisher's Note: This is a work of fiction. Names, characters, places, and incidents are a product of the author's imagination. Locales and public names are sometimes used for atmospheric purposes. Any resemblance to actual people, living or dead, or to businesses, companies, events, institutions, or locales is completely coincidental. No AI was used in the creation of this story.

Cover design: Deranged Doctor Design
Map design: Tora Moon
Map illustrations licensed from Map Effects Fantasy Map Builder

Paperback ISBN: 978-1-946132-11-6
Ebook ISBN: 978-1-946132-05-5

ACKNOWLEDGMENTS

An author may sit alone at the computer, but no book is completed without help. A big shout out to my beta reader team: Angelique, and Kelly. I appreciate your comments and feedback which made this a much better story.

Thank you to all the authors I've had the pleasure of reading their stories and making me want to tell my own. Without story, this world would be a much poorer place.

And especially to my daughter, Sasha, you have made me become a better person by being your parent. I couldn't have asked for a more amazing daughter.

Thank you to all my readers. Thank you for spending time with my stories and letting me be a part of your life. I hope you love them as much I loved writing them.

To my daughter, Sasha.
Thank you for making me a better person. I love you.

EXTRAS

The world of Lairheim isn't a re-imagining of Earth. It has its own culture, language, and landmasses. I've created several extras and resources to help you enjoy this fantasy world more. You can find these on my website at: ***ToraMoon.com/Legends-Extras***.

Extras you may like:

Pronunciation audio - While the appendix includes a cast and glossary, fantasy names and words can be difficult to figure out how to say. I've recorded audios for each name and Posair word.

Maps - There is a map at the beginning of the book to help you orient into the world of Lairheim. A black and white pdf map is available to download for free. Or if you love maps, I've created a beautiful, hand-drawn, color map you can purchase.

Merchandise - I've created some fun merchandise centered around the books and the world of Lairheim. Check them out in my shop!

MAP OF LAIRHEIM

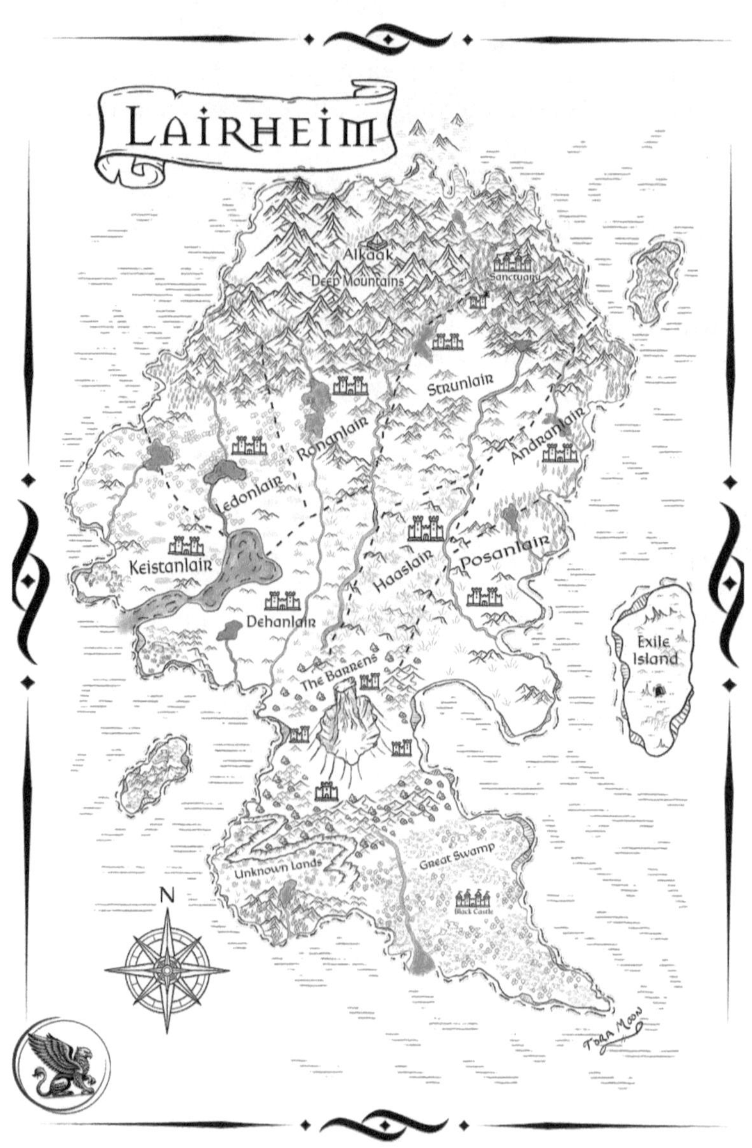

Prologue

Pe-te-tak, the captain of the scout ship, paced the tiny bridge. The vast star system assigned to them to explore was turning out to be a dud. So far, they hadn't discovered many life-supporting planets, and nothing worthwhile to take back to the Empire. Not even slaves. Tightly locked behind his personal shields, he trembled in fear. The punishment his ruthless conclave commander, Ke-ke-tak, would inflict on him if he returned empty-handed would be horrible. He'd rather not return home.

Except, if he failed to report, his sons would suffer a long time before finally being allowed to die. His concubines would endure even more. He had no choice but to return and face the consequences of his failure.

Plopping on his chair before his terminal, he punched up the most recent supply inventory and inwardly groaned. Only a double handful of slaves brought for food remained. They could drain slaves of emotions and blood for a finite period. Then he, as the captain, would get the honor of siphoning off the soul of the worthless body.

The translator slaves were still alive, but they couldn't touch them. He'd pay for it out of his hide if the expensive translators didn't survive because his crew was hungry. Consuming the junior officers would be more acceptable.

He tapped a fang with a long claw, pondering his next actions. He winced at the number of unused nucla fuel bars. Three. Not enough to go much farther and make it back home. Pe-te-tak glowered at the empty space zooming past the view screen. Time to turn around and face the punishment of his failure. Maybe the star charts he'd made of this system would keep his crew alive, although they'd be insufficient to save him.

"Captain, Captain!" his science officer cried, an unusual amount of emotion wafting off him in his excitement. "Look at this reading."

"Take care," Pe-te-tak cautioned. He looked at the report, then punched in the code to get a printout. He snatched it from the slot and scanned it carefully. Their luck had just changed! The readings showed the highest concentration of nucla from outside of their home star system, yet discovered. The precious mineral fueled the Empire's ships and machines. They'd almost exhausted their supply. Without it, they couldn't continue their glorious expansion and conquest.

"How far?" he asked, carefully tamping down his elation. One excited, emotional officer was more than this small ship needed. If the hungry crew smelled it, they'd storm the bridge. He noticed the officer had tucked most of his emotion behind his personal shield.

"A few paraclicks. We can be there in a few cycles. We have enough fuel to investigate it and get home."

"Let's go." He pointed a claw forward.

Four rotations later, they entered a cluttered star system. Fifty planets among thousands of asteroids orbited around one large sun. Their instruments went mad with danger warnings from the bright light spectrum. But the pull of the riches to be had from the huge nucla concentration would be worth the risk. The pilot guided them through the maze to where the readings originated.

Below them spun a small planet with two landmasses. One, a continent with an attached subcontinent, and the other a large island.

The science officer scanned the planet, revealing a modest population of a few hundred thousand on the continent. The island held a few dozen people, but no nucla. Nothing worth investigating.

As the scout ship dipped into the atmosphere, an enormous crater loomed on the screens, nearly covering the isthmus between the continent and the southern subcontinent. Pe-te-tak stifled a whoop of delight when the readings showed a mother lode of the mineral in the crater's core. Commander Ke-ke-tak would reward him with this find, enough to be rich and raise his status within the conclave. There'd be ample nucla to fuel the Empire's fleet of starships for many years.

With this discovery of nucla, Pe-te-tak couldn't risk not returning home. His ship orbited the planet for a quarter cycle—all the time he dared—gathering the intelligence necessary for the coming invasion. The scans revealed a low tech society. They recorded sufficient samples of the language for the slave linguists to decipher it.

The inhabitants would fall quickly to the Scourge's greater technology.

Chapter 1

Deep in the swamp, trees knocked knees and intertwined arms with dangling mossy fingers. The filtered green light shone on a huge cypress. Its multi-triangle depths of twisted roots created a protected cave from the swamp's larger predators. For the past year, the most dangerous one called it home. Blazel's human form made him a lesser predator. But when he shapeshifted into his warrior form, none of the beasts, natural or twisted, could match him.

Three years ago, a vision by his friend, Chariel, sent him exploring the length and breadth of Lairheim. His adventures tested his strength and wits against the dangers of the swamps. His wanderings brought him to the southernmost swamplands, far beyond Shandir's Crater and the Barrens.

Blazel brushed away a questing tendril. Animals weren't the only dangerous swamp denizens. Numerous carnivorous plants sent out tendrils or vines to snare the unwary. A scar encircled Blazel's left ankle where one had caught him sleeping in his first chedan in the swamps.

Another vine reached for him from above, and with reflexes honed from living in constant danger, he whipped out his helstrablade and sliced it off. The stump slithered back up the tree, dripping noxious slime.

He'd found his helstrablade—made from an alloy of helstrim—worked great against the twisted swamp plants and animals. He wiped the blade against his pants before returning it to its sheath. More than once, he owed his life to the keen knife, that through the magic of the helstramiesters, never needed sharpening.

Blazel stepped carefully on the path that lead to his home, testing the ground before committing his weight. The areas of firm and dry land changed frequently, sometimes from the rains, but most often, from the malignant magic pervading the swamps. In every one he'd explored, malignant magic saturated it more than water.

The worst place he'd discovered was on the southernmost peninsula of Lairheim. Malicious magic seeped from every inch. The ruins of a black fortress emanated such evil he'd quickly retraced his steps without investigating it. He made his home far away from it.

Blazel shook his head, his shaggy hair hitting his back, to rid himself of the memory. But it only allowed another one to surface. When he had lived in the Sanctuary as a boy, Blazel's place of refuge had been the library, and he had delved into its dusty corners. He'd discovered a long forgotten shelf nearly buried with cobwebs. His hands tingled, recalling the magic laid on the ancient books, urging him to walk away and forget about them. His curiosity drove him to resist the impulse and read them. They told the history of a group of people who worked evil magic, the Malvers. The Posairs had destroyed them in the Great War.

But had they?

After dealing with the malignant pools in the swamps for so long, he questioned the veracity of the books—and of the Supreme.

The subtle movement of air warned him—he'd let his mind wander and wasn't paying attention. Blazel slid to the side, slashing the angulete with his helstrablade as it flew past him. The flying serpent hit the ground a few feet from him, hissing. A shallow cut ran along the last third of its nine-foot length. It spun around, coiling and readying to strike.

In his human form, the angulete's fangs would penetrate his thin skin. If it coiled around him, it would crush his bones. He didn't dare shift to his warrior form; this area wouldn't support its weight, nor did he have time. But Blazel was stronger and faster as a wolf, and his pelt would protect him from the snake's fangs.

Blazel drew on his magic. In a blink, a large red-brown wolf with a gray streak along its back and nose stood where the man had been. The angulete reared in surprise, but then spread its wings and struck. Blazel ducked and caught the serpent behind its head with his teeth. *Damn, I missed.* He'd grabbed it too far back to sever the head. He tossed the angulete to the ground, where it skidded in the dirt before crashing into the knee of an old cypress tree.

Before the dazed serpent coiled to launch another attack, Blazel sprinted to it and attacked. His claws swiped deep gashes, which oozed ichor. He slashed again and again, trying to slice through the thick body. The serpent twisted and turned, hissing furiously, and struck again. Blazel leaped, avoiding the snake. He landed on the outstretched body, and using his claws for leverage, crawled up it to clamp his jaws just below the head. The serpent's tail writhed, attempting to wrap around him.

Dark green ichor drenched the ground. The scent would draw any swamp inhabitants close by to the feast. He had to finish this before they arrived. Blazel snarled. He hated biting through the neck. Angulete tasted horrible. Trying not to swallow, he clenched his jaws tighter together.

At times like this, Blazel wished he had the ability to turn just a part of himself into his warrior form. His warrior jaws could easily crush the serpent, or his longer, sharper claws could have torn it to pieces. He sensed movement to his right. With a growl, he snapped his jaws closed and jerked, severing the serpent's head from its body. He spit it, wishing he had time to lunge into the water and rinse out his mouth. But first, he had to deal with the creature sitting at the path's edge.

The normal appearing rabbit sniffed and lifted its lips, showing large front teeth. However, they weren't the blunt teeth of an herbivore, but the fangs of a carnivore—a twisted beast. It dug its long, sharp front claws into the soft earth. Behind it, more twisted rabbits hopped to the path, their noses twitching and their eyes glowing.

It would cost Blazel in time and strength to fight them all. He'd let them have the angulete's corpse—he certainly didn't want it. He ran, and using the surrounding trees as a springboard, leaped over the herd.

His sensitive nose caught the scent of other predators and scavengers moving toward the dead angulete. Death here brought even more death. This area wouldn't be a safe place for several days. He snatched a twisted rabbit sitting on the herd's outskirts in his jaws, shaking his head to break its neck. Nothing twisted tasted good, but the rabbits weren't poisonous or too foul tasting. They were also one of the few things edible in the swamp's depths.

He could find more palatable food closer to the edges, but the trade-off was the proliferation of Malvers' monster nests. Although Blazel had more magical ability than most men, his strength wasn't anywhere a match for a female Red's magic. He couldn't cover a nest with super-heated fire, nor was he strong enough to fight a monster's nest alone. He was safer to stay deeper in the swamp.

With predators now rummaging near his home, Blazel took a circuitous route. He'd been in sight of it when the angulete attacked. Carefully ensuring the dead twisted rabbit didn't touch anything but the tall grasses, he crossed several water paths to cover his scent. After almost an octar, instead of a few milcrons, he finally reached home and safety.

Blazel trudged to the perimeter of his camp in the deepening twilight, now throughly wet, hungry, and tired. His dinner was a sodden mess. He debated whether to change back to his human form and cook the twisted rabbit, or just eat it as a wolf. Blazel shook his head. There had been too many meals lately in his wolf form.

He jumped over the herbs warding the boundary of his home, lifting his tail high so it wouldn't break the line. He dropped the rabbit to shift back to his natural form. A whine escaped him as the magic sizzled along his nerves, and his body refused to change.

Panting, he reached for his magic again, then howled. Blazel stood with his head hanging between his front legs, shivering with pain and fear. He'd never before had trouble changing forms. *It's more than eating too much as a wolf. I've spent too much time as one.* Terror skittered along his spine, remembering Histrun's admonishment to never stay too long in his wolf form. He risked staying a wolf for the rest of his life.

Gathering his willpower, Blazel dipped again into his inner magic pool, allowing the power to wash over him, and willed the change from wolf to man. His legs lengthened, his muzzle receded, and his pelt melted into his body. Finally, he felt the cool breeze brush against his skin—his human skin.

How much am I a wolf now, even when I'm a man? I haven't seen or talked to another Posair for three years. He pulled out the band holding his waist-length hair from his face and shook his head. Matted and tangled hair flopped into view. Grime coated it so throughly he couldn't distinguish its true color.

A few fresh-water ponds in the swamps existed where he could bathe, but he had to do so quickly while watching for other predators. Blazel sniffed himself and snarled. *Yep, it's been a few chedans—or more—since I've taken a bath. Living in the swamp is easier as a wolf than a man.* He washed any lingering blood from his paws and face, then rolled around on some coarse sawgrass to clean his wolf pelt.

It's too late tonight to go to the pond. Tomorrow I will. Blazel blinked. *How many times have I promised myself to do that and then not bothered the next morning? Quite often. This time will be different. This time, having trouble shifting gives me added incentive. I need to be more man than wolf, or I will become only a wolf.*

Blazel cocked his head to the side, considering it. *Do I want to be a wolf? No, I can't do that to my mother and grandmother.* They'd risked challenging the Supreme White Priestess in order to keep him in the Sanctuary when no other males were allowed. He had to stay human and return to them, eventually.

With great care, Blazel skinned and cleaned the twisted rabbit. He saved the entrails. They made good bait. Carrying his meal, he crawled through the small opening in the huge cypress tree's roots and entered his temporary home. In the center, a natural chimney drew away the smoke from his fire. He threaded the rabbit on a stick to roast it and set it aside. He knelt in front of the fire pit and stirred the ashes.

No coals.

Blazel gaped and his breath came in shallow pants. He hadn't had a fire in days, maybe even several chedans. Blazel looked around his home with new eyes. Bones of past meals were tossed to the side. A bed of leaves showed the imprint of his wolf form. *Great Mother! I've spent most of my time as a wolf.*

He placed a small pile of kindling in the fire pit. He took a deep breath, held out his hands, and called on his magic to create a tendril of fire. More than a trickle leaped from his hands. The kindling flared, and the fire quickly consumed it.

Pacing the confines of his tree-cave, Blazel searched his memory for the last time he'd used his magic. When he arrived in this swamp and found this tree, he'd created the magical boundary wards to protect his claimed space. Blazel's face screwed up as he thought hard about how long ago it that had been. The heat of late summer had made the swamp a humid hell when he'd arrived. Currently, the spring air was warming.

Six lunadar! It's been over six lunadar since I've used my Talent—or been a man. Great Mother!

Blazel shook, and his mind jibbered.

Unlike most Posair men, Blazel had as much fire Talent as a weak Red. With the greater Talent, came the responsibility to control it. Blazel didn't know if being raised in the Sanctuary, and not part of a pack, caused his anomaly. He slumped to the ground, sitting in a cross-legged position. Closing his eyes, he recalled his childhood drills. Slowly and carefully, he moved through each one until he was sweating. Only then did he rebuild the pile of kindling in the fire pit. With great care, he again accessed his fire Talent. This time, it stuttered. He'd called too little.

Blazel took a deep breath and let go of his fear, then reached again for his birthright. And there it was, flowing in his veins. A tendril of fire spread from his fingers and jumped to the kindling to gently light it afire. Blazel breathed a sigh of relief. Controlling his magic was as important as restraining his wolf-self. He fed fuel into the fire until it burned brightly, then put the rabbit on the spit over the flames. Blazel felt better watching the fire cook the meat.

Fire was the dominion of man, not wolf.

Tonight, he was a man.

What would he be tomorrow?

Blazel woke to the scent of smoke tickling his nose. He sneezed to clear it, but the stink still remained. He shook and rolled to stand on his feet, sniffing more carefully. *Was there a fire in the swamp?* His gaze landed on the remains of his fire. Tiny tendrils of smoke rising from the coals.

Blazel stepped toward it—on his paws. He had changed into his wolf form during his sleep. *Not good. I'm becoming more comfortable as a wolf than I am as a man.* Blazel tried shifting to his human form, howling with the pain as the magic jerked through his system. His tongue lolled out as he panted. He shoved his fear away and calmed himself down. This time, when he willed the magic, it flowed easier, giving him uncomfortable pinpricks under his skin—his human skin. He rubbed his arms and face to erase the last of the prickly sensation. Shaking, he stirred the coals and fed it bits of wood until it again blazed.

The day was warming up, but he needed the fire to warm his cold soul. Shifting forms was his birthright, an essential part of himself. It defined him as a Posair man—a warrior. Without it, he would be nothing more than a rogue. His hands trembled. Blazel had never belonged to a pack—by the circumstances of his birth—but even so, he considered himself a lone wolf, not a rogue. He didn't hunt and kill people. But would he begin to do so if he remained a wolf and lost the ability to change shape to his human form? He'd like to believe he wouldn't, but he couldn't be sure.

Blazel reflected on yesterday's incident with the angulete. He'd been a man when it had attacked him, hadn't he? *Yes, I was a man. I had to shift to my wolf form to fight the flying serpent. But how long had I been in that form?* Tracing his activity, he discovered he had only been in man form for a couple of octars before the attack. It had been the first time in days, if not chedans. He lifted his canteen to his mouth, but he was shaking so badly he couldn't hold it still. Water dribbled down his chin.

Blazel needed to the leave the swamps and associate with other people to remember what it meant to be a man. He plucked at his dirty clothes, wrinkling his nose at the stink wafting from them and his body. *No Posair will accept me into their company in this filthy condition.* Digging in his pack, he finally located a small sliver of soap.

First, he'd eat a breakfast of leftover roasted twisted rabbit and seeds. Eating helped to ease his shaking. He grimaced at the water's staleness in his container, then placed the bottle with the soap near the entrance.

His messy living space begged to be cleaned. *No use getting clean just to get dirty again.* Blazel gathered the scattered bones and carried them to a nearby sink-hole. He dumped them in, watching them sink below the mud where predators wouldn't be able to track them to his home. On his way back, he cut off a tree branch and tied twigs to it to make a broom. Leaves swirled from the trunk opening as he swept out the remains of his wolf bed. He picked up his dirty and tattered clothing. It looked and smelled like he'd washed his clothes the last time he'd bathed. He bundled them into a bag, along with the last of his soap and his water bottle.

By the time he bathed, did his laundry, and waited for it to dry, it would be too late to leave the swamp today. Even he didn't tempt fate enough to travel the swamps after dark. The nocturnal monsters were much worse than their daytime cousins.

Blazel looked around his now clean home with satisfaction, noting the pitiful pile of firewood. He'd used the last of his stockpiled kindling and wood last night. *I need a fire tonight to remind myself I am a man, not a wolf.*

Walking carefully, testing each step to determine the ground's sturdiness, he crossed the glade. Seemingly dry ground gave way under him and he sank to his knees in muck. "Blasted stinking mud!" Blazel cursed. He caught himself just before shifting into his wolf form. It would be easier to walk the trails with his weight distributed over four feet instead of on two. "No," he said firmly, his voice creaky. "I need to stay in my natural form without shifting today. I am a man!"

He climbed several trees to find dead branches that were only slightly damp. Once he had an armload, he returned to his home. He laid them in a single layer on the ground a few feet away from the cypress tree. Using his fire magic, he sent gentle heat into the branches to dry them out. When no more steam rose from the wood, he stopped heating it. Even with the swamp's humidity, it would stay dry enough for his fire that night.

With nothing left to clean except himself and clothes, he grabbed his bundle and made his way to the fresh-water pond. The afternoon light shone brightly on the water. A tree draped with brilliant green moss stood sentinel over it. Blazel searched the tree branches for any hiding anguletes or other nasty creatures, but his passage only disturbed a few harmless birds.

He crouched and silently watched the pond, watching for any telltales of the reptilian predators that lurked just under the surface. An ibis dropped to the water and waded along the shore, looking for insects and small fish. When the bird stalked its own prey for some time without becoming prey, Blazel deemed the pond free of predators—for now. He could safely wash his clothes and bathe.

Blazel stripped. Whenever he shifted from man to wolf, or even to warrior and back to man, he returned in the same clothes he had worn. They might be torn or dirty from whatever fight he'd been in, but he'd have clothes. Once, he asked the Supreme about it. She told him it was an aspect of the spell that had gifted men with the ability to shapeshift. Personally, he was glad he didn't return to human form naked. It would be hell to find clothes deep in the mountains or in the swamp when the fight had taken him measures from where he had first shifted.

Slowly, Blazel waded into the pond. When nothing reacted to his presence, he slid under the water, relishing the warmth. He liked this one because it was always warm, even in winter. Blazel picked up a lock of his dirty, matted hair, and his lip curled in disgust. He briefly considered cutting his hair, but to get rid of all the tangles, he'd have to shave his head. That wasn't an option—he'd never seen a bald man. The color of a man's wolf and warrior pelts was the same as his hair. Blazel didn't want to chance shifting into a naked wolf from shaving his head. He dropped the lock of hair. After he washed the twisted coils, he'd see what they looked like clean.

It took several times soaping both hair and body to remove all the dirt. Running his hands over his face, and feeling his coarse beard, he considered shaving. Except, here in the swamp, shaving was dangerous. The scent of blood from even a tiny nick would draw predators in moments. Instead, Blazel used the last of his soap to launder his clothes.

He climbed out and spread his now clean clothes out on bushes to dry. He could hurry their drying time with fire magic, but he'd already used most of his reservoir when he dried the wood. Blazel envied the Reds, the female fire Talents, and their ability to work greater magics and their larger magic stores on which to draw. He glanced at the sky; there was enough sun left to dry his clothes and himself.

A quick search provided Blazel with the plants needed to create a ward boundary. He strewed them on the ground in a circle and fed a touch of his earthy Brown Talent and his Red Talent into the herbs. Shaping the spell in his mind, he formed a bubble of fire and earth where the herbs touched the ground. He extended it into a dome to protect him from attack from above as well as from the side. No one had taught him the spell. After years of wandering alone in the wilds, he'd developed it to protect himself.

As safe as he could be outside of his tree-cave, Blazel stretched out on the soft spongy grass. The afternoon sun felt good on his naked skin while he waited for his clothes to dry.

Blazel's mind wandered as he lightly dozed—a part of him still aware of potential danger. His memories of how he had ended up wandering and living in the swamps floated to the surface.

"Blazel, you have to leave," Chariel said.

"What?" He shook his head at the non sequitur from his story about one of his adventures deep in the mountains. "Is someone coming who isn't supposed to see me here?"

"No. You have to leave the Sanctuary."

"But I just got back two chedan ago. Is the Supreme angry at me? I swear whatever it was, I didn't do it."

"Go to the swamps." Chariel's voice changed into a deep monotone, and a silver sheen covered her eyes.

Chariel was an anomaly. Her dark charcoal-gray hair and eyes made many people think she was a weak Black. She wasn't, nor was she a Gray, either. She was a prophetess. Chariel's prophecies always came true. Now she was having a vision about him. He listened closely.

"Immerse yourself in the swamps. Travel and explore every swamp in the land. Learn all you can of what is hidden there. It will save us."

Save us? Blazel wondered what she meant, but once in the oracle trance, she wouldn't hear or see anything but the vision unfolding for her. And once she came to, most often, she had little recollection of what she'd seen.

"Do not come back until you are called. When you are, the madness will be approaching."

Blazel waited for more. *What madness? How could the evil in the swamps help save them? Who? The priestesses? All the Posairs?*

Chariel blinked her eyes to clear the vision. "I did it again, didn't I?"

"Yes, but this time it was about me. And I have to admit, Chariel, some of it was scary. What does going to the swamps have to do with saving us? Us who?"

"I don't know. This one was weird." She rubbed her arms. "Even though I don't remember the vision, the fear in it lingers. Whatever is coming is awful."

"How long before I have to leave?" he asked.

"Now. Do not tarry." Her eyes glazed again. "There is so little time. Hurry, hurry, hurry. They are coming."

Blazel left the Sanctuary that afternoon. He had traveled the length and breadth of the continent of Lairheim, exploring every swamp he found. Blazel had fought—and won—every twisted beast or horrendous monster inhabiting the swamps. He knew the flavor of a malignant magic pool. The taste of it in the air could lead him to it. He had tested and cataloged the effects of thousands of plants. Blazel knew which were poisonous—most of them—and the few healing ones. There wasn't much more he could learn from the swamps.

It had been three years since Chariel's vision. Maybe the danger had passed, and it wasn't coming. Sometimes events would change and the oracle visions wouldn't happen.

He shook his head. For other Grays, perhaps, but never for one of Chariel's prophecies.

He stood up and quickly gathered his still damp clothes, and he fought the urge to shift to his wolf form to return to his tree-cave. Grimacing, he put on a shirt and a pair of trousers. When he returned to society, he'd acquire a set or two of good leathers, supple and tough like the Reds wore to fight the monsters.

He crouched at the edge of the pool to fill his water containers. Looking at his reflection, he decided he liked the tight locks of hair when they were clean. As the bottles filled, his skin began to twitch. He looked around and sniffed. No predators or monsters were in the vicinity, but the small hairs on his body stood at attention. He repressed the need to run. If predators were watching him, running would only attract them.

He remembered Chariel's prophecy, and a sense of urgency filled him, telling him to hurry. *But to where?* His nerves twitched, making him feel ready to jump out of his skin. *Why did I recall that vision today? I haven't thought of it for a long time. Is this a message from Chariel calling me back to the Sanctuary?*

Home! Homesickness rushed over him. The loving faces of his mother and grandmother rose in his mind's eye.

He was tired of being alone and ready to leave the swamps. *I'm ready to go home.*

The dusky mist of twilight deepened as Blazel made his way to his tree-cave. A large swamp rat darted across the path. A quick flick of his dagger, and Blazel had dinner. Swamp rats looked ugly, but they were good eating. His step was light as he crossed the boundary into his refuge.

While the rat roasted over the fire, he dried his clothes with a little fire magic. Then he gathered his few possessions and packed everything in his backpack. His hands touched, then caressed the smooth wood of the flute he had made years ago while in the Deep Mountains. He lifted it to his lips, realizing it had been a long time since he had played. This too was the dominion of man, and he played while his dinner cooked. After he ate, the sweet tones of the flute filled the air deep into the night. The sound soothed his itchy skin and his lonely heart. Finally, wrapped up in a blanket, he curled up near the fire.

Blazel awoke at dawn from a dream about Chariel. Even awake, he could still hear her calling to him. Calling him home. In a matter of moments, he tied his bedroll to his pack.

He appreciated the safe refuge the tree had given him, so he completely smothered the fire. It wasn't good manners to repay the tree by setting it on fire. Blazel ate some of the leftover swamp rat and saved a small portion for his lunch. He crawled from the cleared out tree, then he scattered the herbs forming the ward boundary around it. Now others could find the haven he had enjoyed in the tree.

Without another glance, he settled the pack on his back and strode away, heading north.

Home. He was going home.

Chapter 2

Blazel followed a mostly dry path through the swamp. Cypress and alder trees towered over him, moss dripped between their branches. Deep-throated frogs croaked, and a fish plopped. His stomach growled in hunger. He turned off the trail and carefully crossed the roots of an alder until he stood over the edge of the water.

Another fish jumped, and Blazel stared at the ripples, wondering how to catch a fish as a human. He knew he could as a wolf. Another twist of hunger made his decision, and he called on his magic. The wolf settled over him in a heartbeat. He intently watched the water and quickly ducked his head. When he lifted it, he held a fish clamped in his jaws. Saliva filled his mouth, and he tilted back his head to gobble the fish.

And stopped.

If he wanted to retain his humanity, he must eat as a man. The fish thudded to the ground, and a whine escaped him as he looked longingly at it. A shiver snaked through him from nose to tail. Taking a step back, Blazel reached for his magic and willed the change to man. It stuttered, then zapped him, and he pulled for more. A few moments later, he rubbed the twinges of pain from his arms. When the pain passed, he squatted and carefully cleaned the fish, wincing at the holes from his wolf teeth.

His meal cooked and eaten, Blazel sat in front of the fire that pushed back the darkness. He removed his flute from his pack and played, ignoring the gleam of eyes staring at him from across the light. His ward would protect him. The mellow notes of the flute soothed his restlessness. *'Hurry, hurry, hurry'* ran through his mind, day and night. This was the first time he'd stopped to rest and eat in four days. The pull to get home tugged at him mercilessly.

He moved swiftly through the swamp over the next five days. As he jogged along the path, his senses jangled. Slowing, he peered into the shadows, seeking the nearby danger. His foot broke through the thin dirt, and he fell through up to his thigh. Cursing and struggling to pull it out, he didn't notice the silence drop over the swamp. His fine-tuned instincts screamed at him. He leaped from the hole, ripping his trousers and leg just as a jallopitar's jaws snapped where he had been.

The reptile's long body covered the path; its tail disappeared into the water. Its red eyes followed Blazel as he scrambled away from the water's edge. A tree blocked his retreat. He grabbed his magic, let it flow over him, and willed the change to his warrior form. He roared from the heady rush of power and strength. The jallopitar hissed back, showing jaws full of teeth, and took another sliding step onto dry land. It released a pulse of energy, attempting to disorient and paralyze its prey. Blazel jumped, caught a lower limb, and pulled himself out of the energy's trajectory. The tree quaked, raining leaves.

Blazel leaped to the ground, flexing his six-inch claws and releasing the venom under them. He ripped into the reptile's side, pumping venom into the wound. The jallopitar squealed, bent nearly in half, and snapped its jaws at Blazel. The sharp lower tusks grazed across his leg. Snarling, Blazel vaulted, landed on its back, and clamped his arm around the snout, locking it shut. His other hand reached under its jaw and shredded the soft tissue. The reptile bucked and thrashed, its movements growing slower as Blazel's venom ate into its innards. Soon, it lay still.

Three or four of the beasts shared territory, and the others would rapidly arrive to investigate the death of their mate. Blazel—still in warrior form—ran and kept running until he was far from the jallopitar's pool. His gait slowly turned into a limp-hop. By the time he stopped, mud coated his legs, and the gash oozed blood and stunk of infection.

Exhausted, Blazel stood, panting and examining the clearing. Fresh water filled a nearby pool. Plenty of wood littered the ground for a fire, and a hollow cypress provided shelter. He waded into the water and washed the mud, blood, and residual venom from his pelt. Once clean, he closed his eyes and let go of the magic holding him in his warrior form. It sloughed from him with ease, and in a moment, he stood shivering in wet clothes.

He examined his wound, and his warrior's pelt had stopped most of the jallopitar's thrust. The long gash wasn't too deep and dripped droplets while he gathered firewood.

The sweet scent of lengo drew him deeper into the clearing, where he found a large patch of the herb. He harvested a double handful of leaves, dug some roots, and returned to his camp. With a sigh of regret, he tore one of his few remaining shirts into bandages. He then smashed the lengo leaves into a paste and tied them onto the gash with the strips. The leaves would stop the bleeding. A poultice made from the boiled root would fight the infection from the swamp creature's bite.

Blazel marveled at how the swamps could produce such a healing herb as lengo. He stuffed the unused leaves and roots into his pack, along with samples of other plants he'd collected. A few of them were beneficial, but mostly, they were baneful. More plant specimens filled his pack than clothes; and those he did have were threadbare.

The next three days passed uneventfully as Blazel made his way through the swamp, always traveling north. When he stopped to check his gash, he pulled the lengo root bandages off to reveal it mostly healed and the infection gone.

The path ahead disappeared into a dense tangle of vines. Blazel halted, tilting his head and narrowing his eyes. Long runners covered the ground, thorns stuck out in sharp angles, and enormous leaves waved in the breeze. Only there wasn't a breeze. A long, cylindrical leaf shivered, and Blazel heard a muffled squeal.

A skinny tail dangled from the leaf—a swamp rat caught by the carnivorous vines. The vines quivered, and the leaves turned to face him. A runner snaked toward him. Blazel drew his helstrablade—wishing again he could feed fire magic into it like the Reds did—and faced this new foe.

He reached back, keeping his eyes on the deadly vine, and dug into his backpack, pulling out an innocuous looking herb. He ground it into a powder in his hands while muttering a spell to add potency to it.

"Wait, wait," he told himself when he'd rather run. "Let it get closer."

The runner inched its way toward him. When it was an arm's length away, it rose, waving hypnotically side to side. Blazel threw the powdered herb. It hung in the air momentarily, burst into sparkles of light, and then zipped into the vine. Starting at the tip, the runner immediately turned orange. The discoloration quickly spread to the mother vine. Leaves shook violently, and the vines wiggled, attempting to escape the poison. Fifteen milcrons later, rust orange covered the tangle of vines, and the leaves dropped to the ground.

Blazel walked to the vines blocking the path and stomped on one. It crackled and disintegrated in a cloud of orange dust. Satisfied the vine was dead, he covered his nose and mouth with his shirt and strode through it.

The next morning—two chedans after leaving his tree-cave—Blazel finally stood at the swamp's edge. Black sand glittered before him, stretching into the distance. He lifted a hand to shield his eyes from the harsh reflection.

Before him lay the Barrens, an area of utter desolation. It wasn't a desert; deserts held life. Once upon a time, the legends said, this land had been a vast forest. Huge trees had covered the peninsula that was now swamp. The Posairs had fought the last battle of the Great War here. In a desperate attempt to end the war, the White Priestess Shandir had gathered all the magic from every living thing in the area and from the land. After she unleashed the tremendous force, only a vast, deep crater and the Barrens remained. And the ghosts of the dead, or so Blazel had heard.

Water was nonexistent in the Barrens, whereas the swamps had an excess of it. The great river Storengher traversed Lairheim's entire length, from the ice fields in the north to the marshland at the southern tip. One of the side effects of

Shandir's magic was to drive the river deep underground on its journey through the Barrens.

Blazel didn't relish the thought of crossing the Barrens. The journey to the crater and then around to the northern edge would take nearly a chedan. That is, if he was very lucky and didn't encounter any Malvers' monsters along the way. Wishful thinking, he knew. For some unknown reason, the crater spewed the monsters out every few days. Whereas, in the north, it took at least a chedan for a nest to reform after destroying one.

Without a horse, the only option for Blazel to travel through the Barrens was in his wolf form. His stomach twisted in knots at the thought of spending so much time as a wolf. The last few times he had shifted from wolf to human had been easier and not as painful. *After a solid eight or nine days as a wolf, will I even remember I am a man?*

Turning his back on the dark sands, he returned to the swamp to prepare for his journey. He filled his water bottles at a fresh-water pond. A successful hunt nearby provided him with a family of swamp rats and a twisted rabbit, which he put them over a smoky fire to cook. Then he located a marsh with cattails lining the shore and gathered the roots and seedpods. A spicy-sweet scent drew him deeper into the marsh.

"Yes!" he whooped, gleefully picking juicy, ripe fruit hanging from the branches of a marsh ragtile tree.

That evening, he played a mournful tune on his flute. Blazel hoped he had enough food and water to make it across the Barrens and to the plains beyond.

By the pale light of dawn, Blazel packed, put out his fire, and stood at the demarcation from swamp to black sand. On the horizon, a butte jutted into the sky—Shandir's Crater.

It filled the middle of the narrow neck of land connecting the southern peninsula to the continent. The Barrens encircled Shandir's Crater from coast to coast of the isthmus. Even the coastline was barren with sharp reefs that no boat could pass.

Blazel considered going through the crater, as it would cut his journey in half. Instinctual horror squeezed his throat shut, and he doubled over. He breathed deep to settle his roiling stomach.

From this perspective, the Barrens appeared to be flat, but hills and valleys cluttered the landscape. On his previous trip, he'd used the natural debris to avoid the guard-packs patrolling the crater's vicinity. As he made his run this time, Blazel would have to watch for the guards who wandered away from the crater rim when chasing Malvers' monsters.

Besides facing wayward monsters, Blazel dreaded encountering the guard-packs. Most Posairs considered lone wolves as rogues and dangerous, and usually killed them on sight. Blazel had never been in a pack, and after being alone for ten years, he wasn't interested in joining one. It meant he avoided contact with most Posairs. They didn't understand someone like him, who chose not to be part of a pack. He only visited the large territory keeps where a strange man traveling alone from one Keep to another didn't attract undue attention.

Chariel's voice whispering in the back of his mind, *'hurry, hurry, hurry,'* interrupted his ruminations.

During his trip to the southern swamps, he'd traveled along the coast to keep away from the fighting-packs guarding the crater's perimeter. The rocky shore had provided him some protection from the Malvers' monsters, but it had taken him over three chedans to cross. He wasn't at leisure to follow that route, or pace, on his return journey.

Blazel tightened the straps of his backpack more snugly to keep it on while he shifted. He took a deep breath for courage. The prospect of staying in his wolf form for so long terrified him, but it was more practical to travel as a wolf. His wolf's feet were much faster and surefooted. As a wolf, his long, loping strides, which he could maintain for octars, ate up the measures.

"I am a man." The words came out hoarse and croaking.

"I am Blazel." This time, his voice was stronger.

Even knowing the sound would attract unwanted predators, Blazel filled his lungs and shouted, "I am a man! I am Blazel." With his shout ringing in his ears, he allowed the magic to flow through his body. He shook his fur to settle it and raced into the Barrens.

He ran for several octars and then dropped into a walk. Blazel stopped only for a short time to rest, shifting back to his natural form to eat, then took off again, following the same pattern. Running up and down the low hills and barrows was exhausting. As he leaped over another petrified log, he could believe the legends that this area had been a vast forest before the cataclysm of magic formed Shandir's Crater. The amounts of petrified wood strewn across the ground made Blazel leap over or twist around the resulting boulders. He slipped and stumbled on the slick sand, flailing to regain his stride, before racing forward.

A large patch of sand-glass caught him unawares. His steps tossed glass shards into the air, striking his legs, body, and even his face. He yipped in pain when he put weight on his shredded paws. Shifting into his natural form, Blazel examined his injuries. His wolf pelt had protected the rest of his body. He rubbed a salve made from swamp plants onto his cut hands and feet. The ointment stunk of old animal fat. He hadn't had any purified fat or oil to make it while he was in the swamp. It smelled nasty, but it healed his wounds.

Blazel ran in a course parallel to the crater, keeping it in sight, but far enough away—he hoped—to not draw the guard-packs' attention. Other than the natural hazards, he traveled quickly, covering twenty or thirty measures in the first two days.

On the third afternoon, as he raced up a hill, snarls and growls accompanied by clicks and hisses echoed across the Barrens.

A monster battle!

Blazel scurried behind a massive piece of petrified wood. Tremors shook his body as he suppressed his instinctual urge to shift into his warrior form. Transfixed, he watched the age-old battle between Posairs and Malvers' monsters.

Eight-foot-tall warriors, a perfect blend of wolf and human, fought the monsters. The warriors howled, revealing mouths full of sharp teeth, and their six-inch long front claws dripped with venom. Their pelts were predominately red, brown, gold, with a few with green thrown in the mix. Seeing the ferocious and deadly men in action—doing what they were created to do, kill Malvers' monsters—Blazel finally appreciated the sacrifice of his ancestors. He often lamented his fire magic wasn't as strong as a Red's, but the trade-off of strength and the ability to become a warrior was worth it.

A janack trundled along the ground, using its ten tentacles to form a ball, keeping the head on top. In an orchestrated move, a Red sent a line of fire bursting in front of the escaping janack. Heat stalks on the top of its head swiveled toward the woman. Its maw gaped open, clicking in irritation, and then it turned back to the fight. A tentacle flicked at the Red, not quite reaching her. She grimaced and gripped her glowing helbraught tighter, the blade pointed at the monster. She scowled, and instead of attacking, she waited for it to come to her.

Spittle dripped from the janack's jagged teeth, and the ground hissed from the acidic saliva. Blazel tensed, wanting to jump to the woman's aid. At the last moment, she leaped forward and plunged the sharp blade of her helbraught into the janack's belly. It screamed as the weapon tore open a hole, the edges smoking from the heated blade. A warrior jumped on the head of the careening janack and ripped into it, his claws pumping venom.

A yowl rent the air, and a brecha raced toward the killers of the dying monster. Its rear claws threw black sand, its huge mouth opened wide, and its back spines stood straight up. Both the Red and the warrior turned to face this new attack. The man crouched in a ready position, his arms outstretched at his sides and his knees bent. The brecha released a barrage of spines. Even through all his ducking and dodging, a spine pierced the warrior's throat, and gurgling blood, he fell to the ground. The Red's eyes widened as the brecha barreled into the warrior, head bent, intent on eating. She dropped behind the downed fighter. When the brecha closed on its meal, the Red surged to her feet and drove her helbraught like a spear into the monster's head. It crashed to a stop inches from the woman, who calmly retrieved her weapon.

Blazel dragged his attention to the rest of the fighters. The Reds wielded their fire efficiently and sparingly, only using it to drive the monsters toward the warriors. Unlike what he'd seen them do elsewhere, where they surrounded and held the monsters inside of a fire-ring. Blazel surmised the lack of fuel caused this change of tactics. There wasn't anything to burn other than their own fire energy.

Two octars later, the brutal fight ended with all the Malvers' monsters destroyed. The Posairs fared better, with only one dead—the warrior killed by the brecha spines—and several injured, including three Reds. The fighter's feet dragged with exhaustion as they mopped up after the battle.

Blazel stayed hidden until the fighting-pack rode over the horizon, then he came out of his crouch and ran again. He only traveled ten measures when another clash with the monsters forced him to hide. Throughout the day, he had to stop to wait for battles to be fought before he could continue on his journey. A raging headache plagued him from using all of his self-control to keep from shifting into his warrior form at the sight and stench of the Malvers' monsters. But the fighters wouldn't want his help, anyway. He'd only get in their way from his lack of daily training to fight the monsters.

As he hid yet again, he reflected on the stories he'd overheard about crater guard duty. He believed they fought frequently, but nothing like this. If it continued the entire route through the Barrens, it would take him more than the single chedan he planned.

He made up for the lost time by running through the night, even though traveling in the darkness was more dangerous. *'Hurry, hurry, hurry,'* dogged his heels as he ran.

Chapter 3

Over the next two days, Blazel could only travel a few measures before he'd have to stop and hide from a battle. Several times, as he barreled across the Barrens, he nearly crashed into a fight and scrambled to find a hiding spot. More often, the loud clash between Posairs and monsters would alert him. He'd creep forward until he found the battleground—he didn't want any marauding monsters behind him—and wait until it was over.

The waiting gave him a chance to rest. At night, he stopped only when he was stumbling with exhaustion. As soon as he recovered somewhat, he'd take off again. His nerves jangled and his body hurt from the constant struggle to keep from shifting to his warrior form. He needed to get past the crater before he made a mistake and the guard-packs spotted him, or he stumbled into the middle of a battle.

The afternoon of his sixth day in the Barrens, Blazel passed the invisible boundary between the eastern quadrant guard-packs and the northern ones. The fighting-packs he now ran into were fresher, more alert, and stronger than the others he'd crossed. A hint of pride warmed his heart.

Warriors from the north and northeastern packs, especially those from Strunlair Province, had visited the Sanctuary often just to teach him and ensure he was a trained warrior. Histrun had been a favored teacher. For several years after his mate died, Histrun frequently stayed many lunadar with Blazel. But he hadn't seen the old warrior since he'd left the Sanctuary at seventeen. Maybe he should stop at the eastern fortress and ask the Strunlair guard-packs about his mentor. By now Histrun would be past his century mark. Then he remembered they would consider him rogue, and chase him away, if he was lucky, or kill him if he wasn't.

That night, he only dozed a couple of octars before pushing back to his feet and continuing to run. The next day began as bad as the last three. Within a few octars after dawn, Blazel scurried behind a jumble of boulders. His sides heaving, he waited for the battle to finish and for the fighters to leave. As soon as it was clear, he set off again.

He was so tired he ran over a hill rather than creep up it.

Blazel skidded to a halt. In front of him was the largest janack he had ever witnessed. It towered over the warriors, its great maw snapping and its tentacles waving. Blazel crouched, flattening his belly to the ground. With his race's ancient enemy so close, the instinct to shift into his warrior form and fight battered against his mind. His bones began to lengthen and his jaw protruded. Whining softly, he forced them to return to their normal size.

A woman yelled, "Run!" and without thinking, Blazel obeyed the command, running away from the hill. An explosion rocked the ground. He ducked under a large piece of petrified wood just as the first janack pieces plummeted to the ground. Panting, he scooted deeper into his shelter and cowered. He wrapped his tail around his feet with the tip covering his nose.

From his observations, he knew the Reds in the group would be by soon to incinerate any bits not burned to ash by the explosion. Blazel held his breath when a Red walked by his hiding place. When she continued on without noticing him, he trembled in relief.

That was too close. I should stay here for the rest of the day and only travel at night. The thought sent tremors through his body. The Barrens and its toxins were too dangerous to remain in for long. And Chariel needed him home—now. *'Hurry, hurry, hurry'* banged against his fear of being caught. He waited until he was sure the fighting-pack was gone, then slunk up the hill.

Ahead of him, the crater rim loomed. He was closer to it than he expected—or wanted—to be. With all the monster attacks, traveling along the rugged coast would be faster. Blazel changed direction, running east, toward the ocean, forcing himself to keep going when his feet shuffled and dragged.

A strange humming broke into Blazel's reverie. He slowed, cocking his head at the battle sounds ahead of him. He climbed a pile of petrified wood boulders and lay on top of them, his red-brown fur blending with the rocks. From his vantage point, he safely watched the peculiar scrimmage.

A huge janack, unlike any he'd ever seen, stood on three of its tentacles in the center. A strange protrusion on its head stuck out from its sensor stalks. It moved as the battle raged around it. Two dead janacks and six brechas, bodies hacked into pieces, lay strewn on the black sand.

Surrounding—guarding?—the strange janack were eight brechas and a regular janack. Blazel gaped at the odd behavior. Once their lead janack was down, the brechas normally devolved into cannibalism.

Two Reds raced in, and a line of fire burst between the smaller, regular janack and three brechas, driving them away. Two other women separated four more brechas from the group around the strange janack. Men in their ferocious warrior forms leaped over the fiery lines. As soon as they did, the fire blazed and surrounded the groups, burning higher and hotter. Blazel sensed the pop of energy shields being raised within the fire rings.

Unbelievably, the monsters separated by the fire rings turned their backs on the fighters. They lumbered toward the unusual janack and bounced back, roaring with rage when they crashed into the shield. The warriors savaged them from behind. The monsters were so intent on reaching the strange janack, they didn't even put up a fight. In milcrons the warriors killed the contained janack and brechas.

Meanwhile, the remaining three brechas stayed close to the weird janack, making it impossible for the Reds to separate them. A large warrior, with a dark-red and thin yellow striped pelt, attacked the huge janack. As the man harried it, a Red used her helbraught to catapult to its head, staying away from the teeth-filled maw. Her helbraught blade glowed bright red with flickers of orange from the amount of fire magic she had fed into it. The blade sped through the air, slicing through the unusual protrusion. It flew twenty feet away. Another Red chased it, incinerating it as it landed. As it disintegrated, the eerie humming in Blazel's ears stopped.

With all the normal monsters destroyed, everyone focused their attention on the strange janack. The Red still stood near its head as it bucked and thrashed. The warriors and Reds on the ground leaped to avoid its flailing tentacles.

A brecha rose from under a dead janack and raced due north. Blazel waited for a fighter to notice the renegade brecha, but its spiny back disappeared in the distance. Blazel swore. Everything about this nest and fight was crazy. Histrun had trained him too well to allow the creature to escape. Even one brecha reaching populated areas could be devastating.

Still swearing, Blazel shifted to his warrior form, forcing himself to transform more quickly than he ever had before. He howled in pain. As the change completed, he hurtled after the brecha.

He caught up to it in a few strides and swerved to avoid the sharp spines spewing from its back. An explosion boomed behind him, and a tremor raced over the ground, but Blazel kept running.

Past the brecha.

He skidded to a halt and spun around. The monster stood on its hind legs, its head weaving from side to side. Blazel didn't stop to wonder what was wrong with it. He leaped, his claws dripping venom, and slashed the creature's back, severing the remaining spines. It turned and swiped. He twisted to the side. A warrior with red and yellow fur barreled into it. His jaws ripping into its neck.

The two warriors circled the brecha, taking turns rushing in and slicing it with claws or teeth. Putrid green ichor dripped from its multiple wounds. A noisome odor wafted off it, making Blazel gag, and reminding him of the malignant magic pools he'd encountered in the swamps. The other warrior made one last slash across the brecha's neck, and it finally staggered and dropped dead. Ichor drenched the ground.

The unknown warrior immediately turned from the brecha and circled Blazel with a low snarl. He stretched his claws in front of him, ready to attack.

"Who you? Not our pack." The stranger took a deep breath. "Not any pack here."

"No, I not," Blazel agreed. No one was very articulate in their warrior form, and neither man had shifted into their natural one. It was a struggle to get words past elongated jaws. "Traveling. Sanctuary."

The warrior drew closer, still menacing. "Not alpha. Why go Sanctuary?"

Blazel shook his head. He didn't have time for these games. "My business."

"No pack smell. Not alpha. Business at Sanctuary," the man murmured, more to himself than to Blazel. "Ha!" His claws twitched together, trying to snap his fingers. "I know who you."

This could end in trouble. The clan-packs believed all lone wolves were dangerous rogues without any control. None would understand Blazel's desire to be alone.

"Blazel." A grin stretched his muzzle.

Snarling, Blazel crouched into an attack stance.

"No need." The warrior thumped his chest. "Know Histrun."

Blazel relaxed slightly. If this person knew Histrun, then maybe this pack wouldn't kill him outright.

"No more talk. Hard," the warrior grimaced.

Blazel nodded in agreement.

The stranger howled, "Maheli!"

A few moments later, the Red who had climbed on the strange janack jogged into view. "Rolstrun," she said as she rolled her eyes then slugged the warrior's shoulder, "only you would chase a brecha and end up with another warrior." She frowned at the corpse. "Whew! It stinks. Did you have to shred it like that?"

Both warriors nodded.

Maheli laughed. She touched her glowing helbraught to the mess and ignited it. The flames hungrily lapped at the ichor and consumed the monster bits.

"So, boyo, who are you?"

"Blazel," he answered. He couldn't help it. She had the aura of an alpha around her.

"Ahh..." she sounded like she knew who he was. "Come on, you can tell us your story at the fortress. Let's get out of here. This place gives me the creeps. No life, except the boyos and the monsters. Sometimes even a fly would be a nice change." She laughed as she slapped Rolstrun on the back, then jogged off.

Although on the surface it seemed an invitation, Blazel heard the command in it. Since Maheli wasn't his alpha, he could ignore it, instead he shrugged and followed her. She held out the lure of company after so long alone in the swamps. Rolstrun loped to his side, a grin on his face and his tongue hanging out like a young wolf.

They walked past the battlefield and over a small rise where the fighting-pack waited. The brecha hadn't traveled far before Blazel and Rolstrun stopped it.

"He's okay," Maheli told her people. "He's the one from the Sanctuary Histrun told us about."

The others regarded him warily. A few growled.

"Enough!" Maheli snapped. "I vouch for him. No arguments." The ones who had growled lowered their heads in submission. "Good. Let's go." Maheli strode off.

The rest followed her. A few had injuries from the fight, but none appeared serious. Blazel and his companion brought up the rear. They hadn't walked far before encountering two men and a woman holding the reins of numerous horses. Maheli and the other five Reds greeted the horse handlers. When the breeze shifted, blowing the monster stench on the warrior's fur toward them, the horses shivered and blew nervous snorts. Maheli threw a container of water to the men. As soon as they had washed the worst ichor stains off themselves, they all transformed back to human, even Blazel. He swayed on his feet. Rolstrun's strong hands caught him before he fell.

"You okay, buddy?" he asked.

Before Blazel could answer, Maheli walked over to him. "Boyo, you look awful. Who's chasing you?"

"No one," he answered, his voice gruff. He took a quick swallow of water, and when he continued, his voice was stronger. "I need to reach the Sanctuary, fast."

"Where did you come from? You're a long way from any safe place."

"I'm traveling from the southern swamps."

Maheli tapped her helbraught staff against her thigh. "Hmm. The swamps, huh? Must be some story. Come on. You're not going anywhere until you get a hot meal and some rest. You could use some time out of the Barrens' nasty air, too."

Blazel wasn't quite sure if it was good luck or bad that he'd run into the bossy, nosy Alpha Maheli. He should turn his back on her offer of friendship and continue on his way toward Chariel. Instead, he followed Rolstrun. Everyone mounted their horses, except Blazel, who glanced around lost. The group hadn't brought an extra horse.

"Alpha, he can ride with me." The woman, who had stayed with the horses during the fight, offered. She took off her scarf and shook out her long chestnut-brown hair.

Blazel's eyebrows rose. He'd never heard of Browns going into battles with the Malvers' monsters. This clan-pack must be different to let their skilled healer so close to the monsters.

"You sure, Faelyn?"

Faelyn dipped her head. "When he passes out, I can do some healing for him while we ride." She studied Blazel with her deep blue-green eyes. "You really have pushed hard."

"I won't pass out," he ground out.

"I have no doubt you will." Faelyn smiled, then lifted her foot off the stirrup for him to mount the horse and sit behind her. When he tried to put his hands on the saddle pommel, the healer tucked them around her waist.

"Lean on me, Blazel. I'm strong."

Her hands gently cradled his. Soft, warm healing energy spread throughout his body. Without meaning to, he leaned against her back and laid his head on her shoulder.

Damn, he thought as he passed out.

Blazel woke with a start. Unfamiliar scents clogged his nose. He groaned from the luxury of sleeping on a soft mattress, something he hadn't experienced for years. He blinked his eyes, finally recognizing the healer from the battle standing over him.

"Shh... you're safe." She gently soothed his forehead. "I'm Faelyn. You're in the eastern fortress. We're from Strunland Keep."

Blazel stretched. All the aches and pains he'd acquired over the past three chedan were gone. "How long?" he croaked, his voice hoarse from talking only to himself for over a year.

"Last night and most of this morning."

"It feels longer." He felt like he'd slept for days, not one night.

She patted his hand. "I do good work. Here." She handed him a mug.

His hands trembled when he took it. He hadn't eaten much in his grueling run. Nothing tasted right with Barrens grit for seasoning. Lifting the cup, he sniffed, inhaling the aroma of a spicy taevo. He groaned with pleasure when he took a sip. "I haven't drunk any good taevo for over nine lunadars."

The taevo bush didn't grow in the humid swamps. When he'd exhausted his supply of leaves, he'd resorted to brewing an herbal concoction. Luckily, mint grew in abundance, which he used to disguise the less palatable flavors of the other herbs.

"How long have you been in the swamps? No, don't answer." Faelyn waved her hand in a negating gesture. "Maheli will be mad if you tell me before she gets to hear the tale. She loves a good story, so no bare-bones recitation. Come to think of it, we could all use a good story. We've been here half a lunadar, but it seems longer."

Faelyn replaced the mug of taevo with a bowl of rich broth with bits of meat and vegetables. Blazel drooled. After the first bite, he shoveled it in his mouth. Low growls of pleasure escaped him. He had forgotten the joys of well-seasoned and cooked food.

Faelyn laughed, and his gaze flicked up at the sound. Her smile was kind. "You must have had some adventure. My cooking isn't that good. Now, Teledon ke-Strunlair, on the other hand, has a strong Green Talent. Anything he cooks tastes sublime. I'll let you finish while I tell Maheli you're awake."

She left before he could thank her.

He considered Faelyn's unaccustomed kindness. Maheli's acceptance still puzzled him. During the biannual Alpha Competitions at the Sanctuary, he'd met the young men of the various alphas' parties—Rolstrun may have even been one of them. They'd exchanged polite conversations, but none of them ever stayed long enough for a friendship to develop. He liked the men who had taught him, like Histrun, but they were mentors. Chariel was his only close friend. Blazel sighed heavily. *What would it be like to have a group of friends?*

After draining his soup bowl, Blazel was still famished. Another bowl waited for him on the table next to him. This one, he ate more slowly, savoring the deliciousness. He'd been eating his own cooking for a very long time, and it was a treat to eat someone else's cooking, especially when they had a flair for food.

Finished eating, he surveyed the sparsely furnished room. The bed he lay on, as well as a table with a chair next to it, and a trunk for possessions were all utilitarian. Sheadash stone, quarried from far to the north, formed the walls. A necessity in this environment where its properties repelled the Malvers' monsters.

His backpack sat on the trunk. The thick leather was still sound but showed signs of hard use. Stains of various colors made it difficult to tell its original color. The pack drooped, half-empty.

Blazel swore as he jumped from the bed. Someone had gone through his pack. He opened it and paused when the door swung open.

"No worries, boyo, we took your clothes to clean them for you," Maheli said from the doorway. "Didn't survive the cleaning, though. Nothing left but rags."

Maheli leaned against the door frame. Her head nearly touched the top. Her lean, compact build showed her strength. Small scars on her hands and arms attested to her numerous fights with the Malvers' monsters. She wore her fiery-red hair short with a few tight curls framing her pale, creamy face. Her light-green eyes tipped up slightly at the corners.

Faelyn walked in, pushing past Maheli, holding a bundle. "Here are some clean clothes. They should fit."

Blazel took the pile and flipped through it. He pulled it tight to his chest. The clothes were new, not someone's cast offs. "Thanks!"

"We only bring a few spares with us," Faelyn told him. "That's what we could scrounge from the men."

"Any chance I can get some leathers like the Reds wear?" Men wore tough woven trousers, not the durable leather made for the women fighters. The warrior's pelts protected them from the monster's ichor. "The way I travel," Blazel explained, "and the things I run into, they sure would come in handy. Besides, they'd last a lot longer than these."

Maheli stared at him. "I don't know..."

"I am a Red, see." He held out his hand, and after a moment of concentration, a small flame danced on it.

"Wow!" Rolstrun said, striding into the room. "That is so cool. I can't do that."

Most men's Talent was too weak to do much with elemental magic. They only used their magic to shapeshift or for such things as cooking, like the man with Green talent. Fire magic seemed to take more Talent to work even small spells, such as the one Blazel used now. The Supreme had allowed him to stay in the Sanctuary after he'd turned five only because of his strong Red Talent—and his Gray Talent. Both made him an unusual male. Being outcasts had drawn him and Chariel together as children.

"Very few males can do magic like that," Maheli echoed his thoughts. She stepped away from the door.

Blazel detected a hint of admiration in her voice. He had expected scorn.

Maheli reached out to touch the gray streak in his hair, now in a tight coil. "Hmmm..." she said under her breath, "maybe, just maybe..." Still holding the lock of hair, she chuckled. "Depends on your story, boyo."

"Um, Blazel," Rolstrun said, wrinkling his nose. "No offense, bro, but you need to bathe!"

"Can't disagree with you there."

"Rolstrun will show you to the bathing room," Faelyn said, explaining Rolstrun's presence.

"When you're done, he'll bring you to me," Maheli added. "Then, boyo, it's story time. Your story."

The two women left the room. Without their strong presence, the room felt larger.

"Come on, man," Rolstrun waved his hand in front of his face and curled his upper lip. "Let's get you to the bathing room, pronto!" He strode out the door.

Blazel gripped the bundle of clothing to his chest and followed.

Chapter 4

Blazel listened with interest to Rolstrun's running commentary as they walked through the fortress about the building, but tuned him out when he talked about the people. He didn't want to know about them; they would never be friends.

The corridors were narrow and winding. The few open doors led into small rooms similar to the one he'd just left. Rolstrun led him down steep steps that wound deeper into the keep. Sheadash stone lined every surface, even deep in the keep's bowels.

Rolstrun stopped at a large door, and Blazel stepped back up the stairs to avoid trampling his guide.

"This is my favorite place in the keep." Rolstrun threw open the door. "It's warm!"

"Wow! I've never been in a bathing room like this before." Blazel clamped his mouth shut, sure his comment made him sound like a rustic. The Sanctuary had a big bathing room, but only the priestesses used it. He'd had to make do with a bucket of hot water in a corner of the kitchen. Even though the men's ward for the visiting males had a bathhouse, he hadn't had access to it.

Rolstrun studied him critically for a moment. He wore a cheery smile. "No worries, bro. I'll show you around. I could use a bath too. You can put your things here."

Following Rolstrun's example, Blazel carefully placed his new, clean clothes on the wooden bench.

Rolstrun turned back to the large, open room and pointed to several deep tubs made from fragrant redwood and filled with steaming water. "Those are for soaking. There's a spell on the water to keep it hot. The men with Blue Talent work with the Reds to maintain the spell, since Blues aren't assigned here. We get plenty of Reds," he laughed. "We're really lucky Faelyn came with us this time. She may be a Brown, but she's a pretty strong Blue too. She and Maheli work well together. We never run out of hot water. Hey!" He stopped Blazel from dipping his filthy hand in the warm water. "You can't get in those until you're clean. Faelyn would skin our hides getting in there dirty."

Rolstrun picked up two small buckets and handed one to Blazel. "These are for cleaning." He carried his to a spigot on a smaller tub and turned a knob. Hot water streamed out. Once his bucket was filled, he pointed to Blazel's. "Now yours."

Afterward, Rolstrun led him to an area with stools, cloths, brushes, and several pots filled with thick, white soap. Blazel inhaled the fragrant pine scent. His throat tightened and tears sprung in his eyes as homesickness swamped him.

Rolstrun placed the bucket by a stool, then stripped off his clothes. He grabbed a cloth, dunked it into the water, and splashed it over himself. After dipping a small soft-bristled brush into a pot of soap, he lathered his body.

Blazel watched for a moment. He'd been bathing alone, outdoors and in streams, for most of his life. He'd never bathed with anyone else before. Rolstrun didn't seem to mind.

"Aren't you washing?" Rolstrun's eyebrows furrowed. "Do you need help?"

"No," Blazel mumbled and turned his back to take off his clothes—and to hide his blush. The thought of being truly clean quickly overcame his bashfulness. The hot water felt wonderful, and the refined soap was a pure luxury he rarely experienced. He'd always used a harsh lye soap. "What about my hair?"

"What's up with the matted, twisted locks, anyway, bro?"

"Too long in the swamps. I'd have to shave my head to get rid of them." Blazel shrugged. "I like them now."

"Oh, okay."

Blazel didn't think anything would faze Rolstrun's easy-going nature.

"There's another place for washing your hair and for rinsing. Wait 'till you see it! Are you finished soaping?" Rolstrun stood, soap dripping off him.

Blazel hurried to finishing scrubbing his body.

"This way." Rolstrun led him to a huge barrel raised off the ground. A big, wide spigot on a pipe stuck out of the top and a chain hung next to it. He stood under the spigot and tugged on the chain. A lever lowered and water swooshed out, like a mini waterfall. The soap slid off him and circled down a drain in the floor. Rolstrun ducked under the water, soaking his hair. He yanked the chain again, and the lever popped up, stopping the flow of water. He stepped aside. "Your turn."

Blazel stood under the spigot, pulled on the chain, and reveled in the warm water sloshing over him. Rolstrun held out a pot of clear liquid soap.

"For your hair. Bro, I don't know, but you might need to wash it more than once. Hold out your hand."

Blazel did as asked, and Rolstrun poured the liquid into his palm. Blazel picked up one of his dreadlocks and rubbed in the soap. As he squeezed a coil hair, he curled his lip at the foul water pouring from it, then worked with a vengeance on the other locks. A touch on his back startled him, and he jerked away. He'd been warned about how promiscuous the packs were. They had sex with whomever they pleased; gender wasn't an issue. He'd never been with anyone before.

"Hey, no worries," Rolstrun said softly, "just helping, bro. You have a lot of hair!"

Rolstrun worked on the back of his hair while Blazel cleaned the front. Rolstrun was right: it took two washings for the water to run clear.

"Now for the good part!" Rolstrun ambled to an enormous round tub and climbed in. "There's room for both of us." He made a welcoming gesture as he settled on a bench.

Trying not to feel prudish, Blazel joined him, moving to the opposite side, as far away from Rolstrun as he could get. He felt less self-conscious once he sat and submerged his body.

"Usually after a fight," Rolstrun informed him, "this room is filled. We left it empty for you."

"Thank you for thoughtfulness."

"Faelyn insisted. She might not be the alpha, but you listen to her."

"I can understand that." Blazel leaned back and fully relaxed for the first time in three years. Rolstrun seemed to sense his need for quiet and stopped talking. Blazel drifted into a doze.

"Why aren't you in a pack, bro?" Rolstrun broke the silence. "I thought we had to live in packs."

"I was born and raised in the Sanctuary with my mother and grandmother. The only pack there are the guards, but I wasn't part of it. When I left, I traveled north, to the Deep Mountains where there aren't any Posairs, let alone packs." Blazel smiled as he remembered the flight of Gryphons who had taken him in. For the first time, he had felt like he belonged somewhere, even though he was an outsider and a different species.

"How old were you? Why did you go north?"

"I was seventeen." He debated whether to tell Rolstrun why. It was the same reason he had spent the last three years in the swamps—Chariel. He decided to risk it. Rolstrun just might be the friend he'd never had. "My friend Chariel sent me."

Rolstrun looked at him with awe. "Chariel's your friend?"

"Yep. We grew up together. How do you know about her?"

"When Wisah, a White Priestess, came home from the Sanctuary, she constantly talked about Chariel. I've heard she's a powerful Gray."

"Yes, she is. When Chariel has an oracle vision about you, you go where she sends you."

"Well, that explains why we haven't seen you until now. Histrun expected you to come to Strunland Keep when you left the Sanctuary. He knew it was only a matter of time before the Supreme made you leave, and you'd need a pack. He speaks highly of you and ordered us to be on the lookout for you."

Blazel slapped the water in irritation. "He never told me. I thought no one would take me into their pack. Since I didn't have any place to go, I happily went wherever Chariel sent me. But now, I've been on my own so long, I don't know if I can be in a pack." He heard the longing in his voice. Men were meant to live in packs, not alone. He treasured his time with the Gryphon flight.

"If you decide you want to join a pack, come to Strunland. We'll welcome you. Histrun still has his fingers in running things there. He'd find a place for an ugly wolf like you."

Blazel self-consciously touched the stark, thick scar on his face. Even a thick beard couldn't hide it. It began at his right cheekbone and ran down his cheek, barely missing his mouth. It continued over his chin and across his neck and chest, ending at his left elbow.

"Hey, sorry, bro," apology filled Rolstrun's voice. He ducked his head. "Didn't mean it like that. Sometimes I speak before I think."

"It's okay. I've had it for a long time, and I forget it's there."

"How did you get it?" Rolstrun's eyes lit up.

"I was seventeen and had just left the Sanctuary and traveled to the Deep Mountains. I knew nothing about them or living in the wilds. Thank the Mother, the wolf instinct is strong in our wolf form. I would have starved otherwise."

"You really didn't know how to hunt as a man or a wolf? It's the first thing they teach us when we're little. Most of us go hunting as much as possible." Rolstrun grinned. "It gets us away from the girls. Especially the Reds! I mean, they're nice and everything, but they can be so bossy. Rizelya, for instance, isn't an alpha, at least not yet, but you'd think she was one already. She bosses everyone around." His voice took on a wistful quality. "But then she could boss me all the time."

"Is she your mate?"

"Oh! No! Just wishful thinking," Rolstrun sighed. "We're from the same pack, but I'm younger, and she doesn't even know I exist. But oh, bro, you should see how beautiful she is." Rolstrun sighed again. "Back to your story. You obviously learned how to hunt successfully."

"At the time, I was very inept at living in the wild. I wasn't paying attention and didn't realize I was being hunted. A sabertiger jumped me." Blazel twisted around to show Rolstrun the four parallel lines from his shoulder to waist. "I got these on the first swipe. I must have moved just as he leaped."

Rolstrun whistled. "Bro, those are nasty."

Blazel turned back around and indicated the scars on his face and chest. "I got these when it tried to eat me. Lucky for me, a Gryphon was flying by, and he saved me."

"A Gryphon! Really? I thought they were myths."

"They're real. If it wasn't for Graak, I wouldn't be alive today. He and his flight taught me how to survive in the wilds." Blazel fell silent as longing filled him. He hadn't seen his Gryphon friend for several years. Maybe he could travel to the flight's home after he discovered why Chariel wanted him to return to the Sanctuary. No longer in the mood to continue soaking, he stood.

Rolstrun climbed out of the tub ahead of Blazel. "We've stayed here too long. I'm surprised Maheli hasn't sent someone down to fetch us yet." He handed Blazel a thick towel, then grimaced. "Not a good thing."

They quickly dried and dressed. Blazel ran his hands over the first new clothes he had worn in several years. They fit his tall and muscular frame well. Woven yellow geometric shapes dotted the fabric of the turquoise shirt—the work of a skilled weaver. Complementary designs were embroidered around the edge of the neck, sleeves, and hem. The deep-blue pants were in the sturdy, thick weave most men and women favored. It withstood the rigors of fighting and daily living. Trousers made with this fabric lasted a long time, unless they met with the acidic monster ichor.

Blazel sat on a bench near the wall and lifted his boot to put it on. "Ugh," he grimaced, making a face. Swamp gunk plastered it with a deep coating of Barrens particles layered over it. His stomach turned at putting the filthy boots on his clean feet.

"Here." Rolstrun held out a pair of slippers. "Wear these until we get back upstairs. We might have a pair of boots that will fit you."

"That would be great. Mine have had it." He tossed his worn-out boots into a trash bin.

Blazel followed Rolstrun to the main section of the keep. They dug into a storage closet and found a new pair of boots in his size.

Being clean and wearing clothes that weren't rags inspired confidence. Blazel pulled his shoulders back, ready to face Alpha Maheli.

Blazel followed Rolstrun into the courtyard filled with people practicing, the men wrestling and the women spinning their helbraughts. One by one, they stopped to stare at Blazel as he passed by.

"No worries, bro. They're just curious." Rolstrun patted Blazel's shoulder. "No one here is going to hurt you."

Blazel quit growling and rubbed his arms to smooth the hair standing on end. Keeping his gaze on the ground, he walked at Rolstrun's side. It would be poor manners on his part to challenge these men after Maheli's hospitality.

Finally, they crossed the courtyard and reached a door. Rolstrun knocked and Maheli called for them to enter.

"Well, well, boyo, you clean up nice," Maheli said as they entered the room. She sat behind a desk with a large man next to her. "This is Bohandran ke-Strunland, my co-alpha."

Blazel ducked his head in acknowledgment of the two alphas. Rolstrun left, shutting the door behind him.

"Now, boyo, I want to hear a story. Your story."

"It could take a while to tell all of it." Blazel knew he was walking a thin line. He wasn't used to dealing with the hierarchy of a pack.

Maheli's lips lifted in a smile. "We have the time."

Bohandran pulled his mouth in a tight line, and menace radiated from him. "Why aren't you in a pack, *rogue?*" He leaned forward, hands pressed on the desk, and rose slightly.

Blazel narrowed his eyes, then took a deep breath, letting the insult slide over him. Male alphas had a problem with wolves who weren't part of a pack, and for good reason. Rogues killed people, and it was the alpha's responsibility to put them down.

"I was born and raised in the Sanctuary. Not any packs there. No need, no men."

"Why didn't you join one when you came of age and left the Sanctuary?" Maheli sounded curious, not annoyed.

Blazel hunched his shoulders. "I thought no one wanted me."

"Strunland would have accepted you. Histrun likes you," Maheli said.

Blazel shrugged. "He never told me. Besides, Chariel sent me north. That's why I left."

"Chariel?" Bohandran's eyebrows furrowed in disbelief. "The Gray Oracle? Why would she send a rogue like you anywhere?"

"I don't know why, but she's had a few visions about me." He pushed down his irritation. Bohandran's attitude was like most people Blazel had met. If you didn't belong to a pack, you must be a rogue—a dangerous menace, exiled from the packs for the safety of all—and not alone by choice. "Because of her visions, I lived in the Deep Mountains for almost five years, and it's why I've spent the last three traveling to every swamp I could find. I certainly didn't do it because it was fun." Blazel turned to Maheli, who seemed to like him. "Besides, Chariel's my friend. She's calling me back to the Sanctuary now. It's important I get there quickly."

"Then we'll help you do so." Maheli gestured for him to sit down.

Bohandran looked aghast at Maheli. "You don't believe his bullshit story, do you?"

"Yes, I do. You're fairly new to our clan-pack, so you don't know Histrun well. He's been talking about this boyo and his relationship with Chariel for years. Thinks he's something special." Maheli gazed for a long moment at Blazel. "I think Histrun might be right. But why is it so necessary for you to return to the Sanctuary?"

Blazel shrugged, then surged to his feet in frustration and paced the small room. "Her voice whispers in the back of my head saying, *'hurry, hurry, hurry.'* Just before I left the southern swamp, I remembered her vision that sent me there." He looked directly at Maheli, for some reason wanting her to believe him. "I'm scared, Alpha. I'm scared something horrible is coming, worse than the Malvers' monsters. When fire is in the sky, the madness is near." He slapped his hand over his mouth, unsure why he'd said that.

Bohandran raised an eyebrow and cocked his head. It was hard to imagine anything worse than their ancient enemy.

Maheli scowled. "Why do you think that, boyo?"

"Something I remembered about her vision." Blazel sank onto his chair and leaned toward the desk. "She said there was madness approaching and what I learned in the swamp could save us. Even she was frightened of what she saw, and she couldn't remember much of it." Blazel paused, his eyes widening as he continued. "Come to think of it, when she sent me north, I was to find that which would save us all."

"What are you to save us from?" Doubt laced Bohandran's voice.

Blazel shot up from his chair again. "I don't know," he all but howled. "She couldn't tell me, only that it's awful."

"We've been seeing a much higher activity of Malvers' monster nests," Maheli commented, rubbing her chin, "even a new type of janack."

"I noticed. It's been difficult to cross the Barrens without being seen or getting caught this time." Blazel smiled ruefully.

"Didn't quite make it, did you, boyo?"

"No, ma'am. I couldn't allow that brecha to escape, though." He turned his attention to Bohandran. "I may be a lone wolf, sir, but I understand my duty when it comes to Malvers' monsters. We never let them get away. We kill them."

"Rolstrun told us you fought well." Bohandran grudgingly admitted.

Blazel's ears burned at the unexpected praise. "I've had to learn to fight all sorts of twisted creatures in the swamps. After them, a lonely brecha wasn't much of a challenge."

"I want to hear the rest of your story," Maheli said with a grin. "Now. It's too late for you to leave today."

"But—"

"No." She put up a hand and stopped him. "We need to gather supplies so you can finish crossing the Barrens quickly, and it will take some time." Bohandran left the office grumbling about rogues.

Maheli settled back in her chair, her hands over her stomach. "Now, tell me the rest of your story. Don't leave anything out. I want to hear it all."

Blazel resigned himself to having to tell this pushy alpha his life history. He took a deep breath. "Well, I came to be born in the Sanctuary like this." Someone brought the midday meal into Maheli's office while he continued telling her. At last, he reached the end. "I hid, waiting for the battle to end, but instead saw a brecha running away with no one following it. You know the rest."

"Thank you, Blazel. I understand why Histrun thinks so highly of you." Maheli pushed away from the desk. "Now, I have work to do."

Blazel left the office and found his way back to the courtyard.

Rolstrun waited for him, lounging against the wall. He gave Blazel a sympathetic smile. "She must have grilled you horribly. You were in there for a long time."

"It wasn't too bad. I need to burn some excess energy from sitting so long. Spar with me?"

Rolstrun nodded with enthusiasm. They were well matched, and soon sweat coated both their faces. A warning bell clanged, and Rolstrun stopped mid move.

"Brave Warrior!" Rolstrun swore. "Another nest is forming. Sorry, Blazel, but I gotta go." He raced across the courtyard toward the stables.

Blazel followed, using his shirt to wipe the sweat off his chest. He found an extra horse and led it out of its stall to stand next to Rolstrun's.

"Why is everyone so frazzled?" Blazel watched how Rolstrun put the tack his horse and copied him. He'd hadn't saddled or ridden a horse in years.

"The nests are forming all out of whack." Rolstrun adjusted the saddle blanket before tossing on the saddle. "Even here near the crater, the nests have always formed on a predictable schedule, but not any longer. We weren't supposed to have a nest to fight for another two days. Blast these damn monsters anyway."

"Well, that would explain why the southern guard-pack south looked so exhausted." Blazel wiggled the saddle to make sure it sat on the horse's withers correctly. "I could only travel a few measures before running into another battle."

"Thank the Crone, it hasn't gotten quite that bad here." Rolstrun finished cinching his saddle and slipped the bridle over his horse's nose.

"Just what do you think you're doing?" Faelyn demanded.

Blazel jumped at her sharp tone. She stood in front of him, her hands on her hips.

"Going to help. There are monsters to be fought." He turned back to tighten the cinch.

"No, you're to stay here," she informed him. "You're on the injured list."

"What?" Blazel whirled around. "I'm not injured. Let me go fight."

"No, we have enough fighters, while you, on the other hand, have a long journey ahead of you. You need to rest." She reached up, standing on her toes to cup his face between her hands. "I know you're a capable fighter, but more than that, Blazel, you're special. We need you to reach the Sanctuary."

He blinked his eyes, holding back tears. No one except his mother, grandmother, and Chariel had ever cared for him. No one told him he was special and needed. And now this delicate healer touched his heart. He turned his face away from her.

"You don't need to be alone anymore, Blazel." Faelyn softly stroked his back. "There's a pack waiting for you. Friends, too."

He looked over his shoulder at her. "Are you an oracle to know this?"

"No. All I have to do is open my eyes. We would be that pack, if you'd let us in."

Deep in thought, he removed the saddle from the horse. Her offer was tempting. He liked Faelyn and Rolstrun, and Maheli seemed like a good alpha. They held out a hand of friendship to him. All he needed to do was take it. Then he heard Chariel's voice in the back of his mind, 'hurry, hurry, hurry.' Now wasn't the time, but maybe someday he'd be able to accept the offer.

He watched Rolstrun and his pack-mates race from the fortress, then trudged to the room assigned to him and laid on the cot. *Have I accomplished what I needed to do in the swamps or the Deep Mountains? I don't think I found anything to combat the monsters we aren't already using. Why is Chariel calling me back now? What is this madness?* In the quiet, he drifted to sleep, dreaming of fire in the sky and the ground soaked in blood.

After dinner, the guard-pack sat around the dining hall, needing company to ease the grief of losing a pack-mate during the afternoon battle. Blazel lounged with Maheli and a few others in front of the fire. He replayed his headlong dash across the Barrens and dodging fight after fight with the Malvers' monsters.

"Why don't you go into the crater and destroy the monsters while they're in the nest?" Blazel asked. "It would have to be much easier to kill them then instead of when they're adults and are out in the Barrens."

"No one goes to the crater floor." Rolstrun made a sign of protection. "There are horror stories passed down from the first guard-packs, who didn't understand the danger. A huge fighting force, almost two hundred men and women, went into the crater and fought for six lunadar. They only came back to the rim for supplies before going back down. Their mission was to destroy the source responsible for the monsters. Of those two hundred, only an eighth returned." Rolstrun shuddered.

Pity haunted Maheli's eyes. "Of those twenty-five, none of the men could ever shapeshift again into their wolf or warrior forms. The women had been among the strongest Reds in the land, but afterward, they could work only the minor magics. Sadly, their magic never returned to their former strength."

"Any children born to them later were horribly deformed," Faelyn said, picking up the story. "Many were so malformed they had to be killed."

"Surely they didn't kill infants?" Blazel interrupted, horrified.

Faelyn nodded sadly. "If they didn't, those who lived turned into monsters and attacked pack-mates. All twenty-five survivors died within five years."

"But that was a long time ago, wasn't it? The magic causing the problems has probably dissipated by now."

Bohandran shook his head. "No, it hasn't. It's worse. Part of our job is to make sure no foolhardy youngsters try to climb down to the crater. Every year, we get a few who slip past and make it. They do it on a dare. Those who reach the bottom and survive to come up again lose the ability to shapeshift. Sometimes, it's temporary, other times it's permanent, depending on how long they stayed. It's always worse when they climb on the monolith. So no, we don't go to the crater floor."

Blazel started shaking.

"Hey, what's wrong, bro?" Rolstrun asked.

"I'm so glad now I didn't cross through the crater. I like being able to shapeshift too much to lose it."

"It's a good thing you didn't," Faelyn concurred. "I doubt I could have healed you. The crater sickness is nasty."

The talk turned to other things. Blazel listened to the easy banter between the pack-mates. It reminded him of his time with Graak's flight. At first he'd been shy and uneasy, but after a few chedans, he'd relaxed into their acceptance and became part of the flight—and their teasing. He looked longingly at the pack sitting casually around the fire.

Maybe he could be part of a pack like this one day. If the camaraderie of this group was any indication of pack life, he'd go to Strunland Keep when he finished whatever it was Chariel needed him for. He sat listening until Maheli sent everyone to bed, even him. An unusual feeling suffused his heart as he drifted to sleep.

Belonging.

Chapter 5

An octar before dawn, Rolstrun walked to the stables with Blazel. "My feet, whether two or four, get me where I'm going just fine," he grumbled under his breath, kicking a pebble out of his path.

"Hey, bud, what's wrong?" Rolstrun raised an eyebrow at the skittering rock.

"Alphas!" Blazel exploded. "I don't want or need a horse. Maheli wouldn't listen to reason and ended our argument by ordering me to take one."

Rolstrun made a face and shuddered. "It's a long way from here to Strunlair Keep, and longer still to the White Mountains. I can't imagine traveling that far without a horse! Doing it in a straight shot would kill my feet, or paws. Besides, don't you need to reach the Sanctuary fast?"

"I do. Perhaps it will be easier and faster riding a horse," Blazel grudgingly admitted. He hadn't told Maheli his true reason. He hadn't ridden a horse since leaving the Sanctuary, only traveling on foot.

Blazel expected a horse to be ready and waiting for him, but instead, Colstrun, the horse-master, met him at the stable door with four horses on lead lines.

"Choose one of these," the horse-master told him. "They be plains horses, caught and raised by the Haaslair Clan."

Blazel had heard about the odd speech pattern of the Haaslair Clan. Most of the horse masters were from that clan, and those that weren't adopted the mannerism. This one was no exception.

"Alpha Maheli told me you needed to travel far and fast. These lovelies have stamina and speed to spare, not to mention being sweet-tempered. They be the best available here. Any one of them will get you where you goin' to. Go on, take a gander."

Blazel approached each horse and looked them over. They seemed to study him as intently. He wasn't any judge of horseflesh, good or bad. He simply wanted a horse who liked him.

"They won't run from you in either your wolf or warrior forms. The Haaslair be right fine horse trainers. Hear tell some of 'em even shift to horse instead of wolf." Colstrun was rightfully proud to have horses of this caliber. Not all clan-packs were fortunate enough to have Haaslair horses, and if these horses were evidence, the Strunland pack seemed to have an abundance of them.

Blazel had turned to face the horse-master as they talked. A clop sounded behind him, and then he felt a gentle pressure as a chin rested on his shoulder. He stepped back to gaze at the beautiful mare. She was a big bay, with a black mane, tail, and socks, and her fine black stripes were only visible close up. Her nose had a white blaze that looked vaguely like a lightning bolt.

"Ah, good choice." The horse-master sounded pleased. "She be Lighzel. She's a fast one." He ran a hand down her shoulder. "She has a good heart and will carry you until she drops." He turned to Blazel and shook a finger at him. "But don't you take advantage of her and treat her ill."

Blazel shook his head fiercely. "No, sir, I won't. I'll treat her right. She's a beauty." He rubbed her muzzle and talked quietly to her as the stable hand led the other horses away.

"She's a good horse, bro," Rolstrun told him. "I've ridden her a few times. She has a lovely, smooth gait."

"Come on, then," the horse-master said. "Let's get you geared up. Alpha wants you outta here by dawn." He sauntered into the stable. Blazel picked up Lighzel's lead line and followed him.

Colstrun started pulling tack out and placing it on a stand next to a rail. He stopped when he noticed Blazel still standing with Lighzel's lead in his hand. "Well, what you waitin' for? Tie her up there and start gettin' her tacked."

Blazel looked around and panicked. Rolstrun had disappeared. Only the horse-master and Blazel were in the stable, and there wasn't anyone he could copy.

"Um, sir, I could use some help," Blazel confessed. "It's been a long time since I've ridden." Putting the tack on his new horse wrong terrified him. It could cause both of them problems if he did. Without Rolstrun around, he didn't know what to do.

"No shame in admittin' you need help, boy," Colstrun said. "Shame comes from not askin'."

The horse-master showed him basic horse care. He had Blazel clean the frogs of Lighzel's hooves of any dirt and small stones. "Don't care how much of a hurry you be, you do this every day before you ride. Keeps her from going lame." Afterward, Colstrun demonstrated how to put on the various gear and then proceeded to pull it all off. He led Lighzel into a stall and took off her halter.

"Now, you," he directed. "Start from the beginning."

Blazel went into the stall and put on Lighzel's halter. "Come on, sweet girl," he said, leading her out. As he put on her tack, the necessary steps came back to him from his childhood lessons. He had a moment of panic when he picked up several additional pieces he didn't recall using at the Sanctuary.

"It's barding, boy," Colstrun explained. "It be used when we cross other provinces than our home one."

At Colstrun's direction, he put the extra tack on Lighzel as well. Colorful barding straps with decorations ran across her rump and attached to a fitted chest piece. Over the saddle pad, a long silky turquoise draped past her belly. Symbols embroidered in rose and a darker blue decorated the bottom of it. All of it was in a beautiful rose and a turquoise blue. After it was all on, he remembered seeing similar getup on the visiting Posairs' horses when they arrived at the biannual gatherings held at the Sanctuary.

"Good job, lad," the horse-master told him. Then he walked away before Blazel could thank him or ask him about the barding.

"Don't mind him," Rolstrun said, "he's always like that."

Blazel jumped. He'd been so engrossed in readying his new horse, he hadn't heard Rolstrun come in.

"Here are your supplies and backpack." Rolstrun held a set of saddlebags stuffed full and Blazel's old pack.

A quick inspection revealed the saddlebags held food, travel utensils, a small medical kit, grooming tools, and another shirt. Blazel spotted an oilcloth for shelter at the bottom of one bag. The amount and quality of supplies stunned him. He'd easily reach the plains and beyond before needing to resupply. A quick examination of his backpack assured him he still had his dried herbs and plant specimens. Someone had removed the last of his dried swamp rat, replacing it with travel bars.

"Oh, and this." Rolstrun lifted a bedroll off his back and handed it to Blazel, along with a map.

The map showed all the territories he would travel through on his northern journey. Marked on it were all the known nest sites and safe-house locations. It would allow him to travel in relative safety. He studied the map for a moment and discovered the Barrens, as he suspected, had only a few distant shelters. If they couldn't reach one, he and Lighzel would have to make do with whatever they could find.

"Thanks! This will be a great help. I haven't seen a map like this before." Blazel settled the saddlebags and bedroll behind Lighzel's saddle, fastening them on tightly. He picked up her reins and led her from the stable, with Rolstrun pacing beside him. To his surprise, Maheli and Faelyn waited for him outside. The first rays of dawn streaked across the sky. Faelyn held a bundle in her arms.

"Thank you, Maheli." Blazel bowed. "Your gifts were generous."

"No thanks necessary, boyo, and we're not done yet. We have one more gift for you." She leaned in and said in a low voice, "Mind you, Bohandran had fits about it." She gestured Faelyn forward, took the bundle from her, and gave it to Blazel.

He opened it and stood stunned, gaping and sputtering.

Maheli laughed. "Boyo, a Red needs the proper leathers. Go change, the sun's arising."

Blazel handed Rolstrun Lighzel's reins and ran into the stable. A few moments later, he returned dressed in the supple red leathers. They fit perfectly and moved as though they were a second skin.

"My, you're a pretty sight in those, boyo," Maheli commented. "When you get to the Sanctuary, tell the Supreme about what we've been fighting. Between the increase in nests and the new monster, we're barely holding on. We need more help."

"I'll tell her," Blazel promised.

He was in for another shock as first Faelyn, then Rolstrun, hugged him and wished him safe travels.

Maheli grabbed him in an embrace and said in his ear, "You're a good kid, boyo. Look us up at Strunland Keep. We could use someone like you in our pack." She released him and stepped back before he could say anything.

"Up you go," Maheli ordered him. "Oh, you needn't worry about being seen by the other guard-packs. You're wearing our colors." She indicated the barding. "They'll think you're from our pack and won't bother you. Safe travels, boyo. I hope to meet you again one day!"

He climbed into the saddle, less graceful than he wished. In a daze, he kicked Lighzel into a trot and headed out of the fortress. *They've accepted me as one of their own. Otherwise, they wouldn't have given me the barding and the leathers.*

A strange feeling fluttered in Blazel's chest. For the first time, he left the company of Posairs feeling like he was leaving friends behind.

Blazel rode from the fortress at a fast trot. Lighzel's smooth gait made her a pleasure to ride. He'd been riding for over an octar when ahead of them the black sand glittered. The sun bounced off a large glass patch. Before, while traveling in his wolf form, he hadn't been able to see the glass patches before running through it and shredding his paws. Now, higher off the ground, they were easy to spot. He wasn't sure if it would hurt Lighzel to cross it, but going around it would be measures out of his way. Blazel slowed Lighzel, guided her carefully across the sand-glass, and once they were through, reined her to a stop.

He stopped in mid-climb off his horse. His rear and thighs screamed in pain. It would take a few days for his body to acclimate to riding a horse. Finally, he managed to slide out of the saddle and hung onto Lighzel's side. She turned her head to look at him and snorted, as if asking him what he was doing.

When he could move, he lifted each of Lighzel's feet, breathing a sigh of relief when there wasn't any damage. He limped back to inspect the sand-glass and discovered her heavy hooves had pulverized it into fine dust. "Thank the Mother!" He pumped a fist in the air. "I can travel faster across the glass fields without worrying about hurting Lighzel."

He drank from the water container and then poured some into a dish he'd found in his saddlebags for Lighzel. Her care was now his responsibility. He marveled at the new experience of someone else depending on him. When she finished drinking, he gritted his teeth, hauled himself onto her back, and urged her forward.

His long-ago riding lessons gradually returned. He settled more comfortably into the saddle, then pushed Lighzel into a trot and then a canter. The ground flew under her hooves. She slowed when a jumble of petrified wood blocked their way. Had Blazel been in his wolf form, he'd have just leaped from boulder to boulder to traverse the pile. He nudged Lighzel into an opening between two large rocks and followed a path threading through the maze.

When they exited, the unmistakable sounds of a monster battle floated to him. Blazel stood in the stirrups, scanning the area, finally sighting the plumes of Barrens dust kicked up by the fight in the distance. He lowered back into the saddle and spurred Lighzel into a canter to put even more space between them and the fight.

Blazel remembered the horse-master's warning and eased Lighzel into a walk once the battle was far behind them. They fell into a pattern of walking, trotting, cantering, and stopping every few octars to rest. Each time he stopped, he was a little less saddle sore.

Late in the afternoon, he studied the map. It showed a single shelter in this quadrant used by the guard-packs on their way to and from the crater. He angled his route toward the shelter, reaching it before the sun dropped below the horizon. He snugged Lighzel into a stall and stumbled into the small building. Blazel ate a travel bar before falling exhausted onto a cot, which was almost as welcomed as the relief of being out of the dust.

The next day followed the same pattern. Suddenly, Lighzel started dancing, refusing to go forward. Her eyes were white with fear. Blazel breathed deeply, trying to scent what his horse did. All he could smell was Barrens dust—a lot of it. His heart hammered at the wall of black dust, fifty feet high or more, barreling at him. He jabbed his heels into Lighzel's flanks.

They raced toward the only shelter in the area—a pile of petrified wood boulders. He yanked on her reins and leaped from her back when they reached them. Hastily rummaging through his saddlebags, he found the oilcloth and extra shirt. He tore the shirt into strips, then coaxed Lighzel to lie down by the rocks. Working quickly, he tied a strip over her eyes and another around her muzzle to protect her from the damaging dust and glass particles in the windstorm. He fought the wind as he tucked the oilcloth around her, bits of glass cutting his hands and face as the sandstorm overtook them. He slid under the oilcloth, curled against Lighzel, and pulled the oilcloth tight over them. Blazel used the last strips of the shirt to tie a mask over his own face.

The wind howled and particles beat against the oilcloth. The afternoon light darkened. Blazel huddled next to Lighzel, relaxing into her warmth and falling asleep. He still wasn't recovered from his ordeal of crossing the first portion of the Barrens or living in the swamps. Much later, Lighzel's snort woke him as she struggled to stand, alerting him that the storm had stopped.

"Easy, girl, let me get us unwrapped."

Blazel crawled under the edge of the oilcloth. Night had fallen. The moons, Kelar and Zelar, were both nearing the end of their cycle. Only a thin crescent of the smallest moon, Chelar, shone in the sky, indicating a new chedan. He called fire to his hand so he could see. Black sand, glittering with glass shards, covered the oilcloth. They were lucky the glass hadn't shredded it—and their hides with it. Carefully lifting the covering so the sand wouldn't get on her, he slid it off Lighzel. She stood and shook off the last bits of dust.

The boulders provided some shelter. Without the bigger moon's light, he couldn't risk Lighzel breaking a leg sliding on an unseen patch of sand-glass. They didn't have to worry about any predators. The Malvers' monsters went into a stupor after dark, and Blazel had never seen narhili beasts in the Barrens. He decided to stay where they were for the night.

Shaking off his supply pack, he dug out a small lamp. The light provided comfort. He fed Lighzel some grain and watered her before eating a travel bar filled with dried fruit and washing it down with water. To his surprise, the travel bars were tasty, much better than his smoked swamp rat.

The next day, as he rode through the desolate landscape, the tumble of petrified wood thinned. Within ten measures, it disappeared completely and only black sand stretched before him. In the afternoon, Blazel crossed the demarcation of the Barrens. There was no gradual easing of the black sand. It just ceased, and the tall grasses of the plains sprouted.

Lighzel whinnied, picked up her pace, and there was a lightness to her step. The plains were her home. Blazel had a long way to go before he reached the place he'd grown up. He wasn't sure he could call the Sanctuary home anymore.

A few measures from the Barrens, Blazel caught sight of the Storengher River. The immense river flowed from the ice fields in the far north, beyond even the Deep Mountains, through the entire length of Lairheim. It disappeared, going underground, when it reached the Barrens, reappearing on the other side as part of the great southern swamp where Blazel had spent the last year. Once, he had traveled to the southern peninsula's tip and had seen the swamps give way to a large marsh where the Storengher River emptied into the ocean.

On his journey south, Blazel had followed the swamps in the western provinces, then traveled along the coast where no one lived. He had avoided the plains and river. Unlike most people, who stayed close to the safety of the Keeps, the Haaslair clans followed their horse herds as they wandered the plains. There was no telling where they would be in the ocean of grass.

Then, he had all the time in the world to meander south. Now, he was in a hurry, and the quickest way north was following the Storengher River through the plains. Although he risked running into a wandering Haaslair pack, skirting the plains and going north along the coast would take more time than he had. Even as he contemplated the longer—but less likely to meet anyone—route, the whispered, *'hurry, hurry, hurry,'* in his mind grew louder.

Blazel groaned in despair. Any Haaslair packs he met would unlikely give him the easy acceptance he'd received by the Strunland guard-pack. Rather, he expected a hostile reception. He fingered the colorful saddle blanket's edge and hoped the barding would allow him to pass through the plains without being molested for traveling alone. If accosted, he could claim membership in the Strunland pack. It was, after all, what Maheli implied when she gave the barding to him. Whatever happened, he didn't have time to take any other route. He turned Lighzel toward the river and kicked her into a trot.

Chapter 6

Blazel rode for several octars following the Storengher River. As it meandered through the plains, it was wide and lazy. Farther north, it turned into a fast, rushing beast.

Birds flew overhead, small rodents rustled in the grass, and insects buzzed. He spotted a ducorn herd bounding across the plains in the distance, too far away to attempt catching one. Life filled the plains, a stark contrast to the lifeless barrens he had just left. His pace slowed as he swiveled his head side to side, drinking in the sights and smells of living things. The afternoon sun beating down on his back reminded him it was nearly the beginning of summer. The warm, dry heat tempted him, and he took off his leather shirt to soak up the sun as he rode. It had been a long time since he felt sunlight that wasn't filtered through swamp trees.

Every few steps, Lighzel reached her neck out to snatch at the lush green grass growing along the riverbank. Blazel let her. She'd spent several chedans in the Barrens with no fresh fodder. As the day deepened to evening, fish jumped and plopped back into the water, and a rabbit darted in front of Lighzel's hooves. His stomach growled with hunger. The fresh food would be nice after eating only travel bars.

As he rode, Blazel kept an eye out for firewood, but the open plain was devoid of any trees. Just as he was about to give up, an eddy in the bend of the river formed a pool with some driftwood caught in it. A sandy beach made it a good place to spend the night. The river provided some protection from narhili beasts, which avoided rivers.

After taking off Lighzel's saddle, rubbing her down, and feeding her, Blazel set up camp. He remembered the rabbit, then shifted into his wolf form and loped away from the river, his nose low to the ground questing for scents of prey.

It didn't take him long to pick up a fresh scent trail. Suddenly, a rabbit scampered from a bush and he chased it, putting on a burst of speed as it zigzagged ahead of him. Sliding in front of it, he snapped his jaws and missed. Growling in frustration, he continued the chase. He caught the rabbit on his next attempt, shaking his head to break its neck. He dropped it to the ground and nipped off its head. Rich blood filled his mouth, and the skull crunched in his teeth. Fur tickled his tongue.

What am I doing?

Blazel howled, spat out the mangled head, and backed away from the rabbit.

I don't need to eat as a wolf. I am a man, not a beast. I have the means to build a fire and cook it.

Shuddering with effort, Blazel shifted back into his human form and stared at the rabbit and its chewed-up head. It was so easy for him to revert to his wolf self. Shifting from wolf to human was getting easier, but it was still painful. A whinny floated from the river, reminding him his horse awaited his return. Her presence grounded him and helped him remember his true shape. He vowed he'd practice shifting every time he stopped to rest Lighzel.

Blazel picked up the rabbit, walked back to his camp, and dropped it next to his packs. He searched the flotsam and found several suitable pieces of driftwood. Carefully using his magic, he dried them out. When the first piece was dry enough, he added a bit more fire magic, and the wood burst into flame. From long practice, Blazel quickly skinned the rabbit and skewered it to roast over the fire.

Returning to the riverbank, he gathered some wild onions, watercress, and carrots growing nearby. He tossed the vegetables into a pot, seasoned with a few herbs from his bag, to boil. Along with the travel bars, Maheli had included a stash of taevo mixed with spices. Blazel dug out a kettle, filled it with water, and set it by the coals. The meal restored his equilibrium.

After eating, he returned to the comfort of his flute to remind him he was a man. There hadn't been time to play it in the Barrens. He'd been in too much of a rush to cross it.

Blazel continued to parallel the river the next morning. A few octars later, a stone Keep rose out of the sea of grass in the distance. It guarded a stone bridge spanning the river with another Keep on the other side. The temple dome glittered in the sun and longing gripped him. He hadn't been to a temple service in years, and he missed the gentle presence of the Goddess and Her Consort he experienced in the temples.

He kicked Lighzel into a trot, heading toward the Keep. Dust rose as riders left the Keep on his side of the river, and his throat tightened. This wasn't the friendly Strunland pack he'd met at the crater; he doubted they'd understand the difference between a lone wolf and a rogue. His old mentor, Histrun, hadn't been the Clan Alpha of Haaslair to vouch for his trustworthiness. He slumped in his saddle with the realization he couldn't ride to the Keep and ask the White Priestess there for a blessing. Before the patrol could see him, he quickly turned Lighzel away from the Keep and rode deep into the plains.

As they paused on the top of a rise, a herd of ducorns bounded away. A crow cawed as it flew over them. Lighzel's ears pricked forward and then swiveled. Her nostrils flared. Blazel's hands tightened on her reins as he looked all around him for danger until she whinnied a greeting. On a low hill not far from them, a golden stallion with silver stripes gazed at them. He pawed the ground, reared onto his hind legs, neighed, and then took off. The stallion's beauty and grace took Blazel's breath away. Throughout the day, the same stallion, or one exactly like him, appeared on distant hills.

The sun dipped in its westerly journey. Blazel guided his horse toward the river, where they could stay the night in its relative safety. But, only a few measures later, a warrior's deep howl broke the silence. Blazel pulled Lighzel to a stop and tried to place where the sound had come from. Another howl caused Lighzel to dance under him, and he fought to remain on her. A flock of pheasants burst from the ground, close enough to startle Lighzel into rearing. As she landed, she bolted in the direction they had been heading. Blazel glanced over his shoulder. A swirl of dust heralded a battle several measures away. Lighzel sped across the plains. When she slowed, the battle was far behind them, and no one had followed them.

Ten measures later, he caught sight of a battle in progress off to his right. Too embroiled with their fight, the fighters didn't notice him as he galloped past.

The monsters were more active here as well.

He finally reached the river and found a suitable place to camp. Every time he had stopped to rest Lighzel, he had practiced shifting from wolf to human, then back, over and over. Each time he did, the change became easier and less painful.

He called the magic to him and thought of the form he wished to change into. Unsurprisingly, the wolf came easy. He took a breath and willed the change back to human. A thrill of magic coursed through him, this time a pleasurable sensation, and then a moment later he stood in his human shape. A laugh escaped him—it had been as easy as shifting to his wolf form. Still laughing, he willed the shift to warrior, then back to human.

"Thank you, Goddess!" he yelled to the stars. Once again, it was a simple matter of thought to change from one form to another.

That night, Chariel appeared in his dreams, yelling at him to hurry. Behind her, a star fell from the sky, a long trail of fire streaming from it. As it hit the ground, it morphed into a strange monster, unlike anything he'd seen before. Wherever it stepped, blood and death covered the land. Sadness and disappointment pulled on The Supreme's face, and she asked, "Why, Blazel? Why didn't you hurry?"

He woke before dawn, unsettled by the dream. He pushed Lighzel to her top speed. They raced along the river, crashing through the tall grass, stopping only for short breaks. They continued long into the night, with only Chelar's weak light to guide him. When Lighzel stumbled, nearly falling to her knees, Blazel drew her to a halt. Guilty, he walked her to cool her down, then fed and watered her. His hurry had almost cost him his horse. She wasn't some beast he could run to the ground; she was his partner. When he had agreed to take her as his mount at the crater, he had accepted responsibility for her.

If Maheli ever found out about his mistreatment of Lighzel, she'd take it out on his hide. He had no doubt the feisty Red could hurt him. Thoughts about her brought up memories of the others. He wondered what Faelyn and Rolstrun were doing now and if they were unharmed. It surprised him how much he cared about them and how much he missed them.

Exhausted, he fell asleep. The strange monster, fire in the sky, and madness haunted his dreams. Chariel appeared next, terror filling her eyes. She stretched out her hand to him, imploring him to hurry. As he reached for her hand, she turned into someone else. Someone filled with hate and bitterness.

Blazel woke at dawn, panting and sweating from his nightmares. Chariel was in trouble, and he had to stop her from becoming the embittered woman in his dreams. The strange dreams pushed him to increase his pace even more. What would make hate consume her? Lost in his thoughts, he almost galloped into the territory of another Keep bordering a bridge across the Storengher River. A quick turn took him deeper into the plains and saved him from being seen.

Sweat foam flicked off his galloping horse as they raced on. Chagrined, he gradually slowed her down to a walk, then walked her until her sweat dried. Ahead on a small knoll, the shade of a lone tree with spreading branches beckoned him to stop. Lighzel had poured her heart out for him and needed to rest. His growling stomach reminded him it was mid-day and time to eat. He loosened Lighzel's saddle and let her graze. Leaning against the tree, he ate a travel bar and his eyes drifted closed. His horse's munching on the sweet grass, her tail swishing away flies, the sigh of the breeze, and the warmth of the sun lulled Blazel into a doze. He'd been moving full pelt for nearly half a lunadar, except for the two days spent with the Strunland guard-pack at the crater.

A familiar noxious stench jerked him awake. Lighzel's squeal of terror had him sprinting toward her. He tightened her girth strap, grabbed her reins, and hauled himself into the saddle just as the first horse thundered past him, eyes white in fear.

The spiny backs of half a dozen brechas poked out of the grass as they lumbered after the horses. Janack tentacles roiled not far behind. The gold and silver stallion Blazel had seen yesterday tailed the herd, weaving back and forth in front of the monsters. When he passed Blazel and Lighzel, he trumpeted to them. Lighzel took the bit in her teeth and raced after him.

There was nothing Blazel could do except hang on. Alone, he was no match for so many monsters. The ground blurred beneath Lighzel's hooves. She caught up to and outstripped the stallion. He nodded his head, directing them to follow the herd banking west toward the river.

The monster stench grew stronger, and Blazel glanced over his shoulder. The lead brecha nipped at the stallion's heels, who galloped faster. He turned forward again. The herd disappeared from view as they sped down a ravine Blazel hadn't known existed in the rolling plains.

From his left, pounding hoof beats drove toward him. He nearly fell off his horse as two figures rarely encountered outside of the plains dashed past him. Both centaurs had longbows and a quiver of arrows. One nocked an arrow and let it fly. It burst into flames as it sank into the leading brecha. It screamed but kept running. Other men—normal men riding horses—joined the fight, flanking the brechas and shooting more fiery arrows into the monsters.

"Get off your horse, now!" a Red yelled at Blazel. Lighzel barreled past the woman and toward the horse herd milling in a clump at the bottom of the ravine. Stallions were on the outside facing the danger, while the mares and colts stood in the center. The gold and silver stallion was missing. Two young Reds guarded the horses, the tips of their helbraughts on the ground.

Blazel jumped off his horse, rolling as he hit the ground. As soon as Lighzel passed the young women, magic fire burst into a circle, surrounding the horses and protecting them. Another line of fire magic flared around the monsters, caging them and blocking their path. The warriors swarmed up the sides of the ravine and attacked.

Blazel quickly shifted into his warrior form. With a howl and a snap of his jaws, he ran to fight the janack. A tentacle flew toward him, and he swiped his claws across it. A warrior with gold fur and silver ears and paws snarled at him, but when the warrior saw the ichor on Blazel's claws, he nodded.

In accord, they leaped on the tentacle, slashing and biting until they severed it. The janack's movements grew slower and less coordinated as the warriors' venom worked through its system. The warrior and Blazel continued to harass the janack until it crashed to the ground, finally still. Blazel spun around, ready for the next fight, only to find this janack was the last beast to be destroyed.

The Reds walked the battlefield, burning to ash all the monster bits. One broke away from the others and stalked toward him. Her long, copper-red hair lay in two braids over her shoulders. She was medium height and had beautiful citrine-yellow eyes. The blade of her helbraught shimmered with her fire magic. She had the aura of an alpha.

Blazel glared at the pile of monster ash. Just like in the Barrens, he'd been caught because of a monster battle. The last time had worked out well. He hoped this one would too, since he had proven himself a capable warrior and not a cowardly rogue.

With a prayer to the Mother, he shifted to his natural form. Only the gold-and-silver warrior also shifted. Several of the warriors and the centaur with a chestnut horse portion formed a circle around him. Blazel had a hard time keeping his attention on the alpha, whose posture was stiff with anger.

"Who be you? Why do you travel alone?" she spat as soon as Blazel finished shifting.

"I'm Blazel."

"What kind of name be that? What clan be you?"

Hatred and suspicion filled her glare. Blazel's shoulders drooped. He had forgotten the last part of a man's name indicated his birth clan-pack. The names of his new friend Rolstrun or his mentor Histrun reflected they were from the Strunlair Clan. He could never pretend he was part of the Strunland fighting-pack, regardless of what colors were in his horse's barding.

"Why you be wearing Strunland colors?" she demanded.

"I was born in the Sanctuary." Blazel lowered his eyes to the ground and clenched his teeth. The alpha's hostility was more like what he expected than Maheli's friendliness had been. This fighting-pack wouldn't accept him. He looked the woman in the eye and sneered. "There isn't a clan-pack at the Sanctuary. The Strunlair fighting-pack guarding the crater gave me the barding."

"I saw him enter the plains from the Barrens," the warrior he had fought with said. In his human form, the man's hair was a golden yellow, and he had silver-gray eyes. "Although he has avoided the Keeps and tried to stay unseen, he hasn't caused any trouble."

Blazel's jaw dropped. "You're the gold and silver stallion that's been watching me."

The man nodded and held out his hand in greeting. "I be Kaelhaas. This be Lorstal."

At some signal Blazel couldn't see—or hear—the others surrounding him dispersed, leaving the three of them. He guessed Lorstal had communicated in mind-speech, but since he'd never been part of a pack, he'd never experienced it.

Lorstal continued glaring at Blazel. "Where you be going to push your horse so hard?"

"Back to the Sanctuary. The Supreme needs to be informed about what's happening in the crater." Blazel paused, considering how much to tell Lorstal. He decided she didn't need to know about the other reason he was racing back home. "There's a new janack showing up, and the nests are bigger and forming more frequently."

"We be experiencing the same," Lorstal said with a jerk of her head. She relaxed a little. "That batch of monsters escaped from a huge nest. It be luck we had extra fighters and could save the horses. You fought well." She looked around. "The girls be done. We can leave now. You'll come with us to the Keep. The Keep Alpha will want to hear your report." She strode off toward her horse.

Blazel glowered at her retreating back. He wasn't used to being ordered around.

"I can't wait to hear your story," Kaelhaas said. "The only people who go to the Barrens be the guard-packs."

"Someday, perhaps."

"Blazel! Kaelhaas! Get your arses moving," Lorstal yelled. "We be leaving now."

Blazel and Kaelhaas shared a guilty look before Blazel ran down the ravine to retrieve his horse. Lighzel was the only one still waiting for her rider. As he mounted, he caught a shimmer on the top of the hill. The golden stallion stood where Kaelhaas had been. "I guess he doesn't need a horse," he murmured to Lighzel. Without any urging from him, she moved out in a trot, following the other horses. Her gait seemed lighter.

A wide road appeared in the plains ahead of them. Blazel didn't remember seeing one during the headlong flight to the ravine. When he reached it, he realized the monster's slime had killed the grass.

"Don't worry, it'll grow back quickly."

Blazel turned his head to find the inquisitive centaur running beside him. He had rich chestnut-brown hair and slate-blue eyes in a strong face. Blazel couldn't help staring. The centaur's horse portion was the same chestnut-brown and had dark blue-gray stripes. He had thick feathering starting at his knees, and a long tail the same color as his stripes. He wore a brown shirt with yellow trim around the neck and sleeves.

"Greetings," the centaur said, smiling at him and holding out a hand. "I be Jaehaas. I haven't ever met a rogue before."

"I'm Blazel, and I haven't met a centaur before," Blazel said with an answering grin as he gripped the other man's wrist in a warrior's greeting. "And I'm a lone wolf, not a rogue. I've never been in a pack, so I've never been kicked out of one."

Jaehaas threw back his head and laughed. "Good one, man."

"So, what Keep are we heading to? I've lost track of where I am in my mad dash north."

"We be from the Haasneh Keep. You be making good progress. You be about half-way through the plains."

Blazel noticed they weren't riding toward the river, but deeper into the plains. "We're not going back to the river?"

"No, our Keep be in the plains. We won't reach it for another couple of days."

Blazel's eye's widened as he looked around the undulating grass spreading across the horizon. No stone structures intruded the vista. He sank heavily into the saddle, causing Lighzel to sidled into Jaehaas.

Jaehaas stroked the mare's neck before moving away. "We will stop for the night at a safe house. Narhili aren't the only beasts to plague the plains at night. You did well to stay near the river while traveling alone."

"I was more than all right," Blazel snapped.

"No need to get huffy. I be complimenting you." Jaehaas held up a placating hand. "People don't usually travel alone. It not be safe."

Blazel snorted. "I spent the last three years alone in the swamps. I can protect myself."

Jaehaas whistled, rearing slightly, and then hopped a few steps to catch back up with Blazel. "Why in the Crone's fires would you go into a swamp, let alone spend three years there?"

"I had my reasons." Blazel's mouth was in a tight line.

"That must be some story! I agree with Kaelhaas. I can't wait to hear it."

Blazel shrugged. "Someday, maybe."

Lorstal increased their speed, and Blazel kicked his horse into a canter. Jaehaas sped up, easily keeping pace, but it wasn't conducive to talking, which suited Blazel. He was unused to having someone to talk with while he traveled.

Chapter 7

Blazel and Jaehaas rode in the rear of the fighting group he had reluctantly joined. They traveled for the rest of the afternoon and into the evening. Blazel kept scanning the ocean of grass, trying to catch sight of the safe house. But nothing disturbed the waves.

"Are we close yet?" he asked Jaehaas when the setting sun streaked the sky with purples and golds.

"Yes, very close," Jaehaas laughed.

They topped a slight rise, and suddenly, like the ravine where they had fought the monsters, below them appeared a safe house tucked into an unseen valley. The gates were thrown open, and the courtyard was filling with the fighting-pack. Their noisy commotion reverberated on the stone walls of the small structure.

Blazel's skin flushed, and his breaths came in fast, short pants. He considered turning Lighzel back toward the river, but instead, he slowed her to a walk. The tiny space held a lot of strangers. A wave of fear swept through him and black closed in his vision. *Too many people! They hate you. They'll kill you.* His terrified mind gibbered.

Lorstal hadn't truly accepted him. Jaehaas walked beside him with a pleasant smile curving his lips. He seemed to be offering Blazel friendship—or guarding him. Blazel wasn't sure which.

If he didn't have Lighzel, Blazel would just shift into his wolf form and spend the night in a hollow. The nocturnal predators, including the narhili beasts, wouldn't bother him. He reached down and patted Lighzel's neck. She'd proven to be a good companion, and he couldn't leave her now. Grabbing his courage, he smothered his fear. He could do this. He could face the crowd and trust they wouldn't hurt him. Jaehaas gave Blazel an encouraging nod, as if he knew Blazel's internal struggle.

The courtyard was empty when Blazel and Jaehaas rode through the gates. Blazel blew out a breath in relief. He curiously noted the doors of the safe house were taller and wider than normal. The other centaur he hadn't met yet clopped through the door, and with his greater height and breadth, they now made sense. He wondered what other differences the Haaslair clan had developed to accommodate those who had chosen to become both man and horse.

There wasn't anyone in the stable when Blazel entered it. He climbed out of the saddle and led Lighzel to an empty stall which already had fresh, sweet hay in the bin and a bucket of grain. She happily dipped her head in the pail and munched contentedly while he stripped off her tack. He located a curry brush, and as he worked out the sweat and dirt from her hide, he found the motions soothing.

"If you brush her much more, you will take the hide off her," Jaehaas said, leaning against the stall door.

Blazel jumped. He hadn't paid attention to the sound of a horse's hooves clip-clopping through the stable. Taking a step back, he examined Lighzel critically. In the flickering lamplight, she gleamed. He put the brush away and caressed her muzzle.

"Dinner be ready," Jaehaas said. "We have some good cooks, so you don't want to let it get cold. And Lorstal be looking for you."

Blazel sighed. He knew he was stalling the inevitable. Eventually, he would have to go in and face the crowd. He filled Lighzel's water bucket and dished out another generous helping of grain for her. She deserved it; she'd worked hard the last few days. With nothing else to do, he eased out of her stall.

"Is Lorstal more than a platoon alpha?"

Jaehaas nodded. "She be groomed to become the next Keep Alpha."

Blazel snorted. It meant he had to answer her questions. He hoped she'd wait until after he ate. A delicious smell wafted from the building. The last time he'd eaten more than trail food was at the crater with the Strunland guard-pack. His lips quirked up as he remembered the friendly banter and his inclusion in it. He glanced sideways at his companion, who seemed to be a good man. *Perhaps here is another friend.*

Jaehaas pushed open the door, gestured for Blazel to go in, and then followed him inside. His hooves echoed on the stone floor, turning everyone's attention toward them. When the crowd saw Blazel, the noise of many people eating and talking stilled and quieted.

Blazel's first instinct was to bolt, but Jaehaas standing behind him blocked his exit and kept him from running outside. Blazel breathed deeply and took another step into the room. Jaehaas put a hand on his shoulder.

"Hey, everyone, this be Blazel," Jaehaas said into the quiet. "He assures me he be no rogue, just a lone wolf."

"He fought with me, and together, we killed the janack." Kaelhaas stood and walked around the tables until he stood on Blazel's other side. "A rogue wouldn't help us. They would flee, like the cowards they be."

"I may have been raised in the Sanctuary and not in a pack," Blazel said, directing his words to Kaelhaas and Jaehaas rather than to the crowd. "But I know my duty when it comes to the Malvers' monsters. We can't allow them to run rampant and destroy our world. They must be killed."

"Well said," Jaehaas murmured to him.

The fighters nodded and returned to their interrupted dinner and conversations. A few gave Blazel a quick smile. Kaelhaas patted him on the arm and ambled back to his place, stopping now and then to talk to someone.

Jaehaas led Blazel to the stove and filled a bowl with thick, savory stew, adding a piece of pan bread balanced on the bowl's rim. Jaehaas dished up another bowl for himself and then headed to a high table. The other centaur stood at it, while several fighters sat on tall stools. Blazel took an empty stool and kept his attention on his food. It surprised him when someone passed him a mug of steaming taevo. Jaehaas put his dish on the table and stood next to it. Their companions were quiet until both of them had eaten most of their food.

"Be it true you traveled through the Barrens?" the other centaur asked. He had pale red-gold hair and green eyes. His horse hide was the same color as his hair, but with darker red socks above his hooves. "I be Oldhaas, by the way."

The others introduced themselves.

"Yes," Blazel answered. "I spent the last year in the peninsula south of Shandir's Crater."

"Be that just swamps now?" Dolhaas interrupted.

Blazel nodded. "It's why I was there."

Lorstal and Kaelhaas came to their table. Several men quickly vacated their stools to allow them to sit. Blazel wondered if Kaelhaas was Lorstal's alpha partner. Most Posairs were able to sense who were alphas, or even potential alphas, but Blazel hadn't been around enough people to tell the difference.

"Why be you in the swamps?" Lorstal pinned him with her gaze. He could feel power wafting off her. "Only those who be crazy and suicidal go there. Be you crazy?"

Blazel laughed. "I guess in some ways I am, to spend so much time in the swamps. I'm not even sure why, except my friend said it was necessary. That's not important to you. What is important, is the weird janack and unusual monster activity. The guard-packs at the crater aren't going to be enough."

Lorstal pulled back and blinked hard. "Not enough? Why do you say that?"

"They are fighting every day, and sometimes three or four battles in a day. The nests are huge and the strange janack seems to be controlling the rest. Unless they get help, the monsters will escape the Barrens."

Fear, quickly followed by determination, flowed across the nearby fighter's faces. The plains would be the first place attacked by marauding monsters. Lorstal and Kaelhaas exchanged an agonizing look.

"The keep alphas need to know this," Lorstal said. "It be worse than we suspected."

"I'll send out couriers to the others in the morning." Kaelhaas rubbed his forehead. He turned to Blazel. "The nests here also be bigger and more active. We had hoped it be isolated in our territory. Now we know it not be so."

"Do you know how they killed the strange janack? It be difficult to kill. It be much larger, and the hide be tougher than the others." Worry creased Lorstal's forehead. "We've had too many killed or injured while attempting to kill it."

Blazel thought about all the fights he had observed while hiding and the battle when he met Maheli and Rolstrun. "Explode it..." he said slowly. "Keep the brechas away from it, although they will fight to protect it."

"So we've noticed," Lorstal said with a grimace. "I'd hoped you'd have better news. Exploding the monsters causes other problems, like injury from falling debris. We'll just have to deal with it until we can figure out something else."

Sometime during the conversation, Lorstal had quit glaring at Blazel. She gave him a puzzled look. "Now tell me, why in the Crone's Fires, you be wearing a Red's leathers?"

Blazel laughed. "I talked Maheli de Strunlair into giving them to me. The leathers wear much better than anything else, and I have a long way to travel. I am a Red, after all." Grinning, he twirled a lock of red, matted hair. He hoped he didn't have to give her a demonstration. Besides being different enough without adding his magical abilities, he didn't trust her as he had Maheli.

She and the others chuckled. Talk turned to other things, and Blazel was able to sit back and just listen. It wasn't long before people drifted away from the tables to curl up in the cots lining one end of the room. Dawn would come early. Jaehaas and Oldhaas opened a cupboard and dragged out a large pad for each of them, which they laid near the fire. Kaelhaas pointed Blazel to a cot near the centaurs.

Blazel tossed and turned, but sleep evaded him. He clapped his hands over his ears to stop the noise of so many people breathing deeply in sleep—or snoring. The fortress at the crater had rooms where only six to eight people slept. That had been bad enough, but to have forty people surrounding him was more than he could stand. The fire had died down to low coals when he jerked the blanket off the cot. Blazel wrapped it around his shoulders, slipped outside, and entered the stable. He made a bed in the hayloft and, with the much quieter sounds of the sleeping horses, finally fell asleep.

The dim gray light preceding dawn was enough for Blazel to see to saddle his horse. Smoke from the newly stoked fire rose lazily from the safe house's chimney. The smell of cooking grains almost made him change his mind about leaving before the Haasneh fighters. He dug a trail bar from his pack and grimaced at it before taking a bite, wishing it was the hot porridge. He filled his water bags from the well.

The prod of Chariel's *"hurry, hurry, hurry,"* in his mind pushed him to leave the others behind, but if he was being honest, he didn't want the company, anyway. Jaehaas came out of the house, stretching, while Blazel led his horse to the gate.

"Blazel?" Jaehaas squinted. "What you be doing? Breakfast be ready."

"Leaving." Blazel shoved the bar up, unlocking the gate. The clopping of horse's hooves approached him until Jaehaas stood close by, frowning, his arms crossed. His front right hoof tapped the ground.

"That's apparent. But why? We'll be leaving in less than an octar."

"I can't waste the time going to your keep will take. I need to reach the Sanctuary, fast."

"Surely you have time to eat before you go?"

Blazel held up the partially eaten trail bar.

Jaehaas shook his head. "That not be food. Well, not good food. Come on. Come eat." When Blazel didn't budge, Jaehaas added, "There's mookti—"

"Mookti! Where did you find those?" Blazel's mouth watered at the thought of the sweet purple berries. They were the first berries to ripen in the spring, lasting only through early summer. They were his favorite treat. He hadn't seen any mookti plants on their ride. It had been a long time since he'd tasted them. They didn't grow in the swamps.

"Here." Jaehaas laughed at Blazel's confusion. "Ages ago, one of our alphas loved mookti so much she planted them at all of our safe houses to ensure she'd always have them. Mmmm, fresh mookti. It's almost the end of their season. Another couple of chedans and they'll be gone." Jaehaas turned away from Blazel and took a few steps. He twisted around, raising his eyebrows and his tail swishing. "I guess I'll get to eat your share."

Blazel tucked the trail bar into his pack, relocked the gate, and grabbed Lighzel's reins. A few moments later, he was keeping pace with Jaehaas. When they reached the house, he tied Lighzel's reins to the hitching rail and followed Jaehaas in.

Next to the pot of porridge sat a big bowl—mostly empty— of mookti berries. Blazel dished some porridge into a bowl. He filled his bowl to the brim with the berries, after a scan around the room assured him everyone had had a serving. Jaehaas grinned as he piled berries into his own dish. Blazel couldn't help making happy sounds as he ate mookti berries and porridge. Hot spicy taevo rounded out his breakfast.

While Blazel and Jaehaas ate, the fighters cleared out of the building, except one young man, who was washing the dishes. A few milcrons later, Blazel heard several horses pounding out of the courtyard.

"They be heading to the southern keeps you avoided to warn them of the problems in the crater. An additional guard will be set up at the border between the Barrens and our plains."

Blazel nodded and bent back to his breakfast.

Jaehaas's spoon clattered into his empty bowl. He pushed it away and refilled both of their mugs with taevo. Blazel could feel Jaehaas's gaze boring into him. He spooned the last bit of porridge and berries into his mouth. Pushing his own dish away, he leaned back in his chair. The young man hurried to their table and took their dishes. In a few milcrons, only the two men remained inside. Blazel gritted his teeth against the delay.

"Why you be in such a hurry to reach the Sanctuary?" Jaehaas asked, his forehead furrowed in confusion. "It's true the Malvers' monsters be behaving strange and there be a new one. While the Supreme needs to know about this, it doesn't explain your rush."

Blazel studied him for a long moment, letting the milcrons stretch. Jaehaas didn't twitch or look away and wore a sincere expression. Blazel took a deep breath and blew it out, making a decision.

Even though they were alone, Blazel leaned forward and lowered his voice. "My friend, Chariel, is a Gray, a powerful one. She is also an oracle and sent me to the swamps to prepare for a great evil coming to our land. I'm unsure if it's this new janack or something else. She's calling me back home." Blazel paused, then said hurriedly, "I hear her voice in the back of my head, urging me to hurry. Tell your people when there is fire in the sky, the madness is here." Blazel shook his head, his matted locs thumping his back, wondering why he said that. Again.

Jaehaas flicked his tail over his hindquarters and rubbed his neck with a hand while he considered Blazel's revelation. "Then, my friend," he said at last, "we'll have to make sure you get there quickly and safely. Our Keep be on your way. Travel with us." He held out a hand to Blazel and smiled encouragingly. "I'd like to get to know the rogue who isn't a rogue."

Blazel laughed and gripped Jaehaas's wrist. "In that case, I'll ride with you. I'd like to get to know one who is man and horse."

Jaehaas clopped to his sleeping pad and picked up his bow, quiver, and pack. Together, they left the house to find the others were all mounted. As soon as Lorstal saw Jaehaas and Blazel, she issued the order to leave. Blazel scrambled onto his horse and followed the others as they trotted out the gate.

Lorstal led them at a fast pace, slowing only to rest their horses. The first time they came upon a herd of horses, it surprised Blazel when the herd joined them as they ran. Kaelhaas traveled in his gold and silver stallion form, and the wild stallions seemed to love racing with him, but they avoided the two centaurs. The young colts and fillies, however, would race up to a centaur, run a few paces with them, and then peel off as if on a dare. After a few measures of this, at some unknown signal, the herd wheeled away from the riders. A little while later, another horse herd ran with them.

Late in the afternoon, a large stone structure appeared on the horizon. A few octars later, the tall plains grass gave way to cultivated fields and pastures surrounded by stone walls. A crushed sheadash stone roadway cut through the fields leading to the Keep. By the time the riders passed the fields, it was twilight and everyone, including the animals, had returned to the Keep for the night.

The keep walls soared twenty feet tall above the plain. The gates stood open to allow the fighters in. When the last person rode through the gateway, guards pushed the massive gate shut. They lowered the bar with a boom, locking the gates for the night.

Blazel jumped at the sound. His heart palpitated with the reminder he was stuck inside with over seven-hundred people. It took all of his control to not turn Lighzel around and race to the gate, demanding they open it so he could leave. He hadn't felt like this with the Strunlair guard-pack. Jaehaas reached out and put a hand on his arm in reassurance.

"You be with friends," Jaehaas murmured. "I'll tell Keep Alphas Telekhaas and Belistril about your need to hurry to the Sanctuary. I be sure they will have questions for you." Jaehaas beckoned Dolhaas to join them and spoke quietly to him.

Dolhaas eyed Blazel, then nodded.

"Once you settle your horse, Dolhaas will show you around the keep. By then, we'll have moved a bed into my room, where it will be just the two of us. Seeing how uncomfortable you were last night, I thought you'd be more at ease in a place with as few people as possible. Oldhaas will sleep elsewhere while you be here."

"Thank you for your kindness." Blazel swallowed rapidly, blinking his eyes as he turned his head away. He hadn't expected such courtesy. Jaehaas patted Blazel's arm again and then trotted to the large Keep-House to find the keep alphas.

"This way to the stables, Blazel," Dolhaas said as he urged his horse forward.

A pang of longing clutched his heart as they passed the Temple next to the Keep-House. Before Blazel left, he'd seek solace in the Temple's sanctuary. He missed the comfort of the rituals to the Goddess and Her Consort.

They passed three large fighting-pack houses before turning on a roadway beyond the last house. At the end of the lane stood a cozy stable with a large fenced pasture in back of it. A number of horses grazed on the rich grass. Inside the stable, Blazel raised his eyebrows at the long lines of shelves and rails for tack and the few stalls.

"We let the horses roam in the pasture," Dolhaas said. "They'll come when we need them." He stopped at a mostly empty line of rails near the entrance. "You can put your horse's tack here. It be a guest station. Remember your number." Dolhaas then took his horse deeper into the stable.

Dolhaas was much quicker than Blazel in taking off his horse's gear and helped Blazel finish rubbing down Lighzel. Blazel swapped her bridle for a halter and led her out the stable's back door and into the pasture. Paddocks, where the horses could shelter during bad weather, were near the stables, and a small grove of tall trees lined the fence to the east. Lighzel whinnied in delight when Blazel unhooked the lead rope. She trotted several feet away and dropped to roll on the grass.

"Well, she likes it here," Blazel laughed.

"Of course she does. She came from our herds."

"How do you know?"

"Her stripes," Dolhaas said. "The patterns they form and their size indicates which herd and stallion each horse belongs to. Besides, she was part of the dozen we took to Strunlair Keep a few years ago. It be one reason I, and several others, knew you were telling the truth. There be no way you could steal a plains-bred horse. They'd find a way to escape and return to their true master. Lighzel chose you for her partner, didn't she?"

Blazel remembered the horse putting her head on his shoulder. "Yes, she did. The horse-master at the crater brought out several horses, and she picked me. I'd never owned a horse before then."

"We don't own them." Dolhaas put his hands on his hips and frowned with indignation. "We be partners. Without them, we couldn't survive."

"My apologies."

Dolhaas harrumphed and turned away from the pasture. Blazel stepped quickly to catch up to him, and together, they walked to the fighting-pack house nearest the stable. Inside, Dolhaas followed the wide hallway leading to the back of the house, with several doors wider than normal.

Dolhaas pointed to a door on the corridor's opposite wall. "That be the necessary room. Because the centaurs can't go to the bathing rooms below, it has tubs and such in it. I can show you to the bathing room, or you can use this one. And this be where you'll sleep."

Dolhaas opened the left-hand door to reveal a large room with shelves holding clothing, books, and other personal items. Between the shelves was a plank with writing materials laid out on it. The wall opposite the door had a thick pallet with blankets and next to it a cot. Beside the cot was a small table with a lantern and a small trunk. The cold stone floor wasn't relieved by any rugs or other comforts.

"A bell will announce dinner," Dolhaas said. "If Jaehaas hasn't returned by then, I'll come and escort you to the dining hall."

Thanking his guide, Blazel entered the room, dropping his well-worn leather bag on the trunk, and sat down on the cot. The door closed softly as Dolhaas left. Blazel took a deep breath and started coughing. *Crone's fires, I stink.* He thought about the delicious hot water in the bathing room at the crater. He dug in his bag for a clean shirt and trousers, then looked down at his red leathers, which he'd worn constantly since leaving the crater.

"Someone around here has to know how to clean these. Maybe they'll teach me." He put his bags in the trunk and then went to the necessary room for a luxurious bath.

Chapter 8

Blazel climbed out of the deep tub and tugged on the clothing given to him by the Strunland guard-pack. The turquoise shirt and dark blue trousers were the only clothes he owned, other than the set of red leathers. He tied his thick ropes of hair behind his neck with a new leather thong he'd found with his clean clothes.

He looked in the mirror and scowled at his long, bushy, scraggly beard brushing the top of his chest. Now that he was back in civilization, it made him appear wild and unkempt. Stroking the damp strands, he wondered if he even had a razor. He placed his dirty clothes on the floor next to the trunk and rummaged in his bag. He found his razor buried in the bottom. Returning to the necessary room, he sharpened the razor and worked on trimming his beard.

He paused in stamping into his boots at the unmistakable clip-clop of Jaehaas's gait in the hallway.

"Good, you be cleaned up," Jaehaas said. "The keep alphas want to meet with you, but not until after dinner."

Blazel had expected them to call for him immediately. A deep bell reverberated throughout the house.

"The dinner bell," Jaehaas explained. "Let me wash up, and we'll go eat. Our Green and Brown Talents be quite good, and so our meals be excellent. I even heard rumors there'd be mookti berries for dessert." He waggled his eyebrows at Blazel as he crossed the hall to the necessary room. In a few milcrons, he returned with his hair brushed and his own beard trimmed close to his face. Jaehaas wore a thin line of facial hair along his jawline and around his mouth, which highlighted his square jaw. He'd removed his tunic while washing. He examined a stack of folded clothes on a shelf, and withdrew a dark brown tunic with yellow and blue designs embroidered on the neckline, sleeves, and hem.

Jaehaas smoothed the shirt over his chest. "Let's go."

Long tables with benches for seating filled the dining hall. Blazel staggered against the door frame at the rainbow of hair colors. "Sweet Goddess, so many!" In the Sanctuary, the majority consisted of Whites or Grays, priestesses of the Goddess, and the Posairs' spiritual and soul workers. Greens and Browns from the various keeps rotated in serving the Sanctuary as cooks, gardeners, stonemasons, carpenters, and other help needed to keep the Sanctuary working. Rarely, a Yellow or Blue Talent would arrive and stay for a short time. Reds only visited during the Clan Alpha competitions or for the biannual gatherings.

His stomach dropped at facing the five or six-hundred people crammed into the room. He'd only seen so many people at the biannual Alpha Gatherings. *How do they stand to be around each other all the time?*

"No one be bothering you," Jaehaas murmured. He led Blazel along the wall to a large, high table where seven centaurs stood. Blazel recognized Oldhaas, leaning forward in deep conversation with the man across the table from him. Jaehaas settled next to Oldhaas and motioned Blazel to an empty tall chair situated on the other side of him.

Not long after, young people marched into the dining hall loaded with platters of food. Blazel scanned the room, searching for the familiar white or gray hair of Whites and Grays. His shoulders slumped, remembering the priestesses would eat in the Temple, along with their acolytes.

The others at the table soon included Blazel in their conversation as they ate. He answered their curious questions about how he had become a lone wolf and had survived as long as he had alone. He regaled them with a few tales, including how he'd received the scars on his face and back from the sabertiger.

"How many centaurs are there?" he asked, curiosity finally trumping his shyness.

"In this keep, only us." Jaehaas indicated the eight men sitting at the table.

"It be difficult to manage the shift to split your form," Oldhaas explained. "Not many of us can accomplish it. There be not any young centaurs. It takes great discipline and long practice to complete the shift."

"And," Jaehaas added, "most do not want to live our lifestyle. It has its own challenges—"

"—like not ever having sex again," Oldhaas grumbled. "We usually try to get it out of our systems before our final shift. Obviously, we can't have sex with humans." He gestured to his hindquarters. "And sex with a horse be just wrong, sick even. And since women don't shapeshift, there be no female centaurs." Oldhaas leaned his elbows on the table and put his head in his hands with a huge sigh. "I didn't think I'd miss female company so much."

Blazel's eyebrows scrunched. "So why do you do it? Why become a centaur?"

"We be stronger and can run longer distances," Oldhaas said.

"We have the best of both worlds," Jaehaas added.

"Well, except for the sex." Oldhaas sighed again.

A girl, about thirteen, scurried to their table and stared at Blazel. Suspecting why she was there, Blazel clenched his hands under the table. He dreaded the coming meeting and the inevitable judgment and questions.

"Jaehaas, sir," she stammered, "the alphas decided to meet with you and your guest tomorrow after breakfast." She waved tentatively at Blazel before racing away.

Blazel unclenched his hands at the news of the postponement. Dinner ended soon after, and he and Jaehaas returned to their room.

The next morning, Blazel joined Jaehaas, Oldhaas, and the other house residents in the dining room. The congenial gathering relaxed Blazel. Surprisingly, more than one Red flirted with him over fried tubers, eggs, and steaming mugs of dark taevo. Bewildered by the new experience, he stirred his taevo before smiling shyly at a pretty woman, then dipped his head, flustered, when she ran a finger over her wet lips. He was still blushing when Jaehaas backed away from the table.

Together, they walked the short way to the Keep-House and to the alpha's office. The keep alphas sat behind a large wood desk that dominated the room. The woman had pulled her dark red hair into a ponytail. Fine lines crinkled around her brown eyes as she gave Blazel an open, friendly smile.

The man slumped in his chair with his arms crossed over his chest. Green flecks dotted his bushy red-brown eyebrows, furrowed in a dark scowl. He wore his hair cut short and sported a thick mustache that drooped past his chin.

"Telekhaas, Belistril," Jaehaas said, "this be my friend Blazel. He has an important message he carries to the Supreme."

"Blazel, welcome to Haasneh Keep." Belistril gestured to a chair in front of the desk. "Sit. We have questions for you."

As soon as Blazel's butt hit the seat, Telekhaas grumbled, "The first thing I want to know be, why you not be in a pack? It not be right for a man to be alone and without the company of a pack."

"As you may know, I was born and raised in the Sanctuary. There were no packs—"

"But we came every two years," Telekhaas interrupted. "She could have been given you to one of us to raise."

"I'm told Histrun tried several times to talk the Supreme into letting me go with him. But she wouldn't hear of it." Blazel pursed his lips and folded his arms over his chest. "For some reason, and I don't know why, she decided I had to stay. There hasn't been a boy raised in the Sanctuary before or since. I left when I turned seventeen. I didn't travel south into the provinces but north into the Deep Mountains. By the time I returned five years later, it was too late for me to join a pack. I believed no one would have me because I had been alone for too long."

Telekhaas scrutinized him for several milcrons until he grunted and relaxed. "Histrun told me the same. No one could understand why she would handicap a young boy like that. It be why he stayed to train you whenever he traveled to the Sanctuary. He went there when you turned eighteen to take you to the Strunland Clan, but you had disappeared."

Blazel ducked his head. The Supreme hadn't told him Histrun wanted him. *Would I have gone with him?* He didn't know.

"Jaehaas informed us about what you learned at Shandir's Crater." Belistril sipped her taevo. "We too have been having trouble with the Malvers' monsters changing their long-standing behavior. The new janack be difficult to kill. We need to know if the other provinces also be having this trouble, or if it be localized here in the south. We also want to know if the Supreme has any direction for us about how to kill the monsters."

"So we be sending Jaehaas with you to the Sanctuary." Telekhaas smoothed his mustache. "We considered sending a platoon with you, but Jaehaas convinced us the two of you could travel faster and would be safe enough. A fighting-pack will escort you out of our territory."

"When do you want us to leave?" Jaehaas asked.

Belistril ran the tip of her finger around the rim of her taevo cup. "The nest north of here, which you'll have to pass, be active today. If you wait until tomorrow, we'll have cleared out the monsters, and it will be safe for you. Besides, Blazel, you look like you could use a few good meals and time to recuperate."

Blazel had to admit she was right. Exhaustion weighed him down from too many days of traveling hard and not eating much.

After Blazel's meeting, a young man guided him to the quartermaster, a stern matron with Brown and Yellow Talents. She took his measurements for shirts, pants, and boots, even though he had a good pair he'd received from the Strunland guard-pack. When he left her office, he carried in his arms two new shirts, a tunic, another pair of sturdy trousers, and four sets of small clothes. And for reasons he couldn't fathom, she had given him a set of dress clothes in the Haaslair colors of brown and yellow. He also had three new pairs of socks. He hadn't had such bounty for many years. When he returned to Jaehaas's room to drop off the new clothes, his cleaned red leathers lay neatly folded on the cot. He tucked the garments into his pack. Not knowing what to do or where to go, he laid down.

"Yo, Blazel," Dolhaas said, knocking on the door frame. "Be you sleeping?"

Blazel swung his legs off the cot, sitting up and rubbing his face. "No, just resting."

"Telekhaas wants you to train with us this afternoon. We fight differently and if you be riding with us, it be best if you know what to expect."

"Sounds reasonable." Blazel had developed his own fighting style against the dangerous swamp beasts. If he continued to ride with others—as it appeared he'd be doing—he needed to learn to fight with them.

"Here. You missed lunch."

Dolhaas handed Blazel a sandwich, which he ate while walking to the practice field. As the training progressed, his old lessons with Histrun came back, and he soon did well while fighting on the ground. The Haaslair, unlike any other clan, took their horses into the monster battles and fought on horseback. No matter how he tried, Blazel couldn't master the techniques while on horseback in one afternoon, especially since he was so new to riding.

Exhaustion pulled at Blazel, making him sloppy. Rather than risk hurting someone, he wandered over to watch the centaurs practice their archery. Jaehaas pulled back on his longbow and let an arrow loose. It thunked into the target, quivering among the other arrows already crowding the center. Blazel leaned forward to gaze down the line and raised his eyebrows. Quite a few women filled the archery ranks. The centaur's large bodies had hidden them from view.

Blazel blinked, shook his head, and looked again. Besides the usual Reds, Browns, Greens, and Yellows nocked their arrows. His mouth dropped open when two women with blue hair stepped up to the line for their turn. Blues were empaths, sensing and feeling other people's emotions. They rarely fought, even in training, because they were so affected by violent emotions. Blazel moved to study them more closely. Green strands mixed with pale blue in one woman's hair, while brown streaked another one's. He nodded. *Ah, that it explains it. They're all weak Blues.*

A loud, shrill whistle blew, and the archers lowered their bows. Blazel sank to the ground, crossing his legs, balancing his elbows on his knees, and resting his chin on his fists. A team hauled the spent targets off the field, and replaced them with fresh ones, several yards farther away. Each archer placed a full quiver of dark red fletched arrows at their feet, within easy reach. The previous arrows had white feathers.

A woman strode onto the field and stood to the side a safe distance from the targets. Her deep navy-blue hair indicated she was a powerful Blue.

The archers aimed and released their arrows, murmuring a word Blazel didn't recognize. The flying arrow burst into flame before they landed. Within a few moments, the fire on the burning targets died out. The arrows flew again. Blazel studied the targets and noticed water bubbles surrounding the flames. When he looked over at the strong Blue, her fingers moved as she directed her water magic to put out the fires.

In the next round, an arrow flew wide, missing its target. Water drenched the flaming arrow. The Blue's ability to keep track of so many moving objects impressed Blazel. Fascinated, he continued to watch while the archers emptied their quivers. During the practice, the Blue snuffed out several more wild shots before they could hit the ground.

Jaehaas swung his bow over his shoulder. "Blazel, I be finished. Let's go get cleaned up. Dinner will be ready soon. I be starving."

Several young fighters gathered the equipment, including Jaehaas's empty quiver, and put it away. A group of children pulled the arrows out of the targets. The field quickly emptied.

"How do you make the arrows flame?" Blazel asked.

"We have some Reds who spell them. You noticed we said a word before they flamed?"

Blazel nodded.

"The word releases the spell. Without it, the arrows remain unlit. It be genius. We don't always catch the monsters in the nest, like they do in the other provinces. Our plains be too vast. We often fight them as they chase the horses. The arrows allow us to fight them on the go."

"I remember seeing them the other day. Do the other clans know about the arrows? I'm sure they could also use them."

"Huh?" Jaehaas tilted his head, frowning. "I don't know if they do or not. It not be something we've ever taken to the Gatherings since the other clans don't have to chase the monsters like we do. I'll mention it to Telekhaas before we leave."

Blazel followed Jaehaas into the necessary room, happy to find it empty, and he didn't have to clean up with dozens of men—and women. Just having Jaehaas there made him self-conscious and uncomfortable. He hurriedly washed and then dressed in his new shirt and trousers in the Haaslair colors. The clothing made him feel like he fit in better at the dining hall.

After dinner, Blazel carefully packed his backpack and saddlebags. One pouch bulged with all his new clothing. It appeared lopsided, so he took out the extra shirt and pants.

Jaehaas flicked his tail, catching Blazel's attention. "Leave a pouch empty for supplies. The quartermaster will give us provisions in the morning."

Blazel ducked his head, heat burning his cheeks, and stuffed the clothes back in.

A light tap on the door woke Blazel. He rubbed his eyes, disoriented in the dark.

"It be time to go," Jaehaas murmured as he lit the lantern.

Ten milcrons later, they slung their bags over their shoulders and left their room. The jingle of bridles, soft neighing, and the slap of leather bombarded Blazel's senses as a large group of fighters busily saddled their horses. Blazel hurried to where a stable hand had tied Lighzel to a rail for him. She greeted Blazel with a whinny and thrust her head into his chest, demanding he scratch her jaw. Laughing, he complied. He soon had her saddled, his bags and bedroll attached to the saddle, and led her from the barn.

Jaehaas waited for him outside the stable door. He handed Blazel a packet and a ceramic canteen. The packet held a warm bread roll filled with eggs, meat, and cheese. The canteen contained hot, rich taevo.

Lorstal led the fighting-platoon escorting them out of the Haasneh Territory. She nodded a greeting to him before calling out the order to mount up.

The gold and orange light of sunrise blazed across the sky as they trotted out the gate. They rode east until they passed the fields and pastures surrounding the Keep. Once in the tall plains grass, they turned north. Lorstal set them on a fast pace that still allowed the horses to rest and recover. The measures flowed under the horse's hooves.

After the morning break, Kaelhaas chose to travel as a stallion. Lorstal took the lead line of his horse. Soon after, a herd of horses broke over the horizon and joined them in their run across the plains. They continued on, stopping every few octars to rest the horses. As evening closed around the group, a safe house rose over the waves of grass.

The next two days followed the same pattern. With no signs of monsters, Blazel suspected they traveled along a route that avoided the nest sites.

When they stopped for their first morning break on the third day, Blazel let Lighzel drink from the spring bubbling from the ground. Inlaid rocks formed a shallow basin. After the horses drank, the basin refilled with fresh water. Blazel took the opportunity to fill his water skin. He wandered away from the others and sat on a rock, gazing over the plains while Lighzel cropped the grass.

A rustling alerted him. He slid silently into a crouch and waited. A rabbit nosed out of the grass. Without thinking, Blazel shifted into his wolf form and pounced on it. His powerful jaws clamped on its neck, severing its arteries. A couple of quick gulps, and the rabbit disappeared down his throat. A strange quiet made him look up as he licked his snout clean.

Everyone stared at him, some in shock, while fear clouded most of their eyes. Concern filled both Lorstal's and Kaelhaas's faces. Blazel lowered his muzzle onto his paws and whined. He didn't understand why they were so scared of him. It had just been a rabbit.

Kaelhaas approached him cautiously, crouching down to be eye level with him. "Blazel," he said softly, "you still be with us, buddy?"

Blazel lifted his head and cocked it. *What does he mean? Of course I'm still here.*

Kaelhaas looked pointedly at the bits of fur on the ground and then back at Blazel. "We have food. You don't have to hunt."

Blazel had forgotten about the food in his saddlebags. He had spent too many years alone, killing food when it presented itself, so he wouldn't go hungry. Hunting in his wolf form was still second nature to him. Apparently, it wasn't acceptable behavior. Blazel whined again and scooted back.

"It be okay. I understand," Kaelhaas said in a gentle voice. "It be instinct for you." He stood and turned to the crowd. "He not be a ravening beast. Go back to your business." He made a shooing motion. The group dispersed, returning to their horses and re-tightening girth straps or filling water skins.

Kaelhaas turned to face Blazel, who still hadn't shifted into his human form. "We be leaving you here."

Blazel's upper lip raised, revealing his teeth.

"No, it not be because you killed a rabbit." Kaelhaas sounded exasperated. "This be the boundary between our territory and Haasper's. I had planned on telling you before the incident. I be sure the Haasper scouts will spot you soon. They know Jaehaas, so you'll be fine." He stepped toward Blazel and petted his head. "It's been a pleasure, Blazel. Take care of yourself and be safe. Mother's blessings on your journey."

Blazel reached out a long tongue and licked Kaelhaas's hand. He was still too shaken by the fighter's disapproval and rejection to shift.

Lorstal called the order to mount, and in a few milcrons, only Blazel, Jaehaas, and a Red remained at the spring. He hadn't expected anyone besides Jaehaas to accompany him. Knowing they'd only be traveling with him a short time, he hadn't paid much attention to the other fighters in the group, especially the women. Curious, he shifted back to his human form.

The woman had vibrant red-brown hair, and red ringed her dark brown eyes. Her hair was chin length, with bangs cut straight across her forehead, brushing the tops of her eyebrows. She was medium height and wore red leathers, like every other Red when out fighting monsters.

In addition to carrying her helbraught, she'd strapped a long helstrablade to her waist. The staff portion of the helbraught was the height of the woman, and hers had a twenty-inch blade made from the helstrim alloy attached to the end. The blade was sharp enough to penetrate the thick, tough Malvers' monsters' hide.

"I be Ambrelya." She held out her right hand, still gripping her helbraught with her left. "I be coming with you as far as Strunlair Keep."

Blazel gripped her wrist in a warrior's greeting. "Why?"

"You made a valid point yesterday," Jaehaas said.

"I know the spell for the fire arrows," Ambrelya said. "Belistril and Telekhaas thought it be important for us to share this knowledge with the other Clans. We hadn't realized they not be aware of it until you mentioned it."

"Good." Blazel nodded sharply. "The more information we share, the better it will be when the madness arrives." His forehead crinkled in a frown. *Why did I say that?*

"What?" Jaehaas jerked back. "What be that about?"

"Great, now I'm channeling Chariel." Blazel shook his head. "She said she would recall me home when the madness was approaching." He paced, gazing at the ground. "She didn't know what it meant, only it was bad. I don't know if she was talking about the new janack and the strange behavior of the monsters, or something else. Whatever it is, we have to hurry."

He leaped into Lighzel's saddle and kicked her sides. She jumped forward into a gallop. An octar later, he finally slowed down to allow the other two to catch up to him. He had to get to the Sanctuary before the madness hit.

But what madness?

Chapter 9

As the small group rode, the plains seemed empty of life to Blazel. Since entering Haasper Territory, they hadn't seen any horse herds. He missed the thunder of hundreds of horses' hooves pounding the ground as they ran.

Late in the afternoon, a man watched them from a distant rise. Jaehaas waved at him, whistling a pattern of notes. The other man whistled, waved back, and turned his horse away, disappearing in moments.

"The Haasper know we be here," Ambrelya explained to Blazel. "They'll keep an eye out for us and let us know if there be any danger. Otherwise, they'll leave us alone."

When they stopped at a safe house for the night, they had it to themselves. Jaehaas took Blazel outside, set up practice targets in the courtyard, and to Blazel's surprise, handed him a bow.

"Here, it be for you," Jaehaas said. "Archery be a good defense against the monsters and be good for hunting."

They practiced until it became too dark to see the target. At the end, Blazel could hit it at least once every three shots. He admired Jaehaas and Ambrelya's skill. Their arrows landed dead center two out of three times and hit somewhere on the target every time.

After they ate and washed the dishes, Ambrelya opened a cupboard, brought out a board game, and set it up. Blazel smiled and indicated he wanted the red pieces. Keshe was a popular game played even by the Gryphons.

After a few rounds, he asked in what he hoped was a nonchalant voice, "Why was everyone so scared this morning?"

"You don't understand, do you?" Jaehaas moved his piece. "We be worried you had gone rogue. You shifted, killed, and ate that rabbit without thought. Once we reach adulthood, we rarely hunt in our wolf forms and never eat as one. It be believed to lead the man into losing control and turning rogue, an ill thing to become, and dangerous to everyone in their bloodlust and insanity. And to eat while everyone else be hungry be an act of selfishness, something rogues do."

Blazel scrutinized the game pieces while he tried to understand. He kept his head down and said slowly, "I have been alone for a long time. If I didn't snatch a rabbit or something else when I found it, I would go hungry or waste precious energy trying to catch other prey later. I was not being selfish."

Jaehaas patted his arm. "Of course you weren't."

"I am not a rogue." Blazel lifted his head and stared into Jaehaas's eyes. "I do not tear my prey to pieces. I do not kill people."

"No, you not be," Jaehaas agreed. "You be a lone wolf who sometimes forgets his manners." Jaehaas smiled.

Blazel lowered his eyes. "I will try harder to remember them."

Ambrelya reached across the table and patted Blazel's hand. "You be doing fine. We understand and will help you. From what I've seen, you be a good guy."

Blazel's ears and faced burned, and he ducked his head. Soon after, Jaehaas won the game, and they went to bed.

Over the next few days, they quickly covered the measures. With only three of them, they could travel faster and longer, cutting down their rest times. As they rode farther north, the plains began to undulate with rolling hills. Every so often, a scout would whistle and wave to them from the top of a hill. The three safe houses they stayed in for the night were empty. Not once had they run upon a monster battle.

This worried Blazel. "Why haven't we encountered any monsters?"

"Our route takes us away from the known nest sites," Ambrelya told him.

"And the only way for new sites to form," Jaehaas added, "be from malicious deeds such as rape or murder. It be one reason we put down rogues as quickly as possible. We don't want their misdeeds to form new nests. Besides, the plains have always been sparsely populated. We have fewer nest sites than the other provinces. It seems to take more than horses to attract the monsters. They need people. Have you ever noticed there are ruins of our ancestors wherever there be nest sites?"

Blazel nodded. He'd discovered a multitude of ancient ruins as he traveled the length and breadth of Lairheim.

"There has to be a reason for it," Jaehaas continued. "I believe the Malvers' monsters be here to destroy us. But why or for who, I don't know."

"I've thought the same thing." Blazel rubbed his beard. "Perhaps it's time to ask the Supreme about it. I'm sure she knows."

"But that be sacrilege!" Ambrelya made the sign against evil.

Blazel laughed. "I grew up with the old woman. I'm not afraid of asking her a simple question."

Ambrelya still looked scandalized, and she wouldn't talk to him.

At their next rest stop, trees surrounded a pool of water fed by a stream, rather than a spring. The long, thick grasses of the plains had thinned considerably. Birds twittered in the trees, and chipmunks crawled on the rocks.

"We will be entering Strunlair Province this afternoon," Jaehaas said. His tail flicked across his rump, disturbing the flies. "I imagine we'll pick up an escort soon."

They left the small oasis and continued their journey north. The tall plains grass gave way to low-lying grass and brush. The trees grew thicker. Lighzel's hindquarters bunched as they entered the foothills, her hooves clicking on pebbles. Squirrels chittered at them, and birds flitted over their heads.

Suddenly, everything quieted. Blazel reined Lighzel to a stop, gazing around, searching for the danger. A crow burst from the tree canopy, followed by the rest of its flock. A black tentacle reached into the air, plucking a bird from the flock. The noxious stench of the monsters carried on the breeze burned Blazel's nostrils. The sound of battle broke the silence.

Jaehaas pulled his bow out of its case and quickly strung it. He adjusted his quiver of arrows so he could easily reach them. Ambrelya's helbraught glowed as she fed fire magic into it. When she held out her hand for Lighzel's reins, Blazel tossed them to her and leaped off the saddle. By the time his feet touched the ground, they were the massive paws of a Posair warrior.

Blazel now stood at nine feet instead of his normal six and weighed 150 pounds more. His long claws could slash and rip through the tough monster hides. Sharp teeth filled his powerful jaws. His saliva was now a deadly toxin to the monsters, and he had venom sacks under the pads of his front claws. The warrior form was built for one thing: to destroy and kill the Malvers' monsters.

He lifted his head and howled. A howl answered him. He raced off in its direction, with Jaehaas and Ambrelya close behind him. At some point, Ambrelya stopped, and when she caught up with them, the horses were nowhere in sight.

Blazel shook his head, trying to clear the odd humming in his ears, but as he ran closer to the fight, it became louder. Ignoring it, he continued to run. When they came to a large clearing, he skidded to a halt, the marsh making the ground soggy. A platoon of fighters surrounded the nest. The fighters systematically cut the eight normal-sized janacks, and their accompanying hoard of brechas, away from the nest. Inside it stood the largest janack Blazel had ever seen—even larger than the ones in the Barrens. A strange protrusion rose above the sensor stalks on its head, and the beast seemed to be directing the other janacks and brechas.

He ran toward the strange janack, leaping over the fire-ring, and landed in a crouch. The fire-ring blazed up to form a dome surrounding the nest. His jaw dropped. He'd never witnessed such magic. A brecha slammed into the shield, sparks flew, and it pulled back, patches of its hide burning. Blue light surrounded the brecha, freezing it in moments. A gorgeous woman, her deep sapphire-blue hair swinging at her hips, sent another blast of freezing water into another brecha. *What in the crone's fires! A strong Blue is fighting!*

"Don't just stand there gawking!" A woman with bright canary-yellow hair yelled at him. "Go fight!" Suddenly, the air around him was ice cold.

He ran to the janack and stopped when it didn't attack him or act like it was aware of him. *Huh? A cold-air shield?* Taking advantage of the opportunity, he leaped, slicing his claws into the nearest tentacle and pumping venom into the wound. He continued to slice into the janack, twisting and turning to keep away from searching tentacles.

A Red ran past him, used her helbraught to leap onto the janack, and raced to its head. Blazel sliced again and jumped back as a piece of tentacle flew off. He glanced up, wondering what the Red was doing. She slammed her helbraught into the head, sinking the blade deep.

The humming turned into a scream. Blazel roared, fighting the pain in his mind. A warrior came out of nowhere and pushed him out of the way of a tentacle flashing toward him.

"Run! It's going to blow!" the Red yelled.

The other warrior grabbed Blazel's arm, and together, they raced to the fire shield's edge. They crouched down, throwing their arms over their heads to protect them. The janack exploded. Blazel tensed, expecting monster debris to pound onto his back. When it didn't, he peeked under his arm. A shield wavered around him and his new friend.

The Red did something to the strange protrusion. Blazel's head burst with the sound of fury in his mind. Darkness pressed on him, and he let it take him.

Blazel awoke on his back on the soggy ground with a petite woman kneeling over him. At first, he couldn't understand how Faelyn had made it to Strunlair Territory before him. Rubbing the fog from his eyes, he noticed the almost black curls framing the woman's heart-shaped face were a much deeper brown than Faelyn's. This woman was an extremely strong Brown.

"Rizelya's the only other person I know about who passes out from the control-janack's screams," the woman said.

"Nobody else seems to hear them, except for now you. Hmm, I wonder if this is why?" She fingered a loc hanging in front of his face, the one with the gray streak.

He pushed her hand away and struggled to sit up. "I thought everyone could hear them."

She shook her head. "Nope. Until now, only Rizelya. Unlike you, she doesn't have a drop of Gray Talent, as far as we know. She's a strong Red. I'm Kaieli by the way."

"Blazel. Who is this Rizelya?"

"My heart sister and Histrun's daughter. He's been worried about you, Blazel. He'll be happy to see you. Here, eat this. It will help with the headache and weakness."

She handed him a trail bar. He took it and bit into it. After a few bites, the pounding in his head started to ease. "Thank you, it is helping."

"You're lucky I have one of those with me. Another healer developed it for Rizelya, and I thought I'd try it with the others. Saffren also has trouble with the damned control-janack."

"Is Histrun here?"

"Of course he is. Do you think he'd stay away from something this important?"

"No, he wouldn't."

The distinct clomping of Jaehaas's hooves heralded his approach. An older woman of medium height, with the air of authority around her, walked alongside Jaehaas and Ambrelya. Gold streaked her bright red hair pulled back in a thick braid. Behind her strode another Red, in her early thirties. She had copper hair, brown eyes, and was tall and wiry. A man still in warrior form guarded the older woman.

Blazel struggled to his feet. Kaieli put a hand under his arm and surreptitiously helped him. He swayed slightly, and she left it there as subtle support. Whatever the control-janack had done, it had made him weak.

"Ah, so you be awake," Jaehaas said. "You scared us there. What happened?"

"The control-janack," Kaieli answered, looking significantly at the older woman. "It affects some people more than others."

"Blazel, let me introduce you to our fighting mates." Jaehaas gestured to the older woman. "This be Strunland Keep Alpha Naila and the warrior be her alpha partner, Kelstrun. The other

Red be Laynar de Strunheim. We've lucked out and arrived at Strunlair Keep in time for a clan meeting. We'll be able to talk to all the Strunlair Territory alphas."

Blazel shook hands with each of the new arrivals. His forehead furrowed, remembering the strange sight of a Blue participating in the monster battle. "Was there a Blue fighting or was I hallucinating?"

Naila tilted her head. "You did. Good fighter." Her voice was rough and Blazel could see it took her a lot of effort to speak. A ragged scar ran across her throat. Naila made an impatient gesture at Laynar.

"Rizelya figured out the other Talents could fight," Laynar said. "We now have Yellows, Greens, Browns, and a few Blues in our fighting force. You must have seen Saffren. It sounds like we have much to discuss."

Jaehaas folded his arms over his chest and cocked a hind foot. "I told them about our mission."

"Now isn't the time to chat," Laynar said. "Besides, the other alphas would feel slighted if we heard your news first. I know my grandmother would be. Blazel, are you steady enough to ride?"

He nodded, taking another bite from the travel bar. It worked wonders, and he was feeling more like himself again.

"Good." Naila turned and strode off, Kelstrun loping next to her.

"Ambrelya left your horses with ours," Laynar said. "Let's go. The others will follow when they're done with the cleanup."

The group trudged through the marsh grass, pulling Blazel in their wake. Kaieli patted his arm before slipping away. Blazel imagined there were other injuries for the healer to treat.

As they walked across the battlefield, Blazel gaped at the strange sights. A brecha appeared to be rotting at an incredible rate. Within moments, the carcass heaved. Giant slug-like creatures crawled over it and devoured it.

"Is that the other Talents' work?" He pointed to a brecha oozing lava.

"Yes, they can do amazing things," Laynar answered. "Wait until you see Saffren's ice curtain."

This Rizelya must be some woman to convince women with other Talents to fight.

"Where is Rizelya?"

"Gone. She's on her way to the Sanctuary."

"Then perhaps I'll meet her there. I'm also traveling to the Sanctuary."

At the battlefield's edge, Kelstrun shifted into his human form. Blazel winced in sympathy when it took him a long, painful time to do so. He blessed all the practicing he'd done. He could change back and forth between warrior and human almost as easily as to his wolf form.

Several teenage boys guarded the horses. They waved and their shoulders relaxed when the alphas came into sight. Lighzel whinnied a greeting to Blazel and hurried to meet him at the corral gate.

As they vacated the enclosure, the other fighters arrived, including a group of women with canary-yellow hair, or dark forest-green hair, or sapphire-blue hair wearing red leathers. His jaw dropped, and he sat back in his saddle. He rolled his eyes, chuckling softly. It wasn't as if he didn't look any odder in his own red leathers.

The fighters quickly mounted. Quite a few stared openly at Blazel and Jaehaas. Together they made a strange sight.

Naila, the apparent alpha of this fighting-pack, set a fast pace away from the battleground. Blazel gathered a blend of people from each of the eight Strunlair territories formed this platoon. After an initial uneasiness, the fighters welcomed Jaehaas, Ambrelya, and Blazel into the group. Many had witnessed Jaehaas's prowess with his bow and fire arrows and expressed their excitement about learning this new skill.

During the ride, Laynar guided her horse to stride beside Blazel. He glanced over at her, opened his mouth, then promptly shut it again. After several measures, he finally gathered his courage. "What can you tell me about Rizelya?"

"How to describe Rizelya?" Laynar idly slapped the end of her horse's reins against her thigh. "I don't know what she's seen in her dreams. She never shared them with me. But they have made her believe the old ways of engaging the Malvers' monsters will soon no longer be effective or useful. She stresses we have to find new methods or risk losing the battle for survival. Her passion infects everyone she meets. So now we have other Talents fighting alongside the Reds and warriors."

He studied the unusual group of fighters with new respect. For some reason, he imagined Rizelya to be an older woman, like Naila, to have so much influence. "What Keep is she Alpha of?"

Laynar laughed. "None. She's only twenty-three and was only recently made a squad-alpha, and from what I understand, it was under protest. She has a way about her that makes people listen."

Blazel sat back, stunned. *Now, I have to meet this woman!*

The platoon soon reached the safe house where they would stay the night. Blazel quickly took care of Lighzel and entered the building. Jaehaas stood to the side, his tail lazily swishing while he chatted with Laynar. At first, the safe house appeared to be the same as the ones in Haaslair Province, except something seemed off about it. *Oh, there aren't any tall tables for the Centaurs. This clan-pack isn't used to having a centaur around, and doesn't have the special modifications needed to accommodate them. What are they going to do so Jaehaas can join us for the evening meal?*

A whiff of a hot, spicy scent drew Blazel's attention to the stove. Someone had already started the ubiquitous large pot of stew. When forty or fifty people needed to eat, stew was the easiest and fastest thing to fix. A woman with forest-green hair stood with one hand on her hip and balanced on a block of wood so she could peer into the pot. Her eyebrows furrowed in intense concentration as she stirred the stew. Intrigued, Blazel sauntered over to her.

"Hi," he said.

She jumped, the long wooden spoon clanking on the pot's edge. She spun around, the spoon in her hand raised to strike.

"Sorry." Blazel put his hands up. "I didn't mean to startle you. I wanted to meet you."

"Oh, you're the guy who doesn't have a clan-pack."

Blazel grimaced, and his shoulders slumped. "Yeah, that's me. I'll leave you alone."

"No, don't go. I was rude." She put the spoon down and held out her hand. "I'm Grazeen de Strunven, but now I'm with the Strunland pack."

"Blazel." He gripped her wrist in a warrior's greeting and smiled at her widened eyes. "I was curious how you became a fighter. Not that I think anything is wrong with it," he hurried to add when her eyes narrowed. Undoubtedly, there were people still attached to the old traditions against women other than Reds fighting.

"Rizelya. She came to Strunven Keep and found us. Let's go sit down." Grazeen hopped off her block, poured hot taevo into a couple of mugs, and sat at the table nearest the stove. When Blazel settled onto the bench across from her, she handed him one of the mugs.

He took a sip and raised an eyebrow. Instead of the spicy taevo he expected, it was minty with a hint of fruit. "This is good. Your blend?"

Grazeen nodded, pleased. "I made the stew spicy, so the taevo needs to be cooling. Although cooking isn't my specialty."

"What is?"

"Growing food and..." she paused, swallowed hard, and leaned forward. "Raising snelks. Someone has to. If not, how would we get rid of all the garbage? Snelks serve a great purpose."

Apparently, this was also a sore issue for Grazeen. He smiled at her in reassurance, even though he didn't know what a snelk was. "Yes, it's important work." Then it dawned on him what she meant. "You're the one who made the brecha rot! Are snelks the slug-like creatures that were swarming it?"

"Yep, that was me." She cupped her mug with both hands, staring at him intently. "Rizelya isn't nauseated by my magic, like some. She thinks it's great. She was traveling all over Strunlair Province because of the new control-janack, finding ways to kill the darned thing. By the time I met her, she'd already discovered Yellows were very useful in the fight. They form cold-air shields to hide the fighters from the control-janack. But she believed the other Talents could also fight. And we can!

"Our group was training with Maendy in secret, and were trying to prove to our Keep Alpha, Sujeen, that we could fight. She wouldn't listen." Grazeen took a breath in her non-stop narration, making a sour face. "But then Sujeen tried to kill Rizelya, just because she's Histrun's daughter. Can you believe an Alpha would do such a thing?"

Blazel shook his head.

"Saehala fought her, and I'm so glad she did! Rizelya took us to the next monster battle, without Saehala's permission or knowledge. We proved we could kill monsters as well as any Red." Grazeen lowered her voice, adding, "Even better than some." She sat back with a smug smile. "Saehala listened to Rizelya, and now we're part of Rizelya's pack. We'll be going to Strunland Keep with her when she returns from the Sanctuary."

Blazel smiled into his mug at how fast Grazeen could talk. He sipped his taevo. "Wow! Rizelya sounds like an extraordinary woman. I hope to meet her when I reach the Sanctuary."

"You'll like her." Grazeen stood. "Everyone likes her. Sorry, I need to finish dinner. The wolves are getting hungry and impatient."

"Thank you for talking to me."

"I hope we can be friends." She gave him a shy smile, grabbed their empty mugs, and returned to the stove.

Jaehaas clomped to the table and waved toward Grazeen. "Looks like you made a new friend."

Blazel grinned, nodding. "Yeah, she's a good kid. Even though she talks so fast, I had trouble keeping up with her. Are you being treated well?"

"Yes. Naila be a good alpha and takes care of her people. Since we fought together, apparently we now be considered her people. Did you know she be sister to this Rizelya everyone be raving about?"

"No, I didn't." Blazel resolved to speak with Naila after dinner. "Rizelya seems to be a resourceful person."

Jaehaas threw back his head and laughed. "That be one way of putting it. I be reserving judgment until I meet her. She sounds like a glory seeker. Although, she did come up with a genius technique of fighting and killing the control-janack."

The woman with canary-yellow hair stood and, in a voice obviously enhanced with her air Talent, bellowed, "Food's ready! Form a line."

Ambrelya joined Blazel and Jaehaas, and together, they fell into the queue. By the time they had bowls in hand, someone had placed blocks under a small table, making it high enough so Jaehaas could eat as part of the group. A lump formed in Blazel's throat at Naila's kindness.

Chapter 10

After eating, Blazel made his way to Naila's table and asked her about Rizelya.

"She's a good alpha." Naila swallowed several times. "Excellent leader. You want to know more, ask Laynar. Hurts to talk." She put a hand over the scar on her throat.

"You're not part of her pack," Laynar explained, "and so she can't communicate mind-to-mind with you through the pack links. I've traveled with Rizelya from Strunheim Keep to Strunlair Keep, going the roundabout route so we could warn the other territories. She's amazing. Rizelya is bright, resourceful, innovative, and most importantly, a compassionate leader."

Laynar told him several stories of their travels and monster battles. He learned Rizelya was usually the first one to attack and destroy the control-janack. By the time Blazel finally went to bed, he was anxious to meet this amazing woman.

But instead of dreaming of Rizelya, Blazel dreamed about Chariel. As he watched in horror, Chariel morphed into a gaunt woman with pale gray skin, hollow eyes, and long black claws instead of fingers. The woman screamed in frustration at something out of his field of vision. She turned her baleful gaze on him. His stomach churned with dread. "I'm coming for you," she sneered. A meteor flamed through the sky, struck, and the land burned with blood and fire.

Blazel woke with a start, sweating and breathing hard. He quietly eased out of the safe house and peered at the night sky, and his breath whooshed out when only the stars shone in the dark. He sat on the well's rim and continued to watch the sky until it began to lighten with the rising sun. Danger was coming, and it would come from the sky. *But is it the madness from Chariel's visions? Why am I dreaming about it?*

He hadn't told anyone about his dreams. Blazel doubted even his mentor, Histrun, would believe him something horrible was on the horizon. All of their attention was on the Malvers' monsters and the new control-janack. But Blazel knew in his bones they weren't the only hazard to the Posairs' survival.

Blazel rode in a swirl of companionable chatter. His silence was a quiet eddy in the stream of conversation. A frisson of tension ran under his skin, making him irritable and jittery.

"Hey," Jaehaas said quietly, "what be wrong? You look like you be jumping out of your skin."

"Nothing. I just feel odd."

Jaehaas scanned the forest on either side of the road. "You hearing a hum? Be there monsters near?"

"No... that isn't it... I don't think..." Blazel paused. He cocked his head to the side and listened intently, to be sure. "No, there's no hum, so I doubt my jitters are because of monsters. I had a weird dream last night."

"I be here, if you want to talk." Jaehaas patted his arm, and slowed until he walked next to Ambrelya, who was behind Blazel.

By mid-morning, Blazel's odd nervousness vanished. He urged Lighzel forward to ride alongside Laynar. He hoped she'd tell him more stories about Rizelya. The forest thinned and opened to a wide valley, and the road cut through fields and pastures.

"We're almost to Strunlair Keep," Laynar said. "These are the Keep's lands."

High sheadash stone walls surrounded the fields to protect them from marauding monsters. In addition, in the pastures where people tended animals, an adolescent team, consisting of a Red on a horse and a young wolf, carefully stood watch.

"What are they doing?" Blazel pointed to a pair.

"Protecting the herders. If needed, the wolf will call for help while the Red helps the herders escape to safety. We've had too many monsters escape us. Even worse, nests have thrown out a single janack and a trio of brechas unexpectedly, leading to civilian deaths. It's an innovation of—"

"Let me guess, Rizelya."

Laynar shook her head. "No, it wasn't her idea. But she did make sure to tell everyone she met about it. My grandmother Layhalya dreamed this up, or rather, remembered it from her childhood. Histrun was quite chagrined when he found out. She isn't much older than he is, and he hadn't considered setting guards."

Blazel grinned. "We have to remember he's an old man and getting forgetful."

Laynar burst into a fit of laughter so hard her horse stopped in its tracks. Finally, she stilled and wiped her eyes. "Oh, please tell that to Histrun. I'd like to see his reaction. He'll bellow about insolent youngsters while he chases you."

"In his warrior form." He shuddered. "A horrible sight to a six-year-old."

"He didn't!" Laynar put a hand to her chest, and her eyes widened.

"He did." Blazel nodded. "I don't remember now what he did to make me mad, but I called him a senile old man, and he chased me. Although, he must not have wanted to actually catch me, since I evaded him and hid in the hay loft the rest of the afternoon. I've never been disrespectful again."

Laynar chuckled. "No, he didn't want to. If he had, as a warrior, he'd have caught you in two strides. The chase was the lesson. He's here, you know."

"Kaieli told me, I can't wait to see him. It's been a long time."

"How long?"

"Fourteen years. The summer I turned sixteen. Chariel sent me to the Deep Mountain when I was seventeen, and I have been a lone wolf ever since."

"It must have been hard." Compassion filled Laynar's voice.

Blazel shrugged. "I'm used to it. After I left the Sanctuary, I spent five years with a Gryphons flight, having a glorious time."

"Really? Gryphons exist? They must be an awesome sight in flight." She sighed, gazing at the sky as if watching them soar.

"It is. And they are real. I miss them, especially my friend Graak." Blazel sighed. Even though the Gryphons were a different species, they had welcomed and accepted him. Well, he admitted to himself, eventually they had.

Blazel dropped his reins and tilted his head back. "What is that?" A huge stone wall reached into the sky and stretched for many measures in either direction.

"Strunlair Keep. It's the oldest and, I believe, the largest Keep in all of Lairheim."

Blazel stared at the wall. "I think it is. In my travels, I've seen numerous Keeps, but this has to be the largest one by far."

Jaehaas and Ambrelya trotted to ride with them. They rounded a curve in the road. A massive gate, so wide four horses could ride through it abreast, blocked the way. Blazel craned his neck to gaze at the top of the wall. Yellow-haired women walked the battlements, their eyes trained to the distance. With their air Talent they could bend light waves to see great distances.

"What are they searching for?" He pointed to the women.

"Marauding monsters. This Keep hosts nearly six-thousand people and is a magnet for the monsters, especially now their behavior is changing. I was with Rizelya when we battled our way across Strunlair Territory. The moment we crossed the border from Strunheim, monsters attacked us constantly as we tried to reach Strunlair Keep. By the end, we fought five, six, sometimes seven, times in one day." Laynar closed her eyes and shuddered. "The attacks have decreased back to almost normal since Rizelya left."

"Why do you think they've done that?" Jaehaas asked.

Laynar shrugged. "The intelligence behind the control-janack wants Rizelya for some dark purpose. Nobody knows why. It's one reason she's gone to the Supreme. We hope she can figure it out and help Rizelya."

"What intelligence?" Jaehaas's face twisted in confusion. "The Malvers' monsters be mindless beasts driven by hunger."

"You've noticed the control-janack is different?" Laynar rested her wrists on her saddle's pommel.

Both Jaehaas and Blazel nodded.

"From what Rizelya has said, there is someone, we don't know who, instructing the janack. It, in turn, uses the strange protrusion to control the other monsters."

"Yes, I've seen it." Blazel cocked his head to the side and wrinkled his nose. "Is that what the hum is doing? Directing the other janacks and brechas?"

Laynar turned to him, her eyebrows raised quizzically. "You can hear it?"

"Yes..."

"Why can only Rizelya, and now you, hear it?" She stared at him for a long moment. "Although she suffers greatly from its effects. I'd rather not hear it if I had to deal with the debilitating headaches. Have you had any strange dreams?"

Heat blossomed under Blazel's skin, nodding. "I thought my strange dreams were the effect of Chariel's calling," he mumbled. "If the strange, gaunt woman in them is the intelligence Rizelya mentioned, we are in deep trouble." Blazel shuddered and rubbed the goose bumps off his arms. "The Supreme should be able to help Rizelya. The old woman knows more than anyone else. And if she doesn't know, she has access to a vast library of history."

"How would—" Ambrelya started.

"He was raised by her," Jaehaas finished.

The horse's clops echoed in the tunnel formed by the gate entrance through the keep's thick walls. All conversation stopped as they entered the courtyard.

Blazel gawked at the noise and bustle of the keep's vast plaza. It seemed all six-thousand residents were jammed into the space, all vying for attention. He huddled on his saddle, unused to being surrounded by so many people. His eyes darted around, taking in the chaos, and afraid to make eye contact with the strangers, while at the same time, curious.

He followed in the wake Naila and Kelstrun made in the crowd as the platoon rode through the plaza toward the Clan-house. Built from granite flecked with mica, it sparkled in the sun. A sweeping white marble porch skirted the front of the building. Black marble columns held up a balcony. Dark ironwood double doors were polished to a glossy shine and had wide bands of helstrim affixed to them, giving them added strength against the monsters. The enormous building could hold a thousand people or more in case of an attack on the keep.

A large group of people waited on the veranda. A huge man, nearly seven feet tall with broad shoulders and thick legs, stood with his arms crossed and watched the fighting-pack's arrival. His close-cut red hair had streaks of green. His powerful presence exuded power. Next to the giant, the compact woman seemed small. She had deep, dark red hair and extremely pale skin.

Naila and Kelstrun strode up the stairs, nodded to the Clan Alphas, and joined the other territory leaders on the porch.

An old man leaning on the railing caught Blazel's attention. His red hair had dulled, and his once-powerful shoulders were now stooped with age. His mentor, Histrun, had grown old since Blazel had seen him last. The old man squinted and then slowly straightened. His advanced years didn't slow him down as he quickly brushed past the alphas to stand at the top of the stairs.

"Well, well, well," Histrun said, staring down at Blazel, his voice rang out strong. "I heard rumors you still lived. Didn't I teach you better manners, boy?"

Blazel slid off his horse and rushed to the steps. He stopped, kneeled on one knee on the bottom step, and bowed his head. "My apologies."

"You were supposed to wait for me, boy, not run off and worry me. What are you waiting for? Come here and say hello."

Blazel raised his head. Histrun held his arms opened wide. Blazel raced up the stairs, and Histrun enveloped him in a strong embrace. It surprised him to discover he now stood several inches taller than Histrun.

Histrun patted Blazel's back and whispered in his ear, "Good to see you, boy." He pushed Blazel away and held him at arm's length. "You've grown well, a bit thin and scraggly looking, though. And you've found new friends. Good for you. It's not healthy to always be alone."

"You look good too, old man." Blazel's throat tightened. He'd missed Histrun and his gruff affection. "Seems like you've managed to find yourself in the thick of things again."

Histrun laughed. "Of course I have. Introduce us to your friends."

Ambrelya had dismounted and stood next to Jaehaas as they waited at the bottom step. Laynar waited on the other side of Jaehaas.

"Alphas," Laynar said, "this is Ambrelya de Haasneh and the centaur Jaehaas de Haasneh."

The alpha couple stepped forward. Blazel's eyes widened. The woman was a rare double Red. Not only did she have red hair, but her red eyes were ringed in gold.

"Welcome to Strunlair Keep," the woman said. "I am Beladi, and this is my consort, Nestrun."

"You have news for us?" Nestrun asked, his deep baritone reverberating in the enclosed space.

"We do, and an offer of skills." Ambrelya bowed.

Nestrun waved them up the stairs, then gestured for the other fighters to disperse. He led the way into the Clan-house, Beladi at his side. The rest followed them. Blazel wished he'd had time to wash the travel grime off before having to meet with the clan alphas. Laynar walking beside him in the rear soothed his nerves. Nestrun turned and went through a door.

A large group of people occupied the room, all of whom had the air of powerful alphas. They stopped chatting and stared at Blazel and Jaehaas when they entered. Blazel's stomach dropped. There were too many people, too many powerful people, for him. He took a step back and ran into Jaehaas.

"It be okay," Jaehaas whispered to him. "All be friends here."

"There's so many," Laynar added, keeping her voice quiet, "because a clan meeting is in progress. These are Clan Strunlair's territory alphas. None of them will harm you. Histrun will make sure of it."

"That I will, boy," Histrun said. Even though he was no longer a clan or keep alpha, he had followed the group into the meeting room. No one seemed upset by his breach of etiquette.

Histrun glared at the alphas, and they turned their attention from Blazel.

"I need to talk to my grandmother." Laynar patted Blazel on the shoulder as she walked away.

A few people sat at a conference table in the center of the room. A buffet placed along the wall held food and drinks.

Blazel longed for a glass of cool water to cut the dust from his throat, but the alphas guarded the refreshments.

"There's nothing to be afraid of, boy. I bet you could use a drink."

Blazel nodded. Histrun gripped Blazel's upper arm and led him to the refreshment table. As they approached, all but one older couple left. The woman's copper hair had faded to almost pink, and wrinkles lined her dark brown eyes and face. Her companion appeared to be a few years younger and had light brown hair with red streaks and green eyes.

"Blazel," Histrun said, "these are Strunell Keep Alphas Keshanal and Bestrun."

They murmured greetings and then moved away. Blazel sighed in relief and poured a glass of water from a pitcher covered in condensation. He drank it in one long gulp and refilled it. Jaehaas and Ambrelya joined him at the table.

"This spread looks delicious." Jaehaas rubbed his hands together. He heaped food on a plate.

Blazel gazed at the food and then back at the group of people. His stomach roiled. "I think I'll wait."

Once everyone, except Blazel, had filled plates, Histrun led them to the table. Next to a space wide enough for Jaehaas stood a tall tray where he could comfortably put his plate. Blazel's heart warmed to have his friend's needs met by these strangers. Even Histrun was a stranger, after not being in contact with him for thirteen years. Blazel gratefully slipped onto the chair next to Laynar, a recent acquaintance.

On the other side of Laynar sat an ancient woman. Her red hair had faded to a pale pink, and her back curled, making her appear stooped. When she smiled at Blazel, her emerald-green eyes shone with intelligence and humor. Next to her was a man many years her junior, with cinnamon-red hair and brown eyes flecked with green. He seemed to be only several years older than Laynar.

"Blazel, Jaehaas," Laynar said, "this is my grandmother Layhalya and her second, Selestrun."

They nodded in greeting.

A bell rang through the room, cutting through the conversations. Beladi stood at the head of the table, ringing the bell. "It's time to reconvene our meeting. Come, sit down."

A few moments later, everyone found seats at the conference table and focused their attention on Beladi and Nestrun.

"We have visitors who can add to what we know about the change in the monsters," Nestrun said. "Anything we can learn will help us in our struggle to survive."

"Welcome, Blazel, Jaehaas, and Ambrelya." Beladi smiled at each one in turn. "We are anxious to hear your report. Blazel, we are most eager to find out what you have experienced. Why were you so far south?"

Blazel's mouth suddenly felt as dry as the Barrens. "I... I..." He took a long drink of water. Laynar gave him an encouraging smile, and Jaehaas patted his shoulder. He inhaled a deep breath, let it out slowly, and began again. "Histrun, I am sorry, but I was unable to wait for you. If it had been my choice, I would have gladly left the Sanctuary to live with you. But that wasn't what the Goddess had planned for me. Instead, my friend Chariel had a vision that sent me to the Deep Mountains."

"Who is this Chariel, and why would you listen to her?" Nestrun leaned forward on his crossed elbows.

"She is a Gray," Histrun answered, "an Oracle gifted with visions from the Goddess. The Supreme listens to her, as all her prophecies come true. She's not one you ignore."

Nestrun nodded, apparently satisfied.

"Why were you sent there?" Beladi asked.

Blazel shrugged. "Perhaps to meet and become friends with the Gryphons."

A collective gasp followed the mention of the mythical Gryphons. Everyone's eyes turned to Blazel.

He swallowed hard and rubbed his sweaty palms on his pants leg. "But that isn't important for now. More importantly, she had another vision three years ago and sent me to the swamps. I spent the last year in the great swamp south of the Barrens. She told me I would return when the madness was near." He held up a hand to forestall their questions. "No, we don't know what it referred to. I'm guessing it is this new control janack that has shown up and the Malvers' monsters strange behavior."

A flash of a meteor flaming through the sky, bringing with it blood and death, intruded into Blazel's thoughts. He shook his head. They'd just think he was crazy. Chariel, or even the

Supreme, might know what his dreams meant. But with this group, he'd stick with the facts.

Blazel told them about his journey across the Barrens and his stay with the Strunland guard-pack at the crater. When he reached his travels through the plains, Jaehaas added his observations.

Darkness fell, and lamps were lit. Still, the alphas grilled Blazel and Jaehaas, until at last, they were dismissed from the meeting.

Chapter 11

Aloud clanging bell startled Blazel awake. Confused, he pried his eyes open and promptly shut them again, groaning. The room spun, his head pounded, and his stomach lurched. The last thing he remembered was talking with Histrun and drinking—a lot. They'd finished three bottles of wine before Histrun had brought out a jug of moonshine. The bonging bell reverberated painfully, echoing in Blazel's head.

"What in the Crone's fires is that racket?" he grumbled, holding his head in his hands.

"The alarm," Jaehaas answered. "There be sightings of three different groups of marauding monsters where they shouldn't be, and a nest be maturing today rather than tomorrow. Fighters be scrambling to stop them."

Blazel cracked an eye open. Jaehaas leaned his hindquarters against a wall, his left hind leg cocked, and he held a book. A pot of steaming taevo sat on a table near him.

"Why are you still here?"

"I be waiting for you to wake up," Jaehaas drawled. "And since midmorning has come and gone, I thought I'd read."

"But why aren't you mustering to fight?" Blazel rolled over and gradually pushed into a sitting position. The clomping of Jaehaas's hooves made him groan again.

"Here." Jaehaas handed him a mug.

Blazel sipped the potion. It had a bitter aftertaste, but it did make his head and stomach feel better. Wrinkling his nose at it, he took another sip.

"The healer, Kaieli, brought it for you. She said she also had to brew one for Histrun," Jaehaas smirked. "I be sure the whole Keep heard you and Histrun bellowing. We think you be trying to sing. And then there be the dancing naked in the courtyard."

"I didn't!" Blazel's memory was fuzzy after they had started on the moonshine. "Did I?" He squinted at Jaehaas.

Jaehaas burst into laughter, making Blazel cringe. Every time he looked at him, Jaehaas would laugh harder.

"Please stop," Jaehaas said between breaths, "just stop giving me puppy eyes."

Blazel had no idea what Jaehaas meant. He rubbed his face and finished drinking Kaieli's brew. Ignoring Jaehaas and his continuing chuckles, Blazel wobbled to the necessary room. He grimaced at the sour stench of his body and clothes. The hot bath cleared his head and revived him.

"So, did I really dance naked?" Blazel pulled on trousers.

"No, not naked, but you did dance. How be your head?"

"Better." Blazel shrugged into a clean shirt. Someone had gone through his clothing and cleaned everything. "So why aren't you out with the fighters?"

"I be going with you, and we were supposed to leave today, remember?"

Blazel paused from putting on a boot, one foot in the air, and scowled. "No, you're not! I don't need a babysitter."

"You don't have any say in it." Jaehaas crossed his arms across his chest and glared back at Blazel. "I be traveling with you to the Sanctuary. I have every right to go there and seek the Supreme's counsel. Besides, you agreed to it."

"When?" Blazel's forehead furrowed in confusion. "I don't remember agreeing."

"Well, you did. Drinking as much as you did will do that to you." Jaehaas flicked his tail.

Blazel thought back over the night. He had a foggy memory of Jaehaas finding them and joining them in their festivities.

"Hey! Why aren't you suffering from a hangover? You were with us." Blazel glowered at Jaehaas.

"Ah, but I didn't drink as much, and I stopped sooner. We can't leave until later this afternoon. It be too dangerous to travel until the monsters be cleared out."

The brew settled Blazel's nausea and wiped away his headache. His stomach rumbled, this time in hunger. "Is there any chance I can grab breakfast?"

Jaehaas grinned. "No, breakfast be long gone. But you could get lunch. The Keep-House's kitchen always be open."

While Blazel ate, Histrun wandered into the dining hall. His eyes were bleary, and he was walking carefully. He sat heavily on the bench with a grunt.

"Didn't Kaieli's brew help you?" Blazel asked.

"Hmf, doesn't work as well on old men," Histrun grumbled.

"Or you were more drunk than I was."

"I'll get you some food," Jaehaas offered. "You look awful, Histrun."

"Thanks." Histrun made a face. "Just toast and taevo, please. It's all my poor stomach can handle."

Histrun perked up, and the three men chatted, while waiting for the clan alphas to give Blazel and Jaehaas permission to leave. Finished with their taevo, they wandered to a practice field where Jaehaas showed Histrun his archery. This time, instead of standing still, Jaehaas shot his arrows while at a run, zigzagging around the target in a simulation of how he fought the monsters.

"You say the arrows flame and burn the beasts?" Histrun asked when Jaehaas trotted back to where they had watched.

Jaehaas nodded as he removed and nocked a red-fletched arrow, murmuring the spell as he let the arrow loose. Fire bloomed on the arrowhead while in flight. The arrow landed, sizzling, in a bucket of water.

"Ambrelya be here to train other Reds the spell. She be an excellent archer and can teach your people the skill. He" — Jaehaas pointed to Blazel — "reminded us we needed to share."

"Sounds like my daughter," Histrun said, grinning. "She insists we share our innovations with the other clans. As soon as we train enough people, we'll be sending teams to the other provinces."

"Will the teams include fighters from the other Talents?" Jaehaas asked. "They seem to be quite effective."

Histrun nodded. "They are. Those girls can be downright vicious." He studied the bow held in Jaehaas's hands. "Archery could be right handy with rogue monsters leaving the nest before the rest and wandering all over. If Rizelya is right, and I believe her, we'll need every advantage we can to win this war with the monsters."

"What if she's correct, and there is someone directing them?" Blazel mused, thinking about his own dreams. "Where are they? Who are they? Could they be the 'madness' Chariel saw coming?"

"Good questions, boy." Histrun scratched at his short beard. "One none of us can answer, except perhaps the Supreme. I fervently pray the Goddess guides her, and she knows something about it."

"There's a huge library at the Sanctuary." Blazel loved reading the old chronicles hidden in the library's dusty corners and had spent many happy hours wandering its depths. "If she doesn't know, the information might be buried in the ancient histories." He turned to Jaehaas with a wicked grin. Time for payback for teasing him about dancing naked. "Can you read?"

Jaehaas reared slightly. "Of course I can! I wasn't holding a book earlier for nothing."

"Then you'll be of some help when we search the records. You have to have some purpose besides keeping me company." Blazel smiled to take the edge off his words.

Jaehaas crossed his arms, flicking his tail. "Oh, you know you will be lonely without me."

Blazel wouldn't admit it to anyone, but he was happy Jaehaas was going with him. He'd come to enjoy traveling with the other man.

A young wolf loped across the practice field and slid to a stop in front of them. It shifted into a boy, around nine years old. "Histrun, sir, the alpha said to tell you the north road is clear." He stared at Jaehaas, then blurted, "Did it hurt to split yourself like that?"

"Yes, so don't you go and try doing it." Jaehaas bent his front knees to be at eye level with the boy. "Promise me you and your friends won't try something like this. I only did it after years and years of shifting. If you try it, and don't know what you're doing, it could kill you. Or worse."

The boy's eyes grew wide. "Wha... What's that?"

"You might end up with a human arm and a wolf paw, or a human upper jaw and a wolf muzzle on the bottom. Can't eat then. Once you be mixed up like that, you can't go back. You be stuck in the jumbled form."

"No way, that can't happen!" the boy cried.

"Yes, it can. How do you think I ended up like this?" Jaehaas waved a hand at his human half and then swept it back to indicate his horse half. "I can't shift to any other form now. Promise me you won't play around."

The boy nodded and ran off, slipping into his wolf form within a few steps.

Histrun watched the child and rubbed his chin. "I'll tell the teachers to keep a sharp eye on the boys. I'll spend more time with the youngsters just to make sure they don't have an opportunity to attempt foolish ideas. As if I needed anything else to do. I'm supposed to be retired!" He threw his hands into the air.

Blazel and Jaehaas exchanged a glance and laughed. Histrun was no more retired than they were.

Together, the three men walked to the stables. Jaehaas grabbed his packs from the stack by the barn. A stable hand led Lighzel from the pasture. She whinnied a greeting to Blazel, bumping her nose into his chest, demanding attention. After he scratched her cheek, he saddled her. When he finished, he searched for Jaehaas. He stood talking with Histrun and Laynar under the shade of a tree. Blazel joined them.

"Take care, boy," Histrun said, his voice husky. "Come back to us and don't wait fourteen years. I might not be around."

"I promise."

Histrun pulled Blazel into a tight hug, slapping his back. Histrun blinked suspiciously and rubbed his eyes when Blazel stepped away.

Laynar handed him a small package. "Grandmother wanted you to have it."

Inside, he found an amulet with the symbol of the Consort on it.

"Grandmother said it was to remind you of what you are, and what you can become. It is no longer time for you to wander alone. Open your heart and let love enter."

Blazel fingered the amulet. He'd had one when he was young, but had lost it during the sabertiger attack. He'd never had the courage to ask the Supreme for another one.

"Thank your grandmother for me. It means a great deal to me." As he slipped the chain over his head, his fingers brushed his scar. The amulet rested against his heart, warming with the contact of his skin.

Laynar stood on her toes and brushed a kiss on his cheek. "Of course. It was a pleasure meeting you, Blazel. Don't be too long in coming back. We need you in this fight."

Blazel fingered his cheek. "We'll be back."

"Tell Rizelya and Aistrun when you see them, their pack misses them."

"I will. Goddess willing, we'll return together."

Farewells finished, Blazel climbed into Lighzel's saddle. A young warrior rode up and saluted.

"Sirs, I'll be your guide to the north road and the first safe house. There's only one roadway leading from there to Strunhelos Keep, and the pass it guards into the White Mountains."

Their escort led them away from the busy plaza and through narrow streets. Traffic thinned the further they rode from the Keep's center. The less impressive north gate only allowed two horses to ride abreast through it rather than four.

The horse's hooves echoed on a sheadash stone road weaving through orchards of apple, peach, and other fruit trees. An octar later, they left the orchards behind and rode through a forest. The farther north they traveled, the more wild the land grew.

"Goddess, it feels so good to be going home!" Blazel leaned back in his saddle, dropping Lighzel's reins, and threw his arms open wide. He inhaled deeply the crisp smell of pines and smiled at the chatter of blue jays in their branches.

He urged Lighzel to catch up with Jaehaas. "No more living in swamps and suffering with my clothes and fur always being damp. No more twisted animals and trees."

"It be that bad?" Jaehaas flicked his tail, chasing away an errant fly.

"Unbelievably so. The only danger we'll face is from Malvers' monsters and narhili beasts. Here, the rabbits aren't twisted into blood-crazed fiends. Snakes don't fly." Blazel drank in the forest's smells and sights, like a man dying of thirst.

Home. In less than a chedan, he'd be home.

The safe house they stayed the night in seemed cavernous with just Blazel, Jaehaas, and their guide. To ease the quietness, Blazel pulled out his flute and played, losing himself in its melodious tones. In the morning, their guide returned to Strunlair Keep.

Blazel and Jaehaas traveled deeper into the mountains. In Strunlair Keep, spring had given way to summer, but this high summer was still a few chedans away. Blazel was shivering with the dropping temperature by the time they stopped for a rest late in the afternoon. He rummaged through his pack for another shirt or jacket. Last night, when he'd taken out his flute, his pack seemed fuller, but he hadn't paid much attention to it. Now, as he pulled out a thick cloak, he knew why. He snugged it tight around his shoulders, silently thanking whoever had gifted it to him as he warmed up.

Across the clearing, Jaehaas also dug through the contents of his pack. He withdrew a jacket and put it on. It reached to his withers, covering only the human part. His horse pelt would keep the back half warm enough, Blazel supposed.

Blazel and Jaehaas galloped from the clearing. They'd have to hustle to reach the next safe house fifteen measures away. It would be full dark soon—a dangerous time to be caught outside. Although they were too high, and the weather was too cold, for narhili beasts, other predators roamed the mountains. Blazel kept a sharp eye on the bushes and trees on either side of the road.

Dusk filled the forest. Blazel twisted in his saddle as the undergrowth rustled. He slowed Lighzel to a trot. If a predator was around, her running would attract it. He whistled, hoping to alert Jaehaas, who had disappeared in the gloom. Lighzel shied from a shadow on the road, the whites of her eyes showing.

Something was there.

Blazel slid his helstrablade out of its sheath, his attention on the shadow. A long, lean, mottled gray body slunk on the ground. Sharp tusks jutted from the creature's lower jaw. It had four eyes. Two in the regular position and two on the top of its head.

A paether. They never traveled or hunted alone, but in packs of ten or fifteen animals. The beasts could take down a large billocks—or a horse.

Blazel touched his heels to Lighzel's flanks. Needing no other urging, she leaped into a gallop, flying down the road. Several gray shapes kept pace with them on either side. Blazel gripped his helstrablade, wishing it was the longer helbraught the Reds used. The extra length would be useful.

One of the beasts darted from the brush, speeding toward Lighzel. Blazel swung his blade, slicing off an ear. The beast yowled and turned away. He had to keep them from slashing his horse's belly open with their tusks. The eyes on the top of the paether's head meant they weren't running blind under the churning feet of their prey.

Another one rushed from the other side. Blazel whipped his blade toward it, while a third paether nipped at Lighzel's heels. The pack attacked them from every direction. Blazel tied the reins to the saddle and fought with his helstrablade, barely keeping his balance as he slashed, while Lighzel raced forward. They would both be dead if she stopped. *The safe house has to be close! Dear Mother, please help us.* It had been a long time since he had prayed.

Unexpectedly, the paether leaping at him fell away. Blazel glanced over his shoulder. An arrow protruded from its chest. He turned his attention back to the beasts attacking Lighzel. As he fought, another arrow whizzed by his head and thunked into a paether's side. It yelped as another arrow pounded into it, and it tumbled end over end, dead.

Only two more creatures still harried him. Trusting Jaehaas, Blazel clamped his legs around Lighzel's belly and leaned as far over the right side as he could and not fall off. With all of his strength, he thrust the blade into the skull of the paether running next to them. As it dropped to the ground, he pulled himself upright, searching for the remaining beast. It sprawled on the road, dead, an arrow protruding from its eye.

Ahead of him, Jaehaas stood in the middle of the road. He saluted Blazel with the tip of his bow and continued to guard Blazel's escape. As he passed, Jaehaas pivoted and ran beside him. They rounded a bend, the safe house came into view, and they thundered through the open gate. Jaehaas reared, slammed the gates shut, and dropped the bar to lock them.

"That be close." Jaehaas wiped the sweat from his forehead. "What be those things?"

"Paethers. They slice open their prey's abdomen." Blazel slid off the saddle and crouched to examine Lighzel's belly. Several long gashes dripped blood. "Here, hold her." He threw her reins at Jaehaas.

Blazel raced into the stable, found a clean rag and a pail, which he filled with fresh water, and ran back to his horse. Carefully, he washed Lighzel's wounds. Straightening, he let his breath go in a whoosh. "None of her injuries are serious, thank the Mother. I'm really glad now you're with me. Without your arrows, I don't know if we would have made it. Thank you."

"I told you, you needed me," Jaehaas said with a smile and a raised eyebrow. He followed Blazel into the stable and watched while he unsaddled his horse. "How did you survive on your own? It be a long way from the Deep Mountains to the southern peninsula."

"I didn't have to worry about a horse." Blazel patted Lighzel's neck and filled her manger with fresh hay. He scooped out a large portion of grain for her. "I only had myself to take care of, and I traveled mostly either as a wolf or in my warrior form. I've been a wolf more than a man over the last few years."

"You not be a rogue." Jaehaas put a hand on Blazel's shoulder. "It takes more than staying in wolf form for long periods of time. You aren't slavering to kill people. Come on, I be starved. Let's go fix something to eat."

Blazel wondered how he had found such a good friend. Together, they made an edible dinner from the supplies in the safe house and their packs.

The next morning, he insisted they practice archery before leaving. He'd witnessed the bow's value and its long distance-ability firsthand. Now, he had an incentive to improve and hit the target's center three times.

Blazel inspected Lighzel's belly and found the lacerations were all scabbed over. He carefully placed the girth strap around her, ensuring it didn't rub any of her wounds. They should reach Strunhelos Keep before sunset, so another attack from the nocturnal paethers was unlikely.

Once the sun topped the mountain peaks, the day warmed. Flowers bloomed in the meadows they passed. A herd of ducorns bounded from a meadow and disappeared into the trees. They were one of Blazel's favorite foods, and he tightly gripped Lighzel's reins so he wouldn't chase after them. *I won't starve if they get away. I have plenty of food in my packs. So does Jaehaas.*

He glanced down. "What in the Crone's fires!" Fur covered his hand. *I haven't ever done that before. I didn't even know it was possible.* Concentrating hard, he returned his hand to flesh. He surreptitiously patted his face and ears to ensure they were still human, then looked sideways at Jaehaas. But he didn't act like he'd seen Blazel's slip.

When they passed the trees where the ducorns had fled, Blazel relaxed—or tried to. His body quivered with pain. He heard a soft growling, and realized it was him. Other than the brief periods to hunt, he hadn't spent much time as a wolf since meeting the Strunland guard-pack. The last time he'd shifted had been two chedans ago. It had been years since he'd remained solely in his human form.

He gritted his teeth with the effort to restrain the wolf inside of him. He relaxed when he remembered Histrun telling him none of his forms were better or worse than the others. To be healthy, all Posair men had to spend some time in their three shapes. It was all a matter of balance.

Jaehaas glanced over at him and stumbled. "Blazel! Sweet Mother, what be wrong? Pieces of yourself be shifting."

"Gotta run... gotta shift..." Blazel ground out.

"Give me Lighzel's reins." Jaehaas held out his hand for them, concern in his eyes. "Go. Go run in wolf form for a bit. Catch a rabbit or a squirrel, and join me later."

Blazel nodded, tossed the reins to Jaehaas, and slid from the saddle. As soon as his feet touched the earth, he ran, shifting into wolf from one heartbeat to the next, just as easy as it had always been. He put on a burst of speed and wove through the trees, running until he panted for breath. He slowed, sniffing the air in a search of water, and followed the scent to a fast-moving stream. It was ice-cold, filled with snow runoff. He drank deeply, then flopped to the ground to rest in the shade of a huge spruce. His breathing slowed, and his eyes drifted close.

He dreamed again of the gaunt, malnourished woman. She was gray and sickly looking. She wanted something from him, but he couldn't understand what she was saying. The woman's claw-like fingers gripped his arm. A slimy energy plucked at him, making him feel dirty and ill. He jerked away from her, hissing in pain as her claws sliced into his flesh. The dream disappeared, and his arm burned.

Shuffling and scurrying in the underbrush woke him. Forgetting the strange dream, he came fully conscious. His nose twitched, and he cocked an ear forward, listening. Slowly, so slowly, he eased into a crouch. A rabbit bounced from the bushes, and Blazel sprung, jaws snapping. The rabbit didn't have a chance. Blazel carried the body to his sleeping place and laid down, crunching the bones.

The snack awoke his appetite. He stood and shook his fur. *Time to hunt.* Loping from the clearing, a warning niggled the back of his mind. But he licked his chops at the thought of a tasty ducorn. After running a few steps south, he stopped. He was going in the wrong direction. He needed to travel north. North to home.

Blazel trembled. He was a man, not a wolf, and Chariel needed him. His friend, Jaehaas, waited for him. He had almost lost himself in his wolf form, and he'd only been in it a few octars. He'd have to be more careful.

"I am a man. I am Blazel," he chanted with each paw beat as he ran toward Strunhelos Keep.

Chapter 12

The spires of Strunhelos Keep pierced the blue sky. A pennant snapped in the stiff breeze. Hawks flew in lazy circles high overhead. No one traveled the road leading to the keep gates.

Where's Jaehaas? Did he go on without me? Blazel lifted his head and howled. He loped in the direction of the answering yodel, toward a grove of trees. When he arrived, Lighzel happily cropped the grass. She whickered a greeting to him and went back to her grazing. Blazel followed the sound of a bow being drawn and arrows thunking into a target.

Jaehaas methodically filled a circle on a tree with arrows. He let the last one fly and turned to Blazel. "Did you have a good run?"

Blazel dipped his head in a nod and tried to shift. The magic pulsed through his body, building into a ball of intense pain. He howled, the sound turning into the scream of a man, as the magic finally released him. He bent over and emptied his stomach. The base of his skull felt like it had exploded. Bright pinpricks of light danced in front of his eyes, and black encroached on his vision. His legs gave out, and he dropped to the ground in a heap, panting. The pain eclipsed anything he'd ever experienced while shifting, even in the swamp.

Jaehaas rushed over to him, squirting cold water over his face, and urged him to drink. After several long milcrons,

Blazel's vision cleared, and the pain in his head receded. He struggled to sit up, gulping to keep the rest of his stomach contents where they belonged.

"What happened?" Worry creased Jaehaas's forehead.

"I don't know." Blazel rubbed his face, encountered crud in his beard, and wiped his hand clean on the grass. "The magic was there and then suddenly it was stuck. It hurt like the eighth hell."

"It looked awful." Jaehaas shuddered. "You morphed some parts of you into wolf, while others be human. It be a nightmarish mishmash. I almost lost my lunch along with you. Has this ever happened to you before?"

"No!" Blazel thought back to the swamp. "Well, I've had trouble because I stayed too long as a wolf. But it wasn't ever this painful." He put his weight on his right arm to push himself off the ground and hissed with pain.

"Let me see." Jaehaas pulled Blazel's arm closer to him. "Did you fight with another predator while you be gone?"

Blazel shook his head, confused. Something had slashed his sleeve and arm to ribbons. Blood oozed from the cuts. He clenched his jaw against the pain as he removed the shredded shirt.

Jaehaas used a rag to clean the wounds. He wrinkled his nose at the stench and poked at the gray tinged edges. "If I didn't know better, I'd say you be poisoned by monster toxin. But we haven't fought any monsters. How in the Crone's Fires did you get infected?"

"I don't know! I only chased and ate a rabbit, then took a nap." Blazel paused and examined his arm again. Phantom black claws gripped his bicep, exactly over the cuts. "But it was only a dream..." He whispered.

A dream can't hurt me, can it? His injured arm proved something different. He needed to reach home soon. Chariel and the Supreme could tell him what had happened to him—he hoped.

Neither man had enough fire magic to burn the poison from Blazel's arm. Jaehaas wrapped a bandage around it to stop the bleeding. Blazel weaved and stumbled across the grove to Lighzel, while Jaehaas retrieved his arrows. After Blazel's second attempt to climb into the saddle, Jaehaas levered him onto Lighzel's back and tied him to her saddle.

"It be a good thing the keep not be far," Jaehaas murmured.

Blazel groaned as he nodded in agreement. His arm throbbed in time to the pounding of his heart. His head clamored with the cadence of Lighzel's hooves. The bright spots in front of his eyes returned. He slumped over Lighzel's neck. With his last strength, he wound his fingers into her mane and let the darkness take him.

He awoke with a groan and a cool hand touched his forehead.

"You were lucky," a woman's voice said. She reached forward and twisted the knob to turn up the light on the lantern. Like all the other healers Blazel had met, she was a Brown. She'd pulled her medium brown hair into a bun. There wasn't any fringe around her face to give it softness. Summer-blue eyes gazed down at him with kindness.

"If you had waited any longer to receive treatment," she continued, "you would have lost your arm. How long ago were you poisoned? And why weren't you in your fur? I usually only treat this type of injury on Reds, not on warriors."

"I wasn't in a fight," Blazel said. He twisted his arm to look at the wounds. Thin scabs crossed his upper arm. It was red and swollen, with fine spiderweb streaks radiating from the lacerations. "I'm not sure what happened. Thank you for healing me."

"Not to worry, it's my job," she patted his leg. "Watch the red streaks. If they grow larger, go to a healer immediately. Are you hungry?"

Blazel's stomach rumbled. "Starving."

He sat up and took the bowl she handed him and slurped the soup while she left. Blazel searched for his pack—there were still travel rations in it. The tiny bits of meat and vegetables floating in the broth hadn't tempered his hunger. Before he could find it, a call of nature distracted him. Wobbling across the room and hanging onto furniture, he made it to the necessary room. His head had calmed to a dull ache, and the bright lights were gone. His arm was stiff, but as he moved it, the stiffness eased.

When he returned, Jaehaas waited by his cot. He had on a clean shirt, and he'd brushed his pelt to a shine.

"You be looking better," Jaehaas said. "There be a decidedly gray cast to your skin the last time I saw you. The healer told me it be monster poison, and that it be a good thing we be so close to the keep."

"Before you ask again, I don't know what happened. I remember bits of a strange dream I had, where a creature clawed me. When I was in wolf form, I didn't have any injuries. They only appeared when I shifted into my human form. Do you know where my bag is?"

"I do, why?"

"I'm starving." Blazel sat on the edge of the bed. "The broth the healer gave me didn't help much. I also want to get dressed." He shivered in the thin healer's gown.

Jaehaas laughed. He opened a cupboard and tossed his bag onto the bed. "Here. Wait, and I'll bring you some heartier food. You don't need to eat a travel bar." He made a face of distaste before clomping from the room.

Blazel put on a pair of soft, loose pants, which served as sleeping attire, and pulled on the matching shirt. Jaehaas entered, holding a tray.

The smell of roasted billocks and caramelized onions made Blazel's mouth water. Crunchy fried slices of tuber accompanied the sandwich, and a pot of steaming taevo rounded out his meal. Blazel poured a cup of taevo for Jaehaas and himself, then devoured the food.

"Histrun mentioned Rizelya saw a woman appearing in her dreams," Jaehaas said when Blazel's eating slowed. "Could it be the same one you saw in yours?"

Blazel shrugged as he ate the last bite of sandwich and took a gulp of taevo to wash it down. "All I remember is black claws. She'd have to be powerful to hurt me physically through my dreams." He gazed into his mug for a long moment. "I doubt the Supreme could do that. Rizelya told Histrun and Naila she thought someone was controlling the Malvers' monsters. If so, they'd have to be very powerful."

"Something strange be happening." Jaehaas refilled both of their mugs. "It be a mystery I hope to Goddess the Supreme can solve. Let's talk about something else. Tell me about your experiences in the swamp. I've heard bits and pieces. What be they like? Be there twisted animals?"

"Yes. You've seen narhili beasts, right?" At Jaehaas's nod, Blazel continued. "They come from the swamps. There are other things, flying snakes, rabbits who eat meat."

In the quiet, Blazel opened up and shared his experiences about traveling and living in the swamps. He told Jaehaas about the various beasts he'd encountered and fought. He'd never had any male Posair friends to whom he could talk freely. Histrun had always been a mentor. At the crater, he'd found a friend in Rolstrun, and now he had one in Jaehaas. Blazel sent a silent prayer of gratitude to the Warrior for the gift. They talked late into the night, finally sleeping, when the healer came in and scolded them.

The next morning, nothing showed of Blazel's ordeal, not even faint scars. He and Jaehaas left Strunhelos Keep shortly after dawn. Blazel shivered and blew on his chilled hands. The sharp scents of pine and cedar filled the fresh air. Sullen guards watched them leave through the north gate.

They entered a tunnel, which narrowed until Blazel could touch either side with his fingertips if he stretched out his arms. Focusing on the dim light ahead, he took deep breaths to calm his nerves. Once he'd been stuck in a tiny cave for more than a chedan while two huge sabertigers paced outside, waiting for him to leave. He'd nearly died of starvation and thirst before the pair left to hunt easier prey. Ever since, Blazel had problems with small, close spaces. After a hundred breaths, they finally exited, and Blazel's breathing eased.

Jaehaas and Lighzel's hooves echoed as they stepped into the canyon beyond the tunnel. Steep cliffs rose to tower over them on either side of the narrow road, which was barely wider than the tunnel. No one could climb the smooth surface without the guards noticing. A guard on the top of the cliff followed their progress through the pass. The cliffs and tunnel made the pass easily defended. Strunhelos Keep was a legacy of the Great War. Even after a thousand years, the garrison still guarded the entrance to the Posairs' treasure—the Supreme and the Sanctuary.

The cliffs receded abruptly, and the landscape opened to reveal forest and meadow. A winding road wove through the trees marching up the slopes. The rising sun hit the snow-covered peaks, bathing them with golden light while the rest remained in blue shadow.

Blazel kept his eyes on the mountain range, trusting Lighzel to stay on the path. Home was in those peaks. Deeper into the mountains, at the top of the world, the Gryphons made their home. He wondered what his new friend Jaehaas would think of his old buddy Graak. Blazel snorted as his gaze fell on Jaehaas's horsey rump. Both of his friends were unusual.

Near Strunhelos Keep, the mountains were waking up with spring. Trees were in bud, flowers poked their heads from the ground, and birds twittered and sang. The slope steepened, and the signs of spring lessened. Snow still blanketed the canyon's north-facing slopes.

The sun rose higher. Its fingers reached deeper into the forest, and the day began to warm up. At midday, they stopped in a clearing near a stream to eat and rest. When Blazel remounted, Jaehaas clomped back to the road.

"No, Jaehaas, not that way," Blazel said. "I know a different, much shorter route. The road meanders and twists, and it will take us three days to reach the Sanctuary. If we use my shortcut, we'll be there tomorrow."

Jaehaas raised an eyebrow. "Be it safe?"

Blazel nodded. "As safe as the road. The mountain holds its own dangers, but it isn't as dangerous as below the pass."

Jaehaas stared between Blazel and the faint track. Finally, he shrugged. "If this shortcut be faster, then let's take it, even if it be more risky."

Blazel led the way through the forest. Jaehaas continued to look skeptical. His tail flicked in agitation.

"Jaehaas, it is safe. Here, there are no monsters, no narhili beasts, nor any other creatures twisted by the malignant magic pools. The predators are simply animals, and most of them know it isn't a good idea to hunt men. We'll be fine. If there's any trouble, I can shoot it with my arrows."

Jaehaas smirked. "There must not be much to worry about. You still not be a good shot yet."

"But I'm getting better."

"Not much."

"Hey, I hit the center three times!"

"Yes, you did." Jaehaas inclined his head.

The route took them higher into the mountains, skirting cliffs and ravines. They came upon a river cutting through a canyon. A thundering waterfall dropped a hundred feet into the churning water below.

"Wow," Jaehaas breathed, awe filling his voice. "I've never seen anything like this!"

"This is nothing. Above the Sanctuary is the Seven Falls. The first fall is a thousand feet up and drops seven times. The roar is so loud, you can't hear yourself think, and the spray soaks you to the skin."

"I would love to see that!"

"I'll make sure you do, my friend."

"I've only seen the Storengher River, which be wide and placid, nothing like this wild thing."

Blazel rested his hands on the pommel and laughed. "This is the Storengher River. It begins in the far north, deep in the mountains. The Gryphons say its roots are in the ice that holds the world in place."

"Really?" Jaehaas shook his head and studied the river again. "I knew the river flowed from the White Mountains to cut across the land until it disappeared where the Barrens begin. But I didn't know it started so much farther north."

"It goes underground and reemerges past the Barrens." Blazel urged Lighzel into a walk. They still had a long way to travel before reaching the cave he wanted to stay the night in. Jaehaas reluctantly followed, his attention constantly pulled back to the river and waterfall.

"When it flows on the surface again, it forms the great swamp," Blazel continued. "It covers the entire southern peninsula. Once upon a time, the area was dry land. I saw the ruins of a black fortress there."

"Did you explore it?"

"No." Blazel shuddered at the memory. "Beasts I've never seen before guarded it, and I didn't want to fight them. Evil exuded from the place."

The path they followed opened into a wide meadow dotted with yellow wildflowers. Blazel kicked his horse into a gallop, and they raced across it, Jaehaas hot on his heels. They crossed the meadow and reentered the trees. Anytime they came upon a meadow or a break in the thick trees, Blazel pushed them to make up for the time lost navigating through the dense woods.

The purple shadows of twilight filled the forest when Blazel led them to a large cave. While Jaehaas made camp, Blazel gathered firewood and refilled their water skins. He glanced at the darkening sky. Dark gray clouds boiled over the peaks.

"It's going to storm tonight," he said, nodding upward. "If we're lucky, it won't snow. Either way, we'll stay warm and dry."

"You've stayed here before?"

"Many times. Histrun brought me here to learn how to be a Posair man. I first shifted into my warrior form here." He sat quietly, remembering, then stood with a shake of his shoulders. "Rabbit or some type of bird would be good for dinner. I think I'll go hunt."

"Be that wise?" Jaehaas pointed to Blazel's arm. "The last time you shifted, you became ill."

Blazel shrugged. "I need to try." He turned away from Jaehaas and drew on his magic. It pulsed, and he pushed it out to his limbs. A heartbeat later, he stood on all fours as a wolf. He gathered the magic again. The tingling told him he'd returned to his man form.

"Good." Jaehaas let out a strong gust of breath. "I be worried about you."

"I'll be back soon." Blazel shook the last tingles of his change from his wolf fur and loped into the forest.

It didn't take him long to find a plump rabbit. On his way back to the cave, he ran across a pigeon and quickly killed it, too. He shifted into his human form, carrying the dead bird in one hand and the rabbit in the other.

"Nice," Jaehaas commented when Blazel stepped into the cave entrance. "We be having a good feast tonight. I'll skin the rabbit."

"Great, give me the bird to pluck," Blazel said with a sardonic grin.

He tossed the rabbit to Jaehaas, who followed him outside. While Jaehaas efficiently skinned and dressed the rabbit, Blazel methodically plucked the bird's feathers. When he was done, Jaehaas threaded it along with the rabbit on spits, sprinkled herbs on them, and placed them over the fire. Soon, the smell of roasting meat and the sizzle of fat dripping into the fire filled the cave.

They practiced archery while the food cooked. Blazel's arrows landing in the target more times than not, and he hit the center four times.

After eating, Blazel set a small pot of water on the coals to heat. He pulled out his helstrablade and carefully shaved off his beard. A matted, twisted lock of hair fell into his face, and he examined it critically before deciding not to cut his hair. He'd become used to the weight and movement of his locs. He chuckled. The image of his mother scolding him about his long hair delighted him.

"Now, I'm ready to go home," he said, patting his smooth cheeks.

Chapter 13

Blazel set a pot of water on the coals for taevo. Outside, it was still dark. He pulled his cloak tighter around him to ward off the predawn chill. Across the fire, Jaehaas stirred on his pallet.

"You be up early," Jaehaas grumbled as he threw off his blanket and surged to his feet. He hugged his jacket tight against his chest.

"If we leave soon, we can reach the Sanctuary before midday."

Jaehaas tromped outside. When he came back in, Blazel handed him a ceramic travel mug filled with hot taevo. Jaehaas took it and sipped. After a few sips, he shook from head to toe. "I needed that. Now I be awake."

"Here, hold this." Jaehaas gave him back the mug. He went to his pallet, rolled it up, and threw it and his pack over his shoulder. "What about breakfast?"

"We can eat on the way." Blazel handed the cup back to Jaehaas, along with a package wrapped in a cloth. He had a similar one—toasted pan bread filled with leftover rabbit and pigeon.

They left the cave as the light on the horizon brightened. Blazel pushed them as fast as possible through the thick forest.

After two octars of travel, the sound of rushing water greeted them as they rounded a bend.

"It's not much farther." Blazel pointed to the spire rising above the trees.

They topped a rise, and below them lay a broad valley, the river forming its eastern boundary. Tall, white sheadash walls enclosed a large keep situated in the valley's center. Fields, now dormant, spread out from it, unusual in the absence of stone fences. Sheep, multas, and horses grazed lazily on the bright green spring grass. A huge temple dominated the left side of the keep, its crystal dome sparkling in the sunlight. Behind it, another, smaller wall enclosed gardens and a number of long buildings—the cloister where only the Goddess's priestesses could enter. Except for one small boy.

Blazel searched along the outer wall until he found a tiny cottage off on its own. Memories assailed him, and a lump formed in his throat. *Does my mother still live alone there, or did she move back into a cloister-house?* He swallowed the lump.

"The Sanctuary." Blazel waved his arm to indicate the valley.

"It be much larger than I expected."

"See the building next to the temple?" Blazel pointed to the massive building vying for attention with the temple. Built from granite and sheadash stone, it should have been imposing, but instead, the columns and arches turned it into an elegant and airy structure. Its soaring towers narrowed into spires. The central spire was the one they had glimpsed from the trees.

"That's the library. It has thousands of books. Mostly histories and tomes on magic. I spent many long, happy hours in there."

"Haasneh Keep's library only has a few hundred books. I couldn't image thousands of them."

"I promise you'll get to visit it. We need to do some research in there while we're here. The compound over there is the guest quarters, where we'll stay." Blazel pointed to an area opposite from the cloister.

The walled in area only had a few access doors to the public sections of the keep. Inside were three large pack-houses, a few cottages, an indoor and outdoor arena, a practice grounds, and a garden next to a wooded area.

"The arenas are for the alpha competitions," Blazel explained. "Have you attended one?"

"No, just the ones we have in the keep. I've never been to the Sanctuary before. What be those large buildings beyond the wood?"

Blazel shrugged. "I'm not sure. I sneaked into one when I was little. The doors were huge, made for beings much larger than humans, and so were the rooms. Everything was empty, and the fountains didn't work. It wasn't very interesting for a boy of six."

Blazel urged his horse into a trot. They rode across the fields and clattered back on the road. Two large men stopped them at the Sanctuary gates.

"What is your business?" the younger man asked.

Blazel ignored him, instead peering at the older man. "Celedon? Is that you?"

The older man stared at him with a quizzical expression before his eyebrows rose. "Blazel? Welcome home, lad."

"What are you doing here, again? I thought you were done causing trouble."

"So did I." Celedon rubbed his beard. "We got a new alpha, a young one, not ready for the position. I said it aloud too often and found myself back here."

"The Supreme can't be happy about it." Blazel leaned forward, his forearm resting on his saddle pommel, and grinned.

"No. No, she isn't. She said if I come back again, she'll mind-wipe me." Celedon shivered.

Although the Supreme used the threat of mind-wiping troublemakers to keep them in line, as far as Blazel was aware, she had never done it.

"Well, with what's happening, I doubt you'll have time to get in trouble."

"Does it have something to do with the Red who came in yesterday?"

"Rizelya?"

"Yeah, she's the one. She was in pretty bad shape, really sick."

"It might. Can we go in?"

"Of course, of course." Celedon saluted them and let them pass through the gate.

The horses' hooves clattered on the cobblestones of the empty courtyard. A woman with light brown hair hurried from the stables to meet them.

"Blazel?" she asked.

He smiled and quickly slid off his horse. "Shaela, good to see you! You still here?"

"Where else would I go? This is my home." She raised a shoulder, then fingered one of his locs. "I didn't recognize you at first with this. Chariel told us to expect you today."

Blazel laughed. The cloisters' door opened, and he looked toward it, hoping Chariel had come to meet him. Instead, Wisah strode out with a beautiful woman with dark auburn hair swinging in a braid against her back. Her almond-shaped eyes reminded him of Histrun. Their eyes met, and shock zipped through Blazel. *She's here!*

He waved at Wisah as his horse moved. The two women stopped and gaped. He twisted around, noticing Jaehaas was now in their view. He smiled at them. When Blazel turned back, they had disappeared through one of the courtyard's many doors.

"You just caught sight of our new celebrity." Shaela absently rubbed Lighzel's neck. "She has an appointment with the Supreme."

"Who be the White with her?" Jaehaas asked in a dreamy voice.

"Wisah," Blazel said, then looked at him askance. "Why? You can't have sex."

"But I still be a man." Jaehaas glared at Blazel. "I can fall in love."

"She's Rizelya's niece," Shaela added.

Blazel's mouth dropped open. "What! How?" He knew Wisah only as Chariel's friend. She'd only been nine or ten when he'd left the Sanctuary. He'd met her a few times since when he returned for visits, but didn't know her well. He was going to change that. She could tell him more about the fascinating Rizelya.

"Wisah is Naila's daughter, who is also Rizelya's half-sister," Shaela said.

"We'll be here a few days, Shaela," Blazel said. "Is there a room that will accommodate Jaehaas?"

"There is. He's not the first centaur to visit here. A room's being prepared for you too. You can't stay in the cloister any longer."

"I know. Will you tell my mother and grandmother I'm here?"

"Sure." Shaela looked over his shoulder. "Ah, I see it's ready."

A young girl stood in the open door leading to the guest area. He pulled his packs from Lighzel, petted her nose, and whispered to her, "I'll be around to visit you." He handed the reins to Shaela. "This is my friend, Lighzel. You'll take good care of her for me, won't you?"

Shaela rubbed Lighzel's neck. "Of course, it's what I do. Come with me, my beauty. We have some other guests, so you won't be alone."

At the mention of guests, Blazel stopped walking. How would they treat him and Jaehaas? A new bounce entered his step when he realized they must have traveled with Rizelya.

"Come on, Jaehaas, let's go meet these other people." He walked to the open door and gestured for the young girl to lead the way.

The young girl, unused to males, walked far ahead of them. The last time he had been here, Blazel had stayed in a cottage reserved for the Sanctuary workers. No longer a small boy, he wasn't allowed in the cloister where he'd grown up. Before, he'd only entered the guest area during the biennial Alpha Competitions when it teamed with people.

Blooming trees lined the deserted cobblestone road they walked along. Early harbingers of spring poked their heads from the ground in festive yellows, reds, and purples. Patches of bright green dotted the otherwise brown grass.

The girl stopped in front of the first pack-house in the row. Several tables and chairs were strewn about on the porch for guests to gather outside. Jaehaas easily walked through the wider than normal door.

The girl led them down the right-hand hallway and stopped at an open door at the end. Inside the room, a window on the opposite wall provided light. To the left of the window, stood a wide bed similar to Jaehaas's in Haasneh Keep.

Blazel thanked the girl, went into the room, and sat on the normal sized bed. He bounced slightly on the springy, but firmly stuffed mattress. Next to the bed was a clothes chest and desk. On Jaehaas's side, the clothes chest was at the foot of his bed, and the tall desk, without a chair, was tucked in the corner.

"This looks nice," Blazel said.

"It does," Jaehaas agreed. "Shaela was right. They do know how to accommodate the special needs of a centaur." He unpacked his bag, shaking out the wrinkles from his clothes before placing the folded articles in the chest. He dropped his dirty clothes into an empty basket.

Blazel followed Jaehaas's example. The necessary room across the hall had a bathing setup specific to a centaur's needs. After a soak and change of clothes, the men were ready to meet the other guests.

They made their way back to the entrance foyer and down the hall toward the other side of the house. Voices came from behind a partially closed door. The talking stopped when Jaehaas stepped off the rug and his hooves hit the wood floor.

The door popped open, and a man almost as tall as Blazel peered out. His long red-gold hair with gold streaks fell past his shoulders, and his eyes were gold. He wore a turquoise tunic with rose embroidery over brown woven pants. His eyes widened, but instead of stepping back, he held out his hand.

"Hi, I'm Aistrun. Welcome! Welcome to our humble abode while in the Sanctuary."

Blazel gripped Aistrun's wrist. "I'm Blazel, and this is my friend Jaehaas."

"Blazel! Histrun has talked about you frequently. Glad to finally meet you." Aistrun stepped around Blazel and offered his hand to Jaehaas. "Welcome, Jaehaas."

Jaehaas's eyebrow raised, perplexed, as he gripped Aistrun's wrist. Blazel thought back through the journey. Most people, men in particular, generally didn't approach Jaehaas with such outward friendliness and welcome.

Blazel stepped into a large room with a fireplace along one wall and a bank of windows on another. Shelves filled with books, games, and other entertainment covered the third wall. In front of the fireplace sat comfortable sofas and chairs, with small tables to set drinks on nearby. Tables and chairs for eating or playing games were scattered around. Individual chairs sat near the bookshelf so people could sit and enjoy reading.

Another man lounged on a winged chair by the fire. At their entrance, he quickly stood. The six-foot tall, muscular man brushed his pale blond hair away from his golden-brown eyes.

"Eidstrun, you can't believe who showed up! Rizelya is going to be mad that I met Blazel before she did." Aistrun strode into the room and plopped onto a small couch, picking up his abandoned mug. He glanced back at the door where Blazel and Jaehaas still stood. "Hey, come on over here. We don't bite. There's a fresh pot of taevo we'd be happy to share with you."

Blazel glanced at Jaehaas, who lifted a shoulder. Aistrun was like a friendly puppy.

After filling a cup, Blazel settled into a big overstuffed chair. Aistrun's face screwed up in puzzlement when Jaehaas stood balancing his cup in his hands. Aistrun popped off his chair, crossed the room, and came back with a tall table the right height for Jaehaas.

"Now, we can all be comfortable," Aistrun said. "This is Eidstrun, one of my squad-pack. We're expecting Leistral and possibly Rizelya soon. Rizelya's here to talk to the Supreme about her strange dreams. Have you seen the new control janacks? Nasty monster, those. So why are you here?"

"Do I have to have a reason?" Blazel scowled, crossing his arms over his chest. "This is my home."

"Hey, don't get in a huff." Aistrun held up his hands. "All sorts of strange things are happening, and I wanted to know if you're adding to them."

A commotion in the front hall interrupted them before Blazel could answer. He turned toward the door. Joy lightened his heart at the sight of Chariel pausing in the doorway. She nervously fingered the end of her sidelock braid in her unusual charcoal-gray hair as she took in the small gathering. A pretty woman with copper-red hair and dark green eyes strode into the room.

Blazel understood Chariel's skittishness around so many strangers. Grinning, he stood and opened his arms.

"Blazel!" Chariel cried, then raced across the room and threw herself into his arms. "You're back. I knew you were coming."

He hugged her tight, swallowing at the tightness in his throat. It had been too long since his last visit with her.

"I returned home because you called me," he chided as he released his hold on her. "Although I'm happy you did. I was getting tired of living in the swamps. It's so good to be dry."

She stepped back to gaze at him. "You know what this means, don't you?"

"I do. I came as fast as I could."

"The madness is close, so close."

The pretty woman settled on the arm of Eidstrun's chair. "Does this madness have anything to do with Chariel's recent prophecy?"

"Prophecy?" Blazel asked.

"She had one this morning," the woman said. "By the way, I'm Leistral, part of Rizelya and Aistrun's squad-pack."

"Hey, I haven't had a chance to do introductions yet," Aistrun complained. He proceeded to introduce everyone.

"So, Chariel, can you tell us about your prophecy?" Jaehaas shifted, cocking a rear leg.

"No. It isn't that I don't want to. I can't. I rarely remember my prophecies once I speak them. Although..." She tilted her head and studied Jaehaas. "You may be the horse I saw."

Jaehaas pulled back, a sneer on his face.

"It wasn't an insult, Jaehaas," Chariel said gently. "My visions are in images. You are half horse, so a horse is what my vision showed. I wish Wisah or Rizelya were here. They heard the prophecy, but they're with the Supreme right now. I remember bits of this one, which is unusual, like the horse. And... something in it means Wisah and I are going on a journey. But I've never left the Sanctuary before in my life! It's all so strange. We'll have to wait for them to finish to know exactly what I said."

"I heard it," Leistral said in a soft voice. "I'd gone to the necessary room, and when I returned, you and Wisah were talking to Rizelya. I hung back to allow Rizelya some time with her niece, when you started speaking in a weird monotone."

"Well, what did she say?" Eidstrun poked Leistral gently in the ribs.

"Give me a moment, I have to think." She closed her eyes.

Everyone quieted, giving Leistral the opportunity to recall the odd wording prophecies took.

"Newfound friends," she began, each word stretched out, her eyes still closed. "New Talents appear. Unlikely travel—"

"Blazel! You're here!" came a shout from the door.

Leistral's eyes snapped open and everyone turned to the door. Wisah and the beautiful Red Blazel had seen in the courtyard walked in. Rizelya appeared pale and shaky, like she'd just experienced a terrible ordeal. Blazel recalled some of his meetings with the Supreme when he was young. They could indeed be a trial. Wisah also seemed shaken. Whatever had happened in their audience with the Supreme, it wasn't good.

"Is there any taevo in there?" Wisah nodded to the pot.

Eidstrun opened the lid and peered in. "Enough for two cups. You both look like you could use something stronger." He started to push up from his chair.

"No, taevo will be fine," Rizelya said. She trudged across the room and sank onto the couch next to Aistrun. He put his arm around her.

Blazel growled low in his throat. He swallowed it before anyone heard him. Rizelya wasn't his. Yet.

"Hey, Little Red, you look awful." Concern filled Aistrun's voice. He pulled her tighter to him. "Was the audience that bad?"

"If the Supreme ever offers to pull the memories from you," Rizelya groaned, "don't let her do it. It hurts. Thanks." She took the cup Leistral handed to her. It shook in her hands.

A matronly woman pushed in a cart laden with food. She nodded at them as she silently distributed the food onto an eating table. Once finished, she trundled back out.

"So, Leistral, what else do you remember?" Chariel asked.

"Not now," Rizelya broke in, struggling out of Aistrun's grasp to stand. "I'm starving. I didn't have any breakfast before the Supreme drained me. My stomach is touching sides."

She strode to the table, wobbling and weaving slightly. Blazel bit his lip to stop the smile as he joined the others in the migration to the food. *Maiden help me, but she is beautiful.*

Chapter 14

Rizelya spooned another bite of soup into her mouth as she watched the intriguing man from under her eyelashes. Aistrun regaled the party with the tale of their squad-pack's adventures. Wisah and Chariel leaned forward, elbows on the table, food forgotten as they listened. The story also engrossed the two new men. Rizelya had heard it before—had lived it.

Whatever the Supreme had done, it had drained her. Not as much as the damned janacks did, but close. She reached across the table to grab another slice of bread, and her eyes met the strange man's. She experienced a zing of attraction as he smiled at her. Chariel's words came back to her: "Blazel's gonna love you."

She sensed strength and power about him, but also innocence. Rizelya's gaze dropped to his broad, muscular shoulders and slid down to his taut belly. *What kind of lover would he be?* She tossed aside the thought. There was too much danger, too much to do. The last relationship she'd had was with Kaieli, and it had passed quietly into simple, deep friendship. She didn't want a relationship. He reached for the pot of taevo, and his muscles rippled under his shirt. *But a fling? Maybe.*

Aistrun paused in his story, and Rizelya broke into the conversation. "I know everyone here, except you two." She pointed her spoon at the strangers.

"Sorry about that," Aistrun said. Then he pointed to the centaur. "This is Jaehaas de Haasneh and that is Blazel." Aistrun gestured at her, then smirked.

Oh no, what is he going to do?

"And this is Rizelya, our intrepid leader." He paused and raised an eyebrow. "The monster whisperer."

"What!" She felt her cheeks flame and tossed her spoon at him in retaliation. It missed, clattering on the table.

"Well, you do hear the monsters while no one else can," Aistrun said, unrepentant. "Makes you a monster whisperer."

"I can hear them," Blazel said slowly, as he caught her gaze. "At least I hear humming around the control janack."

"You do?" Rizelya sat forward. "Do you see a strange woman? Have bizarre dreams?"

Blazel dropped his eyes and shook his head.

"Wait, what about your dream just outside of Strunhelos?" Jaehaas said. "You be pretty messed up afterward."

Blazel glanced down at his arm as if seeing something under the cloth. He took a deep breath. "I guess you've all seen strange things. This was weird. I only remember bits and pieces of the dream. A gaunt woman dominated them..." He paused and considered Chariel. "She looked a little like you."

"Damn!" Chariel grimaced, exchanging a look with Rizelya before turning back to Blazel. "You're the second person to make the comparison. I scared the daylights out of Rizelya this morning. She thought I was some kind of evil woman."

"I think it's the hair and the eyes." Rizelya indicated Chariel's face. "The woman I see has the same dark charcoal-gray hair as you do and dark eyes, although hers don't have any pupils. And she has claws."

"Yeah, I remember the claws now." Blazel rubbed his upper arm. "She clawed me in my dream, and when I tried shifting, I was sick."

"Tell the truth, Blazel," Jaehaas chided as he glared at him. "He be poisoned. The healer told me it be a mix of monster and narhili beast toxins. If we hadn't been so close to the keep when the poison be activated, he'd have died."

Rizelya shuddered and rubbed her calf. "I recently suffered narhili poison. It isn't fun. The woman in my dreams seems to be linked with the monsters and causes harm through them." She shook her head. "I haven't had her hurt me."

"She must be powerful," Chariel mused, tapping her forefinger on her lips. "Only an extremely powerful Gray would be able to use the veil to affect someone from a long distance. I'm not sure I could do it. And I'm the darkest Gray there is."

"But you contacted me in the swamp." Blazel rubbed his forehead. "I was in the southern peninsula when you called me back home. Your voice was very clear, and it pushed me unrelentingly to hurry."

"I could only reach you because I know you so well. Actually, I don't remember consciously calling you. Something dreadful is coming." Chariel put her head in her hands and groaned. "If only I could see what it is, then we'd have a better idea on how to stop it." She dropped her hands. "It would be amazing to help people from a distance. There's so many I could help, but I'm stuck here in the Sanctuary."

"Be careful what you wish for, you just might get it," Jaehaas said. "I once wished to see the Sanctuary, and here I be. Although I'd have wished for better circumstances, not the death of our people."

"The people in my dreams feed off death," Rizelya said in a low voice, closing her eyes. A memory assailed her. "'Come eat, my friends,' the gray woman said, and a needle-like claw dipped into a bowl packed with pus-colored pearls. Pearls created from the deaths of people killed by the monsters."

Rizelya's eyes flew open at the sound of a sharp gasp. Horror filled her friend's faces. Leistral was green and held a hand to her mouth. She gagged and rushed from the room, with Eidstrun right behind her.

"I said that out loud, didn't I?"

The rest nodded.

Aistrun had a stricken look on his face. "You've been seeing that all this time and haven't told anyone about it?"

"What could you have done?"

"Shared your horror, your pain," Aistrun cried. "It wouldn't have made it better, but it would have lessened it. Is that what trapped you in your dreams on the way here?"

"Yes, and more," Rizelya said, her voice flat. "She showed me people getting killed, children even, and as the monsters ate them, smoke and an oily-pus substance gathered wherever she is, forming those awful pearls. She sucked them down with relish."

"Who be they?" Jaehaas asked. "Be there some way we can stop them?"

Wisah shuddered. "The Supreme knew them. She called the woman a Malvers—"

"You were right, Riz," Aistrun interrupted. "The monsters do belong to someone called Malvers."

"It isn't a someone, but a race of people." Wisah tapped the table with her fingers, her rings clinking softly on the hard surface. "They are the people we fought in the Great War. Apparently, they weren't all destroyed, but exiled. The prophecy you had, Chariel, provides us with a way to defeat them once and for all. These Malvers are evil if they are eating the pain and death of others."

"So what is this prophecy?" Blazel asked. He indicated the men in the group. "We don't know what it said. Leistral was starting to tell us when you came in."

"Let me try to get it right." Wisah closed her eyes, then intoned, "New Talents appear. Unlikely travel companions. They find danger. A rogue guides them into the Deep Mountains to seek long-lost allies to fight the ancient enemies coming into the light. A menace comes. If there aren't allies, the enemy wins and we all die. All must go or none returns. Horse and hawk, fire and warrior, white and gray. Rizelya must lead. He will follow. We will follow."

Wisah opened her eyes. As she regarded the people around the table, her face drained of color. "It was us, all of us, in the prophecy." She pointed to each person as she named them. "Horse is you Jaehaas, fire is you, Rizelya, and the warrior must be Aistrun, because the rogue can only be Blazel. You were right, Chariel, you and I are the Gray and White. That leaves only the hawk."

"Another quest," Rizelya sighed, dropping her head to her chest. She'd hoped she could go home soon. "We're going on a quest to search for old allies, who might not be allies any longer, to fight our ancient enemy."

"The hawk is probably my friend Graak," Blazel added. "I'm sure he will help us."

"He must!" Wisah slapped the table. "Or we won't win the fight. The prophecy said if we didn't find our allies, the enemy wins, and we all die. Not just us," she motioned in a circle, encompassing everyone in the group, "but all Posairs."

"Damn!" Blazel pushed away from the table. "I wasn't planning on leaving as soon as I arrived."

"The Supreme hasn't approved the quest yet," Wisah reminded him. "It could be days or even a chedan before we leave."

Blazel nodded, sharply. "Good. It will give me time to research our enemies. Now I know what I'm searching for, I should be able to find the information in the library. When I was younger, I found several hidden caches the librarians were unaware of their existence. We need to discover who these Malvers were and what they were capable of. It might not be true anymore, but it's a start."

"I be joining you in the search." Jaehaas emptied his cup of taevo. "You did promise to show me the library."

"I'll go with you." Chariel tossed her napkin on her plate. "I'm as familiar with the library as you."

"Me too," Wisah added.

Soon, only Rizelya and Aistrun were left in the recreation room. Leistral and Eidstrun hadn't returned. Aistrun stood, walked around the table, and sat back down next to Rizelya. He put a hand over hers.

"Well, Little Red, you've stirred up a hornet's nest again. We'll be haring into the Deep Mountains in search of the Gryphons."

"You can't blame me this time, Wolf. I didn't have the prophecy. That would be Chariel."

"But you'll lead us, and we'll follow."

She stared at him. His words echoed the prophecy. *Why is the Goddess so concerned with me? Where is destiny taking me?*

Sunlight fell in through the high windows of the quiet library, filling the cavernous room with warmth without touching the fragile contents. Long lines of shelves marched the length of the chamber, books stacked in neat order, scrolls in their cubbyholes. This section was reserved for the more modern works, those after the Great War.

The books Blazel wanted were older, hidden, forgotten. It had been over a thousand years since the Great War ended, leaving the Posairs' society in ruins and their once-grand cities destroyed. Their survival hung by a thread and they put all their efforts into staying alive. They thrust the war and its cause aside as the few remaining people struggled to rebuild their world.

Blazel searched the stacks for a book he'd read as a teenager. He'd found the ancient history buried deep in the dusty stacks. It described his ancestor's struggles after the war and the horror of the first attack by the Malvers' monsters. He remembered reading a personal footnote by the author saying something about the Supreme's choice to eradicate all memory of the enemies fought in the war. The historian had cautioned it would be a detriment, for one day, their enemies would return. His words were proving true. Blazel hoped the book would give them clues of what they now faced.

Sometime during the afternoon, he lost his companions somewhere in the library's depths as they conducted their own searches. He wandered to the far back corner of the library as evening dimmed the light through the windows. Dust covered everything. A patina of cobwebs laced the shelves, and he heard the skittering of mice. In the gloom, he glimpsed a door.

Dirt encrusted the frame, and age rusted the bar locking it. Blazel shifted into his warrior form, and with his greater strength, wrenched it open. A dark hole lay behind it. Blazel transformed back to human and grabbed the lantern from a nearby reading table. Holding it aloft, the light barely penetrated the depths beyond the door. Steps led down into the darkness. The thick layer of dust showed no one had come this way for a long time. Blazel sneezed from the old-age musty scent as he descended. He held the lantern high with one hand, brushing the wall with his other hand.

Down and down, he traipsed until he finally reached the bottom. The light from his lantern formed a small circle around him, unable to penetrate the oppressive dark. Blazel discovered an old torch in a wall sconce, and calling his fire to him, he lit it. There were more torches along the wall. The increased light revealed a vast room filled with ancient relics.

He touched an antique staff, and a weak pulse of magic thrummed from his hand to the staff. A fireball burst from it, sizzling for a moment before it disappeared. Blazel pulled back his tingling hand, and the staff clattered to the ground.

From the corner of his eye, he glimpsed a reflected light. A crystal ball pulsed with indigo light. Mesmerized, he reached for it. It fit perfectly in the palm of his hand. Again, a feeble throb of magic passed from him to the ball. The indigo light crisscrossed the ball's surface, gathering into a swirl of snapping energy. It released the energy with a crack of lightning, hitting the wall with a muffled boom. Startled, Blazel dropped the ball. Instead of breaking, it bounced twice before returning to an inert piece of crystal.

Afterward, he was careful not to touch anything—until he came upon a stack of books and scrolls, brittle with age. He squinted, trying to decipher the ancient writing. Finally, the titles made sense. Mordar's Reign of Terror, Creation of New Species, Shandir's Great Magic, and The Malvers' Rise to Power: A Treatise on Corruption. These books were written before and during the Great War.

Soft footsteps on the stairs disturbed the quiet, and Blazel whirled around. The Supreme stepped into the torches' flickering light. She appeared even older than he remembered. Her face was wizened with wrinkles and she stooped over a cane. But when she gazed at him with her strange white eyes, he knew her power was undiminished. He hurried over to where she stood and made obeisance to her.

"Ah, Blazel," she said, touching the top of his head. "What am I going to do with you? You've been back less than a day and already you've found trouble." She sighed and then intoned, "Blessing of the Goddess." She stepped away and Blazel rose.

"What is this place?" He gestured at the treasure trove. "What are all of these things?"

"This is where we hide what we once were," the Supreme said sadly. She shuffled farther into the room, her cane tapping on the stone floor, and picked up an object. It glowed as she fed a bit of her magic into it, and a small black cloud rose above her, swirling into a whirlpool. She directed the maelstrom to the stairs where refuse had gathered. The whirlpool sucked it up, shredding it into a minute pieces.

"And what we once could do," she said when the dust settled. "These are the weapons our ancestors used to fight the war."

"Why don't we use them now? The fireball would be effective against the monsters."

A bench sat near a worktable. Blazel helped the Supreme to hobble over to it. She eased onto it and patted the empty spot next to her. "Here, come sit with me."

After he joined her on the bench, she studied him for several milcrons. "Danger is coming. It is time our people knew the truth of the Great War and whom we fought. My predecessors decided long, long ago to hide it. And every Supreme since then has held the secret. They believed that without memory of the war atrocities, our people would heal and be able to begin anew. The war was brother against brother, sister fighting sister. Those whom we called Malvers were once part of us, until they turned to dark magic—magic fueled by death. Our ancestors could not stand by and let them kill innocent people.

"Shandir ended the war by blasting their stronghold into oblivion. You've seen Shandir's Crater. It's a misnomer because Shandir didn't create it by herself. She simply directed the magic. It took many, many Posairs to perform that great magic. The blast crippled the surviving Malvers. We didn't do so well either. The spell drained most of our magic. But it was worth it because it weakened the Malvers enough so we could exile them."

"Why didn't we kill them?" Blazel asked.

The Supreme frowned in distaste and leaned on her cane. "And be like those we hated? No, we couldn't do that. Everyone believed the Malvers would die in their exile, and we'd never have to deal with them again. But after a decade of nothing from them, came the first nest of monsters, the janacks and brechas. Have you ever wondered why the nests are where they are?" Before Blazel could answer, she continued. "Each one is a site where atrocities were committed, by one side or the other. So yes, it was easier for the survivors to forget what they had once done. War is never clean."

"And now their progeny is finding a new way to attack us." Blazel stood and paced in front of the old woman.

"No, not their descendants." The Supreme banged her cane on the floor. The sound reverberated in the vast space. "One thing the Malvers gained from their death magic was near immortality. We will be fighting the same people who were exiled, who hate us for the sins of our ancestors. Perhaps it would have been better to kill them at the time."

"Now it will be up to us to end this war." Blazel looked around the stockpile of weapons. "Are there any of these we can use?"

The Supreme shook her head, then stopped, peering intently at the piles. "Perhaps, but not by you men. You forsook your ability to work the greater magics for the gift of shapeshifting to protect us from the Malvers's creations—their monsters. It has been, and will continue to be, a good exchange. We'll need your warrior abilities in the war to come. That stubborn, insightful Rizelya has shown us our women are strong and willing to fight. I agree with her. We will need everyone before this war is over."

She pushed off the bench. "Chariel isn't the only one who has visions. The Goddess has sent me visions of a great menace coming to our world, even worse than the Malvers' monsters plaguing us now. It is not clear where they come from, only that they bring the madness of war."

"Chariel told me I'd come home when the madness drew near. I heard her call from far to the south telling me to hurry. Supreme, I have had dreams of fiery meteors, bringing blood and death. Is this the madness coming?"

The Supreme grimaced, and her shoulders drooped. "It is. We must prepare for war on two fronts: this new threat coming from the sky, and our old enemies. Come, it is time to go."

She held out her arm for him to help her. Blazel caught a flicker of fear in her eyes as he tucked her hand around his elbow. They strolled across the room in silence. She stopped at the first stair.

"I'm glad you've come home, boy." She patted his face.

Blazel pressed her hand against his face and kissed her palm. He knew it was the only affection she would allow him to show. She patted him once more, and together they trekked up the stairs.

Chapter 15

Rizelya lounged on the couch in the entertainment room of the guest house, reading a book while waiting for the others to return. It was strange not to have anything to do or someplace to race to. Rizelya was determined to enjoy it while it lasted. She hadn't had time to read since the first fight with the new control janack nearly a lunadar ago. The long days of travel caught up to her and her eyes drifted closed, the book falling out of her hands.

Loud hoofbeats on the wood floor dragged her from her nap. *What is a horse doing in here?* A deep voice muttered something, followed by Wisah's ringing laugh. The sound made sense when Rizelya remembered meeting the centaur, Jaehaas, earlier. She rubbed her face in the dim light. She'd slept the afternoon away.

"Is Blazel back yet?" Wisah flopped on a chair across from the couch Rizelya sprawled on.

"No. At least I don't think so." With a groan, Rizelya rolled to a sitting position. Aistrun smirked at her, pointing to her chin as he dropped into the other chair. Rizelya off wiped the drool off her face.

"We lost him in the mausoleum they call a library." Jaehaas stood by Wisah's chair and cocked a hind leg. "I've never seen so many books before. It seems to go on forever."

Chariel sank onto the chair next to Aistrun. "It's rumored that during the Great War, our ancestors gathered all of their knowledge and deposited it in the Sanctuary for safekeeping."

"I can believe it after seeing, and tromping, through the library." Jaehaas let out a loud sigh. "I be beat."

"There are ruins all over Lairheim," Aistrun said, "so it was probably a good idea. Is there anything to eat? A pot of taevo?"

"Taevo would be lovely," Wisah said. "I'll ring the kitchen for it."

She picked up a bell off the table near her chair and rang it. A few milcrons later, the same matronly woman who had served them before came in. Wisah asked for the taevo, and the woman left. Within a short time, she returned with a large pot, pastries, and sweets. They had made significant inroads on the food when Blazel entered the room. His steps were slow, and he wore a shocked expression.

"Hey, you look awful," Aistrun said.

"Where did you go?" Jaehaas asked. "You just disappeared."

Wisah jumped up and led Blazel by the hand to a big, comfortable chair. Rizelya handled him a cup of taevo. A tickle of energy passed between them as her hand brushed against his. He gave her a quizzical look, proving he'd felt it, too. His ears turned bright pink, and he ducked his head, letting his long, twisty locs hide his face. She smiled at the thought of the handsome man being shy.

"Well, I found out about the Malvers." Blazel put his cup down and laced his fingers in front of him. "Only not from a book as I expected, but from the Supreme herself."

He told them about his impromptu meeting. Rizelya nodded at the similarities with what she'd heard from the Supreme earlier.

"Will the Supreme send us to find the Gryphons?" Aistrun asked.

"Yes, I believe so." Blazel leaned back, his long legs stretched in front of him, and crossed his ankles.

Wisah refilled her cup. "Until she gives us permission to leave, we wait."

The next morning, Chariel and Wisah helped Rizelya and Leistral move their belongings to the guest house where the men were staying. Rizelya wanted to be close to her pack-mates, so they'd be ready to leave as soon as they received the Supreme's approval. She'd wanted the two priestesses to join them, but protocol demanded they remain in the cloister.

After lunch, Aistrun rummaged in the lounge cupboards, searching for something to do. "Ah, ha!" He chuckled gleefully as he removed a box. "A keshe set! What do you say? With eight playing, it will occupy us all afternoon."

Jaehaas lifted a shoulder. "Why not? It be better than sitting and staring at each other." He joined Aistrun at the table and helped set up the board.

Rizelya sat in the chair next to Aistrun. "After the grueling trip we've had, I'm ready for some rest and fun. I'll take black."

"Red for me," Blazel said, sliding into the seat opposite from Rizelya.

The others settled around the table. Wisah, with the blue pieces, played the opening move. While they played, they talked and told stories. When Rizelya outmaneuvered Blazel, taking five of his pieces, she winked at him. He ducked his head, blushing. Later, she stretched her legs, her bare toe brushing Blazel's leg. She chuckled softly when his eyes widened and pink tinged his ears.

On the third afternoon, Rizelya paced the entertainment room, too anxious and restless to sit. "What could be taking the Supreme so long?"

Wisah sat primly on the edge of a straight-backed chair by the fire, sipping a cup of taevo while Jaehaas hovered nearby. Aistrun sprawled on the small couch next to Chariel, his arm thrown across the seat back—and over her shoulders. Blazel stood by the cold fireplace, his elbow propped on the mantel. Leistral and Eidstrun sat in the matching wing-backed chairs.

Chariel shrugged. "She likes to take her time before committing to a course of action. If... when we find the Gryphons and bring them back, it will completely change our way of life. She will be considering all the implications."

"Even though you had a prophecy about it?" Aistrun asked. "It seems pretty clear-cut to me."

"Especially because of my prophecy. It has repercussions for all Posairs."

"She is most likely in prayer," Wisah said, "communing with the Goddess. Chariel is right, and this will affect all Posairs and not just because of a renewed alliance with the Gryphons. You have to admit the part about a menace coming and without allies, everyone dies is pretty scary."

"The madness is near," Blazel said in a quiet monotone as he stared into the distance. He shook his head. "When Chariel sent me to the swamps, she told me I'd come home when the madness is near. And here I am, home."

A shiver of dread climbed up Rizelya's spine. She slumped deeper into the couch, and the room quieted, but not in the previously companionable silence.

After a few milcrons, Blazel pushed away from the fireplace. "We can't do anything about it right now, and the Supreme won't rush making a decision. We've stayed cooped up inside too long. Let's get out of here."

"What do you suggest?" Jaehaas asked, with a swish of his tail.

"Remember I told you about the Seven Falls?" At Jaehaas's nod, he continued, "Let's go see them. They shouldn't be missed, and we have the time."

"Ooh," Chariel's eyes lit up. "I haven't been to the falls in a long time. They are amazing. You all should see them."

Everyone agreed, and they tromped to the stables. When they entered, Blazel spoke to the stable mistress, Shaela, who nodded and called a young girl to her, who ran off. Rizelya shrugged and started saddling her horse.

As Rizelya cinched Kymaya's saddle, the girl returned and handed Blazel a picnic basket. She raised her eyebrow in question.

Blazel attached the basket to the back of Lighzel's saddle. "The falls are spectacular. We'll want to spend some time there. At the bottom, there's a good place for a picnic lunch."

"Hey, that's a great idea," Aistrun said, coming up behind them and throwing an arm around their shoulders. He disappeared into the stables and came out, grinning, and tied a bundle to his saddle.

Once the other horses were ready, the group mounted and rode into the mountains above the Sanctuary. The sun filtered through the trees, birds chirped, and butterflies flitted around the wildflowers. Rizelya leaned her head back and breathed in the peace. She'd been going full tilt for nearly a lunadar. The last few days had given her the chance to rest and recuperate.

Rizelya admired Blazel's strong profile and the gentle way he guided his horse. He caught her gazing at him and gave her a slow, shy smile before returning his attention to the trail.

Ahead, she heard the roar of rushing water. The trees thinned as they rode into a rocky clearing. The river cut a deep cleft in the white sheadash stone. Above them, the waterfall thundered as it cascaded from one height to the next. She counted the levels. Only five.

"Where are the other two?" she shouted.

Blazel leaned closer so he could hear, and she repeated her question. He pointed down.

Rizelya swung her leg over the saddle and stepped down. Walking carefully on the slick, wet rocks, she made her way to the edge. Sunlight cast rainbows on the water spray as the river tumbled two-hundred feet to the next shelf of rock, where it plummeted the last thirty feet to a wide pool. The spray soaked through her clothes. The others joined her, gazing at the falls.

Blazel walked along the rim toward the waterfall above them. Rizelya followed him, and when he stopped, she joined him, staring at the amazing sight. Her hip bumped against his.

She stood on her toes, bracing herself on his shoulder, and shouted, "It's beautiful."

He turned his head. She licked her lips. His were so close.

"It is." He searched her face for a moment before turning back to the falls.

Rizelya slumped, frowning. She could see his interest in her in his eyes. So what was wrong?

Once everyone finished admiring the waterfalls, Blazel guided them down the steep path to the lowest pool. Rizelya stepped carefully on the slick rocks. Her foot slipped, and her heart thundered as loud as the falls. Her grip on Kymaya's reins as she lead the horse saved her from tumbling over the edge. At the bottom, the sun warmed the rocks, and a grassy meadow provided grazing for the horses.

Rizelya dipped a hand in the water and quickly pulled it back. "Brr! I'm not going in there."

"In another couple chedans, it'll be warm enough to swim in." Blazel said. "Right now, snow-melt is still feeding the river."

"The sun feels good." Rizelya sprawled out on the rocks, using her magic to dry her clothes. Chariel and Wisah joined her, and she provided the same service for them.

"What about the guys?" Chariel asked. "Their clothes are soaked, too."

"Yeah, what about us?" Aistrun stood next to Chariel and shook his head, sending water droplets all over them.

Chariel squealed and tried to move away, but Aistrun bent over her, and rubbed his hands through his hair, releasing more water on her.

Jaehaas laughed, dancing away. He held out his hand to Wisah. "My lady, would you like to go for a stroll with me?"

"Yes, I would, kind sir." Wisah smiled, took his hand, and stood. Hooking her hand around his elbow, they meandered alongside the pool. Their quiet conversation fading as they disappeared into the trees.

Rizelya watched them wistfully, wishing Blazel would suggest they take a walk together.

"Do you need me to dry your clothes?"

"No, I can." He lifted his hand, then scowled. "Although, I can't with them on."

She stood and faced him. "Stand still." Holding her hands a few inches away, she ran them over his clothes, the heat from her palms drying them. She allowed the heat to penetrate just a little more to lightly caress his skin.

His eyes widened, and he leaned forward.

"Hey, Little Red, what about me?" Aistrun bumped Blazel out of the way.

Rizelya glared at him. Blazel had been so close to kissing her. She waved her hand, drying his clothes all at once, and singeing his chest hair in the process.

"Ouch," he complained, sticking out his lower lip and rubbing his chest. *What did I do to deserve that?*

You interrupted. And it was going so well. She looked significantly at Blazel, who was walking to the grazing horses.

Oh! Sorry. I've just the thing. He strode to his horse and pulled off the bundle, shaking it out to reveal a large blanket, which he spread on the grass under a tree. He approached Chariel and gave her a gallant bow. "Would you like to join me? It's much more comfortable than these hard rocks."

"Good idea!" She grinned, holding out her hand. "My butt's starting to hurt."

He helped her to her feet. With more care than Rizelya had ever seen him give another woman, he made sure she was comfortable.

Blazel returned with the basket and stared at the blanket, chewing his bottom lip.

"There's room for both of you, too." Aistrun patted the blanket. "I'm starved. What's in there?" He took the basket from Blazel and rummaged in it.

Rizelya waited, still sitting on the rocks. When Blazel didn't come over to help her up, she snorted to herself, clambered to her feet, and plopped onto the blanket. Jaehaas and Wisah returned and joined them in their picnic of roasted fowl, fresh berries, and cold tuber salad. Rizelya rolled her eyes at how attentive Aistrun was with Chariel, filling her plate for her and pouring more wine.

Blazel set his dishes aside and leaned back, resting his weight on his arms. "While we wait for the Supreme to give us permission to go on the quest, we should start preparing."

"You be the only one who has been to the Deep Mountains," Jaehaas said. "Tell us what to expect."

"For one thing, there aren't any Malvers' monsters, but there are plenty of other predators. The highland wolves, which are nearly as large as our wolf form, frequently attack people. Black bears will be waking soon from their hibernation and will be hungry and testy. We want to leave those alone. The most dangerous and ferocious are the sabertigers. But the size of our group should deter most predators, including the sabertigers."

Blazel fingered the scar on his face. "The ones we're searching for are the apex predator—the Gryphons. They hunt the other predators and aren't particularly fond of Posairs. But if we find my friend, Graak, he'll help us contact their king. Convincing him to restore the alliance will be difficult."

Rizelya studied Blazel's scar, wondering how he'd received it. The new quest sounded as fraught with danger as the one she'd just completed. They were fortunate to have Blazel and his friendship with a Gryphon flight. Otherwise, they might not have a chance to save their people from this latest difficulty.

She gazed at the waterfall, wishing, praying, her people could do more than simply survive.

Rizelya woke up refreshed and full of energy. Leistral sat on the stool in the bedroom, braiding her freshly washed hair.

"You look perky this morning," Leistral commented.

"I feel good," Rizelya said, stretching. She stopped in mid-stretch and lowered her arms. "Oh! I just realized since coming to the Sanctuary I haven't had any dreams featuring that awful Malvers woman. I hope they're gone, but I suspect they're being blocked by the power of the priestesses living here."

"Two priestesses will be traveling with you. If the dreams come back, perhaps they can help you block them."

"That's a good idea, Leistral. I'll talk to Chariel and Wisah about it."

Later in the afternoon, Rizelya found Jaehaas in the common room, with Wisah sitting next to him. He attached a sharp, deadly arrowhead to an arrow shaft, then handed the bolt to Wisah, who methodically affixed feathers to the opposite end. Jaehaas smiled at Rizelya when she approached.

"You be coming to help?" he asked hopefully and gestured to the pile of arrowheads, shafts, and feathers. "After hearing about the dangers we be heading to, I decided I needed more arrows. I spent all morning in the forge creating these beauties." He pointed to the pile.

"Sure, I could help. Just show me what to do."

Rizelya sat next to Wisah. Jaehaas started to hand her an arrow to fletch when he paused and looked at her funny.

"What?" she asked.

"You're a Red!"

"Yes, and..."

"The Reds at home cast a spell on my arrows." Jaehaas twirled the bolt still in his hand. "They put a delay on it and I activate the flame when I shoot it. Can you do something similar? We probably could use fire arrows where we be going."

"What word do you use? It can't be an everyday word, or you'd have arrows exploding in your quiver when you didn't want them to."

"Yeah, that happened when they first created them." Jaehaas grimaced. "So they made up the word 'oyt.' It be short and easy to say, and you'd never say it any other time."

"Oyt, huh?" Rizelya repeated it several times under her breath while mimicking drawing a bow. "Do you have any of the spelled arrows I can examine?"

"Sure."

He told Wisah where to find his stash. She hurried to his room, returning quickly with a quiver full of red-fletched arrows.

Rizelya pulled one out, closed her eyes, and concentrated. She ran her other hand above the arrow, not touching it. She sensed the spell and how it was held in stasis until the proper word released it. Opening her eyes, she tapped the fire arrow. "Okay, I think I can figure this out. May I have a few of these? And I'll need some blanks to practice with."

Jaehaas handed her a half dozen of each. He smiled at Wisah and asked, "Be there some red feathers around this place? We'll need them to differentiate the two types of arrows."

"I'm sure we could find some," Wisah said. "If not, I know a Green who could change the feathers to any color you want."

Rizelya found Leistral, told her about the experiment, and together, they walked to the outdoor arena and rummaged in the nearby storage shed.

"This is just like old times," Leistral commented, "trying new things."

"Well, this one is recreating what someone else has done."

"It's still new to us. Ah ha! These should work." She dragged a few straw targets from the shed. "Too bad Saffren is in Strunlair Keep. We could use her water abilities since we're playing with fire."

"We'll just have to do it the old fashioned way." Rizelya filled a pail with water and dowsed the targets.

Leistral threw an arrow into the air and laughed when it fluttered a few feet away. "I guess we need a bow, too."

Leistral ran back to the pack-house to borrow Jaehaas's bow. Instead, she returned with Blazel.

He held out his bow. "Jaehaas has been teaching me. This will give me good practice. We haven't worked with the fire arrows yet. It was too dangerous in the wilds."

"For now," Rizelya said, "I just need you to shoot the arrow for me while I try to determine what was done."

He nodded and took the red-fletched arrow from her. Their fingers touched, and a thrill skittered through her. Seemingly undisturbed by the touch, he nocked the arrow and pulled it back, the muscles in his arms and shoulders rippling. He waited patiently for her signal.

"Now!"

He shot the arrow. It arced high in the air before speeding toward a target.

On its downward path, Rizelya barked, "Oyt." The arrow tip burst into flame. By the time the arrow sizzled to the ground, only the shaft with the feathers remained.

Rizelya laughed. "There appears to be an optimal distance from your target to activate the flame."

She directed Blazel to shoot another one. She waited until the arrow was closer to the target to release the spell. This time, the flaming arrowhead punched the straw without damage to the shaft.

Next, she attempted to place the spell on the normal arrows. The first time, the flame erupted in the shaft's middle, and the arrowhead dropped harmlessly to the ground. On the second attempt, the flame burst all along the shaft and burned it to ash in a heartbeat. Rizelya swore when the next time, the arrowhead ignited, but the fire fizzled out before the arrow hit its mark.

She conferred with Leistral and tried several more times. Finally, her spell worked in a similar fashion as the ones Jaehaas had given her.

"This time, you activate the spell, Blazel," Rizelya instructed him.

Blazel took the arrow, and in his excitement yelled, "Oyt!" The arrow immediately burst into flames. He dropped it, and it was ash in moments.

Rizelya frowned at him, perplexed. "That shouldn't have happened, especially for someone with little Red Talent. More fire was used than the spell had."

He lowered the bow and grinned. "I have more than most men. See?" He held out his palm, and in a few moments, a tiny flame danced in his hand.

Rizelya gasped. She had never seen a male able to do the trick. She handed him another arrow. "When you activate the spell, don't add any of your Red Talent to it. Just let it do the work."

Blazel nodded and loosed the arrow. The fire ate it before it hit the target. Three more tries resulted in the same thing. They were out of arrows.

Rizelya scowled as she paced, going over the spell in her mind. "Leistral, go get more arrows and bring Jaehaas with you. We need someone without fire magic to test this on."

Leistral saluted and jogged off.

Rizelya cocked her hip, tapping her chin with a finger while considering Blazel. "Our problem is you keep burning them up with your Talent. You don't need the delay spell. You could ignite the arrows with your own magic. But you must control your Talent better. How often do you use your magic?"

"The Supreme taught me how to use and control my fire magic when I was young. She didn't want me to burn things accidentally. I use it more often than most men, especially when I'm alone. I don't have the luxury of a Red to dry wood for me and such."

"Well, to keep you in practice, I won't do it for you. It's too bad you aren't more talented. I'm the only one with magic effective against predators. Wisah and Chariel's magic won't help in a fight. I'd feel better if Leistral and Eidstrun were going with us."

"It's different high in the mountains than down below." Blazel touched her shoulder. "The warrior gifts and your helbraught will be enough to protect us. I doubt the predators will attack us. Most of them are solitary hunters and wouldn't be a match for a group our size."

Leistral walked out of the building, followed by the others.

"Hey, we wanted to see the show," Aistrun said in explanation.

Rizelya laid the spell on an arrow and handed to Jaehaas. She held her breath as he shot the arrow, hoping she'd set the spell correctly. It worked perfectly with Jaehaas activating it instead of Blazel. The group sat under the trees and made arrows while Rizelya and Leistral placed the fire spell on half of the stock.

Rizelya was concentrating on the fire spell when Chariel came up with another batch of arrows for her to spell.

"When we're on this quest," Chariel said quietly, "I'll need someone to saddle my horse for me."

"What?" Rizelya's eyebrows furrowed in confusion. Chariel sat hunched over and rocking from side to side. "You don't know how to saddle a horse?"

Chariel shook her head. "No, and neither does Wisah. The stable hands have always done it for us."

"That will change. We won't have time for someone to do it for you. We'll teach you. First lesson is tomorrow morning."

Right after breakfast, the group tromped to the stables. The stable mistress, Shaela, met them in the courtyard.

"So, Chariel, Wisah, you're finally going to learn to care for your own mounts, eh?" Shaela asked. "I've picked out a few horses for you to choose from, or more rightly, for them to choose you. Come on in, and let's find out who your mount will be." She pushed open the stable doors and led the group inside. Eight beautiful plains-bred mares waited in the center aisle.

A racket came from one of the closed stalls. Frantic banging from the horse's hooves shook the door. A white stallion with wide black stripes reared, whinnying wildly. Shaela quickly pulled the mares out of the way.

Rizelya raced to the stallion's stall. "Tejen, be easy, boy," she crooned. The big plains stallion had followed her and Aistrun when they left Strunlair Keep and wouldn't turn back. He'd been Keandran's ride until Keandran disappeared. She grabbed his headstall and pulled his nose down.

He quieted, staring at the people assembled in the aisle. When Wisah moved nervously away from Aistrun, Tejen whickered, bobbing his head, and kicked at his door again. Wisah cringed behind Aistrun.

"Wha... what's happening?" Wisah cried. "Why is he after me? I didn't do anything to him."

Jaehaas clattered in, saw the scene, and rushed to Tejen's stall. "What be the matter, boy?" He took Tejen's head in his hands and stared into the horse's eyes. The stallion stilled and whickered softly, then lifted his head to gaze at Wisah over

Jaehaas's shoulder. Jaehaas released the horse and turned to gaze with wonderment at Wisah.

"You be his rider," he said to her. "Tejen be excited to finally see you. He'll behave now." Jaehaas slowly opened the stall door.

The stallion pranced to Wisah and delicately reached out his muzzle until he was nose to nose with his chosen rider. The very large, very tall horse dwarfed the much smaller woman. Where most plains horses had fine, pale stripes, Tejen had bold, wide black stripes on a white hide. His black socks reached up to his knees, and his mane and tail were a deep gray. Wisah rubbed Tejen's nose. He closed his eyes with pleasure.

"Now we know why he followed us," Aistrun said. "The damned horse broke out of his stall in Strunlair Keep and came running after us. Tejen likes Kymaya, and we thought he was just protecting his mare."

"That be part of it, but not all," Jaehaas said. "He knew his rider be here, and you be going in her direction. Plains horses know these things. I've seen horses run off and turn up several territories away, or even in a different province, where their rider lived. There be no explanation, other than that be the way the Goddess made them. Wisah, come with me and get acquainted with Tejen."

Jaehaas led Wisah and Tejen to the back of the stable, where they could be alone to show Wisah how to groom her horse.

Shaela had left when it was obvious what Tejen's problem was and now returned, leading the mares. "Well, Wisah may have a mount, but you don't, Chariel. Come and let these beauties get a look at you."

Chariel approached the horses and held out her hand, letting each horse snuff at it. All except one turned away from her. The remaining mare stepped closer to Chariel and whuffed softly. Chariel reached out and rubbed her muzzle. The mare was a light golden brown with pale cream stripes. Her mane and tail were the same cream as the blaze stretching from her forehead to her nostrils, and her left hind leg had a cream sock.

"This is Chaezreen," Shaela said. "She's a good horse with a nice smooth gait. You'll like her."

"I'll help you, Chariel." Aistrun took the lead rope from Shaela. Together, they found a quiet corner.

Aistrun worked with Chariel, while Jaehaas worked with Wisah, teaching them how to properly groom their horses and put on and remove their tack.

As she watched, Rizelya snorted. There was more going on besides teaching. Between the stolen glances and giggling, it was a wonder they were accomplishing anything. She rolled her eyes when Aistrun stood behind Chariel and wrapped his arms around her waist to show her how to curry her horse's coat.

Rizelya turned away with a sigh, wishing Blazel would flirt with her.

Chapter 16

At breakfast, a messenger brought them news the Supreme would meet with them shortly. Wisah led the small procession, followed by Rizelya and Aistrun. Rizelya was conscious of Blazel a step behind her. If he didn't make a move pretty soon, she was going to have to show him how it was done. Leistral, Eidstrun, and Chariel were next in line, with Jaehaas bringing up the rear.

They passed through the courtyard, and to the grounds beyond, following the garden pathways to the enormous temple. This time, Rizelya wasn't as stunned by the size. The Sanctuary was the home of the Goddess and Her Priestesses, and the temple reflected this.

Inside, murals and statues depicting the Goddess's four faces filled three of the public chamber's walls. Rizelya stared at the wall dedicated to the Consort. Many of the images filling it were familiar as the Consort cycled through the stages of life. Beginning as a small boy, experiencing the joy of shifting to his wolf form for the first time. It finished with the Consort as a venerable sage with a long beard, wrinkled face, and kind, wise eyes.

Rizelya paused, waiting for Aistrun to notice the unfamiliar image—the Consort in his warrior form.

"Hey!" Aistrun exclaimed. "He has a black pelt. I haven't ever heard of a man being a Black."

A warrior's pelt was the same color as the man's hair. A person who could work all the forms of magic had Black Talent—rare for women, and unheard of in men.

"The Consort is the epitome of all that men may become," Wisah explained, her voice a bit pompous. "It is fitting he should be shown in all His glory."

Chariel had stopped next to Aistrun. "Once, we weren't separated by magical Talent. We could access all the streams of magic, even the men. This mural is ancient, predating the Great War."

Rizelya wondered what it would be like to use more than fire or earth magic. Water and fire never mixed. How could one control both at the same time?

Wisah resumed striding toward the rear exit, leading to the Temple's inner sanctum. Beyond it, stunning murals of the Goddess and Her Consort filled the richly painted corridor. But once again, Wisah rushed through the corridors, not allowing Rizelya time to stop and study the murals.

They stopped finally at a huge, black ironwood double door with an illustration of the symbols of the seven Talents in a circle. The black background represented the eighth Talent, Black. The cycle of the three moons, Kelar, Zelar, and Chelar, was depicted on the lintel. Two veiled women stood guard, one on either side, each holding a helbraught. At the group's approach, the one on the right opened the door. Rizelya winced at the tingling along her skin as she passed through the threshold. A spell guarded the entrance just as surely as the two women outside the door did.

Several hundred people could fit in the audience chamber. White sheadash and marble covered the floors and walls, and white curtains hung on the windows. White pillar candles lit the room.

The Supreme sat on her throne carved from one massive piece of clear quartz crystal. Ten paces in front of the throne's dais, Wisah stopped. Together, the group made the gesture of obeisance and honor to the Goddess's representative and dropped to their knees.

"You may rise," the Supreme said, after several long milcrons. "I have weighed all you have told me, listened to the reports of my priestesses, and prayed to the Goddess for guidance. Chariel, your gift is true. There is no doubt in that. What you have seen will come to pass. The six of you will travel into the Deep Mountains and find the Gryphons."

"Six?" Rizelya scowled. "What about the rest of my squad-pack?"

The Supreme frowned at Rizelya for interrupting her. "They will go to Strunlair Keep and wait for your return. There is war coming. The Malvers chafe after all these years at their exile. As both Chariel and I have seen, madness stalks our people. We must have allies if we are to win this war. Blazel, we need your friends, the Gryphons. It is time for them to remember their duty."

Blazel stared at her. "What duty, Supreme?"

"Our ancestors created the Gryphons during the war to fight the flying beasts the Malvers sent against us. It is their duty to protect the Posairs and our world. I fear the Malvers will send such creatures against us once more."

"If they've had such powers," Rizelya said, "why haven't they used them before now? There haven't been any new monsters since the war. The new one is simply a janack variation."

The Supreme's lips thinned and her fingers drummed an irritated staccato on the arms of her crystal throne. Rizelya froze. The Supreme stared at her for a long moment. "After the first monsters appeared in our land, we placed a barrier around their island exile, preventing them from doing such things again." She paused, her fingers stilling as she gazed into the distance. She turned back to them, sighing heavily. "The barrier is failing. Their magic is growing and penetrating the veil. I have mended it, but my repairs won't last long. You must hurry. Blazel, convince the Gryphons to join us once more."

"I'll do what I can," Blazel promised, bowing his head.

"That is all we can ever do. Now, go." The Supreme made a shooing motion. "You have much to do before you leave."

On the way out, Chariel hung back, walking behind Jaehaas. She hugged her arms tight against her body. Her face had lost all color, and pure terror darkened her eyes. Once they were in the main sanctuary, Rizelya waved the others to go on and waited for Chariel.

"Hey, what's wrong?" she asked when Chariel shuffled up to her.

"I'm so scared, Rizelya," Chariel gasped. "I've never been beyond the Sanctuary's borders."

Rizelya frowned. "Surely you've gone home to visit. After Wisah's initial training, she returned for a visit, then completed her apprenticeship in her home temple at Strunland Keep."

"No." Chariel shook her head. Her hands twisted together like writhing snakes. "I was abandoned in a temple as an infant and was immediately brought here. I had no home to go to, no other temple to apprentice in. Besides, as you know, I'm a spitting image of our ancient enemy, and although no one remembers the Malvers, there is still prejudice against someone with my coloring."

"I'll be with you, and so will Wisah and Blazel. We won't let anyone hurt you, and neither will Aistrun nor Jaehaas." Rizelya smiled. Especially not Aistrun.

"But I'm a priestess, not a warrior," Chariel sputtered. "I can't fight."

"Why-ever not?"

Rizelya dragged Chariel to the mural depicting the Goddess as a warrior. Fierce joy filled her face. She stood in a fighting stance with a helbraught in her hands. Her red hair flowed behind her.

"Look at her eyes," Rizelya commanded. "They are white, the color of the Goddess, of her priestesses. In all Her forms, Her eyes are white, because no matter what shape She takes, She is always the Goddess. If She didn't want us to fight, why would one of her forms be a warrior?"

"But that doesn't mean she wants her priestesses to fight," Chariel argued. She crossed her arms in front of her stubbornly.

Rizelya wasn't a priestess and so couldn't answer the allegation. Instead, she took a different tack. "Who was the greatest hero of the Great War?"

Chariel frowned, and mumbled, "Shandir."

"In all the tales about Shandir, one quality stands out and never changes—she was a White Priestess."

"Oh!" Chariel dropped her hands. "She was, wasn't she?"

"We don't expect you to fight," Rizelya said in a gentle voice. "But there is some reason you need to be with us. Why else would your vision include you in this quest?"

"You're right. But... I'm still scared."

"I know. I'm scared too."

"You?"

Rizelya nodded. "I've never been to the Deep Mountains. Nobody but Blazel has. There might not be any Malvers' monsters, but there are sabertigers, bears, and other predators. And there are Gryphons. Blazel calls them friends, but the tales say they are bloodthirsty beasts who hate humans. I don't know what I'm getting myself into. But—" she gazed directly into Chariel's eyes "— but I trust the Goddess. I trust your visions are Her gifts. So I'm willing to go, even though my knees are shaking with fear."

Chariel drew herself up to her full height and threw back her shoulders. "I, too, trust the Goddess and will follow your example."

"Come on, let's go help the others get ready." Rizelya linked her arm with Chariel's. "Together, we can face anything, including snarly males trying to shove things where they don't belong." She'd meant the packing, but an image of Blazel above her, smiling as he thrust within her, flashed through her mind. Thankfully, Chariel didn't notice her blush.

Chariel grinned, and Rizelya banished the pleasant daydream. Laughing, they went to find the others.

They spent the afternoon organizing supplies from the Sanctuary stores. Leistral took charge of requisitioning the winter tents, bedding, and clothing. Wisah ordered food from the kitchens. The travelers sent their dirty clothes to be laundered.

Rizelya walked to the cloister to help Chariel and Wisah pack, especially Chariel. She'd piled practically everything she owned on her bed. Rizelya rolled her eyes at the mess, then helped Chariel to winnow it down to the necessities.

Leistral popped in and whistled. "I hope you're not taking all of that with you, Chariel."

"No," she laughed. "Rizelya will only let me take those." She pouted, pointing to two medium packs.

Leistral raised her eyebrows. "That's much more manageable, but it's still a lot. Rizelya, the support staff has the supplies ready."

"Try to cut a little more, Chariel." Rizelya patted her friend's shoulder. "I want both you and Wisah to spend the night at the pack-house. It'll be much easier if we're all together when we leave in the morning."

Chariel bent over her bags, mumbling.

Rizelya and Leistral hurried to the stables. Eidstrun and Blazel stood by the doors, surveying the huge pile of supplies.

"Let's get this sorted," Rizelya said. "There's more here than what we carried across Strunlair Province. It's a good thing we brought Kressy with us."

"Once we leave the Sanctuary's territory, there won't be any safe houses or Keeps to augment or restock our supplies," Blazel reminded her. "We'll need all of this and hope we have enough."

Rizelya considered the pile. "Kressy can't carry all those packs. Let's go choose another multa." She grabbed Blazel by the arm, leaving Eidstrun and Leistral to the sorting.

Blazel led her to a pen with several multas in it. The pack beasts could carry large loads, and their wide platter-like cloven hoofs enabled the animals to easily walk on the snow. These were still losing their winter coat and had long, curly pelts. Her multa, Kressy, already had her summer pelt in. If it became too cold, they'd put a blanket on her. Rizelya and Blazel chose a multa named Gemmy and led her back to the stable.

By the time they returned, Leistral and Eidstrun had the supplies packed in the bags for the multas, ready for loading in the morning. The weight needed to be distributed so as not to overbalance the animals.

The new multa took to the horses and Kressy and was soon happily munching hay with them. Nothing was left to do except say good-byes and get a good night's rest.

Blazel crawled out of bed, rubbing his sleep deprived eyes. He'd returned late to the guest house after sharing dinner with his mother and grandmother. During his short, but busy, stay, he'd only visited with them twice. It still shocked him how old and frail his grandmother had grown. If he were lucky, he'd see her one more time before she passed, but he doubted it. "Merciful

Crone," he prayed, "may my grandmother's passage back into the Goddess's womb be sweet and gentle."

Fumbling in the dark, he grabbed his toiletries and headed to the necessary room, passing Jaehaas coming out. As he went through his morning ablutions, thoughts of the lovely Rizelya flitted through his mind. His groin tightened as he imagined her in his arms, wishing he'd given into the temptation to kiss her while they worked on the fire arrows. The flush of excitement in her face had melted his heart. The looks they exchanged gave him hope she was also attracted to him. But they were always surrounded by people. Blazel sighed, gazing into the mirror. "Admit it, man," he told his reflection, "you're falling for her but are too damned shy to be more than friendly with her in front of others." He bent over, hanging onto the sink, mentally chastising himself for not being more like Aistrun and openly showing his affections.

Back in their room, Jaehaas tossed the last of his possessions in his bag. "We need to keep our pace slow these first few days. Neither Wisah nor Chariel be accustomed to riding all day."

"I'd planned on it. I remember how it is." Blazel pulled on a tunic and a pair of thick, sturdy woolen pants. He stamped into his boots. "Not so long ago, I had to get used to riding. At least they've ridden for pleasure frequently. I hadn't been on a horse for years when I acquired Lighzel. Those first few days were brutally painful."

Blazel threw his bag over his shoulder, along with his bow and quiver. He and Jaehaas ambled to the stables to find a flurry of pandemonium as their friends readied to leave.

While Blazel hurried to saddle Lighzel, Jaehaas clopped to the packs ready for the waiting multas. He hoisted a pack over Kressy's back, adjusting the weight distribution before securing it in place. In less than half an octar, Rizelya led the group from the stables and into the courtyard.

Blazel's jaw dropped at the sight of the Supreme leaning on her cane in the courtyard.

"My children," her voice carried across the open space, "the fate of our survival is in your hands. We need an alliance with the Gryphons if we are to win this war once and for all. Come forward, one at a time, to receive a blessing from the Goddess."

Blazel waited, wanting to be the last to kneel in front of the Supreme. She lightly touched the top of his bowed head and murmured her blessing. Finished, she tipped his face up to gaze into his eyes.

"Blazel," she whispered, "keep my priestesses safe. They are your sisters. Protect them, and bring them safely home to me. You come home safe, too." She placed a kiss on his cheek. Tears stung his eyes at the unaccustomed affection.

"I'll bring them home," he promised. "Along with our ancient allies. Stay well, Your Grace."

As she gently patted his face, he turned into her palm and kissed it. She was more to him than his spiritual leader. She had raised him as much as his mother and grandmother, and he loved her just as dearly. In the morning light, age sat heavily on her, and he hoped she would live through the coming trials. He stood, mounted Lighzel, and rejoined the group.

"Go with the Goddess's blessings," the Supreme said. "Return home quickly. We need you." She made the sign of the Goddess in the air before them. As she did, a bright, white light streamed from her fingertips. The symbol hovered in the air in front of her a moment before expanding until it encapsulated the group.

Blazel drew in a sharp breath as particles of magic sank into his skin and filled him with energy. He felt stronger and more confident than ever before. His companions also sat straighter in their saddles. Rizelya pressed her hands together, touched her fingertips to the center of her forehead, and bowed to the Supreme, before urging her horse forward.

The horses' hooves clattering on the flagstones echoed in the courtyard. Rizelya rode through the gate, then Aistrun, followed by the others one by one. When it was his turn, he looked over his shoulder. The Supreme lifted a pale hand in farewell.

When they reached the crossroads, the group made additional quick farewells as Leistral and Eidstrun turned onto the southern road, while the rest took the road north.

Travel was easy the first two days on the smooth road, with safe houses strung along it where they could spend the night. Rizelya stopped frequently to allow Chariel and Wisah to dismount and stretch their legs. During the third day, they rested less often and traveled at a faster pace.

After dinner, Blazel approached Rizelya. "We'll leave Sanctuary territory tomorrow."

"I thought so. The road is getting rougher, less maintained. You'll guide us then?"

"Yes, it's why I wanted to talk to you."

"Good." She leaned back, rolling her taevo mug between her hands. "You know this country. I don't. Normally, Aistrun is my co-alpha, but I think while we're in the Deep Mountains, you should be."

Blazel's mouth dropped open in shock at the unexpected request. He was still getting used to being in a group. He'd been alone for so long he doubted he had it in him to play the dominant role.

"I can guide you, but I'm not an Alpha. This is the first time I've ever been in a pack. Why do you want me to lead?"

"You know the dangers and what we need to watch for. Aistrun doesn't."

"But I can do that as just a guide."

Rizelya laid a hand on his arm. "No, you can't. That isn't how a squad-pack works. Those who lead, in this case, guide, are alphas. You are more dominant, and more capable, than you believe yourself to be. The others already look up to you. We're simply making it official."

He swallowed, took a deep breath, and surveyed the room. His gaze landed on Chariel and Wisah. The Supreme had made it clear the safety of the two priestesses was his responsibility. In her subtle way, she'd pushed him toward this role. Did she know this would happen? He couldn't let her down. He turned back to Rizelya, who had her head cocked to the side, and watched him expectantly. Being her co-alpha would mean they had to spend more time together. He perked up.

"Okay, but I'm not part of your squad-pack. Won't Aistrun be mad?"

"No, I won't." Aistrun joined them, sitting next to Rizelya. "I tried super hard not to be an alpha, and I was succeeding until they stuck me with Little Red. I'll be glad to let you be responsible and have all the headaches." He raised his voice, "Hey everyone, gather round."

The others quickly crowded around the table.

"What be going on?" Jaehaas asked.

"We've got a change in leadership." Aistrun put a hand over his heart. "I am no longer the alpha of this little pack. He is." He pointed to Blazel. "So if you have any complaints or problems, talk to him. I don't want to hear about it."

Wisah chuckled. "This isn't a surprise. Blazel knows where we're going. You don't."

The next day, the road became a dirt path, and patches of snow lay under the trees. Whenever their pace slowed to a walk, Blazel urged his horse alongside Rizelya's mare. They chatted about fighting, magic, and their philosophies about life. Other than Chariel, he'd never talked so openly with anyone before. The dappled light highlighted her beautiful face, and as she licked her lips, he worked to gather his courage to kiss them. What would they taste like?

His movement to lean over and find out startled Lighzel, and she moved away from Rizelya's horse. As he caught his balance, he remembered the vow he'd made long ago not to have casual sex, and he slowed his horse to walk next to Chariel. She raised her eyebrow in question, gesturing between him and Rizelya. When he shook his head, she sighed and patted his arm in understanding.

He was the result of a casual encounter, and he didn't want another child to suffer as he had. In the territory keeps, open sex wasn't a problem, nor were the resultant children. They were raised in a crèche and rarely lived with their parents, especially if the parents were fighters. But in the Sanctuary, there were few children as the priestesses lived chaste lives. He'd been an anomaly.

In the afternoon, they stopped at a tall pillar. Blazel threw a warmer cloak around his shoulders. "This marks the boundary of the Sanctuary's territory. From here on, we'll be riding in the wilderness. Stay sharp."

Chapter 17

As they rode farther north, all signs of spring evaporated, and snow covered the ground. The horses' hooves crunched through the snow's icy top layer and sank past their fetlocks.

"Stop!" Jaehaas called after only a few milcrons. He lifted his foreleg, showing the blood dripping from multiple cuts. "The ice be cutting the horses' legs."

Guilt sat like a heavy weight on Blazel's chest with his first failure in leading. He hadn't considered the danger from the ice. As he ordered a stop, he vowed to be a better leader. Chariel found the bandages in their supplies, and he helped wrap Jaehaas's and the horses' legs from knee to hoof.

As they climbed higher, the trees grew denser. They rode slowly under gigantic trees, soaring over a hundred feet high. Dim green light filtered through their wide branches. Here, the snow lacked the icy coating. Blazel scanned it for signs of predators.

Behind him, the group spread out in a long line. His breath caught at the sight of a fresh large paw print in the snow. Dark shapes flitting through the trees. Blazel slowed his horse for Rizelya to catch up with him.

"We have a problem," he said quietly, tilting his head toward the trees. "Highland wolves. The blood attracted them, and I sense it's a large pack, more than enough to challenge us. We need to gather everyone together."

"Should we run for it?" Rizelya's eyes tracked the forms pacing them.

"No, they'd take us down in milcrons. There's a place ahead where we can defend against them. We just have to make it."

"I'll let Aistrun know. He'll bring the others." A faraway look came over her face as she mind-spoke to her pack-mate.

Blazel had forgotten fighters in the same pack could mind-speak to each other. He'd never experienced it. Aistrun immediately quickened his pace, catching up to Chariel, and together overtake Wisah and Jaehaas, he understood the wisdom of it. There hadn't been shouting or anything else to alert the wolves.

They rode in a tight knot, following Blazel as he kicked Lighzel into a trot. The wolves drew closer, no longer hiding. Ahead, an enormous pile of rocks reared out of the snow. The stones resolved into a ruined tower, the lowest branches of the tree it stood under sweeping across the remains of its roof.

With the tower—and the safety it offered—in sight, he kicked Lighzel into a gallop, and the others followed his lead. The wolves howled and gave chase. Blazel raced toward the single, narrow opening into the ruins. Once through, he jumped off his horse. Rizelya raced in after him, slid from her saddle, and ran to the entrance, holding her glowing helbraught in front of her. She tossed her cloak to the side. His landed on top of it. Blazel boiled into his warrior form and joined her.

Chariel sped into the tower. Wisah, right behind her, held the reins of Aistrun's horse. Jaehaas guarded the front of the tower, his bow raised and arrow nocked. Beside him, Aistrun rose in his warrior form, snapping his huge fangs. He now stood seven-and-a-half-feet tall with bulging muscles. Wolves surged around them, snarling. Jaehaas let loose an arrow. A wolf whined, then dropped to the ground, dead.

Aistrun howled, and Blazel joined in. The highland wolves paused. Blazel experienced a moment of hope the wolves would flee, only to have it dashed when a wolf snarled and lunged at Aistrun.

Blazel's focus narrowed to fighting. Swipe, bite, claw. Over and over again. Yelps of pain momentarily intruded as Rizelya sliced into the wolves. He leaped back, astonished, when a severed head flew past him.

Not long after, the few remaining wolves fled into the trees. Blazel sagged against the tower's wall, gore spattered his fur. Blood seeped from a gash on Rizelya's cheek and flowed down her leg. Jaehaas hobbled toward the tower with deep claw wounds in his flanks and a wide slash across his chest. Aistrun's warrior pelt hid any injuries, as did Blazel's.

"Is there someplace we can wash?" Rizelya asked, her voice thin with exhaustion.

"Stream close, freezing," Blazel's jaws mangled the words.

"I don't care. I just want to get this blood off me."

"Meee, tooo," Aistrun growled out between his fangs.

Jaehaas gestured at the wolf corpses. "We can't remain here too long with all this carnage around."

"Not safe," Blazel agreed. He pushed away from the tower wall.

"It's too dark to travel, and we're injured. I'll take care of it so we can stay here tonight." Rizelya heaved a huge sigh and hefted her helbraught. She stumbled when she put weight on her injured leg.

"It wait." Blazel took the two steps separating them and picked her up.

She yelped and pushed against his chest. "Hey, what is it with you boys thinking you can carry me?"

Blazel chuckled and pulled her tighter. It felt so good to have her in his arms, even if fur covered them. He carried her into the tower ruins.

"What's all this?" Rizelya asked. A fire danced in the remains of a fireplace, and a kettle of water hung over it, heating.

Chariel blushed, shrugging. "I had a flash of premonition we'd stay here tonight. Wisah and I unloaded the multas and made camp. Although, we couldn't figure out how to set up the tent by ourselves."

Rizelya beamed at them. "You were correct. Good job, ladies."

Blazel strode to the fire, and carefully lowered Rizelya to her feet. She swayed, but he caught her before she fell, out cold.

"Lay her down, here." Wisah indicated a bedroll. "The gash in her leg needs to be closed." Her eyes widened when she saw Jaehaas, and her hands clenched into fists. She slowly relaxed her hands. "Your wounds need tended as well."

Blazel laid Rizelya down and stepped aside.

Chariel examined Blazel and Aistrun. "Do either of you have any injuries? I can't tell."

"None bad," Blazel said. "Mostly wolf."

"A few," Aistrun said. "Can wait."

"Neither of us are healers," Chariel indicated herself and Wisah, "but we've had first aid training. We can care for minor injuries." Chariel knelt next to Wisah and began to wash the blood off Rizelya.

Blazel caught Aistrun's attention and led him to the stream. Ice didn't cover the surface, but even against his warrior pelt, the water was freezing cold. They both shook hard several times to remove as much water from their fur as possible. Even so, when they shifted, their clothes were damp.

By the time he and Aistrun returned, shivering with cold, a blanket covered Rizelya, and Wisah tended Jaehaas's injuries with a gentle touch. He regarded her with soft eyes. Blazel smiled. It appeared love was blooming.

Chariel glanced up, and her face paled. "You're hurt!" She rushed to Aistrun and grabbed his arm. "Let me take care of it for you."

The corner of Aistrun's lip quirked up, and he gazed adoringly at Chariel as he followed her to the other side of the fire. His cut wasn't deep, and the cold water from the stream had stopped most of the bleeding.

Blazel shook his head. There must be an epidemic of love, even he was feeling it. He found his pack, dug out clean, dry clothes, and quickly changed. His and Aistrun's abandoned cloaks lay on top of the supply packs, and he wrapped his around himself. As he passed Aistrun, he threw a cloak to his friend, while Chariel tenderly cared for the cut.

Blazel crouched to check on Rizelya. Her eyes opened.

"How are you feeling?" he asked.

"I'm fine." She frowned at the blanket and sat up. "The gash wasn't that bad. I just lost too much blood. I'll be able to burn the carcasses after I eat something."

A pot of taevo heated next to the fire, with a stack of mugs nearby. Blazel poured taevo into two mugs and handed one to Rizelya, then sat beside her.

"We shouldn't be bothered by any more wolves." Blazel sipped on his taevo, letting the warmth thaw him. "The survivors will spread the news."

"Good." Rizelya looked at him over the edge of her mug. "You fought well."

"I've had a lot of practice."

Finished tending wounds, Chariel and Wisah fixed a pot of soup. As they waited for it to heat, Blazel told them about the various twisted beasts he'd battled in the swamps. While they ate, Aistrun shared stories of his and Rizelya's adventures, then Jaehaas added his. Blazel sighed in happiness. He hadn't ever had so many friends at once.

Later, he accompanied Rizelya outside their encampment, guarding her while she burned the wolf carcasses. Out in the dark, away from everyone else, Blazel snatched his courage, leaned in, and kissed her. He sensed her momentary hesitation before she returned the kiss. He put his arms around her and drew her close, liking the feel of her body pressed against his. They continued kissing until they both shivered in the cold. He couldn't wipe the ear-to-ear grin from his face as they walked back to the fire.

Rizelya touched her fingertips to her lips as she and Blazel rejoined the others. His unexpected kiss surprised her, especially since they hadn't done any flirting before he leaned in. One moment they were talking, and the next, kissing. She enjoyed his kiss and wanted more.

The fire burned low. Rizelya stretched and yawned. "Who will take the first watch? Now we're in the wilderness, we need to set a guard."

"There's no need," Blazel said. "I can cast a boundary ward to keep us safe."

Rizelya raised her eyebrow. "Huh? I've never heard of such a spell."

"You always stay in safe houses, so you wouldn't need it. I traveled alone and had to find something to allow me to sleep. It won't take long to do." He gave Rizelya an appraising look. "The spell uses Brown Talent. You appear to have enough. Follow me, and I'll show it to you."

Blazel went to his tent and came out a few milcrons later with his old beat-up pack. Rizelya followed him beyond the tower opening. He crumpled a mixture of herbs in his hands. While chanting, he sprinkled them on the ground, forming a thin line as they walked the perimeter of their camp. The brown magic of earth trickled from his fingers to the herbs, creating a circular wall of protection around them.

"Nothing wishing us harm can pass through it," Blazel explained. "It will stay until I scatter the herbs, even while I'm asleep or absent from the circle."

Rizelya examined it, nodding in satisfaction. "Nice! Your shield takes less energy and focus than my fire shield. Either you or I should set the warding spell around our camp every night."

"Agreed."

The next few days were uneventful as they traveled deeper into the mountains. Flowers bloomed in sheltered valleys where the snow was mostly melted. In Rizelya's home territory, summer would be in full swing by now. But this high in the mountains, the middle of Sandar meant the coming of spring, not summer.

Blazel and Aistrun occasionally broke off from the group to hunt the plentiful game. They usually returned with a couple of rabbits each for the evening cook pot. The fresh meat was welcome and would stretch their provision from the Sanctuary.

Rizelya glanced in consternation at Blazel riding at her side. He rode with his head tilted back to catch the sun's warmth on his face. He hadn't kissed her again since the wolf attack. Every so often, he'd hold her hand, but only when the others couldn't see them.

Behind them, Wisah's tinkling laugh was followed by Jaehaas's deeper tenor. Rizelya smiled at their growing closeness.

Chariel and Aistrun rode close together, holding hands and their knees touching. Happiness lit Aistrun's face as he told her a story. The corner of Chariel's mouth turned up, and she tilted her head toward him, listening. Earlier, in the dark of their tent, she had confided to Rizelya and Wisah she hadn't believed anyone to become interested in her. Besides being a Priestess, she'd believed no one would see past her charcoal-gray hair to the woman inside. As Rizelya expected, Aistrun didn't care. He only saw a beautiful woman.

"How long before we reach the Gryphon territory?" Rizelya asked, needing to take her mind off the love life of her friend and the lack in her own life.

Blazel gazed around them. "Today or tomorrow. If we're lucky, scouts will spot us soon to guide us through the pass and into their land." He pointed to a high peak in front of them. "That's where we're headed. To reach it, we'll be crossing sabertiger territory. Without help from the Gryphon's, it will be dangerous. We should pick up our pace." He kicked Lighzel into a canter.

Rizelya sighed and nudged Kymaya into the faster stride. They crossed the valley and ascended the next mountain. The trees here weren't the behemoths like where the wolves had attacked them. Tall, slender pines, blue spruce, and dark cedar intermingled with silvery birch and ash. Spring runoff swelled the streams. The retreating snow left the ground muddy. Outcrops of stone became more common the higher they climbed. Before dark, Blazel led them to a large cave with space for the horses.

Rizelya slid from Kymaya. She rejoiced to be on the cave's dry floor after all the mud they'd slogged through. After nearly a chedan of traveling through the mountains, they'd established a routine for setting up camp. They cared for their horses, located water, and scrounged wood for a fire.

Grimacing at the damp wood, Rizelya dried it with her fire magic. She stepped aside to allow Blazel to light the fire—his control was much better since he'd been practicing. After she ascertained he wouldn't blow it up, she exited the cave to create the ward.

As she sprinkled the herbs and chanted the spell, Rizelya sensed being watched. She slowly straightened. A huge sabertiger sat on a rock pile across from the cave's mouth. The ward flared to life. The sabertiger blinked and leaped from the rocks, disappearing with a flick of its tail.

She hurried back into the cave. "We need to be on guard tonight." Rizelya jerked a thumb at the entrance. "A sabertiger was outside, watching us a moment ago."

"The ward should keep it out," Blazel assured everyone. "It's kept them and other predators away while I slept alone."

"Hey, I don't want to be eaten," Aistrun said. "We'll set a watch to be sure."

Blazel shrugged. He put his hands behind his back and rocked on his toes. He reminded Rizelya of a child wanting to show a favorite adult something.

"I have a surprise for you." Blazel grinned. "I think you'll all love it. Follow me."

He turned around and headed toward the rear of the cave. Rizelya and the others followed him down a sloping tunnel. Ahead of them, Blazel balanced a small flame on his palm, lighting the way. The tunnel opened into a huge cavern. Blazel closed his hand to extinguish the flame. Phosphorescent moss growing on the rock walls illuminated a pool of steaming water.

"There's a hot spring feeding the pool," Blazel said excitedly. "Not quite as good as your hot soaking tubs, but they will get us clean."

"How deep be it?" Jaehaas asked, uncertainty filling his voice.

"Last time I was here, it reached my chest. You should be okay." Blazel's gaze dropped to the floor. "I wouldn't have brought you here if I didn't think we could all enjoy it."

"Hey, this is a brilliant idea!" Aistrun clapped a hand on Blazel's shoulder. "Don't let the horse get you down. He likes it."

Jaehaas had thrown off his tunic and stepped into the pool where naturally occurring steps led into it. He stepped farther into the pool until the water covered his shoulders. "Aha..." he sighed. "This be lovely. Come on in."

Wisah began sliding out of her clothes. Blazel's eyes widened, and his face turned bright red. He whirled around, away from her.

"Blazel," Rizelya said, "let's go get towels and clean clothing for everyone. These sillies didn't think of how cold they're going to be, running up to the cave while soaking wet."

Blazel gave her a grateful look, and together, they walked back to retrieve supplies. When they returned to the underground pool, the others were in the water. Rizelya threw Aistrun a bar of soap, then lifted the hem of her tunic. She noticed Blazel blushing, but watching her with avid attention. She slowly pulled the top over her head and stretched. Blazel gasped and turned around.

Smiling, Rizelya finished undressing and hopped into the pool. Blazel's reaction made her think he'd never seen a woman naked before. She splashed the delightfully warm water over her shoulders, then turned, wondering what was taking Blazel so long. He approached the pool with a towel wrapped around his hips. He dropped the towel and quickly jumped in. She caught a glimpse of a well-endowed man. She glanced at the others, who were trying to keep a straight face. The poor boy was unused to nude people. An embarrassed flush reddened Blazel's face, and he turned his back to everyone.

She gasped. Four parallel scars covered his back from shoulder to waist.

"Sweet Mother!" Chariel exclaimed. "What happened to you?" She reached out to gently touch the scars.

Blazel hunched his shoulders and pulled away from her touch. After a moment, he turned around to face them.

"You never told me about them," Chariel said. "I always wondered how you got the scar on your face, but didn't want to intrude."

"I received them at the same time." A haunted look crossed over his face. When he spoke again, his voice was distant. "I was nearly seventeen, full of myself, and ready to leave the Sanctuary. Chariel, you had a vision and sent me to the Deep Mountains. The Supreme didn't tell me about Histrun wanting me to go with him, and I believed I didn't have anyplace else to go.

"I knew nothing about the mountains or living in the wilds. I may have felt alone in the Sanctuary, but there were cooks, and healers, and gardeners, and—well, people. When I'd hunted, someone like Histrun was with me. I discovered my wolf had strong hunting instincts, otherwise I would have starved.

"One evening, I was so engrossed in finding a place to stay, I didn't realize I was being stalked. A sabertiger attacked me."

Blazel put a hand over his shoulder and touched the scars on his back. "His first swipe gave me these. I must have moved just as he jumped. Afterwards, I was in so much pain I couldn't shift to either form and so had to fight him as a man, with only a helstrablade."

"Sabertigers are big," Aistrun interrupted. "How did you win?"

"I didn't." Blazel touched his face and followed the scars down his shoulder. "These I received when it tried to eat me. The sabertiger had me on the ground, his jaws inches from my neck, when he was tossed from me. A Gryphon saved me. The same one we're searching for. Graak took me to his flight, and I lived with them for five years. They taught me how to live in the Deep Mountains."

"When was the last time you saw your friend?" Rizelya asked.

Blazel paused, thinking. "Eight years. Graak could be mated and a father by now. It will be good to see him again."

They continued to soak and chat for quite a while until Wisah stood. "I'm wrinkled to the bone." She made her way to the steps. "And starving!"

Rizelya and the others quickly followed Wisah's example. This time, Blazel wasn't quite so shy about being naked in front of everyone. He was, however, the first one to get dressed. When they returned to the main cave, the fire had burned to coals. Rizelya added wood to the coals. Aistrun and Blazel strung the rabbits they'd caught earlier on spits and put them over the fire to roast.

After dinner, Rizelya took the first watch, sitting just inside the cave's mouth, a heavy cloak wrapped around her and the fire at her back. The sound of people bedding down for the night soon gave way to soft snores. She thought about Blazel alone in the mountains at seventeen. She had been battling monsters for four years by the time she had reached that age. It reminded her how sheltered Blazel's childhood had been. The glorious sight of him fighting the wolves came back to her. He'd become a powerful warrior. Now, if he'd become a grown man and take her to his bed.

Chapter 18

Blazel swore at the tracks in the mud, unconsciously rubbing the scar on his face. Quite a few fresh sabertiger prints littered the ground. If a pride was stalking them, they were in trouble. The huge felines fiercely protected their territory and weren't afraid of humans, only the much larger Gryphons. He'd hoped their party was large enough to deter the cats, but the various paw prints proved him wrong. He scouted the area around the cave while he waited for the others to get ready to leave.

Jaehaas came out and joined him. "What be the matter?"

"Sabertigers." Blazel stopped his prowling. "Several of them were out here last night."

"But none of us saw anything during our watch."

"They can be quite stealthy and are intelligent." He pointed to the print by his foot. "This is as close as they approached the cave. Nobody would have seen them."

Jaehaas measured the distance between the print and the cave with his eyes. "At this distance, no one would see them. I certainly didn't."

"Hey, what are you looking at?" Aistrun loped toward them. "Oh, those don't look good. Are we going to have problems?"

"We could," Blazel answered. "If we seem weak or have stragglers, they'll attack. Therefore, we need to make sure to stay together, no spreading out like we've been doing. Stick close to your lady today. Don't let her out of your sight."

Aistrun snorted. "That will work with Chariel and Wisah, but Rizelya? Not a chance, unless you want her angry at you."

"Better angry and safe." Blazel crossed his arms over his chest, scowling.

"This is a Red we're talking about, and not any fighter, but an alpha," Aistrun said. "And she could fight circles around you."

"Ahem."

Blazel whirled. Rizelya stood behind him, hands on her hips, her eyes narrowed, and her mouth in a tight line.

"So what is it you're not going to tell me?" Rizelya spat out. "And guard me like I was a fluff with no brain and incapable of taking care of myself?"

Blazel shuffled his feet under her glare. His movement drew her attention to the paw print.

"Oh! A sabertiger's, right?" She scanned the area. "It appears a few were here last night, just out of our sight. Crafty beasts."

Rizelya stepped closer to Blazel, grabbed the neck of his shirt, and twisted. She was a full foot shorter than he was, so she had to stand on her toes to reach. But it didn't stop her from slowly cutting off his air. *By the Warrior, she's strong.*

"Let me remind you, cur," she ground out as she twisted, "who is the alpha and leader of this little expedition. I am. Not you. You will tell me everything so I can keep all of us safe. Do you understand?"

Blazel nodded. She released him, and he bent over, gasping for breath.

"I told you, man," Aistrun whispered to Blazel, "you don't want to make her angry at you. You're lucky she didn't use her helbraught on you."

Blazel stood, rubbing his neck. She hadn't hurt him, only showed him who was in charge.

"Is it safe for us to leave?" The anger had fled from Rizelya's face.

"We should be, if we stay close together and show we're not afraid, and therefore not prey." He studied the multiple tracks again and their relation to the cave. "I think they were curious about who had invaded their territory. At least, I hope that's all they were doing."

"Jaehaas, keep your bow handy today," Rizelya said. "Aistrun and Blazel take turns running in your wolf forms. Your senses are more acute as a wolf."

"What about going in our warrior form?" Aistrun asked.

Rizelya looked the two of them over. "I suspect Blazel can shift quickly between forms, but what about you, Aistrun? How fast can you shift into your warrior?"

Fur boiled over his arms, and bones moved under his skin. A moment later, Aistrun stood in his warrior form. He quickly reversed the process and stood as a man, panting, and with sweat shining on his face. "I've been practicing."

"Then run as warriors. It should be pretty obvious to the sabertigers you are the greater predator." Rizelya gazed over her shoulder toward the cave. "Keep a close watch on the girls. Keep them safe. I'll take care of myself." She glowered at Blazel before stalking back to the cave.

"I'll take first shift," Blazel said when she was out of hearing range.

"Good choice," Aistrun said. "It'll give her some time to cool off."

"It appears the ladies be ready to go." Jaehaas flicked his tail and trotted over to help Wisah secure the packs on the multas.

The sabertigers continued to track them as they rode ever northward. The trees thinned, and the ground grew rockier. The felines leaped from rock to rock above the trail the group followed. Jaehaas had fired a warning shot at them earlier, and now they always stayed out of his range. So far, they hadn't done anything more than keep pace.

The path, wide enough for two horses, switchbacked up the mountain. Aistrun joined Blazel in his warrior form. Rizelya kept her helbraught in her hands, guiding her horse with her knees. When they topped the ridge and dropped back down, Blazel relaxed. On this side of the pass, they were in Gryphon territory. The pride should stay on the other side.

He and Aistrun remained in their warrior form as they traveled away from the pass. Blazel's shoulder blades twitched as if someone were watching him, and he kept an eye on the surrounding trees but didn't see or smell any sabertigers.

They should soon spot Gryphons floating high in the air. The shadows stretched as the sun sank lower on the horizon.

Rizelya directed her horse to pace next to him. "Blazel, is there a safe place to stop for the night? It's getting late."

"I know, look for cave... there!" He pointed with a claw at a black hole not far up the mountain. "Wait. Check." He clambered to it, rocks skittering down the side. A quick examination of the cave showed no critters had claimed it recently. Standing at the edge, he waved for the others to join him.

The horses scrambled up the slope, rocks slipping and sliding underneath them. The multas also scampered up, their large platter-like feet easily gripping the rocks.

Aistrun lumbered over the edge and sank to the ground in front of the cave, puffing. "Whew!" Shivers ran through his body, and after a few moments, his human form sprawled across the ledge. "I've never stayed this long in warrior form. Please tell me this cave has hot pools in it."

Not sensing any danger, Blazel allowed his warrior form to flow away from him. His change was painless and effortless, like it should be. He stretched, relieving the tingles of the change, and reacquainting himself with his natural form.

"Sorry, this one only has a fresh-water spring for drinking."

The horses taken care of, the women exited the cave and searched for firewood. Blazel started to go after them, then stopped when Rizelya glared at him and raised her helbraught. He wondered if he'd made an irrevocable error that morning. She hadn't spoken to him at all, except as necessary.

The next day, they crossed over the rocky mountain cap and dropped into the tree-line. Blazel watched the air above them, hoping to catch sight of a Gryphon. Finally, at mid-morning, he spotted a large shape high overhead.

"Look!" Blazel yelled. "A Gryphon."

Rizelya put a hand up to shade her eyes. "Really? All I see is a dark splotch."

Another blot joined the first, and then another and another, until six humongous forms circled above them. Blazel waved his arms to catch their attention.

"They didn't notice us." Rizelya's shoulders drooped as the Gryphons disappeared from sight.

"No, we must have been too far away. A scout flight will see us eventually," Blazel assured her. "We're in their territory now. They won't let us wander for long without stopping us."

The trail they followed took them through a deep, narrow canyon. Thick bushes hung on the canyon walls. The horses sank into the soft sand with every step. High above in the cliff, dark cave openings loomed.

Something darted from a cave and dived at Blazel. The creature had a flat face with a pug nose, pointy ears, small eyes, and tusks sticking out of its mouth. The sparsely furred body was about four feet long. Leathery wings flapped nearly soundlessly. Sharp talons sped toward him.

"Baethor!" he shouted. He ducked and felt the rush of the hideous creature's wings above his head. Another one streaked at him. He pulled his helstrablade from its sheath and stabbed its belly. Dark green ichor sizzled on his face, burning him.

"'Ware their ichor," he yelled. "It's acid."

Suddenly, a fire shield shimmered above him. He whirled around to find it surrounding the whole group. When the baethor hit it, flames flared, driving them away. Dozens of creatures flapped above and around them, just outside the shield.

"I don't think they're going to leave us alone," Rizelya cried out as a beast slammed into the shield.

"No, they won't." Blazel cringed as another creature hit the shield. "They're single-minded. They won't leave until either they or we are dead."

"You need to shift. I'll put a shield around the girls and horses. And then we fight."

Blazel and Aistrun slid off their horses, throwing their reins to Chariel and Wisah. In moments, two warriors towered above the women. Blazel snarled. Aistrun howled. The creatures flew back and bumped together in confusion. Blazel dropped his jaw open in a grin. *Sound affects them.*

He howled again. A high-pitched tone weaved through it. He let his howl go and turned to gape at Chariel. She wasn't precisely singing—the sound she made wasn't pretty. The baethor flapped in agitation, many crashing into each other or the canyon walls. Wisah joined Chariel in making the eerie tones. Rizelya grinned like a mad-woman and dropped the shield in front of the men.

The beasts who weren't disoriented attacked the men, screeching with anger. One dove straight at Blazel. He swiped his claws at it, tearing a long gash into its belly. Another one flapped into him. He snarled and sank his powerful jaws into its neck. *Gagh! I forgot how awful they taste.* He shook his head, flinging the foul thing away from him. Rizelya's helbraught glowed with orange and red flames dancing on the blade, dead baethor piled around her feet. Creatures burst into flame from Jaehaas's flaming arrows.

No matter how many baethor they killed, more seemed to come at them. More bodies littered the canyon floor than the original swarm. Ichor covered Blazel's fur, and fatigue made his movements sluggish. Aistrun appeared to be in the same condition. Rizelya kicked carcasses to the side so she could move. Chariel and Wisah had quit toning and sagged over the necks of their horses. Somehow, Rizelya kept the fire shield over them even as she fought. Grimly, Jaehaas nocked one of his few remaining fire arrows. They couldn't keep this up much longer.

Rizelya kicked a creature's body out of her way. The baethor seemed to be a never-ending swarm. They had killed hundreds and were still being attacked. Fighting these relatively small creatures was different from fighting the Malvers' monsters, although their ichor was as acidic. After suffering the first burn, she'd wrapped a fire shield around herself. She wished Dehali were with them. They could use her air Talent. As she stabbed her helbraught blade into another creature, she vowed she'd never allow someone to break up her squad-pack again. She needed all of her people.

Rizelya couldn't hold the weakening fire shield around Chariel and Wisah much longer. Blazel and Aistrun continued to valiantly swipe creatures from the air, even though they seemed to be moving through thick mud. Jaehaas pulled his bow back and loosed another arrow. Only a few remained in his quiver. They needed to end this fight soon or risk losing. She gritted her teeth and swung determinedly again at a swooping creature. *I'm not ready to die!*

A deafening screech echoed off the canyon walls. A huge shadow blocked the sun. *Sweet Mother, what now?*

An enormous Gryphon soared above them. His tawny feline body was fourteen feet long, excluding his tail. His head and wings were those of an eagle, and he glowed. The light in the canyon dimmed from his humongous wings. He had to have a nearly forty-foot wingspan. He snapped them back to dive. The thunderous blast made Rizelya cringe. In her shock, she lost her tenuous hold on the shield over the girls, who threw their hands over their heads as they realized they were now exposed.

"Are they here to help us?" she yelled at Blazel, who wore a huge grin.

He nodded.

The baethor immediately broke off from attacking Rizelya and the others to face the menace above them. A smaller shape streaked past the behemoth, this one a hawk-like Gryphon. As he neared the creatures, the nimbus of light surrounding him exploded into flames. Flames shot from the Gryphon, igniting the baethor, which fell from the sky, turning into ash before it hit the ground. Several more Gryphons entered the fight with claws and fire.

Rizelya and the men ran to regroup with Chariel and Wisah. The horses pranced, their eyes white with fear. Rizelya grabbed Kymaya, Jezhan, and Lighzel's reins and held them tight. The poor horses could be around Malvers' monsters without fear, but the strange Gryphons, who were big enough to eat them, terrified them. Jaehaas finally stared each horse and multa in the eye for several long moments, communicating telepathically with them. After which, they settled down. Although Tejen—the only stallion—still pawed the ground and gazed warily at the Gryphons.

Rizelya turned her attention back to the sky. She and the others gaped at the magnificent sight of Gryphons soaring and flaming. After the first smoking baethor crashed inches from her feet, Rizelya tried to reestablish the fire shield around them. She was so tired it took several long milcrons for her to manage the magic.

Soon, the Gryphons destroyed the creatures, and Rizelya released her shield. She sagged against Kymaya's side. The horse snorted at the unusual stench wafting off Rizelya.

A hawk-like Gryphon floated to the ground and settled his brown and white wings over his back. He had sandy-brown feathers along the back of his head, and his chest was creamy white, flecked with light brown and black feathers. An orange band covered the upper part of his beak and continued across his cheeks. His feline body was dark brown.

"My friend, Graak." Blazel grinned, stretching out his arms.

The Gryphon padded over to Blazel, his wings bobbing as he walked. When he stood in front of Blazel, tilting his head in the peculiar way birds did, they were nearly the same height.

Blazel folded his arms across his chest and allowed the Gryphon to examine him.

"Graak!" Blazel smiled and dropped his arms to his side. The Gryphon cocked his head. "Old friend!"

The Gryphon studied Rizelya's group for a long moment, then he looked up. Rizelya blanched in fear. Another Gryphon—the same type as Graak—was diving toward them, talons outstretched. Graak opened his beak and let out a shrill cry. The other Gryphon back winged furiously as it pulled up from its dive, before it turned and flew in a different direction.

Rizelya kept an eye on the other Gryphons, who were checking the baethor bodies, ensuring they were dead. The behemoth continued to circle above the canyon. It was too narrow for him to land, especially with everyone milling around.

Blazel?

The unknown voice in her mind startled Rizelya. She decided the rich baritone was Graak. From the expressions on the others' faces, they had heard him too. The Posairs mind-spoke to each other on rare occasions, such as in the middle of a battle. It appeared to be the Gryphons' usual communication method.

It's been a long time, my friend, Graak said. *Not that I'm not happy to see you, but what in Crone's fires are you doing here? It's a good thing our scouts saw you. You were almost baethor dinner.*

"Hmf, we do okay." Blazel looked pointedly at the bodies strewn around them. He motioned for Rizelya to join him. "Alpha Rizelya."

Rizelya gazed into the Gryphon's face. His sharp beak was slightly open in what, she hope, was a grin. Not knowing how else to greet him, she bowed, keeping her eyes on him. He dipped his head in return.

"We're grateful you arrived when you did," Rizelya said aloud, uncomfortable using so much mind-speech. "My companions and I have been searching for you."

I like her, Graak said. *She shows proper respect, unlike you, Blazel.* He turned toward the rest. *And you've brought a centaur and two priestesses. How odd. I recall a warning from our Silver Beaks that when a White Priestess appears in our aerie, trouble is near. What is amiss, my friend?*

"Chariel, friend, argh—" Blazel snapped his jaws closed and made a frantic movement toward Rizelya.

She took over the introductions for Blazel. "This is Chariel, Blazel's friend. She had a prophecy about you, well, all of us, in one of her visions, so the Supreme sent us here. We need your help."

My help? Or the Gryphons' help?

"Both."

Graak glanced up at the behemoth guarding the canyon opening. *This isn't a safe place to talk. This canyon will be swarming soon with other baethor coming to eat their dead. Follow me.*

He bent his powerful hind legs and leaped into the air, pushing strongly down with his wings. Rizelya felt a jolt of magic, and the Gryphon was aloft.

"Found Gryphons," Blazel announced needlessly.

"Or they found us," Rizelya said. "They are everything, and more, I expected from living myths. Will they help us?"

"Graak, yes. Others?" Blazel shrugged. "Don't know."

Rizelya put a foot into Kymaya's stirrup and bounced to hop into the saddle—and didn't go anywhere. She hung with her foot in the stirrup, panting with exhaustion and embarrassment. Blazel didn't say a word as he stepped behind her and lifted her easily onto her mare. He handed her Lighzel's reins, and she tied them to her saddle. Chariel had already tied Aistrun's horse to her saddle. Wisah held the multas' leads, and they followed placidly behind Tejen.

The group exited the canyon, following the Gryphons flying above them. Rizelya slumped in her saddle. Chariel and Wisah had recovered enough that they were no longer draped across their horses' necks, but they weren't in much better shape than she was. Blazel and Aistrun, still in their warrior forms, walked to the side of her, their feet dragging in the dirt. They were both too covered in gore to shift back to human without washing first. She watched Graak and the other Gryphons floating in the sky. *I hope where they're taking us is close. None of us can travel far.*

Chapter 19

The sand dragged at Blazel's feet. He trudged forward, concentrating on putting one large, clawed foot in front of the other. Aistrun stumbled. Blazel reached out to steady him and nearly fell himself. *This isn't working. I'm too tired, and the Gryphons will protect us.* He let go of the magic holding him in warrior form and slid into his wolf form. The baethor ichor was still on his fur and away from his body so he wouldn't get burned, but now he could walk better on four feet.

Aistrun looked down at him in a stupor. A moment later, a red-gold wolf stood where Aistrun had been. His tongue lolled from his mouth, and his head drooped. He yipped and started following the horses again.

They moved faster after the two men shifted to four feet. The sand gave way to a rocky downgrade, which dropped into a lush valley where spring was in full bloom. Flowers dotted a meadow of bright green grass, and the trees sported blossoms and the buds of new leaves. Blazel's head drooped as he followed the trail, unable to appreciate the beauty around him. When they reached the meadow, he and Aistrun stopped and rolled in the grass, scraping off some of the dried ichor from their fur.

Beyond the meadow, huge trees soared into the sky. Their broad crowns linked together, forming a canopy above the forest. The Gryphons flew to the trees, landed in them, and promptly disappeared—even the behemoth.

Graak alighted near them. *We'll stay here for the night. Follow me.* He led the group into a large clearing.

The trunks formed a ring of huge pillars, and the branches entwined high overhead created platforms, creaking in the slight breeze. Across the clearing, several Gryphons dipped their beaks into a creek. Steam rose from a large pool near where the Gryphons were drinking. A few feet from where Blazel and his group stood, another, smaller pool steamed. Blazel yearned to wash the remaining baethor ichor off his fur and shift into his human form.

You can make camp here, Graak said. *After you've cleaned up, rest and eat. Tonight, you'll tell us why the Supreme sent you.* He leaped into the air and flew to the platforms.

Blazel loped to the hot pool and jumped in. He shifted to warrior form, grabbed a handful of sand from the pool's bottom to scrub his pelt.

Aistrun yipped and splashed into the pool. He dunked under the water, came back up, water sluicing from his body. After shifting into his human form, he removed his clothes, throwing the sodden mess to shore. "There's nothing like getting clean after a monster fight. Well, food is good, and sex is even better."

Blazel laughed. He finished scrubbing his pelt, rinsed, then shifted to his human form. He tossed his soaking clothing to the edge. It surprised him how fast he was becoming comfortable being naked around the others.

"You be hogging the hot water all day?" Jaehaas's front hoof pawed the ground. "The rest of us want to wash the stink off too."

"Sorry." Blazel stepped out, and immediately hugged his arms close, shivering from the cold so hard his teeth chattered.

"Here." Wisah held a towel out to him. She had another one in her hand for Aistrun, and a pile sat beside her feet.

"Thanks!" Blazel snatched the towel and hurriedly wrapped it around his hips. Someone had taken his packs off Lighzel. He raced to them and quickly pulled on warm clothes.

After he dressed, he noticed Chariel struggling to raise a tent. He jogged over to help her. Baethor gunk hadn't covered her and Wisah. Rizelya's fire shield had protected them from it.

But dark circles bruised Chariel's eyes, and her hands trembled as she worked.

"Is it always that bad?" she asked, a tremor in her voice.

Blazel's forehead crinkled in confusion, then raised his eyebrows. "Oh! It was your first battle, wasn't it?"

She nodded, her lips quivering. He gathered her into his arms, and she burst into tears. He held her for a long time. Chariel had grown up in an idyllic environment, untouched by violence. The biennial alpha competitions were the only fighting she had ever seen, and no one was seriously injured or killed in them. Chariel had never even seen any livestock slaughtered.

He glanced over Chariel's shoulder. Jaehaas held Wisah, sobbing into his chest. Although she'd spent time in Strunland Keep and had witnessed fighters return, she hadn't been part of a battle before. Today was an initiation for both of them into the life most Posairs lived. If they were going to remain outside the Sanctuary, they would need to get used to it. If all the signs were true, more—and worse—battles were coming.

The snap of canvas broke into the interlude. Aistrun and Rizelya worked to finish setting up the tents. Rizelya's wet hair dripped down her back. Instead of red leathers, she wore a dark green quilted tunic, which set off her brown eyes, and wool trousers in a lighter green.

Chariel wiped away her tears. "We've work to do. I can't stay protected in your arms forever."

Blazel hugged her tighter before letting her go. Chariel staggered to the fire someone, probably Rizelya, had lit, knelt in front of it, and pulled items from the food pack. Wisah hurried over to help her, and together, they worked to prepare their evening meal. Soon, the scent of savory stew and baking pan bread filled the clearing.

When they finished eating and cleaning up, Graak glided into their camp.

What happened to your head feathers, Blazel? Graak asked.

Blazel put a hand to his hair and picked up a loc. "It seemed easier to keep them than shave my head. I like them now."

It will take some getting used to. Graak peered at Blazel's hair, lifted a long loc with his nimble talons, then dropped it. *So what messes have you gotten into since leaving us?*

"Well, I've spent the last three years living in the swamps," Blazel said.

What? Why would you go to those nasty places?

Blazel frowned and pointed at Chariel. "She sent me. I get in more trouble because of her. She sent me to the Deep Mountains when you found me."

I remember. You were in sad shape. I never did see anyone less suited for the mountains than you—or less capable of surviving on their own. Graak reached out and brushed a knuckle along the scars on Blazel's cheek. *At least you don't have more scars.*

"Ha!" Blazel tugged off his boot, pulled up his pant leg, and pointed to the scar circling his ankle. "This is from a swamp plant that tried to eat me. This—" he lifted his tunic to show the two puncture marks on his ribs "—was from an angulete, a flying snake." He heard Rizelya's indrawn breath.

Blazel put his clothing to rights. "Other than the five years I stayed with you, Graak, and the few short visits to the Sanctuary, I've lived alone and managed to stay alive. There are twisted beasts in the swamps worse than the baethor, and I fought every type of them. I am quite capable of surviving." Blazel crossed his arms in front of his chest and glared at the fire.

"Graak, we're here to ask for your help." Rizelya leaned forward, resting her elbows on her knees. "Down below, there's a new Malvers' monster, one that directs the others. In my visions, I've seen a woman who controls them. The Supreme said she was a Malvers."

Malvers! Graak reared onto his hindquarters, wings flapping. Sparks from the fire flew up. He threw back his head and warbled a frightening shriek.

Blazel grimaced. The Gryphons had long memories, and they told stories about the foul people they'd fought in the Great War. He now believed the hated people in their stories and the Malvers were the same. He'd wanted to gently introduce the subject.

Graak's cry caused a ruckus on the platforms above. Dark shapes leaped and zoomed to the clearing. Within moments, every Gryphon in the camp sat around their fire, tails swishing in agitation. A huge eagle-type Gryphon stalked toward Blazel and his friends. The firelight gleamed on the gold feathers of his head and chest. Gold tinged the edges of his wings. His shoulders were level with Blazel's head. He loomed over them.

What is the meaning of this? he boomed. *Where are the hated Malvers?*

Tell him, Rizelya, Graak said, dipping his head low. *This is Moraak. His father is our king.*

Rizelya stood and bowed low to the prince. "Moraak, I am deeply honored to meet you. I am saddened we could not have met under better circumstances. We've come to renew the ancient alliance between our people and yours."

Moraak reared onto his hind legs, spread his wings, and fire burst from his throat. *We'll never be slaves again!*

He dropped back down and stalked to Rizelya. He lifted his front foot and jabbed a huge talon with eight-inch claws at her chest. It impressed Blazel when she didn't retreat. Her hands clenched into tight fists.

There is no alliance, girl, for us to renew. We had no choice in the things we did for our masters. We fought who they told us to fight. Horrible monsters. The feathers on his head raised.

"We're no strangers to fighting monsters," Rizelya said. "We've been fighting them since the end of the war. They are being controlled by a woman, a horrible woman. She uses the monsters to kill. She eats the victims' death, and with each death, she and her people eat, they become stronger. This is what we've come to ask you to help us stop."

How do you know this? The Malvers were exiled and died.

"They didn't die. She invades my dreams. Shall I describe her for you?" At Moraak's nod, Rizelya continued. "She has pale, gray skin, dark charcoal-gray hair, and black eyes. They don't have any pupils. Instead of fingers, she has long, needle-like claws. She's starving and now is extremely gaunt."

This is how we remember the Malvers. Moraak's tail flipped in agitation. He hunkered onto his back paws and resettled his wings. *I will hear your story.*

Aistrun stood and bowed to Moraak. "So you shall. It started one day, just like any other. Our platoon left Strunland Keep to destroy a nearby monster nest. To our surprise, it was three times the typical size. It disgorged the normal janacks and brechas, only to reveal a new janack. This one outsized the others and had an odd protrusion on its head. A brave Red—" Aistrun pointed at Rizelya "—attacked the strange janack. Much to all of our consternation, we discovered the only way to kill the beast was to explode it."

Aistrun's voice fell into a storyteller's cadence, and everyone around the clearing focused on him. Blazel listened as raptly as the rest of the crowd as Aistrun told the story of his and Rizelya's mad journey across Strunlair Province and their many monster fights. They hissed at Keandran's cruelty and clapped at Rizelya's ingenuity in utilizing all the Talents. The pile of firewood was low when Aistrun came to the end of his story, when they arrived at the Sanctuary.

Wisah told them about Chariel's prophecy. "I'm sure the hawk is you, Graak," she said. "The horse is obviously Jaehaas, here. We need you. We need your people."

"There is something dark coming to our world." Chariel shuddered. "It brings madness, and if any of us are to survive, we need all of us to fight." A silvery film covered her eyes, and her voice changed, becoming deeper. "It comes! Beware the skies. Danger flies on metal wings. Stolen souls to never return to the Mother's Womb. Stop! Stop the madness! Aaahh." Chariel gripped her head in her hands, groaning, and then collapsed. Aistrun caught her and held her in his arms.

At her words, a chill shook Blazel, and he remembered his strange dreams of flaming meteors bringing blood and death. Shaking it off, he strode around the fire to stand in front of the huge Gryphon.

"Moraak, you heard her," Blazel said. "That was a prophecy. You and your people are needed. This isn't going to be a fight for only the Posairs, but for everyone living in Lairheim."

Moraak cocked his head to the side, looking away from Blazel and the other Posairs. Several long milcrons later, he turned back to them. *I can't deny the words of the prophet, Chariel. Danger is coming to our world. But —* he held up a talon *—this is not a decision I can make. It is for my father to* *decide if we are to join you in this new war. You'll come with us to Alkaak and tell him what you have seen. Rest now, we leave at dawn.*

Moraak gave a sharp cry, and the Gryphons swooped to the tree platforms. Moraak and Graak remained on the ground.

I will do all I can to persuade my father, Moraak said. *Our mystics have also seen trouble coming.* He pushed with his powerful hind legs and leaped into the air. A swoop of his massive wings stirred the leaves in the clearing and startled the horses.

It is a great privilege, Graak said, *to visit our city and talk to our king. No Posair has ever been permitted to enter Alkaak. During the journey, I will teach you the proper protocol.*

"I'm honored." Blazel placed his right hand over his heart and dipped his head in a small bow. "Even I haven't been to Alkaak. In the five years I lived with the Gryphon flight, they never took me to the city. They made me stay in the outer camps, like this one."

"I be excited to see it," Jaehaas said. "What a great adventure to tell my people."

"How far is it to Alkaak?" Blazel asked.

For us, only two days. For you, on your horses, four or five. Sleep now. Morning comes quickly. Graak crouched, then leaped. With a few wing strokes, he disappeared into the night.

Rizelya stood, yawning. "Let's get some sleep. It sounds like we have more long days in the saddle ahead of us." She turned on her heel, strode to the women's tent, and crawled inside.

Huddled under her blankets and shivering, Rizelya wished she could convince Blazel to share her bed with her. During the night, Aistrun had crept into the women's tent and snuggled with Chariel. He spent most of his time with the beautiful Gray. Rizelya tried to block out the quiet sounds of their lovemaking. She turned over and caught the longing in her niece's eyes.

"I can't ever have that with Jaehaas," Wisah whispered. "Riz, I'm a White. I'm not supposed to fall in love."

Rizelya snorted, crawled out of her covers, and scurried into Wisah's. "Who said you couldn't?" Rizelya quietly asked, nose-to-nose. "You're still a woman, and the Goddess doesn't expect celibacy from Her priestesses."

"Yes, I'm allowed to have a lover, but not be in love. I've dedicated my life and given my love to the Goddess. How am I supposed to split it with Jaehaas? I'm falling in love with him, but we can't be together. After all of this is done, I'll remain in the Sanctuary, and he'll return to the plains." Tears trickled down Wisah's face. She picked up a lock of creamy white hair and held it out. "I can't change who I am. I was born a White and will always be one."

"And Jaehaas will always be a centaur. Don't give up before you've even given love a chance. There are temples in Haaslair Province. You could serve in one of them and be near Jaehaas. You're not the first, nor will you be the last, White Priestess to fall in love. Things will work out. Take this time to get to know him and then decide later what you want to do with your life. With everything Chariel's been saying, we may not even survive to have a later. So love now while you have the opportunity."

Wisah sniffled. "The same to you. I've seen how you look at Blazel."

"I would, if I could get him to notice me."

"Oh, he looks."

"That's the problem. He just looks. If he doesn't do more soon, I'll go crazy and jump him."

Wisah laughed. "Give him some time. He and Chariel had a much different childhood than we did. They grew up in the cloisters."

"Hasn't stopped her." Rizelya threw her head back, indicating the couple behind them.

A strange warbling sounded through the clearing.

Rizelya sat up, her eyes darting, searching for the danger. They hadn't placed a ward last night, lulled by the safety of the Gryphon flight. "What's that?"

Outside the tent, wings rustled as Graak landed. *Rise and shine,* he called out, his mind-voice startling Rizelya. The Gryphons' ability to mind-speak with anyone, and in the Posarian language, still disconcerted her. Their spoken language consisted of clicks, screeches, and hisses. *Time to leave.*

Aistrun's head poked out of Chariel's blankets. He smirked at Rizelya and Wisah. "I'm already up and shining."

Rizelya rolled her eyes and groaned. She gave Wisah a quick hug before crawling out. She pulled on her knee-length, thick woolen navy-blue tunic and woolen trousers over her red riding leathers. If the day warmed, she'd remove the extra layers. After dressing, she folded her bedroll and gathered her things into her bag.

Throwing on her warm crimson-red cloak, given to her by Keshanal, she stepped outside the tent. A gray day greeted her. Fog covered the ground and dripped from the trees overhead. It spun in eddies around her feet as she walked. Blazel fed wood to the coals of their fire. He smiled at her. He hadn't shaved for a few days, and the beginnings of a beard dusted his face. She waved at him and sauntered across the clearing to find a tree for her morning toilet.

When Rizelya returned, everyone in her group huddled in front of the fire, including Graak. Wisah's thick white cloak seemed to radiate light in the fog. Jaehaas knelt beside her with his arm around her shoulders. As she leaned her head against his chest, Jaehaas gazed down at her fondly. Rizelya's heart warmed to see her niece taking her advice.

Chariel sat in front of Aistrun in her dark, muted gray cloak. He encircled her in his arms and rested his chin on the top of her head. He laughed at something she said. Her friend was happier than Rizelya had ever seen him.

Chariel brushed a strand of charcoal-gray hair away from her face. It, and her dark-gray eyes, bound her to the Sanctuary. All babies born with those characteristics were taken to the Sanctuary, and they never left. At first, Rizelya was certain, these children had appeared too much like the Posairs' ancient enemy, the Malvers, to be allowed to remain in the general population. As time passed, it became a tradition.

But Rizelya doubted Chariel, after experiencing a taste of freedom, would go meekly back into the Sanctuary to hide away again. And this development with Aistrun made it even more unlikely. Aistrun would fight for Chariel and not allow tradition to interfere with their love.

Rizelya inhaled the luscious scent of taevo and the earthy porridge bubbling over the fire.

"You're in time." Blazel held out a mug to her. His eyes crinkled at the corners from his smile. "Here."

Rizelya reached for the mug, and Blazel's fingers caressed hers for a moment before he let go. Inside, she did a jig of happiness. Perhaps with the others becoming lovers, Blazel would catch the hint. He passed out mugs of taevo to everyone else. Graak's nimble talons gripped the mug as he sipped the hot, stimulating drink. Blazel scooped porridge into bowls and handed them around.

I prefer meat to break my fast, Graak said as he declined the porridge. *I'll catch something along the way. It will be a long day of travel, and those grains wouldn't stick to me for long.*

Rizelya dropped her full spoon, spilling porridge, when the booming flap of Gryphons' wings filled the clearing. The platforms above them creaked, and a rustling of wings heralded dozens of Gryphons taking flight.

"They're leaving us!" She put her bowl aside and pushed to her feet. Hands on her hips, she glared at Graak.

No, Graak said, rearing slightly. His head feathers fluffed, making him appear taller. *I'm still here and so are most of our flight. Moraak is going ahead of us to tell the king of your coming. Your news won't please King Zorlaak. Better he hears it before you arrive. Safer, too.*

Rizelya sat back down and finished eating. Half an octar later, they'd folded the tents, loaded the baggage onto the multas, and saddled their horses. Kymaya stared at Graak with wide eyes and shied away from him. So did the other horses. Tejen stepped in front of Kymaya, his attention never leaving Graak. Kressy gazed at him for a long moment, bleated at him, and returned to her grazing. Rizelya heard a strange warbling sound. Puzzled, she looked around, finally realizing Graak was laughing.

Jaehaas whispered to each horse, but Kymaya snorted as if she didn't believe him. He said something else, and this time, Rizelya caught the edges of the images he sent to Kymaya. He attempted to convince her the large predatory bird in front of her was a friend.

I don't eat the horses of friends, Graak said in a placating voice.

Rizelya noticed the qualifier. Apparently, so did Kymaya, since she continued to shy away from Graak.

Okay, Graak said, holding a talon over his chest, *I won't eat any horses while you're with us, nor will my companions. Satisfied?*

Kymaya nodded her head and let Rizelya climb into the saddle. Tejen still watched Graak but allowed Wisah to mount on his back. The other horses weren't as stubborn, and Blazel, Aistrun, and Chariel had already mounted.

We'll scout ahead of you. Graak hunched, preparing to take off. *Follow us.*

"Remember, old friend," Blazel said, "we're on the ground and have trees and boulders to go around. Try to find us a path we can traverse."

I remember. Graak leaped into the air, and again Rizelya felt the push of magic as he lifted off. Watching him climb above the trees, she decided the Gryphons used magic to help them fly. Their bodies were too massive for just their wings to hold them aloft.

She guided Kymaya from the clearing, found a trail heading in the same direction as the Gryphons, and followed it. They didn't have to avoid the tree's high branches, and the path curved around the huge trunks.

Late in the afternoon, they broke from the trees and rode into a wide valley. The melting snow made the ground wet and muddy. Graak and his flight flew over them in great lazy circles. Rizelya urged Kymaya into a gallop across the valley, praying the horses didn't catch a hoof in a hole and tumble. They crossed without mishap and charged back into the forest.

Rizelya pushed the group hard, stopping only long enough to rest the horses. It reminded her of the mad dash through Strunlair Province a few short chedans ago. It seemed as if all her travels now were rushed.

The huge trees surrounding the clearing they stayed in for the night provided roosts for the Gryphons. The next morning, they rode off again before the sun's first rays brightened the world. They continued the relentless pace for two more days.

On the third evening when they stopped, steam rose from a hot spring, forming a mist. Exhausted, Rizelya slid from her horse. Jaehaas lifted Wisah from Tejen's saddle. She whimpered, unused to such a grueling ride. Aistrun helped Chariel, while Rizelya and Blazel set up camp. They fell into an easy rhythm, and soon, they'd raised the tents, lit a fire, and put food over it to heat.

Graak backwinged to land in the clearing. The wind of his wings tossed sparks and dirt into the air. He settled by the fire. *We'll arrive at Alkaak tomorrow. It isn't far from here. Rest well tonight, my friends, and take advantage of the hot springs. You'll be presented to our king.*

While they ate, he continued, as he had every night, to drill them in the proper protocols of attending the king. Rizelya ducked as Graak lashed out his wing to thump Blazel on the head.

No, that isn't correct, Graak grumbled. *Again. More carefully and don't mangle the words.*

"I thought he understands Posarian?" Blazel rubbed the back of his head.

He does.

"Then why do we have to greet him in your language?"

Because it's protocol! You once knew our language. Why is it so difficult for you now?

"It's been a long time since I've spoken it or heard it, Graak," Blazel said. "It isn't easy for us to pronounce."

Graak pointed his beak at Chariel. *You, say it.*

"Oolk keee shree neekalaaak." Chariel dropped her head.

Rizelya and the others stared at Chariel. She had even managed all the little screeches and clicks correctly.

Now, you try, Blazel, Graak ordered.

Blazel again mangled the words. So did Jaehaas, only he was worse because he added whinnies and snorts like a horse. Aistrun said the words right, but missed all the screeches and clicks.

Chariel, work with him, Graak growled in frustration. *At least one of you must greet King Zorlaak with the proper words.*

"Why can't Chariel do it?" Rizelya asked. "She can already say it correctly."

Graak sighed in a whistle of breath. *Unlike you, in our society, only males are leaders. The king will expect a male to be leading your expedition. It is good Aistrun is the one who butchers our language the least. He is your Silver Beak, your storyteller. We value our Silver Beaks and listen to their wisdom. Our king will give him honor.*

Aistrun threw his shoulders back and preened. Rizelya gazed at the sky, shaking her head. He'd be insufferable until she smacked some sense into him. She listened as he said the greeting over and over, with Chariel and Graak correcting him. After several such corrections, Aistrun growled, stood, and paced around the campfire, muttering the phrase under his breath. He made two circuits, then stopped in front of Graak. Aistrun bowed, his arms held out, holding his cloak to make it appear like wings behind him. He cocked his head to the side and recited the greeting. Graak's beak opened wide in what passed for a grin.

Well done, Aistrun, Graak warbled. *Now, the king won't eat you.*

Aistrun quickly straightened, his arm going furry, and his sharp claws extended as he lunged toward Graak. Rizelya hadn't known he could shift only one part of his body. Only the very skilled—mostly old men like Histrun—were able to accomplish the feat.

Blazel leaped across the fire and put his hand over Aistrun's. "Easy, friend. He was teasing you."

Graak shrugged his ruffled feathers back down. *The king does not tolerate foolishness. This way, he will listen to you before making any rash decisions. We can only hope he has taken Moraak's warning seriously. Get some sleep. We'll leave later in the morning than usual.* Graak leaped into the dark for his roost in the trees.

Chapter 20

The tweeting of birds going about their morning routines woke Blazel. In the gloomy light, he made out Jaehaas, still sleeping. His soft snores filled the tent. Aistrun was gone—as he'd been the last few days—staying in the women's tent with Chariel. Blazel grimaced, recalling Aistrun's satisfied smirk as he'd exited with his arm wrapped around Chariel's shoulders. Jaehaas and Wisah were spending quite a bit of time together, too.

Rizelya's beautiful smile came to him, and her luscious body as she sauntered away from him. Simple lust didn't draw him to her, but her intelligence, her quick wit, and her loyalty to her friends. Only his shyness, and his vow, kept them apart. He'd vowed only to have sex with someone he loved. And he was falling for the feisty Red. The one kiss he'd exchanged with her made him want her even more. His manhood stiffened as he thought about her.

Groaning, he crawled out of his bedroll and rummaged in his bag for clean clothes. He hustled toward the hot pool near their camp. Across the clearing, Graak and the other Gryphons splashed in another, larger steaming pool. Graak sprawled out in the water, his wings wide, while smaller Gryphons cleaned his feathers and fur. His friend had climbed in the hierarchy since he'd left. Blazel chuckled to himself as he continued toward the Posairs' pool.

Blazel shed his clothes and quickly slid into the hot water. He soaped down and rinsed. Now clean, he tipped his head back and floated. His fantasies about being with Rizelya paraded through his mind.

He had been floating for several milcrons when he heard a soft, "Oh, my!" He flipped over, nearly drowning himself. Rizelya stood at the pool's edge, amusement dancing on her face. Behind her, Chariel and Wisah walked toward them. Blazel moved farther into the water until his chin rested on the surface. The heat of embarrassment rose to rival the water's temperature.

The women's light laughter floated to him. His face burned even hotter. Suddenly, his vision changed, and he paddled with four paws instead of treading the water with feet and hands. Without consciously willing it, he'd shifted to his wolf form, which he hadn't done since just before the paether attack nearly three chedans ago. All it took to ruin his control was getting embarrassed by the woman he longed for.

As the women undressed, he swam away from them toward some bushes and jumped out. He raced to where he'd left his clothing, snatched them in his teeth, and ran into the forest to find a secluded spot. After shaking the water from his fur, Blazel shifted back to human form and put on his clothes over his still-damp skin. Dressed, he hurried to the camp. Luckily, both Jaehaas and Aistrun were gone. He had the fire going and was cooking breakfast when Graak landed in the clearing.

"You've come up in the world, my friend." Blazel continued to stir the pot of porridge. "I saw you being preened."

Graak stretched his neck and fluffed his neck feathers. *I have. I'm now the flight leader. But I still end up finding strays, like you.*

"It's a good thing you do because I wouldn't be alive without you. Both times."

Two? What about the time with the skeaeter? I saved you then, too.

"Ha! I had it. It was almost dead when you arrived."

It had you wrapped in its antennae, squeezing you to death. "But I had nearly severed its head."

I'll give you that, my friend. Graak chuckled. *I still extricated you from it.*

Laughing, Blazel poured a cup of taevo for his friend.

Graak took it and settled on the ground, his tail curled around him, wings nestled along his back. *Do you trust this Rizelya? Is she telling the truth? Are the Malvers becoming active again after so many years?*

"The Supreme believes her."

Graak snorted.

"And so do I." Blazel looked away and said quietly, "I've seen what she has. On my way to the Sanctuary, I had a dream about a gaunt woman wanting me. When I woke up, I had been poisoned with Malvers' monster toxin." He shuddered and turned back to face Graak. "I believe it is the same woman who haunts Rizelya's dreams.

"The Malvers didn't die. Their monsters plague us and, from Rizelya's visions, the deaths they cause feed the Malvers somehow. Something has happened, and they're getting stronger. How else could they create the new control janack? I've fought them, my friend, and they are every bit as bad as Aistrun told you. I've known Chariel all my life. Her visions are never wrong. If she says there is madness coming to our world, and we need our ancient allies, the Gryphons, to survive it, then it will happen."

"I don't lie, Graak," Rizelya said, standing behind them. Her wet hair dripped down her back. She'd traded her red leathers and woolen tunic for a finely woven turquoise top. Bands of rose-colored embroidery gathered her full sleeves at her wrists. The same geometric shapes were embroidered around the neckline. She wore a mid-calf length, wide-legged split skirt in darker turquoise. She'd polished her black riding boots. Her brown eyes flashed in anger.

Blazel sucked in a breath at her beauty.

"I don't have any reason to make up what I've seen," she said. "I'm not a storyteller, simply a fighter. This woman, and all her followers, want us dead. And when they're done with us, they'll be coming after you next."

Graak pulled his head back and held up a placating talon. *I'm not calling you a liar, Rizelya, nor you, Chariel.* The others had followed Rizelya to the fire. *You've convinced me of your truth. More importantly, you must convince King Zorlaak. But even if he doesn't agree to the alliance, I can still come with you as an ambassador. Our own mystics have visions of a time of trouble heralded by the appearance of a White Priestess in our lands. Now we have not one, but two, priestesses here. Simply by your presence ladies, my lord-king will listen to you.* He bowed to Chariel and Wisah.

They'd dressed in the traditional garb of priestesses. Silver embroidery etched the neck, sleeve bands, and hem of their long gowns. A dark gray belt cinched the waist of Chariel's dove-gray gown. She had braided her hair in the traditional priestess style, with two small side-lock braids framing her face. Wisah's white dress gleamed in the morning light. Around both of their necks hung an eight-pointed star with a small diamond in the center, signifying they were full priestesses of the Goddess. Even here, in the Deep Mountains, the Gryphons knew and revered the symbol.

"I've not seen the witch as Rizelya has," Jaehaas said, "but I have fought the Malvers' monsters. After a thousand years of uniformness, their habits be changed. There has to be a cause for this, and I believe Rizelya has the right of it. I will add my testimony to your king." He, too, had dressed in his finest. He wore a dark brown quilted jacket over a golden-bronze shirt. He'd trimmed his beard and brushed his horse hide until it gleamed.

Aistrun's long, red hair shone, and he'd shaved his beard. His jacket and trousers were a darker turquoise than Rizelya's, and his shirt was a pale blue.

Eat your breakfast, Graak instructed them. *Alkaak is but a short ride. You may leave your tents and baggage here. No one will bother them.*

Everyone ate carefully so as not to spill on their fine clothes. Blazel hadn't dressed in his formal clothes yet and quickly washed the dishes. Afterward, he entered the tent and changed. He grimaced at the Haaslair Clan's colors of brown and yellow. He didn't belong to the clan, but they were his only formal clothes. Sighing at this reminder he didn't truly belong anywhere, he pulled on the butter yellow shirt over light brown trousers. The jacket matched the pants with embroidery in the same yellow. He found a piece of leather and tied back his long locs at the nape of his neck. He rubbed a hand over his freshly shaved face before leaving the tent.

When he arrived at the picket line to saddle Lighzel, Jaehaas had brushed her coat until it shone. She was decked out in her barding, as were the other horses.

Graak floated down to join them, wearing a wide leather collar dyed a deep indigo and embossed with bronze metal. The metalwork's artistry was stunning. The elaborate collar signified his high rank in the flight.

They made a colorful parade as they exited the clearing and traveled on the well-worn path. Graak paced beside them while the other Gryphons soared above.

The road led to a massive granite bluff. Huge Gryphons circled above it. Once they caught sight of Blazel's procession, their loud cries reverberated across the valley. A flight of smaller Gryphons dove toward them. The youngsters zipped over Blazel's head. A stone structure soared above the cliff. It appeared even bigger than Strunlair Keep.

Graak pointed to it. *The king's palace.*

"Hey, how will we get up there?" Aistrun craned his neck to glimpse the top.

You will receive a ride. There are no stairs, Graak chuckled. *We don't need them.*

"But what about our horses?" Rizelya asked.

There is a cave at the bottom where they will remain. I guarantee their safety and no one will eat them.

"How can you do that?"

Because it's my flight's cave, and they will do as I say.

The sky filled with more and more Gryphons as news of their arrival spread through the city. There were fifteen different flights, but Blazel had only lived with Graak's Thorn Claw flight, which predominately consisted of hawk- and falcon-type Gryphons. He'd met a few of the smaller Gryphons, who belonged in the Silent Prowlers flight, and were the Gryphons' messengers and scouts. He had never seen so many Gryphons at one time.

"How many live here?" Blazel asked, drawing his eyes from the aerial displays above him.

About fifteen hundred Gryphons live in the city, Graak answered. *Another four to five hundred live in the scout camps and elsewhere. Ah, here we are.*

Graak led them into a huge cavern. Excited Gryphons filled it, their wings rustling and beaks clicking. At the far end, they'd built a corral for the horses, with piles of fresh grass and a trough of water in it. The horses shied and whinnied in fear from so many large predators around them. Graak let out a cry, and all the Gryphons, except one, hurried out of the cave.

He was slightly smaller than Graak and appeared to be the same hawk-type. He had deep, dark brown feathers and his feline body was the same dark brown. A band of dark yellow-orange covered the top portion of his beak and spread into his cheeks. He dipped his head to Graak.

All is ready for our guests, the Gryphon said.

Thank you, Broogk. Graak turned to the Posairs and extended a talon toward the other Gryphon. *This is my wing second, Broogk. He will ensure your horses are safe.*

The Posairs murmured greetings to the Gryphon. The horses had calmed with only Graak and Broogk in the cave with them. Broogk swung open the corral gate. Blazel and the others led their horses into it. Once they were in and unsaddled, Broogk clicked his beak and muttered soft words to the horses. Blazel rocked back on his heels, stunned, when Lighzel bobbed her head and walked to Broogk's outstretched talon. He carefully petted Lighzel's nose.

Sweet lady, you are gorgeous, he murmured to Lighzel. He turned to the Posairs and dropped his beak open in a grin. *These are magnificent creatures! Be sure I will take good care of them.*

The other horses followed Lighzel's lead and stood by the corral bars, letting Broogk pet them. Blazel shook his head, unbelieving the horses would trust the large Gryphon. They left the cave to the sound of him crooning to the horses.

Rizelya followed Graak as he led the way out of the cave. Six large Gryphons milled nervously outside, wearing a collar on their breasts similar to Graak's, only not as ornate.

When Graak had told them they'd get a ride up to the top of the cliff, she had thought it'd be in a basket or something. Her eyes widened when she realized their ride would be on Gryphon backs. She wondered how the centaur would manage the trip.

When the two White Priestesses exited the cave, the waiting Gryphons reared onto their haunches, opened their wings slightly for balance, and let out a sharp cry. They dropped to the ground and bowed low to the priestesses. Two stepped forward, white feathers on their necks sweeping back to meld with the white and gray fur of their feline bodies. A wide stripe of dark gray started at the tops of their beaks, crossed their heads, and continued down their backs. They dipped their heads to Chariel and Wisah.

It is our great honor to carry you, they said in unison.

Wisah bowed her head slightly in regal acceptance.

Graak directed Blazel and Aistrun on where to place the women on the Gryphon's backs. As they stepped aside, walking carefully with their burden, Rizelya noticed a strange contraption spread on the ground. Lengths of rope snaked from it to the two huge, solid-black Gryphons on either side of it.

Graak gestured to the device. *That is for you, Jaehaas. This is what we use when we must transport an injured Gryphon, so it should support your weight.*

Jaehaas doubtfully scrutinized the mess of ropes. He gingerly stepped on it, lifting his hoofs high in mincing steps. Graak pointed to where he wanted Jaehaas to stand. Shivers cascaded over Jaehaas's back and down his legs as he waited.

The Gryphon who approached Rizelya had light brown and white feathers, and his wings were a darker brown with white stripes. His feline fur was a creamy tan and brown. He stood nearly a foot taller than she was, and his body was nearly thirteen feet long. He dipped his head in greeting.

I am Glork, and I am honored to carry you. He crouched for her to climb onto his back.

As she settled, she found two straps attached to the collar in front of her. "Are these for me?" At his nod, she leaned forward and grasped them tightly.

When Rizelya looked around, Blazel sat on Graak's back, and Aistrun rode a brown-and-red Gryphon. Graak gave the signal, and Glork's rear legs bunched as he leaped into the air. Magic brushed across her senses, and they were off the ground, his powerful wings beating strong strokes. Below her, the two black Gryphons burst upward with the ropes clutched tightly in their talons. The contraption took the shape of a sling, with Jaehaas's belly snug in its cradle. Jaehaas gripped the sling's edge, his knuckles white.

Aistrun whooped with joy. "I'm flying!" He threw back his head and laughed.

Rizelya smiled fondly at him. She wasn't sure she liked the sensation of nothing around her but sky.

I will not drop you, Glork assured her. His voice in her mind was a deep, kind baritone. His wing beats took them higher and higher. He soon soared high above the cliff and the city below. *Is this not beautiful?*

Snow capped the mountain peaks, and they glittered in the sun. Far below, a river snaked through the emerald-green forest. Clouds slid by them. The others landed in a courtyard of the palace, while she and her Gryphon still circled above it. Rizelya wound the straps around her hands and gripped the Gryphon's sides tighter with her legs.

Is it true the Malvers are returning? Glork asked.

"Yes. One has invaded my dreams and shown me terrible things."

"Aaii!" he warbled.

Glork's body trembled, and heat rose from him. She cried out when it threatened to burn her. He mumbled an apology, and his lazy glide turned into a steep stoop as he arrowed to the courtyard. The wind burned her face and stole tears from her eyes. Her heart pounded in terror when she slid backwards, and she wildly clutched the straps on the harness. He dropped down onto his talons and crouched. Rizelya unwrapped the straps, shook the blood back into her hands, and stepped off. "Thank you, Glork, for allowing me to ride you."

Gryphons filled the courtyard. Heat radiated off from them, making the courtyard balmy. A number of them were huge, even larger than Moraak. They dwarfed the rest with their height and weight, and wore gold collars. The other Gryphons stayed away from them. They formed a line and blocked a large gold door.

Graak and her friends stood in a lonely huddle in the sea of Gryphons.

Are you okay? Graak asked when she joined them.

Rizelya nodded, then tilted her head toward the enormous Gryphons. "Who are they?"

Thunder Wings. They protect the king.

The door opened, and the guards stepped aside to reveal Moraak. He glowed as a beam of sunlight touched his golden feathers. An ornate gold collar adorned his breast.

The king will see you, Moraak announced. *Come with me.*

Graak took the lead, Blazel slightly behind him, as they followed Moraak through the doors. Wisah threaded her hand around Jaehaas's elbow as they paced through the cordon of Thunder Wings. Aistrun escorted Chariel. As the two priestesses passed, a murmur passed through the crowd. Rizelya walked alone, her hand on her helstrablade at her side. Her fingers ached to be holding her helbraught, but Graak had forbidden her to bring it. Although it was easier to direct her magic through her helbraught, she could access her magic without it. She murmured the spell for the fire shield under her breath, keeping it ready in case they needed it. She trusted Graak, but not these other Gryphons. Her shoulders twitched when a huge black Thunder Wing stepped after her and joined the procession.

Inside the palace, they walked through multiple corridors. Thunder Wings guarded each intersection. Rizelya caught glimpses of intricately carved stone walls and beautiful sculptures in both stone and wood. They finally reached a golden door, finely embossed with Gryphons in flight, the wooden lintel decorated with carvings. A Thunder Wing pushed it open.

The marble floor was polished to a high sheen. Tall windows with brightly woven curtains provided ample light. Gryphons stood on either side of the aisle leading to the dais.

Rizelya saw female Gryphons for the first time. They were smaller and more graceful, and their coloring was more subdued than the males. They wore beautifully crafted bands on their fore talons, many of them set with bright, winking jewels.

Near the dais stood four Gryphons, who had the same golden feathers and fur as Moraak. Graak had informed them Moraak was just one son in line to inherit the crown from their father. These four Gryphons must be his brothers. They scowled at Moraak and the Posairs behind him.

The Gryphon on the dais had the same coloration as his sons. King Zorlaak was larger than Moraak. He had golden head feathers, his wing feathers were a golden-brown edged with gold. His feline body was a rich, dark gold. Even his talons were gold. He wore a gold collar studded with jewels and a crown on his head.

Moraak bowed to the king. *Father, these are the Posairs I told you about. They have come bearing a message from the Supreme.*

Aistrun stepped forward, holding his cloak to form wings, and bowed. "Oolk keee shree neekalaaak," he said perfectly, with all the screeches and clicks.

The king nodded thoughtfully and motioned to someone behind him.

A Gryphon with silver-gray feathers, a gray feline body, and a silver beak glided forward. He was smaller and shorter, only reaching Rizelya's chest. The Gryphon cocked his head from side to side as he examined the group. He half hopped, half flew, from the dais to land in front of Wisah. His curious head bobbing continued as he studied her, and he did the same thing to Chariel. Sitting back on his haunches, he stretched until he could peer into Chariel's eyes. Tentatively, he reached out a talon and ran it gently down Chariel's cheek.

You have the sight, he stated, his voice a high tinkling sound. He sounded old to Rizelya. *What have you seen, child?*

"Madness coming," Chariel said. Her voice changed to the odd monotone of prophecy. Her unseeing eyes looked upward as if watching something no one else could see. "It comes! The madness is here. All must fight or none shall live."

Aistrun caught Chariel as she fainted. He glared at the Silver Beak.

What say you, Sheekeek? King Zorlaak asked.

She sees true, my lord. the Silver Beak bowed to the king. *It is the same danger foretold in my visions.* He whirled to face Wisah. *And why, White Priestess, are you here?*

"My Supreme sent me." Wisah pulled herself up to her full height and straightened her shoulders. She turned from the Silver Beak to the king. "Because of Chariel's prophecy. It's why all of us are here. We have come to urge you to remember our alliance from ages past and to renew it now."

And what did her prophecy say? asked Sheekeek.

Wisah closed her eyes for a moment, then opened them to stare at the king. She intoned, "Long-lost allies to fight once more, ancient enemies coming to the light. A menace comes. No allies, the enemy wins and all die."

Graak stepped forward. *My King, the Malvers return. It is our sacred duty to fight them.*

That time has long passed, King Zorlaak grumbled. *We are safe here in our mountain homes. The Malvers have never been here, and therefore, can never send their evil against us.*

Your Grace, the baethor have been getting stronger, Graak replied. *A flock attacked our guests unprovoked. If we had not spotted them on our patrol, they would not be here to warn us about the coming evil.*

The king turned to Moraak. *Is this true?*

Moraak nodded. *It is. Baethor haven't been found in the canyon where we rescued the Posairs. Not one, but several flocks of baethor attacked them. I have never seen the like.*

You carry this evil with you! The king sputtered, glaring at the Posairs.

"Your Grace," Aistrun said, bowing again to the king. "We only bring warning and a plea for your friendship. Would you listen to my tale?"

King Zorlaak thrummed his talons on the floor, the sound a dull ring. Rizelya held her breath. They needed the alliance with the Gryphons. After several long milcrons, the king nodded.

"It all began one day, a day just like any other," Aistrun's voice fell into the cadence of a storyteller. "A platoon rode from Strunland Keep to fight a nest of monsters and a brave Red—" he indicated Rizelya "—fought a new janack. It's true! After a thousand years, a new janack showed up in the nest. It controls the rest."

Aistrun told the rapt audience the tale of their journey across Strunlair Province. He told them of Rizelya's awful dreams that proved to be visions. The journey to the Sanctuary, and the meeting of Blazel and Jaehaas, took on new proportions, and Rizelya almost didn't recognize herself. Aistrun made her sound so brave and fearless when, in truth, she wasn't. She'd only been protecting her squad. He ended with the baethor battle and Blazel and Graak's chance reunion.

"And so, Your Grace," Aistrun said, "we are here, begging you to believe us. The Malvers are once again active and trying to destroy us."

King Zorlaak was still for a long time, except for a flick of his tail. *During the Great War,* he finally said, *there were thousands of us. But by the end, only eighty survivors flew to the Deep Mountains to escape the ravages of the war. And we have prospered here. We know the Malvers' malice. Our histories remind us about the depravations of war. Even after a thousand years, our population is still dangerously low. Helping you will decimate us, and I do not know if we can survive a war at this time.*

Rizelya stepped forward. Blazel grabbed her arm, but she shrugged him off. She knew she was breaking protocol. Women, except priestesses, weren't supposed to speak to the king in this formal setting.

The king's feathers rose in agitation as Rizelya bowed deeply to him.

"My lord, listen to me," she cried. "What the Malvers are doing to my people will only become worse as they grow stronger. We can fight their monsters. We have been doing it for the past thousand years. But if they send, as Chariel says, flying monsters, we can't hope to fight them. You were created to battle them." She clasped her hands in a pleading gesture. "Please, help us now."

A boom shook the windows and echoed throughout the palace. The ground swayed. Rizelya fought to keep her balance.

"They are here!" Chariel screamed, hands over her face. "The madness is here!"

Chapter 21

The floor stopped rocking. Blazel moved to help Chariel, but Wisah and Aistrun already knelt beside her. He changed direction and ran for the nearest window, Rizelya on his heels. Graak and Moraak winged to the one next to them. Blazel couldn't see anything.

"Is there a way out of here?" he asked Graak. "We need to discover what's happening."

Come on, Graak shouted. *I'll take you.*

Blazel dashed to Graak's side and leaped onto his back. Graak jumped into the air. Blazel looked down, stunned, when Rizelya climbed onto Moraak. He hadn't thought the prince would allow a Posair to ride him.

Graak flew directly at the window. With a cry, Blazel threw his arm over his face to protect it. He experienced a moment of pressure, and then they were winging high into the air. Blazel slowly lowered his arm. The glass hadn't shattered at their passing. Behind them, Moraak caught up to them quickly. Below, four Thunder Wings rose from the courtyard to join them.

"There!" Blazel shouted, pointing to the red tail of a comet plunging across the sky, far above the Gryphons. Blazel's hands convulsed on Graak's neck feathers. The meteor from his dreams, a baleful fire, slashed across the horizon.

Graak turned and sped toward the flaming streak, with Moraak and the Thunder Wings flying at their side. Even as fast as they flew, the object stayed ahead of them. The leading edge, a bright ball of fire, outpaced them, and soon dropped beyond the horizon.

We can't catch it, Moraak called out. *Let's go back.* He signaled to two of the Thunder Wings, who continued to follow the object's trail. Moraak made a wide turn, with Graak following his lead.

"That isn't natural," Rizelya said. "Right after the boom, Chariel cried that the madness was here. We need to find out what that thing is."

I agree, Moraak said. *Ah, father has sent more scouts.*

Several Gryphons, all significantly smaller than the huge Thunder Wings, winged toward them. Blazel recognized a couple of individuals from the Silent Prowlers he'd met during his time with Graak. Within moments, the scouts overtook Graak and Moraak as they sped after the Thunder Wings. It didn't take long for them to overtake the larger Gryphons and disappear from sight.

We'll know more either later today or tomorrow, Graak said. *The scouts are fast.*

When they returned to the throne room, the Silver Beak, Sheekeek, conversed earnestly with Chariel and Wisah. Aistrun paced off to the side, while Jaehaas talked to one of Moraak's brothers.

The king prowled his dais, casting worried glances between the Silver Beak, the priestesses, and the windows. When Blazel's team arrived, he stopped pacing and gazed expectantly at Graak and Moraak. *What was it?*

We do not know, my lord, Graak said. *It travels fast in our skies.*

The scouts will catch it, Moraak assured his father. *The comet was not natural. It traveled in a direct course toward the south, perhaps the Barrens or the crater.*

This is not good. King Zorlaak rubbed a talon on the edge of his beak. *The southern peninsula was the Malvers's territory, and it is said their evil still lives there.*

Blazel nodded. "It does. I have been there and have seen the ruins of a fortress. Evil permeated the place, so I avoided it. It must have been a Malvers' Keep. There are twisted beasts in those swamps, like no others in Lairheim. I know, I've spent time in all of them."

Sheekeek escorted Chariel and Wisah to the dais. *This is an ill omen, Your Grace. One we must heed. We have compared visions, and they speak of the same things. A madness that knows no fear, no compassion, and no regret comes to destroy our world. If it is in the Barrens, then we are all at risk. It derives strength there where we only find poison. We must ally ourselves once more with the Supreme and the Posairs if any of us are to survive.*

Daelaak, one of Moraak's brothers, snarled, stepping forward. *We are safe in our mountains. There is no reason for us to leave them and fight another war for these ungrateful curs. What have they ever done for us? Nothing! We are prosperous and thriving after all these years. We have our children to think about. Let them fight their own battles.*

My eldest brother urges us to stay here, to stay safe. Moraak paced forward until he stood next to Daelaak. Moraak was larger by more than a foot in height and length, and he was sleeker and more muscular than his elder brother. *But, this is not the right course of action. I have listened to what Rizelya and her friends have said about what is happening below. If the Malvers do return to Lairheim, there is no place safe for us to hide. We fought and destroyed their monsters in the Great War. We were at the final battle and added our magic to the White Priestess Shandir's spell to defeat the Malvers. Do you think they forget this, or forgive it? If you do, you are fools.* He glared at Daelaak.

That was a thousand years ago!

"They don't forget." Rizelya stepped forward and faced the king. "Your Grace, I shared my visions with the Supreme, and she told me the Malvers woman I saw was one of those who had been exiled. How they remain alive after all this time is a mystery."

One of their magics we fought against was death magic, Sheekeek said. *They used it to become near immortal. It appears they succeeded in taking the final steps to cheat their own death.*

If they are immortal, can they be killed? Graak asked, fear in his voice.

"Yes," Chariel answered. "I have seen their deaths, but it only occurs when we fight together."

So you say. We only have this woman's story. Daelaak sneered. *I for one do not believe her, nor do I believe the tales of the mystics. Our people should stay here, where they are safe, and not get involved in this fight.*

We are bred for fighting, Moraak said, exasperated. It sounded like an old argument. *It was, and is, our sacred duty to fight the Malvers's evil. Our warriors need more to battle than sabertigers and baethor. What challenge is there in killing them? I will not cower behind walls of stone when our ancient enemies are beleaguering our world.*

The Malvers are dead!

"No, they're not," Rizelya said. "I'm not a Gray to have visions. I'm a Red, and I fight. But for some reason, I'm plagued by the Malvers, and I've seen them feeding off the death of my people and getting stronger. They hate everyone who lives, not only Posairs. Once they discover they didn't exterminate you during the Great War—"

Exterminated! Daelaak rose onto his haunches, the nimbus of flames outlining his body. *We are not animals to be eliminated.*

"No, you aren't, at least not to me and the other Posairs. But to the Malvers? We are all vermin to be crushed under their boot heel."

Enough! King Zorlaak roared. *I will make no decision until we have more facts. We will wait for the scouts' return and their news. I'll consider what you have revealed here today.* He addressed the Posairs. *You will guest with us until I make a decision.*

They are camped not far from here, Your Grace, Graak said. *They could return—*

No. Zorlaak glared at Graak. *They will stay here. We do not know when the scouts will return, and I want the Posairs here when they do.* He stood and paced with dignity through a door behind the dais.

We have a guest suite, Moraak said to Blazel and the others. *You will be comfortable there while we wait.*

"What about our horses?" Rizelya asked.

They will be safe with Broogk, Graak assured them. *They fascinated him.*

"Our multas are back at camp. Someone needs to take care of them," Rizelya said. "We didn't expect to leave them alone."

Graak tilted his head. *They should be fine, but I'll have Broogk check on them. I doubt they'd let him bring them here.*

"No, they wouldn't. I guess we don't have any other choice, do we?"

No. After the king's command, no one will fly you down, Moraak said. *Not even Graak here would disobey a direct order.*

"Show us to our new quarters, please," Blazel added quickly, before Rizelya could make any more objections.

Moraak lowered his beak in a grin and led the way out of the throne room and through the corridors. A contingent of Thunder Wings quietly followed the group. After several turnings and a trip down a flight of wide, low stairs—easy for Jaehaas and the Gryphons to navigate—Moraak stopped at a door.

The guest suite.

Blazel entered first. The low couches and pillows preferred by the Gryphons formed a circle in the center. To one side sat a table with goblets, a pitcher beaded with condensation, and bowls of nuts and berries.

A hallway led from the main room to three sleeping rooms. The beds were large and well-padded with pillows and furs.

"Ah, one my size!" Jaehaas crowed, dumping his pack on the bed spacious enough to accommodate his bulk.

A necessary and bathing room was off the same hallway. The deep pools were perfect for the Gryphons—or centaurs—to lounge in the water. Fine paintings in bright colors of landscapes and flying Gryphons decorated the walls. On every surface sat beautifully wrought metal or wood sculptures. Blazel hadn't ever seen such artistry.

"This is lovely." Chariel gestured at the room. "We should be comfortable here. Thank you, Moraak."

Wisah sighed. "We didn't bring a change of clothing or our bedclothes. I don't want to sleep in these robes. Is there something we can use?"

I'll send someone to retrieve your things, Graak said. *Tell me where to find them.*

Blazel shrugged. He didn't understand the girls' need for sleeping clothes. His small-clothes were good enough. Aistrun shared a rueful grin with him as he mouthed, "Women." Blazel wandered to the table and sniffed the pitcher. He smiled to discover the fermented fruit juice the Gryphons made filled it. He poured a goblet for himself, the other men, and Moraak.

Aistrun took a tentative sip. "Hey, this is good! It's cool and refreshing."

"Be careful," Blazel warned. "It packs a punch if you drink too much."

We pride ourselves in our art, Moraak said, *and making wine is an art.*

"Yes, it is." Blazel raised his goblet in a toast.

They took their drinks to the main room and sank into the couches' soft cushions. Blazel let out a huge sigh.

"This be nice." Jaehaas settled deeper into a wide couch. "Certainly more comfortable than our campsite."

Graak flew out a window to pick up the women's things. This time, Blazel watched with interest as a hole opened in the center of the glass. It spread to the edges until the opening was big enough to let Graak through. As soon as he was gone, the gap closed. Blazel strolled to the window and tapped on the solid glass. Close examination revealed no sign of where the opening had been.

"How did he do that?" he asked.

Magic, of course, Moraak answered. *Our magic helps us fly, flare without burning ourselves, and do other things, such as create exits wherever we need them. We need to know what is on the other side, which is why windows work well. Just like your women work the various colors of magic, and your men shift forms, we were gifted with magic by the Goddess. Fire destroys the Malvers' creations, so we were made to flare and burn our enemies. Whatever my father decides, I will go with you to fight our ancient enemies.*

"Graak has said the same thing." Blazel returned to the couch.

"It would be better if we had a formal alliance." Chariel approached the couches, holding a goblet of wine. "Before this is over, we will need every able person to fight. As Rizelya reminded me, the White Priestesses were once also warriors, and we too shall have to enter the fray to end the madness."

Moraak asked for more details on the new control janack, and soon they enjoyed a lively discussion and telling tales of past battles. Graak returned with the requested supplies. A crew of servants arrived with platters of steaming meat and tubers for the Posairs and raw meat for the Gryphons.

Blazel leaned back, his legs stretched before him, sipping on his wine. Rizelya and Graak hotly argued fighting techniques. She was magnificent when riled. Warmth flooded him when she turned and winked at him. The desire to carry her to one of the big, comfortable beds and make love to her overwhelmed him, snatching away his breath. Realization hit him. He'd made his vow from a child's anger, and he understood his mother's actions for the first time in his life. Love, no matter how fleeting, was worth sharing and holding onto for as long as it lasted. Soon, he hoped, he and Rizelya would be alone, and he'd do more than kiss her.

Rizelya snickered quietly when first Wisah, then Jaehaas slipped from the common room and made their way to the sleeping room Jaehaas had claimed. Not long after, Aistrun nodded slyly to Chariel, and they sauntered to their bed.

Oh my, Graak said a while later, *look at the time.*

Moraak glanced at the clock and groaned. *My mate is going to skin me.* He hastily pushed off the couch and scurried from the room.

If we hear anything, I'll let you know. But I doubt we will until morning. Make sure you get some sleep. Graak winked at Blazel and Rizelya before leaving.

The door shut quietly behind him. Rizelya gazed at Blazel. They were alone for the first time since leaving the Sanctuary. *If he doesn't make a move, I will.* She leaned forward slightly and licked her lips.

Blazel stretched, throwing his arms wide. "It is late."

Rizelya sighed and rolled her eyes. Unexpectedly, Blazel put his arm around her, pulled her closer, and kissed her. The taste of him burst through her senses. She groaned as he deepened the kiss. His hands fluttered to her breasts, stroking them to tightness. He scooted closer until the length of their bodies touched. The hard bulge in his pants pressed against her.

Panting, she pressed him back among the cushions and trailed kisses along his neck, savoring his spiciness. She skimmed her hands under his shirt and caressed his chest. His muscles tensed as she trailed her fingers to his flat stomach and slid under his waistband.

With a moan, he shifted until she was under him. He pushed her tunic up to place kisses on her belly. He moved his lips and tongue slowly upward to her breasts, tasting every part of her body. Fire flared under her skin wherever he touched her. She pulled his face back to hers for a long, deep kiss. Still kissing, she wrapped her legs around his waist as he put his arms around her. With a tremendous push, he rose to his feet and carried her to the empty bed. His ardor overcame his innocence, taking them both to ecstasy. Afterward, resting her head on his shoulder, her leg thrown over his chest, she drifted to sleep, deeply satisfied.

As dawn lightened the sky, they made love again. Later, in the common room, Rizelya bashfully looked at Chariel and Wisah. They both smiled at her and laughed. They, too, appeared like they had been well-loved during the night. Breakfast consisted of boiled grains and fruit. After eating, they relaxed on the low couches, entwined in their lover's arms. Late in the morning, Graak joined them.

Did you get any sleep? he asked as he surveyed the new grouping.

Rizelya blushed while Blazel chuckled.

"Of course we did," Blazel said. "I'm quite rested."

Graak dropped his beak in a grin. *I'm sure you are. We haven't received any word yet from the scouts. Where could they be?*

Aistrun toyed with one of Chariel's sidelocks. "If the comet was heading to the Barrens, it will take them some time to get there and back. Even if they fly fast, it's a long way to travel."

You're right. Graak ducked his head. *I know two of the scouts well. They've served with my flight. I worry about them.*

"They'll be fine," Chariel said.

Is that a prophecy?

She shook her head. "No, just a feeling."

Graak pulled out a game board and pieces from a cupboard. "Since all we can do is wait, we might as well play."

"First, I be out of fire arrows," Jaehaas said. "We need to make more today while we have time."

Our artisans can craft new arrows for you. Graak chirped and a young Gryphon answered the door, then flew off with Graak's message. When he was gone, Graak lifted the game board. *Until they do, let's play.*

Rizelya raised an eyebrow at the keshe board. "Where did you learn to play this?"

We've always played keshe. When Blazel stayed with us, we learned the Posairs also played it.

Seven players complicated the game, and it took all afternoon to finish. Aistrun crowed with pride when his pieces were the last on the board, and he won. They were setting up for another game when Moraak came in.

Ah, I see you've found something to occupy your time. Moraak waved at the game board. *The scouts have not returned. Set up pieces for me. I need to be distracted. I am losing my patience with this waiting and worrying.*

After dinner, they received a delivery of arrows. Rizelya, not in the mood to lose again to Aistrun, spent the evening setting the fire spell on the arrows. When Moraak won the last game of the night, Rizelya couldn't help teasing Aistrun. He harrumphed and flung an arm around Chariel's waist as he stomped off to bed. As he turned into the bedroom, he winked over his shoulder at Rizelya.

As they ate breakfast, Moraak and Graak hurried into the guest suite. Moraak's head feathers were fluffed out.

Finally, Moraak crowed, *we've sighted the scouts returning. They just crossed the Barrier Range, which forms the border between the Deep Mountains and the White Mountains. It shouldn't be long until they are here. Father wants you in the throne room.*

Blazel squeezed Rizelya's hand as they and the others hurried to their rooms to change back into their finery. A short time later, they followed Moraak through the corridors.

Gryphons crowded the throne room, but moved aside when they saw Moraak. King Zorlaak and the Silver Beak, Sheekeek, sat on the dais, with Moraak's brothers crowding close in front of it. Daelaak sneered at Moraak and his companions as they approached.

The huge Thunder Wing guards stood glowing along the walls, heat waves rising from their fur, and the room grew hot. King Zorlaak motioned to the Thunder Wings' leader, and a few moments later, the glow surrounding the Thunder Wings diminished, and the room cooled to a more bearable level.

Representatives from every flight attended the gathering. Rizelya saw black hawk-types Graak said were Black Feathers, and Gryphons of various types from the White Feathers, Gray Feathers, and Red Feathers' flights.

Rizelya bumped Graak's shoulder, gesturing to the group of Gryphons who stood off to the side with the others, giving them a wide berth. They had light brown head feathers, dark brown wings, and white fur. However, their most striking feature were their green talons. "Who are those?" she whispered.

They are the Green Talons. See the sack on their wrist? They produce a deadly poison that is a holdover trait from the Great War. They are born with the sacks, and the poison turns their talons green.

"But why are the others avoiding them?" Rizelya's brow furrowed.

Many fear their poison. Although, to the best of my knowledge, no Green Talon has attacked another Gryphon.

Rizelya shook her head at the prejudice. She gazed around the room. Among those waiting behind the princes, she recognized Glork, the Gryphon who had given her a ride to the top of the cliff. He caught her eye and gave her a small nod. She hoped it meant he supported her. He ambled toward her, stopping every so often to chat with another Gryphon.

He finally made it to her side. *I heard what your mystic said after the boom. I will go with you to fight the Malvers when you leave. There are others here, besides Graak, who have listened to our mystics and see the signs of trouble before us.*

Before she could respond, he moved away. As he wove his way through the crowd, she heard a commotion. A Gryphon flew through the door with a loud shriek.

He says the scouts are coming, Graak interpreted for Rizelya and the others. He turned to stare expectantly at the big window.

Rizelya intently watched the window with everyone else. After what seemed like ages, but was actually only a few milcrons, a hole opened, and the scouts zipped through it. They swooped to land in front of the dais. A bit later, the two Thunder Wings who had gone with them burst into the room. All of them panted hard, and their head feathers and fur stood on end.

Your Grace, the gray and black scout said, *we caught up to the thing. It wasn't a comet, but a huge metal flying machine. It was several measures wide and landed in the Barrens, close to the crater. As it descended, a half-a-dozen smaller flying machines broke away from it.*

One flew west toward the ocean, a white and brown owl-type scout spoke up. *I followed it out to sea. It headed to a distant large island, but for some reason, I could not pass beyond a certain point. It felt like a magical barrier. The machine easily penetrated it.*

Near dark, the big one disgorged strange people, the first scout said. *They were unlike the Posairs or what our histories tell us the Malvers look like. The strangers didn't stay outside long, so we only caught glimpses of them. They are tall, thin, and willowy and wore black robes, covering the misshapen lumps on their backs, and carried some sort of weapon. None of us liked the evil flowing from them. Once we ascertained what had arrived, we flew back as quickly as possible. I don't think they saw us, because we weren't followed home.*

Sheekeek cocked his head to the side and peered at the king. *These strange people bring madness and destruction to our world. We must join with the Posairs to toss them from our world.*

Daelaak sneered. *They are in the south, far away from us. They do not know we are here. Let those who live in the south fight the invaders.*

If they have flying machines, Moraak said, with a shake of his head, *then it is possible they will find us sooner or later—*

And if they do, we'll fight them. In our home territory.

What about the Malvers? King Zorlaak asked Sheekeek. *Are they still a problem?*

"Yes, Your Grace," Chariel said. "The madness these invaders bring makes the Malvers stronger. I don't know how. My visions have only shown me it does and that we must fight together to survive."

The king paced the dais for a long time, ignoring the crowd's mutters. He finally settled back on his haunches and addressed the assembled Gryphons. *Are there any who would fight with the Posairs?*

A multitude of squeaks and trills, the loudest coming from Moraak and Graak, answered him.

Moraak stepped forward. *My lord, I am willing to go fight, and there are many who will accompany me. We cannot allow these invaders, or the Malvers, to conquer our world. We must fight for our freedom, for our children's freedom, and for our friends' freedom. Their landing at Shandir's Crater tells me the strangers are here for no good.*

We must stay and protect our home, Daelaak cried.

Not everyone should go with me, Moraak said. *I agree we need to leave warriors here to protect our homes and families.* He turned expectantly toward King Zorlaak. *May I go, father?*

King Zorlaak put his head on his doubled-up talon and gazed at his sons. *You are both correct. I will allow Moraak to take a total of two hundred, two flights' worth, to fly below the mountains and fight with the Posairs. Choose only those who volunteer, and select from all the flights so no one flight is severely reduced in numbers. We still have to protect our lands from sabertigers and baethor.*

I will renew our alliance with the Posairs fully only if our ancient enemies, the Malvers, return to Lairheim. Only then, will we join the fight to destroy them once and for all. But until that time arrives, the majority of us will stay in the mountains. Send out the announcement for volunteers.

The Thunder Wings threw back their heads and warbled a call. It reverberated on the throne room's stone walls. As they waited for the volunteers, those in the room rearranged themselves. Those who were staying either left or gathered next to Daelaak. Those wishing to fly with Moraak clustered around him. Glork was one of the first. It surprised Rizelya when the Silver Beak, Sheekeek, joined the group.

We must have someone to make a record of our fight, he said in response to Moraak's questioning glance. *The White Priestesses will need me before this war is done.*

Rizelya frowned at him, but he wouldn't explain further. Mystics and priestesses were alike in their need for secrecy.

Within an octar, nearly three hundred had volunteered to fight with Moraak. When more than the stated two hundred enlisted, the king relented and allowed them all to go. Rizelya sighed with relief. With three hundred Gryphons, surely they could win any battles with the invaders or the Malvers.

Chapter 22

Wonder filled Blazel as Gryphon after Gryphon bowed to Moraak, pledging their service to him in the coming fight. When the number reached two flights, each with one hundred members, he expected the king to halt any further oaths. But Moraak remained silent until the last volunteer presented himself.

Graak guided the Posairs to the guest suite to gather their belongings. Blazel smiled with fondness at the bed where he first made love to Rizelya. She came up behind him and wrapped her arms around his waist.

"I'm going to miss this place," she said, sighing against his back. "There are good memories here."

"We'll make more memories elsewhere." Blazel patted her hands and twisted around so he could embrace her. "Too bad we only have two tents. Three would give us all privacy."

"That would be nice. But you'll just have to get used to creating your own privacy. There isn't much in the safe houses, and our traveling is far from over. We have invaders to throw off our world."

Blazel groaned at the thought and nuzzled Rizelya's neck. They broke apart and gathered their few belongings. Graak paced in the common room when they entered. The others also waited, their packs slung over their shoulders.

Let's get going. Graak led them down the corridor. *I'll take you back to your camp so you can pack up. We'll leave early in the morning. If it weren't so late already, Moraak would demand we depart today. The prince is eager to prove himself and be named heir.*

"Isn't the oldest son the heir?" Chariel asked.

Graak shook his head. *No. It's the most capable male, which usually ends up being the eldest. Many of us hope it is Moraak and not Daelaak. This foray south gives Moraak the opportunity to show his prowess and leadership.*

They followed Graak to an outdoor courtyard where Gryphons waited to transport the Posairs off the cliff. Blazel helped Rizelya onto Glork's back, then climbed onto Graak. As they flew over the city, chaos reigned as the warriors made preparations to leave. Older youngsters flitted about carrying messages and supplies, while the younger ones careened excitedly in the sky. Guards scanned the skies from the towers, where there hadn't been any before.

"At least King Zorlaak is taking the threat seriously," Blazel observed.

Graak bobbed his head. *He is. He's sending flights to patrol our borders. Some of those who go with us will remain at the boundary between our land and yours. Messengers will be sent to all our outposts, warning them to watch for invasion. Our job is to keep the invaders south.*

"Who are they and what do they want? There is nothing but poison in the crater. What would they possibly want with that?"

I don't know. We'll find out soon enough.

Graak backwinged, and Blazel tightened his grip around his neck. Dust rose as he landed in front of the cave.

Broogk came out of it, his beak dropped in a grin. *The lovelies are well.* He assisted Wisah off her Gryphon. *I've had a great time getting acquainted with them. That Tejen of yours is quite the fellow. Too bad I'm too big to ride them.* He heaved a wistful sigh, then helped Jaehaas out of the sling.

Blazel hurried into the cave and raised an eyebrow at the calm horses. When Broogk and Graak entered, the horses lifted their heads and looked at the newcomers with curiosity, not fear. Lighzel whinnied at him and thrust her head over the rails for him to scratch her nose. Rizelya's Kymaya was doing the same.

Blazel ducked under the railing to saddle his horse. The others followed suit. Chariel and Wisah were now as competent at saddling their horses as the rest. In less than half an octar, they waited for Broogk to open the corral. He shoved off the rails. As they clattered to the ground, Lighzel's eyes widened, and she pulled against the reins at the echoing sound. Blazel scowled at Broogk, and he hunched his shoulders in apology. Once out of the cave, they mounted their horses and set off back down the road.

Graak flew above them, guiding them to the clearing where they'd left their tents. He took off once they arrived, saying he'd join them in the morning.

After dinner, Blazel and Rizelya slipped away to the hot pool and made love. When they returned, the fire burned low, and the others were tucked in the tents. He and Rizelya slipped into his tent. Jaehaas lifted his head, smirking at them as he laid back down. As usual, Aistrun was missing, sharing Chariel's bed.

Once they settled into his bedroll, he pulled Rizelya close to him. Her warm breath on his chest lulled him to sleep. She woke him in the cold predawn light, and they quietly made love. While he let his breathing return to normal, Blazel's gaze fell on Jaehaas's back. His posture radiated anguish.

Shame and guilt filled Blazel, and he decided from now on, he and Rizelya would share a tent with Aistrun and Chariel. Wisah and Jaehaas, who couldn't express their burgeoning love in the same way, would be spared from any sounds from the couple's love making. With a last kiss, Rizelya pulled on her clothes and climbed out of the warm bedroll. Sighing, Blazel did the same.

The rest of their group roused to the smell of hot taevo and cooking porridge. After a quick breakfast, they worked quickly to take down the tents and load the multas. The sun's rays peeked through the trees as they saddled their horses.

Graak alighted in the clearing, bobbing his head in approval at the Posairs' readiness to travel. Broogk and Glork landed with a group of thirty Gryphons, each with a large pack strapped to their backs. Lighzel rolled her eyes and snorted at the Gryphons, but quieted quickly.

Moraak says for us to depart ahead of him, Graak said. *There are still arrangements he needs to make. He hadn't realized how much needed to be done before so many of our people leave for an indefinite time. They will follow in a few days. Since you travel slower than we do, they'll easily catch up. My flight will guide you to keep you from becoming get lost or finding trouble.* He chuckled.

Blazel made a face at him, then mounted his horse. Jaehaas slung his bow and a quiver of arrows across his back, and Rizelya hooked her helbraught to her saddle. The weight of Blazel's helstrablade at his side comforted him, and he patted the arrows and bow tied to his saddle. With so many Gryphons, he doubted they would have trouble, but it was better to be prepared. At a nod from Rizelya, he clicked to Lighzel, and they left the clearing at a trot.

With Graak and the other Gryphons giving them directions from the air, Blazel and the others made it faster through the forests. Graak's guidance kept them from going out of their way to find a path through the thick trees and meandering streams. They rode the horses hard, with the valiant little multas with their heavy packs keeping up.

When on the second day they reached the canyon where they'd battled the baethor, Graak flew down and stopped them from entering. *There's another way where the baethor don't roost. It's much safer.* He stalked next to them as they crossed the canyon's mouth.

Blazel drew in his breath sharply when there weren't any baethor bodies littering the ground. The only trace left of the battle was the ichor splashed on the walls. "What happened to all the bodies?"

Other baethor came and ate them. While the creatures don't kill each other for food, they don't have any problems eating their dead.

Bile burned Blazel's throat at the cannibalism. Rizelya, riding at his side, shuddered and gulped a couple of times.

"How awful." She grimaced. "Let's not tell Chariel and Wisah about this. They don't need to hear such foulness."

Blazel nodded in agreement. He kicked Lighzel into a canter so those behind wouldn't have time to study the canyon.

Just before dusk, they reached the forest's edge, and it surprised Blazel when Graak urged them to continue up the rocky mountain.

"Graak, what are you doing?" he called out. "We can't cross the pass in the dark. It's too dangerous for the horses."

Trust me. There's a cave up here where we can spend the night.

Blazel shook his head. The warriors, and Rizelya, rode with hands on weapons and carefully watched their surroundings. Even though they were technically in Gryphon lands, sabertigers sometimes hunted on this side of the pass.

Not far from the trees, true to his word, Graak led them to a hidden cave. The main cavern was large enough for their full contingent. The Gryphons shrugged out of their packs and made their camp. After taking care of their horses, the Posairs set up their camp on the cavern's opposite side. The horses weren't comfortable with so many Gryphons close to them.

Aistrun and Chariel unloaded the multas while the rest gathered firewood. Blazel and Jaehaas carried their bows and arrows. Rizelya had rigged a strap to carry her helbraught across her back, leaving her hands free to pick up firewood. The lower end banged on her legs as she walked. The two men scrutinized the area while the women filled their arms with wood.

Blazel caught movement out of the corner of his eye. He turned quickly, nocking an arrow and drawing his bow's string. He couldn't see anything in the gloom. The hair on the back of his neck lifted. He took a deep breath to sample the air. It reeked of sabertiger. He squinted, keeping his bowstring taut, and surveyed the trees.

"Graak!" he yelled, hoping the Gryphon would hear him. "Sabertiger!"

Rizelya's firewood clattered to the ground, and her helbraught blazed with red light. A few moments later, Graak and Broogk dropped down next to Blazel, their head feathers and fur standing on end. Two more Gryphons hovered above them. They waited, muscles tense, and weapons ready, for several long milcrons. When nothing attacked them, they relaxed.

If only one sabertiger was here, it wouldn't attempt so many. Graak shook, settling his feathers. *Let's hurry back to the cave. We'll guard your backs.*

Rizelya let go of the magic she'd fed into her helbraught, and the light in it dimmed. After slipping it into its holder, she bent and picked up the firewood she'd dropped. Blazel helped her. Wisah leaned into Jaehaas, who gently smoothed her hair. Rizelya gave her a wan smile, and they walked to their shelter. Graak and Broogk paced behind, and the two other Gryphons flew slowly above them. Blazel kept watch with both eyes and nose, but couldn't sense any sabertigers in their vicinity.

The next day, as they raced to the pass, Graak and several other Gryphons skimmed above their heads. The rest of the flight flew so high they were specks in the sky. As they neared it, Blazel glimpsed a sabertiger's white and black fur, pacing them on the outcroppings above the path. He pointed it out to Graak, who shrieked loudly. A Gryphon dove for the sabertiger. It disappeared in the jumble of rocks with a flick of its tail.

Six Gryphons swooped to circle overhead. The Gryphons should be an ample deterrent for the sabertigers. Blazel and Aistrun opted to remain in human form, riding beside their partners. They rode carefully, but quickly, through the pass. On the other side, they picked up speed as soon as the terrain allowed.

More and more shadows paced on either side of the group. Lighzel's eyes shifted from side to side, and she pulled on the bit, rearing slightly and whinnying in fright. Blazel caught Rizelya's attention and pointed at the shadowy forms.

Aistrun, Jaehaas, prepare to fight. Rizelya said in mind-speech. *Chariel and Wisah take care of the horses.*

Blazel rocked back in his saddle when he heard her and the others' responses in his mind. He knew packs could communicate in mind-speech to each other, but he'd never experienced it before. The thrill of belonging coursed through him. He was part of a pack!

The path led into a clearing surrounded by boulders. The first sabertiger leaped from behind a boulder, but a Gryphon caught it in mid-leap from above. Blazel tossed Lighzel's reins to Chariel. Rizelya cast a fire shield around Chariel, Wisah, and the horses. When Blazel's feet touched the ground, he called his magic to him, and a moment later, he stood in his warrior form. He lifted his head and howled. Aistrun's deeper cry answered him.

Horror froze Blazel when a sabertiger pounced on Lighzel. It hit the fire shield and bounced off. Its fur bursting into flame. An arrow thunked into its side, and it dropped to the ground, dead. Another sabertiger rushed from behind a boulder. Blazel met it with a howl. His thick pelt saved him from the feline's slashes. He flexed his long claws, releasing his venom, and sliced across its shoulder and neck. The cat roared in pain, flailing as the venom ate into its innards.

A sabertiger slammed into Blazel's knees, knocking him off balance. Its claws punctured his back just below his shoulders. He grimaced, waiting for it to rip him to shreds. Instead, a rush of flames threw the cat from him. Rizelya saluted him with her helbraught. His heart stuttered when a huge feline attacked her. With grim determination, she thrust the sixteen-inch long blade into the cat's chest. It toppled over, and she pulled the helbraught out.

Jaehaas roared with pain, and Blazel whirled. A feline hung onto the centaur's flanks. Blazel ran across the clearing and bowled into the sabertiger. He dug his front claws deep into its shoulders while shredding its belly with his rear feet. A sabertiger thudded next to him. Its bones shattering from the impact of its fall from a great height.

A cat slinked toward him, but before he could react, a red-gold ball of fur landed on its back. Aistrun sank his claws into the feline and crushed its throat with his powerful jaws. He jumped from the dead cat and waved above him. Graak's screech answered, and a moment later, Broogk dove for one of the few remaining cats. His talons sank into its side, and he lifted it off the ground. Aistrun rushed to shred its belly. Blazel crouched, jaws open, claws held ready to fight.

"It's over," Rizelya cried.

In a daze, Blazel scanned the clearing. The tail of the last feline disappeared into the forest. Sabertiger bodies littered the ground. Blood dripped from Jaehaas's flanks. Blood pooled around a dead Gryphon. Another one whimpered, with his wing drooping at an odd angle. Aistrun wore a maniacal grin. He lifted his bright red snout and howled. He didn't appear to be injured, but until he shifted into his human form, it was difficult to tell.

Blazel hissed as the punctures on his back began to burn. Ignoring the pain, he searched for the one who filled his heart. He finally found her and scowled at the blood spattering her face and arms. He jogged to Rizelya and pulled her into an embrace, being careful with his claws. She returned his hug.

"You hurt?" he asked.

She shook her head. "Not badly. A few scratches is all. You?"

Her fingers reached up his back and touched his wounds. He yelped with pain and jerked away.

"You're wounded. Let me dissolve the shield around Chariel and Wisah, and we'll patch you up. Too bad Kaieli isn't with us."

He gave a quizzical look.

"She's my heart-sister and a skilled healer. We don't have anyone with healing abilities with us. Unless..."

Blazel shrugged, hissing at the unwise move. "Perhaps." He had more he needed to say but couldn't get enough words out of his warrior muzzle. He had understood Rizelya's mind-speech. Maybe he could communicate like that. *Rizelya?*

She jerked him, startled. "You used mind-speech! What do you need to tell me?"

The Gryphons have healers, but I'm not sure any accompanied us. They are usually females. I'm fine, but Jaehaas and a Gryphon are badly hurt. At least one is dead.

"Chariel and Wisah have some first-aid supplies. Let's go get them." Rizelya tugged on his hand, and he followed her to where the women waited. When the shield dissipated, they ran to the battlefield carrying bags over their shoulders. Chariel rushed to the Gryphon with the injured wing while Wisah raced to Jaehaas.

They spoke a moment before he embraced her. Wisah's hand flew to her mouth, and the color drained from her face when she saw Jaehaas's hindquarters and back. With trembling hands, she withdrew bandages and salves from her bag. She lifted a waterskin and poured water over Jaehaas's wounds. His hindquarters quivered, and he let out a shrill gasp, crumpling to the ground.

Blazel and Rizelya raced to him. Blazel knelt by Jaehaas's head. Scratches covered his face, shoulders, and arms, but they didn't appear to be as severe as the ones on his horse haunches. In his warrior form, Blazel couldn't do much to help. Rizelya and Wisah worked to stanch the bleeding from a particularly deep cut. Rizelya grimaced at something Wisah said and stood with her helbraught in her hands.

"Blazel, hold him," Wisah commanded. "This is going to hurt like Crone's fires, but it's the only way to stop the bleeding."

Blazel nodded and carefully placed his paws on Jaehaas's shoulders. Rizelya's helbraught blade glowed red as she heated it with her fire magic. Grimacing, she touched the blade to the cut Wisah indicated. Jaehaas screamed and kicked out with his hooves. Blazel pressed down hard, restraining his friend.

"Aistrun!" Rizelya yelled. "I need you."

The warrior loped over to them. He'd found some water to wash the gore off his muzzle. Blazel wished he had thought to do the same. Every time he breathed, he smelled the unpleasant stench of sabertiger. Jaehaas stopped kicking, falling into unconsciousness.

"We have to cauterize three more of these slashes," Wisah said. "If we don't, he'll bleed to death. We need to keep him from flailing."

"Tie him," Aistrun muttered, then switched to mind-speech. *If we tie his legs together, he won't be able to kick them. Hey, I don't want to get hurt.*

Without waiting for a response, Aistrun jogged to the horses. While he dug through the bags for rope, Blazel picked up the water bag and splashed water over his muzzle and claws. He sighed in pleasure at removing the stink of blood. He took a drink and passed it to Rizelya, who gratefully took it, drank, and handed it to Wisah. She shook her head, concentrating on slathering salve on the cauterized wound. Jaehaas's skin shivered under her touch, but he remained unconscious.

Aistrun gave the rope to Rizelya. She quickly looped it around Jaehaas's legs just above the pastern and tied them together.

Wisah pointed to a long, bloody stripe, stretching from the top of Jaehaas's back all the way across his flank. Blazel set his paws on Jaehaas's shoulders while Aistrun held his rump. Rizelya concentrated, heating her helbraught blade to the right temperature. When it glowed, she placed the length of it on the cut. Jaehaas woke, screaming. His head and shoulders rose in protest, and it took all of Blazel's strength to push him back down.

Wisah put her hands on either side of Jaehaas's face. "We have two more to do, my darling," Wisah murmured. "Be brave, my love, and it will all be over soon." Still holding Jaehaas's face and staring into his eyes, she nodded to Rizelya.

This time, Jaehaas clenched his teeth before finally letting out a loud moan. Wisah gave him a few milcrons to recover before indicating for Rizelya to do the last one. Jaehaas's eyes rolled back in his head, and he passed out again. Wisah kissed his forehead before standing. She opened a jar and carefully dabbed salve on the seared flesh.

"He won't be able to travel today," Wisah said quietly, not looking up from her work. "If he tries to walk, these will break open and he could die." Fear darkened her voice.

"Is there a cave or other shelter nearby?" Rizelya leaned on her helbraught as if it were a staff.

Now the danger was gone—and Rizelya didn't need his warrior strength—Blazel released the magic and nearly sagged as his injuries flared with fresh agony. He gritted his teeth against the pain as he gazed around the clearing, getting his bearings.

"The cave with the hot pool isn't far from here, but we'll have to somehow get Jaehaas there."

"Perhaps the Gryphons can help," Rizelya suggested. "They used a sling to carry him up the cliff to Alkaak. Couldn't they do the same and fly him to the cave?"

"If they could, it would be best." Wisah looked up from applying salve. Tears streaked her face. "I don't want to lose him."

"I'll go ask Graak." Blazel touched Wisah's head in sympathy.

He found Graak beside the Gryphon with the damaged wing. Chariel had bandaged it the best she could. She smeared an ointment on Broogk's neck. The big Gryphon towered over her.

"How many of your flight were wounded?" Blazel asked.

Keeru is the most seriously injured. We have one dead. All the other injuries are minor. We fight the sabertigers often. He rotated his head to gaze at Blazel. *And you?*

"Jaehaas is seriously hurt. We've cauterized his wounds, but Wisah says if he walks, he'll break them open and bleed to death."

I'm grieved by this news. There is a cave nearby. We'll go there to rest and treat our wounded. I'll have two of my warriors bring the sling and carry Jaehaas there. We'll have to lift Keeru as well. He can't fly. Graak indicated the Gryphon with the damaged wing.

"Thank you." Blazel bowed his head in relief.

Chariel approached him as Graak gave orders to his flight. "Blazel, what happened to you? Remove your shirt so I can examine your back."

Groaning, he took off his shirt. He tried to pull away from her touch, but she grabbed his shoulder and wouldn't let him go.

"These wounds need stitching." She wrapped a bandage over them. She handed his shirt to him. "We'll take care of it at the cave. Is it the one with the hot pool?"

He nodded.

"Oh good! The hot water will help all of our wounded. Did I hear right? Jaehaas is badly injured?"

"Yes, but Rizelya cauterized his wounds, so he'll be okay."

He trailed after her as she ran to Jaehaas. Aistrun had shifted back to human and only had a few scratches. He helped Blazel maneuver Jaehaas into the sling under Chariel's and Wisah's supervision. They watched anxiously as the Gryphons lifted the net.

"Please, be careful and not break open his wounds." Wisah's voice was strident with worry. Once Jaehaas was safely off the ground, Chariel and Wisah ran to their horses.

"Go with them, Aistrun," Rizelya ordered. "Keep them safe. We'll follow."

Aistrun saluted her and raced after the girls. The sound of large wings beating echoed off the rocks. Soon, only Blazel, Rizelya, and Graak stood in the clearing.

"Would you like me to burn your fallen warrior, Graak?" Rizelya asked quietly. "It would be more dignified than leaving him here for the scavengers to eat."

Graak dipped his head. *I would be most grateful if you would. Our custom is to burn the dead, so their souls can pass to the Mother's arms.*

"It is ours as well."

It didn't take long for Rizelya's fire to immolate the body. Exhaustion hit Blazel as he climbed onto Lighzel's saddle, and his own back hurt where the sabertiger's jaws had punctured him. Warm blood dripped past the bandages. But as he gazed at Rizelya, he knew that with her he could endure anything.

Chapter 23

The horse's hooves rang on the stones in front of the cave's entrance. Rizelya slipped off Kymaya and hung against her, holding back a sob. She hadn't experienced the pain of having one of her squad-pack so seriously injured before. Fighting the monsters was dangerous, and many of her friends had been hurt, some even killed. But this was the first time someone under her leadership had been wounded.

She shuddered, remembering the deep gashes on Jaehaas's back and flanks she'd cauterized. The stink of burning flesh and hair rose unbidden to her mind. *Please, Warrior, Mother, and Crone, protect my pack. Let nothing more happen to them. And I pray I never have to do that again to one of my friends!*

Kymaya nosed her shoulder and gave a snort. Rizelya pushed away from the security of her old friend. She grabbed Kymaya's reins and led her to the makeshift stables. Blazel walked in front of her, his shirt boasting bright stains of blood. He needed his wounds taken care of soon.

Aistrun waited for them and took the horse's reins. He slapped them against his other hand. "We put Jaehaas in the back where it's warm. Wisah is with him. He hasn't awoken yet, but she assures us it's better for him. Hey, Blazel, Chariel told me to send you to her as soon as I saw you. She's in the same place."

Blazel grunted in reply and turned around. Aistrun whistled. "Sweet Mother, no wonder she's looking for you. You need to get those stitched. Don't worry, I'll take care of your horses. I've got help."

He tilted his chin to indicate Broogk, who carefully brushed Tejen. The curry brush appeared odd in the Gryphon's talon. When Broogk stopped his brushing to look at the newcomers, Tejen snorted and nosed the brush. Broogk dropped his beak in a grin and, chortling, went back to grooming the horse.

Blazel laughed and then bent over, coughing. When he quit, Rizelya gripped his arm and guided him to the fire. He had waited long enough to get his wounds tended properly, and she wasn't going to let him dither any longer. Chariel glanced up from stirring a simmering pot.

"Blazel, sit down before you fall down," Chariel ordered. "You're too pale."

Blazel slumped to the ground, and Chariel hustled to stand behind him. She grimaced at his blood-soaked shirt, dipped a rag in the basin warming near the fire, and tossed it to Rizelya. "Here, soak his bandages."

Rizelya placed the steaming towel on Blazel's back. He hissed through his teeth when it touched him, and it took a few milcrons for him to relax against her hands. When the towel cooled, she removed it, and together with Chariel, gently eased the shirt off his wounds. Rizelya bit her lip as Chariel removed the blood-soaked bandages.

Four deep punctures were on either side of his spine where the sabertiger's front claws had fastened onto Blazel's back. If she hadn't seen the attack and killed the cat, Blazel wouldn't be here now. Tears prickled her eyes. She blinked them away quickly. Chariel gently examined the holes.

"Will I need to cauterize any of them?" Rizelya's hand trembled. She didn't want to hurt her lover, but she would if it would save his life.

"No, they only need stitching." Chariel shook her head and handed a piece of wood to Blazel. "Here, bite down on this." She picked up a long, slender needle threaded with fine, strong thread.

Rizelya turned away, unwilling to watch. Instead, she moved to sit in front of Blazel and took his hands in hers. "You can hold on to me."

He gazed into her eyes as Chariel plunged the needle into his skin. His hands convulsed, tightly squeezing hers. By the time Chariel finished stitching all eight puncture wounds, Rizelya's hands were bruised from Blazel's crushing grip. Chariel slathered on salve. The tightness around his mouth and eyes eased, and his grip on her hands gentled.

Jaehaas regained consciousness, but he could barely hold his head up from so much blood loss. The sabertigers had attacked him the hardest. Chariel had stitched several wounds on his shoulders and one on his chest. If he didn't run or use his damaged flanks, he'd heal.

Rizelya curled next to Blazel, and his strong arms held her close. She gave thanks to the Goddess all her people had survived.

Graak's flight rigged two slings in the morning, one for his injured Gryphon, Keeru, and another for Jaehaas. Jaehaas grumbled about being carried, but didn't have much choice. He'd hobbled outside to relieve himself and shuddered with pain and exhaustion by the time he finished.

Even flying with slings between them, the Gryphons traveled quickly. The snow Rizelya and the others had trouble traversing on their journey northward had melted, increasing the pace the earthbound horses could cover. They raced past the ruined tower where they'd fought the wolves, and she was relieved to see no shadows skulking in the trees.

What had taken them eight days to travel, they now crossed in three. The air was warm, and she caught glimpses of flowers blooming in the meadows as they sped through them. Trees that had just been budding were in full leaf. Their rush startled a lonely bear, who roared as it chased them. A huge eagle-type Gryphon dove on it and snapped its neck. He gloated with pleasure for such a fine meal.

"If we keep this pace, we should reach the boundary of the Sanctuary's territory tomorrow," Rizelya commented as she ate dinner. Her arms ached so badly from gripping the reins, her spoon trembled.

"I might make it." Wisah groaned, staring at her soup bowl. "I'm so tired I can't eat."

"Hey, just think," Aistrun said, sounding much too chipper, "there will be safe houses along the way with real beds to sleep in."

Chariel's eyes lit up. "No more sleeping on the ground."

By the time they finally stopped for the night, fatigue dragged at Rizelya. Lines of exhaustion pulled at her people's faces, and when no one mentioned digging out the tents and setting them up, she didn't argue. They laid out their bedrolls in a circle around the fire.

"Even though I be riding in that damned contraption all day, I'm exhausted," Jaehaas complained, holding his mug of taevo in shaking hands. "My poor belly be sore from being rubbed by the sling's ropes."

"I'll get some salve." Wisah smoothed ointment into his tummy and snuggled beside him. She mumbled something about fixing the sling for him before her eyes drooped shut.

Rizelya had enough energy to kiss Blazel goodnight before her own fatigue dragged her into sleep.

Late the next evening, when the light was failing, and they were about to quit for the night, the trail became a rough road. A tall pillar marked the Sanctuary Territory's boundary.

Rizelya pulled on Kymaya's reins. "We're here. Let's make camp. It's too dark to go any further."

Aistrun and Blazel removed the packs from their multas. Kressy hooted with pleasure, immediately sank to the ground, and rolled in the dirt, quickly followed by her companion, Gemmy.

Chariel and Wisah dug through a pack for the cooking supplies. Rizelya gathered firewood, using her fire magic to create a small light to see. She dropped the armload of wood next to the circle of stones Aistrun stacked for the fire. A few moments later, a cheery fire pushed back the darkness. Graak landed beside them. He settled in front of the fire and watched while the pot of water boiled and Chariel tossed in taevo leaves to brew.

He took a sip, savoring the rich flavor. *I expect Moraak and his group will arrive here sometime tomorrow. We should wait for him.*

"Our horses could use a rest," Rizelya said. "We've pushed them hard."

"Hey, I could use a rest," Aistrun complained. "So could Blazel and Jaehaas. This arduous journey hasn't helped their injuries any."

Then it's settled. Graak held out his mug for more taevo. *We do not have this drink. Perhaps when this is all over, we can begin to trade. I believe our alliance should not end when we have defeated these invaders.*

Blazel nodded with approval. "Trade would benefit both our species. You have many fine things, and we have taevo." He laughed as he held up his mug. "Seriously, there are multiple items we can share and trade between us."

"But first, we have to rid the world of the Malvers' monsters." Chariel rubbed her face. "We can't think about trading when it's so dangerous to travel."

After we deal with these invaders, we will combine our efforts to accomplish this plan. Graak twirled his mug between his talons. *That is, if Moraak becomes the heir. He would support our idea of trade. His brother Daelaak would not. As you saw, he believes we should continue to isolate ourselves from the rest of the world. It is only the mountains that stop the Malvers' monsters from our territory. If the Malvers themselves should escape their exile, they will hunt us down and kill every last Gryphon.*

"Do you think we can defeat this invader?" Wisah turned her cup in her hand and glanced shyly at Graak. "They did come from the sky."

We shall see if we can kill them. If so, then yes, I believe we'll be able to remove them from our world. It has been a long day. I must attend to my flight. Sleep well, my friends.

Rizelya had tried to keep from thinking about the strange people who had invaded her world. *Why had they landed in Shandir's Crater? Who were they? Were they friends or foes?* Her thoughts and worries kept her awake until well into the night.

The chirping birds slowly intruded into Blazel's sleepy mind. He cracked one eye open, squinting at the pale light of dawn. He started to push himself up when Rizelya snaked her arm around his neck and tugged him back down.

"We're not leaving at dawn today," she whispered, then kissed his throat.

He grabbed the top of their blankets and pulled them over their head. Kissing her deeply, he roamed his hands over her body. He cupped her breasts, bent lower, and swept his tongue across a nipple. It hardened, and he sucked on it. Rizelya groaned, and her searching hands found his manhood, stroking it to hardness. He throbbed with need. Their lovemaking this time was hard and fast, both of them too exhausted to prolong it. Afterward, Rizelya kissed his chest, then laid her head on it. Blazel wrapped her in his arms, and they drifted back to sleep.

With a muttered growl, Blazel flung his arm over his eyes to block out the obnoxious light. As he came more aware and awake, he grimaced at the cold seeping under the blanket where Rizelya usually warmed his side. Sighing, he rubbed the sleep out of his eyes and opened them to find a mug held in front of his nose. He took a deep breath, inhaling the savory smell of deep roasted taevo. The sunlight framed Rizelya's face. He leaned forward and kissed her fingers before taking the mug.

"A scout arrived a little while ago." She stood, sipping her taevo. "Moraak will arrive in an octar. It gives us time to eat breakfast and clean up. Aistrun caught a rabbit, and it's roasting now. The last of our gruel is boiling. I'm so glad we're in Sanctuary Territory and there are safe houses with food available besides rabbit stew and porridge."

"I'm tired of it, too." He stretched, throwing his arms out wide. "Ugh! I didn't get enough sleep. I'll be happy when we reach the Sanctuary and can stop moving for a few days, if not a chedan."

Rizelya grimaced. "I wouldn't count on it."

They joined the others at the fire. Jaehaas sat curled on his knees next to Wisah. Blazel walked behind him and examined his injuries. "You look better. Your wounds aren't as swollen or red, and there isn't any oozing from them like there was yesterday."

"I be better." Jaehaas flicked his tail across his back, wincing when it caught the edge of a cauterized cut. "I should be able to run with you today."

Wisah sputtered, spitting out her taevo. "Oh, no you won't! Your wounds need another day to heal." She patted his shoulder. "I know you hate the sling, dearest, but I don't want to lose you."

"I be fine. Really. I be injured before, and it only took a few days to heal."

"Not like this you haven't!"

"We'll see how he moves after we eat," Chariel interrupted. She shook her spoon at Jaehaas. "But mind you, if any of those wounds are still seeping, it will be the sling for you."

Jaehaas ducked his head in agreement.

They finished eating and cleaned up their campsite. Chariel examined Jaehaas's injuries before directing him to go through his paces. Blazel joined her, draping an arm over her shoulders.

"He's stiff and favoring his right side," Blazel noted. "But he's moving well."

"How much farther until we reach the Sanctuary?" Chariel asked as she continued to scrutinize Jaehaas's movements.

Blazel thought for a moment. "It took us three days the last time, but then we were traveling slowly to ease you and Wisah into riding. If we continue at the pace we have been, tomorrow. Two, if we slowed a bit so he could travel with us."

"Let's go slower. It hurts his pride to be carried like he has been." Chariel waved to Jaehaas and yelled, "Jaehaas, come here!"

A light sheen of sweat covered Jaehaas's hide and face. When he presented his right flank to Chariel and Blazel, his wounds hadn't opened. Chariel ran a gentle finger over the cuts.

"No seepage. You can run with us, but..." She held up a hand to forestall Jaehaas's whoop. "If you falter, or it breaks open, I'll have Graak's people carry you."

"I be careful," Jaehaas promised, touching his hand to his chest. "I'd much rather return to the Sanctuary and the Supreme on my own four feet." He ducked to brush a kiss on Chariel's cheek.

The boom of distant thunder shook the ground, and Blazel searched the sky devoid of clouds. A smudge appeared high overhead. It soon resolved into wing upon wing of Gryphons.

The light gleamed off the lead Gryphon, Moraak. Rizelya jogged to Blazel's side and her fingers interlocked with his. The three hundred Gryphons flying in a huge wedge darkened the sky. Aistrun and Wisah joined them. Graak landed near them a few moments before the rest of his flight.

"Oh, what a marvelous sight," Rizelya breathed. "How can we not win with so magnificent a force fighting with us?"

I agree with you. Graak lifted his head to the sky. *I haven't ever seen so many Gryphons in flight all at once. It is so beautiful.* Awe tinged his voice.

Moraak folded his wings and dove swiftly toward the waiting group. A contingent of Gryphons followed him down. The rest lowered their altitude in a slow spiral. The clearing wasn't large enough for all three hundred Gryphon to land.

They will find roosts in the trees, Graak said. *The ones with Moraak are his advisers and guards. Ah, Sheekeek is with his entourage. Good, we need a mystic's advice.* He turned to Chariel. *Not belittling yours, but we will need all we can get.*

Chariel smiled at him. "It isn't a problem. I like Sheekeek. I'm glad he's come. He and the Supreme will get on well."

The Gryphons backwinged to land, throwing dirt and leaves in the air. They alighted in perfect formation with Moraak in the lead, two massive Thunder Wings at his side and one at his back. Sheekeek peeked around another huge Gryphon and waved at the group.

Greetings, my lord. Graak bowed.

Aistrun stepped forward and dropped to one knee in front of Moraak, repeating the traditional greeting to Gryphon lords. Graak gave him an approving nod.

You have been practicing, my friend. Moraak indicated for Aistrun to rise. *It is good we have found you at last. Are you all well? We saw the signs of a battle with sabertigers.*

Graak mantled his feathers. *Yes, they attacked us and killed Telek. Keeru was injured. His wing is healing thanks to the care of Priestess Chariel.*

And were any of you hurt? Moraak asked the Posairs.

"Yes, my lord," Aistrun answered. "The sabertigers nearly killed Jaehaas."

Moraak motioned for Jaehaas to approach him. He examined the claw slashes, a shrill whistle escaping him. *You *are lucky, Jaehaas. Those wounds are deep. I am pleased you survived and are healing. Where are we?*

Graak pointed at the tall pillar. *At the boundary to Sanctuary Territory. It is but a half day's flight to the Sanctuary itself, or so Blazel assures me.*

"But it's two or more for us on horseback," Blazel added, "if we allow for our injured."

Moraak considered the morning sun. *If you leave him here, how long?*

"A day... day and a half."

Good! I will meet you at the Sanctuary's gates at sundown tomorrow. We'll rest here, and my army will camp in this forest until we have spoken with your Supreme.

Blazel and the others bowed to Moraak, who turned away from them, giving orders to his commanders.

"I be not staying here!" Jaehaas cried, grabbing onto Rizelya's arm. "Please, don't make me stay here alone."

Rizelya raised an eyebrow in question at Chariel, who nodded. "Okay, you may come with us. But if you slow us down, we'll leave you at a safe house until after Moraak's meeting with the Supreme."

Jaehaas nodded his understanding.

I will remain here with the prince, Graak said softly. *It wouldn't do to take his surprise away from him. He knows he makes an impressive sight and wishes to use it to his advantage with the Supreme. We hear she is formidable.*

"She is," Blazel said. "Remind him she sent us looking for you. She knows we need this alliance with you to survive the coming madness."

Graak dipped his head, then turned to catch up with Moraak.

Within half an octar, Rizelya's group secured their packs on the multas, saddled their horses, and raced on the rough road toward the Sanctuary. Rizelya set a quick pace, but not one so fast Jaehaas couldn't maintain. They stopped often for short rests to allow Jaehaas to catch his breath and relieve the ache in his wounded flank. Soon, the road became better maintained, and not long after, they passed the first safe house.

The summer sun warmed them as they continued to ride. The sky was the purple of dusk when Rizelya guided the group through the gates of a safe house. As soon as they were in the courtyard, Jaehaas stopped, his head hanging and his hindquarters quivering. Chariel reached for the reins of Wisah's horse. Wisah, bag in hand, slid off Tejen and hurried to Jaehaas. Blazel, riding in the rear, passed them as Wisah was rubbing liniment into Jaehaas's sore back and hindquarters.

When he arrived in the stables, Aistrun cared for Chariel's horse. Blazel assumed she was in the safe house preparing dinner. In the three chedans they'd traveled together, he'd learned Rizelya wasn't much of a cook. If they wanted an edible meal, then anyone in their group, besides Rizelya, did the cooking. Blazel wearily slid off Lighzel, led her to a clean stall, and laid out fresh straw for her bed. After rubbing off her sweat, he filled a bucket with water and the manger with hay. He measured out a healthy portion of grain for her as well. All the horses worked hard and needed the extra rations.

Blazel grimaced at the narrow cots in the safe house. He pushed his and Rizelya's cots together. Aistrun noticed what he was doing, and with a grin, did the same thing to his and Chariel's beds.

"How are you holding up, Jaehaas?" Rizelya asked as Wisah and Jaehaas came into the house.

"I be hanging in there. I'll live."

"None of his gashes tore open," Wisah said, sinking onto the end of the bench. "There isn't any bleeding. He should do fine tomorrow."

"It isn't much farther to the Sanctuary." Blazel stretched his legs in front of him, crossing them at the ankles. "We've made better time than I expected. We should arrive there well before sundown.

They ate a meal of rice, beans, and hot pan bread. It tasted sublime after days of eating rabbit stew and porridge.

Blazel roused at Rizelya's touch on his face.

"Wake up, lover. We need to leave soon."

Blazel elbowed himself to a sitting position, peering at the pale gray light of predawn.

The group ate a breakfast of cold leftovers and a mug of hot taevo.

"Let's go, let's go." Chariel gulped the last of her taevo. "I can't wait to get back home and sleep in my own bed."

Aistrun frowned at her. "But if you sleep in your bed, I can't sleep with you. You live in the cloister."

"None of us will be sleeping with our lovers while in the Sanctuary," Wisah said. "Certainly not us priestesses. The Supreme won't allow it. Only if we were bond-mates."

"Then let's do it." Aistrun's eyes lit up.

"No." Chariel crossed her arms over her chest. "You don't rush into completing a bond-mate ceremony, and we won't do it just so we can have sex. It's a lifelong bond." Her lip trembled, and her eyes watered. "Besides, the Supreme would never allow it for me."

"Why not?" Aistrun's brows furrowed in confusion.

"Because she's a Gray," Rizelya answered softly, and a haunted look flitted across her face. "And not any Gray, but a charcoal Gray. We've become so used to her, we don't see anything unusual. To us, she's simply our friend and pack-mate. But to others, she will awaken the ancestral hatred for Malvers, even if they don't know why they're afraid of her."

"But... but she's part of our pack now. She has to come with us."

"Perhaps the Supreme will allow her to." Rizelya shrugged.

"She must," Chariel said. "The prophecy isn't finished. We've only found the alliance." She gave a small smile to Aistrun. "Don't worry, you're not done with me yet."

Aistrun wrapped her in his arms and kissed her deeply. "I will never be done with you," he said hoarsely.

Rizelya turned away from them and headed out the door. Blazel followed her. At the stable entrance, he caught her arm. "What's wrong?"

"I'm dreading leaving the mountains. The Sanctuary will be just another stop in our journeying. Once we pass its protection, I'm afraid I'll be swamped again with visions from the Malvers. They nearly crippled me. The ride from Strunhelos Keep to the Sanctuary is a blur. I was locked in the nightmare of the Malvers' cruelty, and I'm not sure I can face it again. To see and feel the deaths of so many... children... animals... she showed me all of it." Rizelya covered her face with her hands.

Blazel folded her into his embrace and held her while she cried. She soon brushed the tears from her eyes and leaned against his chest for a moment longer before pushing out of his arms. Rizelya straightened her shoulders and put on a brave smile.

"I won't let her win," Rizelya said forcefully.

He reached out and rubbed the last of her tears away with his thumb. "You're one of the strongest people I know. We'll find a way to block her from your mind. You mentioned you had a Blue in your pack. Perhaps she can help you."

"That's right, Saffren. She mentioned Blues were taught to shield their minds."

When she smiled at him again, it was with hope.

The road to the Sanctuary was smooth and well maintained. The sound of thundering hooves echoed off the crushed stone. They rode over a hill in the late afternoon, and before them sprawled the Sanctuary. A herd of horses and multas grazed in a pasture, and sheep roamed the green hills.

Women wearing broad-brimmed hats, brown tunics, and trousers worked the fields. Young girls, their white hair shimmering in the sun, ran and played in the cloister's central space. Here, life was slow and peaceful. They were far from the depravations of the Malvers' monsters and didn't live in constant fear of an attack. Blazel would do anything in his power to keep this territory from the Malvers' evil.

He guided the group around the pastures and fields to the road leading to the great gates. The guards waved them through, and they clattered into the guest courtyard. He glanced at the sky. Sundown was still an octar or two away. They should have time to clean up before Moraak arrived.

A team of young girls hurried from the stables to care for their horses. He caught the attention of one.

"Tell the Supreme we've returned, and that she will soon have guests."

The girl's eyes widened, and she sped from the courtyard and into the Sanctuary's inner sanctum. Blazel pushed open the door to the guest area. With the others following behind him, even Chariel and Wisah, he strode to the guest house they had stayed in prior to leaving on their quest. All he could think of was a hot bath—and loving Rizelya.

Chapter 24

The saddlebags thrown over Rizelya's shoulder weighed her down as she trudged next to Blazel into the guest house. They'd traveled sixteen days to reach the Gryphon city of Alkaak, but their mad dash to the Sanctuary cut their time in half. Her people, and most of all, her horses needed to rest.

Blazel pulled open the front door, and she tripped on the small step up. His strong arm halted her fall. Rizelya pushed her saddlebags back onto her shoulder. The tired footsteps of her pack staggering on the stone floors made her hope they'd stay here for a few days to recuperate. Jaehaas's stride stuttered and dragged.

"I'll ask a healer to see you," Wisah said to Jaehaas.

"I'm unsure if I want to sleep, eat, or bathe first." Rizelya's voice quivered with fatigue.

"Bath!" the others shouted in unison.

At the next intersection in the corridor, she turned left toward the bathing facility. Steam filled the room. After dropping her bags on a bench, she tore off her clothing and lurched to the waiting wash buckets. She sat on a stool and reached for the soap pot. Blazel's hand on her shoulder made her pause. He held a rag, already soaped. With smooth, almost caressing movements, he washed her back. His hands slid around to cup her breasts. A small gasp escaped her as the heat of desire blazed within her.

Quiet murmuring, and the clunk of someone rising from a stool, returned her to her senses. They weren't alone. Regretfully, she pushed him away and snatched the rag from his hand to wash her own front. He sighed and sat on the stool next to her. With a grin, she swept behind him and soaped his back, being careful of his nearly healed wounds. Hand in hand, they entered to the shower to sluice the soap from their bodies and wash their hair.

Picking up his long locs, she rubbed hair soap into them. When she had first seen him, he had looked wild and strange. Now, he was quickly becoming more than her lover. She slipped into his arms and tenderly traced the scar on his face. Yes, she was falling in love with this extraordinary, courageous, solitary man. Standing on her tiptoes, she kissed him deeply.

"I'm glad you returned to the Sanctuary when you did," she whispered.

"And I'm happy you were here. Especially in this dangerous time, it's nice to have someone to care about you." His thumb traced the line of her jaw. "And I care very much for you."

As he kissed her again, she wondered if it was possible for them to become bond-mates, a rarity in their society. No one had ever touched her heart like he did, Kaieli had come close, and Rizelya dearly loved her heart-sister, but their relationship had never deepened into becoming bond-mates. She'd wait and discover what developed.

Clean of dirt and suds, Rizelya linked hands with Blazel and led him to the deep tub of steaming water where the others soaked. It amazed her how comfortable Blazel had become. She remembered the first time he'd joined them in a bath, and how shy and embarrassed he had been. Well, he wasn't now. He joked with Aistrun as they settled into the tub. Smiling, Rizelya leaned her head back on the tub's rim and closed her eyes. Soon, their chatter quieted and silence ruled the bathing room.

A strident voice broke through Rizelya's reverie. "Blazel, Chariel, the Supreme wants to meet with all of you."

Rizelya groaned and pushed back until she was sitting straight. "Work calls. I'm surprised the Supreme let us have this much time before demanding to see us."

"The runner must have told her how filthy we were," Wisah said as she sat up. "She believes in cleanliness. But if we don't hurry, she won't be happy with us."

"Moraak!" Blazel exclaimed, shooting to his feet. Water sloshed over the sides. "He'll be here soon, and the Supreme doesn't know he's coming. Hurry up! We don't want this tentative alliance to fail because we were bathing."

His words galvanized the group, and they quickly climbed from the soaking tub. Rizelya dug through her bags until she found her formal clothes. As she slipped on her top, she noticed the others were putting on their finery as well. Blazel was handsome in his yellow shirt and light brown trousers. She frowned. Those were Haasneh colors. Once they rode back to Strunlair Keep, she'd find him something in Strunland colors. He belonged to her pack and needed to be wearing her colors. Come to think of it, Jaehaas needed new clothes in her colors, too.

Dressed and with her hair neatly braided, Rizelya was ready to report to the Supreme. Chariel and Wisah arranged their hair in the traditional style for priestesses. Aistrun was the last to stamp his feet into his boots. Without a word, they filed from the bathing room.

Rizelya gave Blazel a small smile as he strode beside her, the customary spot for her co-alpha. She glanced over her shoulder at Aistrun, happily escorting Chariel. When he'd relinquished his position to Blazel in the mountains, Aistrun had neither asked nor wanted to resume the leadership role. She doubted Histrun and Naila would allow him to continue shirking his responsibility as an alpha. She had fully accepted being one when she brought the women with other Talents besides Red into her squad-pack. And now, she realized, she was quite content being the leader. And she liked having Blazel as her co-alpha.

Outside, the sun dropped low on the horizon, but hadn't set. They still had time to warn the Supreme, if they hurried. She increased her pace. The clip-clop of Jaehaas's hooves kept up. The hot water had done all of them good. She paused inside the temple's threshold, again in awe of the beautiful murals. Blazel hooked her hand over his elbow and hustled through the sanctum. Blazel continued to unobtrusively guide her to the audience chamber. They stopped at the huge black ironwood double doors and waited for the guard to admit them.

As she approached the dais where the Supreme sat on her crystal throne, Rizelya studied the white room, gauging if the Gryphons could fit into it. With both doors open, a Thunder Wing could easily pass through them. The high ceiling wouldn't make the Gryphons feel crowded, and the large room would allow all of Moraak's entourage to sit comfortably. She considered the corridor leading to the audience chamber. A Gryphon could walk down it and not scrape his wings. Rizelya wondered if they'd built the Sanctuary to accommodate Gryphons.

The Supreme tapped her fingers on the arms of her throne. Her nails clicked on the crystal, creating a soft chime. The ten rings on her fingers flashed, casting light all around her. She wore a dazzling, long, white silk gown, and a white veil covered her white hair.

This time, when Rizelya stopped the required eight paces in front of the dais, she wasn't frightened or in awe of the Supreme. She dropped to her knees, her companions a heartbeat behind her, and together they made the gesture of obeisance and honor to the Goddess's representative.

The soft chimes of the Supreme's tapping fingers stilled. "You may rise and come closer. So. Don't keep an old woman waiting. Did you find the Gryphons? Are they willing to renew our alliance? Well, speak up."

Rizelya bowed her head, hiding her smile. "Yes, Your Grace, we found the Gryphons. King Zorlaak is not ready for a formal alliance just yet. But he did send his son, Prince Moraak, to help us."

"What good is a single Gryphon?" the Supreme groused.

"Not one. Nearly three hundred." Blazel rocked on his heels, grinning.

The Supreme sat back on her throne, stunned.

"Did you hear the boom and see the comet ten days ago?" Rizelya asked. At the Supreme's nod, she continued. "It wasn't a comet, but a metal flying machine. It landed at Shandir's Crater and disgorged people. We have been invaded."

"How do you know this?"

"Gryphon scouts followed the machine and saw it land. We nearly killed our horses getting back to you."

The Supreme considered Rizelya. "And when will I meet this Moraak?"

"He'll arrive at sundown."

The sun's last rays hit a window high in the wall, and bright colors sparkled and dappled across the dais. A crack of thunder rolled over the Sanctuary. The Supreme's eyes widened, and then a slow smile crossed her face.

"It's Moraak," Blazel explained.

"I never thought to hear the sound of Gryphons landing in my courtyard," the Supreme said. "It has been too long since we allowed our friends to retreat into the Deep Mountains."

Rizelya felt the tickle of mind-speech being used nearby, but not directed at her. A few milcrons later, a phalanx of red-robed, veiled female warriors carrying helbraughts trooped through the doors, followed by numerous priestesses in white gowns. The guards tromped to form a ring around the outside walls, and two hurried to stand at attention on either side of the Supreme's throne.

The sound of claws and talons clicking on the corridor's marble floors reached them, and the Supreme leaned forward. Light globes spaced throughout the chamber brightened as the room darkened with the setting sun.

A guard flung both doors open, and announced, "Prince Moraak to seek an audience of Her Grace, the Supreme of all Posairs, the Goddess made flesh."

Moraak towered over the woman as she stepped aside to let him enter. Gasps rippled through the gathered crowd as they glimpsed his massive form. The gold in his feathers gleamed in the brilliant light. Gems studded the filigree shapes worked in gold, silver, and copper on his collar. On his head, he wore a gold circlet. Leather bands dyed gold covered his fore talons, and gems winked as he moved.

Moraak led his entourage into the audience chamber with slow, ponderous steps. Graak paced in behind him, resplendent in his deep indigo leather collar. His feathers and fur shone. The Silver Beak, Sheekeek, entered next. A beaten silver collar with large moonstones worked into it adorned his chest. Two Thunder Wings, both dark black and wearing unadorned black leather collars, formed the rear guard.

Rizelya and her group had moved to the side when the Gryphons arrived. Moraak stopped one of his paces from the dais and, with great dignity, bowed to the Supreme.

"Oh, you are magnificent," the Supreme breathed. "Welcome to the Sanctuary. We have long awaited the return of your people to our lands."

Moraak placed a talon across his chest and dipped his head. *It is my honor to be the first Gryphon in generations to return south of the Deep Mountains.*

"It saddens us you have come when our world is in danger. Rizelya informed us of what your scouts reported. Are you here to renew our ancient alliance?"

My father, King Zorlaak, assigned me as an envoy and bade me to discover if it would be beneficial for Gryphons to ally with the Posairs once more. The threat these strangers present to all of us is the only reason he agreed to even speak with you. Moraak turned his head to nod at Rizelya. *Rizelya's visions of our hated enemy, the Malvers, also sent us here. If they indeed are not dead and are becoming stronger, an alliance may be what saves us from their evil.*

The Supreme's fingers idly drummed on the arms of her throne. She gazed thoughtfully at Chariel. "Are these invaders part of your visions?"

Chariel nodded. "They are the madness."

They rape the land, Sheekeek cried. *Keeps slaughtered, survivors enslaved. Madness is here...* He wailed and dropped to the ground, his beak tucked into his belly. Chariel hurried over to him and gently stroked his head feathers.

"Is this true?" the Supreme demanded.

Moraak dipped his head in assent. *Sheekeek is a mystic and has true visions, just like your Chariel. I will send scouts to the crater to determine what the invaders are doing.*

"We would much appreciate such tidings. Blazel mentioned you have a large force with you. We have facilities to house two flights of one hundred each. Your remaining people will have to quarter outside in a field."

You are most gracious, Supreme. I and my retinue will stay here tonight. The rest of my flight will join us tomorrow.

"Wisah," the Supreme said, motioning her forward, "guide our new friends to the aviary, but slowly. By the time you arrive, we should have it cleaned and ready for our guests. Moraak, when will you send your scouts?"

I have scouts with me. They'll leave at first light.

"Very good. We can do nothing until we know more about these invaders. Report to me when you have news."

Moraak bowed and turned to the door. Wisah hurried to his side. At a slight nod from the Supreme, Rizelya made a quick bow and followed the Gryphon delegation from the audience chamber, her pack at her heels.

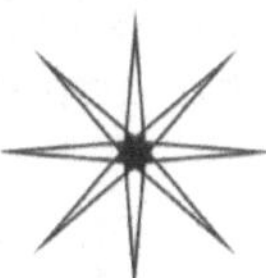

Once they exited the audience chamber, a red guard motioned for them to follow her and led them to a panel on the wall. The mural depicted Gryphons in flight, a contingent swooping down on a beast that put to shame the monsters the Posairs fought. Near the top, a nimbus of flame surrounded a gold Gryphon. The monster directly below him burned.

The guard reached up and pressed the gold Gryphon's beak, and the panel disappeared, revealing the courtyard beyond. In all his years in the Sanctuary, Blazel hadn't seen anything like it. He glanced at Wisah and Chariel, and their faces echoed his surprise. Thirty Gryphons huddled in the inner courtyard. At the sight of Moraak, they stilled. Blazel hadn't expected so many to accompany the prince.

Show us to this aviary, Moraak said to Wisah.

She nodded. "I always wondered what those enormous buildings were and what type of being they were supposed to house. Now, I know." She looked at a door in the east wall, then frowned at Moraak and the two Thunder Wings behind him. "Oh, you're never going to fit through there."

Moraak chuckled. *Do not worry so, Wisah. It is but a short hop for us to go over the wall. We will meet you on the other side.*

Wisah blushed. Blazel and the others followed her through the door. Moraak and his entourage flapped over the courtyard wall.

Wisah led them past the guest houses and beyond the small wooded area, a good distance away from the practice arenas. The trees opened to reveal two humongous buildings, with an extensive field behind them. The tall, wide door would allow a Gryphon as large as the Thunder Wings to enter. Carved Gryphons decorated the door and the lintel.

Wisah gazed at the carvings. "I never noticed those before when I came here exploring."

"Neither did I," Chariel said. "It's obvious now because we've seen Gryphons that this building was built to house them, which explains why the furniture is so strange. Welcome to your guest quarters."

Chariel pushed on the door, which swung silently open into a huge communal space with many of the low couches the Gryphons favored scattered around the room. Tables for eating filled one corner. Blazel wondered how the furniture hadn't fallen to dust long ago. The Sanctuary hadn't housed Gryphons here since the Great War. Then he remembered the store room he'd discovered under the library with the ancient artifacts. Magic had kept them in pristine condition.

The open far wall allowed the Gryphons to fly into and out of the structure and led to a grassy plaza. A large fountain, gurgling as water began to flow through it, was located in the center. Individual rooms lined three walls of the building. The top-floor balconies overhung the bottom floor, and wide railings provided landing grips for incoming Gryphons housed on the second floor. Each floor contained fifty rooms, sufficient space for a full flight of one hundred.

Moraak peered into the first room, nodded in satisfaction, and continued inspecting the building. Blazel peeked in. It held a thick, fluffy bed large enough for even the massive Thunder Wings. The only other furnishing was a wooden chest to hold personal items.

When they returned to the communal room, servants had filled a table with plates of bloody meat, pitchers of chilled wine and juice, and bowls of nuts and berries. Several steaming pots of taevo sat on another table. Blazel's eyes widened at the Posair dishes also laid out, including his favorite spiced lamb dish and creamy roasted tubers. His mouth watered at the smell of the fresh baked bread. He grabbed a loaf and broke it open, inhaling as he pulled the bread apart and stuffed it in his mouth.

"Pan bread just isn't the same as hot, crusty yeast bread," Rizelya said, taking the other half of the loaf out of his hand.

They piled plates with food and found places at the eating tables. Once they satisfied their initial hunger, talk resumed.

Graak, you and a talon of your flight fly to the crater tomorrow. Moraak put down his goblet of wine. *If what Sheekeek saw in his visions has already occurred, I want more than scouts. Your warriors are capable of fighting if needed. Assess the invaders' strength, determine if they have any weakness. If you can, find out why they are here.*

Graak sat up straighter at the praise. *We shall do as you ask.*

But don't take any unnecessary risks.

"I need to go with you," Blazel said. "I know the area. The Barrens are not a place to treat lightly. Besides, I want to make sure my friends guarding the crater are safe. With the invaders landing there, I'm worried about them."

Rizelya covered her plate with a napkin. "Maheli is a good friend of mine. More than our Strunland pack guards the crater. We need to ensure all four guard-packs aren't in trouble. I'm going, too."

"Have you been to the crater?" Blazel asked.

"Well, no. But you need me. You said the monsters were even more active near the crater when you were there. I can protect us from them." She turned to Graak. "If the guard-packs are in trouble, is there any way for us to evacuate them?"

There won't be enough of us. None of the big guys are going with us. They're too slow. At Rizelya's crestfallen face, he added, *If we can help, we will.*

"What about the rest of the pack?" Aistrun asked. "Shouldn't we stick together?"

Rizelya frowned, shaking her head. "We aren't going to be fighting, just looking around. I doubt this is what the prophecy referred to."

This reconnaissance mission only consists of a small party, Graak added. *We can't carry all of you.*

"We'll need to take food and water with us," Blazel warned. "There isn't any in the Barrens. The only things in the Barrens are black sand-glass, petrified wood, and the crater." A shiver ran through him as he remembered his trek through them. It seemed a life-time ago, but had only been a lunadar.

A while later, they finalized their plans, and everyone left to find their beds.

Blazel sank into his with Rizelya, groaning with pleasure. They had the room all to themselves. He stroked her face and kissed her lightly, but his exhaustion weighed his eyes closed.

Chapter 25

Blazel and Rizelya raced to the Gryphon's housing. They each carried a pack of food and a large water skin. Sweat dripped down Blazel's back. He loosened his winter coat, which Graak insisted they had to wear, because as high as they would fly, the air would be freezing. When they arrived, the Gryphon contingent filled water bags from the fountain.

Graak and Glork wore what looked like a modified saddle on their backs. The saddles were longer and flatter than those made for horses, and fit along the Gryphon's upper back. Straps, similar to a girth strap, led from the seat on either side of their wings and under their bellies. Lines attached the saddle—or was it a harness—to the leather collars they wore.

"Hello, Glork." Rizelya bowed to the Gryphon. "Thank you for allowing me to be your passenger."

The brown and white Gryphon ducked his head. *My pleasure. The saddles will make the long flight to Shandir's Crater more comfortable for both of us. Put on your hat and gloves, and fasten your coat before buckling in. As high as we'll fly, you'll get cold.* He crouched low for her to climb on his back.

Rizelya frowned at the multiple straps with buckles hanging from the saddle. "What do I do?"

Blazel shrugged. "I don't know. When I stayed with Graak as a teenager, he didn't have one of these."

The harness is what your ancestors used when we fought with them during the Great War, Graak explained. *We discovered them while exploring the house. It's a good thing too. Otherwise, Blazel, you'd fall off.* He warbled a chuckle, making his sandy brown feathers jiggle.

"Hey, that only happened once!" Blazel protest, scowling at Graak. "And you didn't warn me you were going to fly a loop."

Broogk stepped forward. *Here, I'll help you. We also found instructions with them.* His front talons, with four "fingers", were as dexterous as Rizelya's hands.

Together, they figured out how to strap a person onto the Gryphon saddles. By the time they were done, Blazel felt like a bird trussed up for roasting. His legs were tucked up on either side of Graak, and he laid on his stomach. His feet rested on Graak's back, next to his wings. He had limited room to sit up into a crouch.

Once Blazel and Rizelya were securely bound in the harnesses, Graak gave the order to fly. His leap into the air threw Blazel back, his head snapping. Graak's powerful downstroke of his wings flung Blazel forward again. He reached for the straps and gripped them so tight his hands cramped.

Lay forward, Graak suggested.

Blazel did, and the jerking motions of Graak's pumping wings smoothed. Graak climbed higher, and the air chilled Blazel even through the thick fur he wore. Below them, the land passed quickly. The Storengher River sparkled in the sun. In a matter of octars, they swept over Strunlair Keep. At noon, the Gryphons spiraled down to the plains for a break.

Blazel carefully slid off Graak, keeping hold of the riding straps. When his feet touched the ground, his legs buckled. Riding a Gryphon was nothing like riding a horse. Blazel's butt and thighs were sore in different places, and his arms ached from holding onto the leather strap. Rizelya groaned, shaking her arms and legs to return the feeling into them. Once he steadied, Blazel dug a piece of dried meat from his rucksack and chewed it while walking in circles. All too soon, Graak called him back, ready to leave.

The sun sunk low on the horizon when Graak descended again. He landed near the Storengher River, right before it disappeared beneath the Barrens. The black sand-glass glittering in the fading light created a stark demarcation where the plains stopped and the Barrens began. Blazel cleared the grass and carried rocks from the riverbank to build a fire ring. Rizelya wandered the riverbank and found several large pieces of driftwood. Soon, a cheery fire pushed back the night.

The river's rocky shore wasn't a comfortable place to sleep, but it provided fresh fish for the Gryphons. Glork carried a large trout, still flopping wildly, in his beak, and dropped it next to Rizelya. He sauntered back to the river before she could thank him. As the fish cooked, Blazel stood gazing at the Barrens. His heart thundered in his chest, and bile rose in his throat as a breeze blew over the sand. Instantly, he returned to the awful night the windstorm buried him and his horse with black sand riddled with glass shards. He slept curled around Rizelya, her warmth chasing away the nightmares of his last crossing of the Barrens.

The next morning, they flew into and over the Barrens. They had only flown a short time when Rizelya cried out, her face white with fear. "Oh, Sweet Mother, no!" She pointed below them.

Two janacks and six brechas trundled from the Barrens and into the plains. No warriors chased them. No Reds stopped them with their fire.

"We can't let them get away," Rizelya shouted. "Glork, take me down."

Glork obeyed. Rizelya's helbraught glowed. A moment later, a stream of fire shot from the blade and arced to surround a brecha. It burst into flame and quickly disintegrated. Broogk screamed in anger, flames erupted around him, and he dove at a janack. The monster instinctively reached out a tentacle to yank him from the sky. It jerked away from the heat, but not before fire engulfed the tentacle and raced toward the bulbous body. Screeching, Gryphons dove and darted at the monsters. They swiftly destroyed the beasts, leaving only smoking piles of ash. Graak overflew his warriors, ensuring no monsters had escaped the carnage. A breeze carried the ashes back into the Barrens.

They flew on in large, sweeping circles. Less than an octar later, a plume of dust alerted them to something moving quickly across the sand. As they neared, Blazel swore at another group of monsters. He searched, but there weren't any fighters on the ground. He gritted his teeth at his uselessness and inability to fight the monsters with tooth and claw like he normally did. Before he could ask Graak to let him off so he could fight, the monsters were dead.

We haven't fought this type of creature before, Graak said, winging higher. *This is good practice for us.*

"But it's difficult for me to sit and only watch," Blazel grumbled.

Rizelya gave him a rueful smile. "Since your focus isn't on fighting, your job is to make sure none of them escape."

"I can do that. But I don't like this. Something is wrong. When I crossed here before, the guard-packs were all over the monsters—"

"We're a long way from the crater—"

"Rizelya, it didn't matter how far the monsters ran. The fighters chased them until they caught them."

Her eyebrows crinkled in worry.

After flying twenty more measures, and fighting three more battles, without a single fighting-pack on the ground, even the Gryphons became concerned. Blazel's heart lodged in his throat as Graak flew to the northern fortress, where he'd met the Strunlair guard-pack.

The gate hung open, and there weren't any sentries standing on the wall. An eerie silence filled the fortress.

"No, no, no!" Rizelya fumbled out of her saddle harness. "Maheli! Rolstrun! Bohandran! Where are you?" She ran into the Keep-House, with Blazel on her heels.

The only sound was their boots echoing off the stone floors. Small holes in the walls and the overturned furniture pointed to a struggle. But there weren't any bodies until they entered the stables. A few horses had escaped, but those caught in their stalls had been slaughtered. Whatever had killed them had left only dried husks behind. Blazel ran outside and heaved. *Who would kill horses?*

They found the same thing at the other fortresses. With heavy hearts, Graak led his flight into the upper atmosphere, catching the thermals and resting. They flew farther south. Even from their height, they could clearly see the wound in the earth. Shandir's Crater. An ugly, oblong object squatted on its rim. Blazel gasped at the size of it.

Graak sent Baekeek, a fast-flying owl-type scout, down to the crater, while they continued to circle high above it.

There's activity in the center, Graak explained, his long-distance sight much better than Blazel's.

Baekeek circled the crater once before he dove. Blazel gripped the riding strap as he waited, his fingers hurting with the pressure.

Suddenly, loud pops rent the air, and with a screech, Baekeek zipped out of the crater, his flames extending several feet away from him. As he gained altitude, he wobbled, and his flames sizzled out. Two of the larger Gryphons dove and came up under the injured scout, supporting him with their wings. Graak began to descend.

"No! His injury will get infected if we land in the Barrens," Blazel said.

Graak grumbled, and with a squawk, directed the others to keep flying and to stay together. They caught a thermal that carried them quickly out of the Barrens. Blazel kept glancing over his shoulder, afraid of pursuit. He didn't relax his vigilance until they returned to the edge of the plains, where the black sand-glass met scraggly bushes.

It took a few moments to unhook himself from the riding harness, and by the time Blazel jumped off, the injured scout was keening in pain. Blood covered his left wing where something had punctured a hole in it, and his feathers around it were scorched. Graak padded over to him and poured water over the wound. The scout's flaring had sealed the wound's edges, although blood still oozed from its center. Baekeek screeched as Graak examined the injury.

Grimacing, Blazel stomped away from the injured scout. He stopped at the edge of the Barrens, and he scuffed the toe of his boot into the black sand. The crunch of grass behind him alerted him, and a moment later, Rizelya threaded her arms around him and laid her head against his back. He pulled her hands tights against his chest.

"How can we fight these invaders when they're able to shoot a Gryphon from the sky?" Blazel said.

"We'll find a way. We've survived the Malvers' monsters, so we can survive against this." She scooted around until she faced him. "Perhaps the fire shield will stop whatever shot the scout. It worked with the baethor."

Blazel held her for a long time, staring out at the Barrens. His gaze swept to the boundary marking life and death. He squinted, trying to make sense of what his eyes were telling him. Letting go of Rizelya, he crouched to examine it closer. He stood, scowling. Still confused, he followed the beaten, compacted glass for several paces into the Barrens. He jumped on an outcropping of petrified wood. From this vantage point, he turned around and gasped. Jumping off the rock, he raced to where the scrub lands started, where the crushed bushes indicated a large party had camped. Frowning, he continued to follow the signs of a trail leading back into the scrublands. Rizelya paced behind him.

The trail took them to a wash where the dirt showed the passage of many feet, but no horses. A deep track, from something he'd never seen before, paralleled it. He crouched, studying the markings. Whatever made it, had three toes, with the middle toe longer than the others. The trail led deeper into the scrub. He hadn't paid much attention to where they were when Graak landed, but the scrubland told him they were in Posanlair Territory. He stood and stared at the trail.

"What's wrong?" Rizelya asked.

"A large group of people marched through here. And see here." He pointed to the strange track. "This must be an invaders' print. There's a minor keep in the direction the tracks are coming from."

"Warrior, take them!" Rizelya slammed the butt of her helbraught on the ground. "We have to go and search for survivors." She turned to run toward to the Gryphons.

He reached out a hand and stopped her. "We'll have to wait until morning. By the time we get back up in the air, it will be too dark."

Rizelya glared at the setting sun and swore again. She stalked toward their camp.

Blazel studied the tracks once more before following her. Bile burned his throat. He doubted they'd find anyone alive at the keep.

Early the next morning, Graak's team leaped into the sky, and followed the clearly marked trail made by the marching Posairs. After the night's rest, Baekeek could fly, although not far or fast. Only one place existed in the Barrens for the invaders to take the people from the keep: the crater. Rizelya's team, designed for scouting and quick movement, was too small to fight the invaders and rescue the people taken. Especially since the invaders possessed weapons able to injure a Gryphon in flight. Instead, they backtracked along the trail toward the keep, hoping to find any survivors and to learn more about the intruders.

A measure from the Barrens, a body sprawled on the ground. Rizelya's stomach plummeted when they landed to check it. Blazel carefully turned the dry and desiccated corpse over. Rizelya's hand flew over her mouth at the terror frozen on the young man's face. On closer examination, they discovered a strange wound puncturing his chest, and no blood remained in the body. Using her helbraught, Rizelya burned the corpse.

Bodies littered the trail to Posanreande Keep. After checking the first few, and finding they all had the same wounds, they couldn't bring themselves to look at each one they came across. However, Rizelya insisted on burning each one they found to allow their souls to return to the Mother.

When they arrived at the keep, scorch marks blackened the gates, which hung lopsidedly on their hinges. Rizelya scrambled off Glork's back, with Blazel following her a moment later.

A strange quiet blanketed the keep. No children ran in the streets. No women bustled around houses or in the fields. No men guarded the gates. Blazel shifted to his warrior form, lifted his muzzle, and choked. The stink of death stung Rizelya's nostrils and made her gag. They stalked inside. Half a dozen men sprawled on the cobblestones. Multiple holes punctured their bodies, but when Blazel turned them over, they lacked the strange wounds on their chests and necks.

Blazel stooped and checked a dark splotch on the ground. He inhaled deeply and shook his head. *Something died here, but I can't tell what it was. The only thing I can smell is death.* He stood, rubbing the stench from his nose.

They continued into the keep. Behind them, Graak motioned to the Gryphons, who spread out to investigate the buildings. Clearly, no danger remained, and Blazel shifted back to his natural form.

Rizelya and Blazel jogged to the Clan-house to search for the Keep Alphas. Inside, a Red sprawled in the foyer, her helbraught still gripped in her hands. A man, still in his warrior form, had purple stains covering his claws. The signs of struggle indicated the invaders had snatched people from their beds.

They checked the other houses. Broken furniture showed the Posairs had fought before succumbing to the attacker's greater force. But thankfully, they didn't find any more dead. Their luck changed when they reached the infirmary. Rizelya gagged at the discovery of the corpses of two fighters and an old man, still in their sickbeds, with similar gaping holes in their chests.

"These invaders are inhuman, to kill the sick and injured." Rizelya choked back her tears. They hadn't uncovered any murdered children—the only good thing in this catastrophe.

Shaken, she and Blazel trudged to the stables, hoping they wouldn't discover the same situation as they had at the fortresses. She sighed in relief at the lack of bodies. Blazel paced through the barn to the pasture and stopped at the gate.

"They're here. How could they do such a thing?" His head drooped into his hands, and his shoulders shook.

Rizelya didn't want to see what caused Blazel to break down, but she walked over anyway to stand next to him. A horse lay dead, drained of blood, just like the Posairs they had found on the trail. The lumps of more carcasses littered the pasture.

"Why would they kill the horses?" Tears streamed down her face.

Blazel shrugged and wiped at his eyes. "To keep our people from escaping?"

Rizelya and Blazel left the stables and regrouped with the Gryphons in the main courtyard.

"Did you find anything?" Blazel asked.

Only death, Graak said, his eyes bleak. *They killed all the livestock.*

"I didn't see any bodies of the invaders," Rizelya said. "Surely, our people would have killed some of them."

"I found signs in the courtyard where something had died," Blazel said. "It appears they took any of their wounded or dead. Too bad they did. It'd be helpful to study our enemies."

Have you seen enough? Graak grimaced. *This place makes me feel ill. Can we return to the Sanctuary?*

Rizelya surveyed the keep. Deep sorrow welled up in her heart for those who had died. Rage burned under her skin at the invaders who had taken her people. She gestured sharply at the carnage. "This proves they aren't here for peaceful purposes. The Supreme must know what we've discovered, and so must everyone else. I swear they will pay for this."

"Yes, they will." Blazel put his hand on her shoulder. "They will pay for every death they cause."

Rizelya could perform one service for the Keep's dead. She could burn their bodies to allow their souls to return to the Mother's Womb. She directed Blazel and the Gryphons to gather the dead. Rizelya prayed they weren't too late, and the souls of the dead hadn't begun to wander as ghosts. She wished Chariel had come with them to guide any lost souls to the other side of the veil. It was late afternoon by the time she fired the pyres. Sadness gripped her. She didn't know any of the deceased, and therefore, couldn't enact the traditional ritual of reciting the names of the dead to the Goddess as they burned.

We must go. Graak laid a gentle talon on her shoulder. *Moraak and the Supreme needs our information as soon as possible.*

Rizelya turned from the pyre, rubbing her face to dash away her tears. She was a warrior and had seen death before. But these people hadn't deserved to be murdered like this. And these were only the first to die because of the invaders. She shuddered at the thought.

Drained, she climbed onto Glork's back and numbly tied herself into the riding saddle. She kept her eyes on the ground, hoping against hope someone had escaped.

"Glork! Glork, go down." She tapped his shoulder, and when he turned his head to her, she pointed. "There's someone running. Well, stumbling."

I see them.

Glork dove, and Rizelya held tight onto the straps. As Glork opened his wings to land, she was already working at the buckles. Glork landed softly in front of the runner, who moved as if they were terrified beyond their endurance. Rizelya dropped off Glork before he crouched for her. Her feet thudded, kicking puffs of dust into the air, and she grunted. The person screamed and cowered on the ground, arms over their head.

The frightened bundle resolved into a young girl about ten summers old. "Shh... shh... It's all right. You're safe now." Rizelya knelt and pulled the girl to her, murmuring soothingly and lightly rubbing the girl's back. When the girl stopped shaking, Rizelya held out her water skin. "Drink slowly."

The girl nodded, gulping several mouthfuls of water.

"I'm Rizelya de Strunland. Who are you?"

The girl peered over Rizelya's shoulder, screamed, and flung herself back into Rizelya's arms.

"That's my friend, Glork. He's a Gryphon. He won't hurt you."

"They're dead, all dead!" the little girl wailed.

"No, they're not. We saw the tracks of marching people, so some of your clan has survived."

The soft thud alerted Rizelya of the other Gryphons landing, and a moment later, Blazel stepped behind her.

"It's true." Blazel hunkered on heels. "Can you tell us what happened?"

"Can you save them?"

Rizelya shook her head. "We don't have enough people with us. What's your name, little one?"

"I'm Dreana de Posanreande. I woke up, wanted a drink of water, and went into the kitchens. A loud noise shook the Keep. Lights flared and beamed from the sky. It scared me, and I hid in the pantry. A big sack of flour hid me good. I heard screaming, and I stayed where I was. After a long time, the screaming stopped, and the lights flew away. I waited and waited for the pack to find me, but they never came. When I crawled out, there were bodies everywhere, and I ran and ran. And then you found me."

"How long ago was the attack?" Blazel asked.

"Four, maybe five days ago, I think. I lost track of how long I hid."

Blazel stood, staring south toward the Barrens and the crater and digging his toe into the dirt. "Her clan will be at the crater by now. We need help to rescue them."

"They aren't the only ones." Rizelya rose to her feet, still holding Dreana in her arms. "The guard-packs are missing too."

Then let us fly. Graak snapped his beak.

Dreana cringed and held tighter to Rizelya.

"This is Graak," Rizelya said.

"He's big..." Dreana's eyes widened, and her mouth dropped open.

"Yes, he is. We aren't riding on him. We'll ride on my friend, Glork."

Glork stepped forward and bowed to them. *I am honored to carry one so brave.*

"But I wasn't brave. I hid."

You were brave to hide and survive, so you could tell us what happened. You are but a little girl and did the best you could do. Glork reached out and ran a gentle knuckle over Dreana's cheek. *There is no shame in surviving, little one. Come, I will take you away from here to where you'll be safe.*

Tears slipped down the girl's face. "Will you rescue my clan-pack?"

Glork nodded solemnly and placed a talon on his chest. *We will do our best to bring them home.*

He crouched. Rizelya settled Dreana on his back in front of her and looped the straps around them both. She squeezed his sides with her knees to let him know they were ready. His powerful hind legs bunched as he leaped into the air. Dreana's gasp floated back to her as Glork beat his wings to fly higher.

They flew back toward the plains. When the moonlight shivered off the silvery water of Storengher River, Glork descended. He touched down on the riverbank where soft grasses cushioned the ground. Graak and the other Gryphons alighted a few moments later. Blazel helped loosen the straps and lifted Dreana off Glork's back.

Rizelya scanned the group, and her forehead creased. The injured scout hadn't landed yet. "Where's Baekeek?"

He is coming. He will be here soon.

She assisted him in removing the riding harness. He sighed, dropped to the ground, rolling and moaning with pleasure. She left him there and joined Blazel and Dreana in digging a fire pit. Dreana trailed Blazel to the river's edge, where they gathered rocks. Blazel understood better than she did what it meant to be without a clan-pack. Rizelya walked along the river and found enough wood for a fire. Once the fire was lit, she put on a pot of water for taevo, dug out a travel bar, and handed it to Dreana. She munched on another one.

Graak padded to the fire and perched next to Blazel. His tail wrapped around his feet. *We shall sleep for a few hours and then fly again.*

"What about Baekeek?" Rizelya asked. "He just arrived. He won't be able to keep up with you."

No, he cannot. Only myself and Glork will go back with you. The others will follow at a pace suitable for our injured scout. Get what rest you may. He padded into the dark to rejoin his flight.

It felt like she'd just gotten to sleep when Graak prodded her awake. Rizelya groggily put the riding harness on Glork and fastened it on. Once she'd settled on Glork's back, Blazel handed her the sleeping child. The two Gryphons were larger than the other scouts, and each beat of their wings took them farther. Without the smaller Gryphons to slow them, they raced through the night.

They winged over Strunland at dawn, and homesickness rushed through Rizelya. Even though no one could see her, she waved and blew blessings to her home and clan. Would she ever get to sleep in her own bed, or laugh with her pack mates?

They stopped a few octars after passing Strunland Keep. Groaning, Rizelya climbed back on Glork. The rest stop had been too short. Dreana talked Blazel into letting her ride with him, so Rizelya leaned forward and laid on Glork's back. She watched the familiar country of her home pass beneath them. She recognized Strunlair Keep as they flew over it. Were her sister Naila and her father Histrun still there? Were her girls—the other Talents she'd added to her squad-pack—still waiting for her to return? At the thought of them, tears pricked her eyes. She missed her squad-pack, even Keandran. Where had he gone? She prayed he'd found somewhere he could finally be happy.

The landscape below her changed into mountains and forests as they passed by Strunhelos Keep and into the White Mountains. In another octar, they reached the lands surrounding the Sanctuary. The Temple's crystal dome cast rainbows in the sun. Graak landed in the inner courtyard. Rizelya loosened her stiff fingers to slide off Glork. Wisah, Chariel, and Aistrun ran out to meet them. Jaehaas followed, still limping.

It brightened Rizelya's heart for some of her squad-pack to stride at her side. Her legs were a bit wobbly and, unasked, Aistrun paced beside her, his arm around her waist, giving her support. Blazel carried the lone survivor of Posanreande Keep, her small arms wrapped tightly around his neck.

Priestesses crowded the audience chamber. Standing among them were Leistral and Eidstrun. Rizelya's forehead crinkled in confusion. She'd expected them to be at Strunlair Keep. Moraak crouched by the Supreme's throne. The tip of his tail flicked in agitation.

"What have you found out?" the Supreme demanded. She noticed the little girl, and her voice softened. "Who is this child?"

Blazel stepped forward. "This is Dreana de Posanreande. She is the only one who escaped the attack on her keep. The invaders took those they didn't kill in the fight into the Barrens, and we presume, to the crater."

The Supreme's eyes widened, and a collective gasp wove through the audience.

Rizelya leaned against her helbraught, exhausted. She stood straighter. "The guard-packs weren't in their fortresses, and the Malvers' monsters range unchecked in the Barrens."

The invaders have established a stronghold on the crater's rim, Graak added. *My scout was only able to get a quick glimpse before they attacked him, but it seems the missing guards were prisoners. A great number of Posair men worked in the crater. He did not see any women or children.*

"We saw the invader's ship," Blazel said. "It's large enough to hold thousands of people. This is unmistakably an invasion force."

The Supreme's face tightened in anger, and her fingers drummed a staccato on the arm of her throne. Her rings chiming against the crystal. "We can only pray our people have survived. It is clear the invaders are not peaceful. We must protect our people and our land. We should drive them from our home. But," she nodded toward Leistral and Eidstrun, "word has reached me that the Malvers' monsters are worse than when you first arrived here, Rizelya. Whom do we fight?"

Even though it seemed a rhetorical question, Rizelya answered. "We must fight both if we are to survive."

The Supreme wilted, her shoulders hunched. "So many will be killed."

Blazel's hands fisted at his side. "It will be worse if we don't."

Moraak heaved to his feet. *We will join you. After hearing this, I know this is the madness our mystics have warned us about.*

The color from Chariel's drained, and she trembled. "They will kill and kill until nothing remains but desolation if we don't oppose them."

"Will all of your people join the battle, Moraak?" the Supreme asked.

He shook his head. *No, only the three hundred I brought with me.*

"Then we must pray they are enough." The Supreme stood, sparks of light dancing from the rings on her hands. Her voice filled the room. "Send word to every province and clan. We are at war. With the attack on Posanreande Keep and the guard-packs at Shandir's Crater, the invaders have already declared war. We must stop them, drive them back to where they came from, or destroy them. All who can fight will be called to the Warrior's service."

War!

The word reverberated through Rizelya's mind. The last one had nearly destroyed the Posairs. What would a fight with these strange invaders do?

Epilogue

The Supreme finally sent everyone away from her audience chamber. She staggered into her apartment, reaching her bedchamber when the enormity of her decision hit her. She clung to the door frame as the tremors shook her frail body.

War! Her mind shuddered at the conflict to come. How many people would cross into the Mother's Womb as a result of her declaration? Too many.

She crossed the room and sank into the chair by the fireplace. She held her hands out to the fire, needing its warmth to chase away the chill in her bones—and in her soul.

Why did the invaders travel to their world? What could they possibly want? She considered the area where they landed. Something about Shandir's Crater drew them to the crater and her world. But the only thing inside it was malignant magic. If the kidnapping of the guard-packs and Posanreande Keep didn't prove the invader's evil intentions, their desire to make use of the malignant magic did.

Her people fought to survive against the Malvers' monsters every day. To them, it was a normal way of life. No one alive remembered a time when they didn't have to fight. But this fight would be different. This time, they battled against people not from their world. The technology—the magic—needed to fly between the stars was far beyond anything the Posairs possessed.

She considered the projectile weapon the scout described. How could her people stand a chance against something like that? She trusted the Goddess would provide a way for them to do so. Perhaps She already had by sending the prophecy to Chariel that led to reestablishing the alliance between Posair and Gryphon.

She sighed. The Gryphons far exceeded her expectations. Moraak's golden wings and fur, his size, and his intelligence awed her. During Rizelya and Blazel team's absence, she'd researched the old manuscripts. Her ancestors created the Gryphons during the Great War to fight the Malvers's creatures.

In the intervening years, the Gryphons became much more than those who had created them ever dreamed possible. She anticipated with pleasure learning about their culture. In her mind's eye, she imagined what a city full of Gryphons, swooping and diving, would look like. She experienced a moment of regret that her calling forbade her from leaving the confines of The Sanctuary.

Soon, the Supreme's eyes drooped closed from the warmth of the fire, and with her chin resting on her fist, she fell asleep. The snap of a log jerked her awake, and pain radiated down her left arm and clenched her heart.

"No, not now," she gasped as she clutched her chest.

Struggling to breathe, she fumbled in her dress pocket for the small container of pills prepared for her by her healer. Finally, she opened the tin, and with shaky hands, put one in her mouth, grimacing at the bitter taste. After a few moments, the pain loosened its grip on her heart, and she breathed more easily.

"Please, Goddess," she prayed, "help me survive to lead my people through this hardship. Let me live long enough to teach my successor all she needs to know."

Normally, before the new Supreme became too old, a new incarnation of the Goddess would be born with plenty of time to be fully trained by her predecessor. But a white-eyed child hadn't been born in the Supreme's lifetime, and she was nearing her end. The latest episode with her heart made her fearful there wouldn't be time for her to train the new Supreme.

She slowly and carefully stood and readied for bed. As she lay in the dark, her memories drifted to the vision she'd received years ago when she'd first questioned why her replacement hadn't been born yet. The Goddess had shown her that her people needed a new kind of Supreme and would arrive in a different way. She eagerly searched for the signs in every priestess she trained, but hadn't seen the woman in her vision. *Where is she?*

WHAT TO READ NEXT

Join Rizelya, Blazel, and the team as they fight the alien invasion in *The Scourge Incursion*, the next exciting exciting episode in the completed Legends of Lairheim series!

You can purchase this, and all my books, directly from me at *Shop.ToraMoon.com* or at your favorite retailer.

An alien invasion...
A desperate battle begins...
A quest for survival unfolds...

Rizelya, now a seasoned leader, commands a battalion against the alien invaders, the Scourge, who seek the nucla mineral—and slaves. But when the Scourge captures her heart-sister Kaieli, Rizelya's resolve is tested while navigating the perils of leadership and love in a world under siege.

Blazel returns to the treacherous swamps, searching for herbs to concoct a potent poison to cripple the Scourge. In his new role as the Battle Commander's second, Blazel grapples with being a leader as he and his Gryphon friend lead the charge against the alien menace.

Meanwhile, Kaieli, a gentle healer, discovers a method to purge the nucla poison from the enslaved Posair men. Teaming up with Rolstrun, a fighter who learns the true meaning of courage and love, Kaieli sparks a rebellion within the camp. Amidst the horrors of slavery, a tender love blossoms between them.

The Posairs and their Gryphon allies refuse to yield to the Scourge's subjugation and terror, valiantly fighting for freedom against the technologically superior Scourge.

Can Rizelya and Blazel lead their people to victory? Will Kaieli and Rolstrun's newfound courage be enough to turn the tide?

Rizelya and Blazel fight to save their world on the brink of annihilation. Be prepared to be captivated by this thrilling tale of bravery, cooperation, and the battle for freedom.

The Scourge Incursion is the third book in the epic science-fantasy series, Legends of Lairheim, where amidst the darkness and despair of war, hope shines and the enduring power of love and friendship triumphs.

Explore the exciting world of Lairheim today!

YOU MIGHT ALSO ENJOY...

Are you curious about how Rizelya's mother dies and Histrun's sojourn to the Sanctuary where he meets and trains the young Blazel? Read the story in the bonus prequel novel, **Redemption**.

You can purchase this, and all my books, directly from me at *Shop.ToraMoon.com* or at your favorite retailer.

A tyrant's rule...
A tragic mistake...
A journey toward redemption...

Once a revered Clan Alpha, Histrun now struggles with the relentless passage of time. Alongside his bond-mate, Zehala, he has developed a revolutionary method for battling the Malvers' monsters that is finally offering hope for the future.

The call for help from the last province to learn their technique thrusts Histrun into a confrontation with his past.

In the heart of Dehanlair, Histrun finds not just a province in peril but a leader who has forsaken his honor and embraced tyranny. As Histrun and Zehala seek to liberate the oppressed and restore order, tragedy strikes. Zehala falls in battle, leaving

Histrun consumed by grief and guilt and haunted by the what-ifs of his choices.

Broken, lost, and spiraling into despair, Histrun returns home, only to find an unexpected path to redemption—guiding a group of young priestesses-in-training to the Sanctuary. There, he crosses paths with Blazel, a boy on the brink of becoming a warrior, with no one to teach him.

Can Histrun find the peace he so desperately seeks?

Histrun must discover that redemption often doesn't lie in the past, but in the promise of the future. Be prepared to be captivated by this gripping, heartfelt tale of courage, loss, and the search for forgiveness.

Set eighteen years before the events of *Ancient Enemies*, **Redemption** is part of the *Legends of Lairheim* saga where magic and monsters collide.

For fans of epic science-fantasy, this prequel delves into the origins of the characters you've come to love and the dark secrets that shaped them.

Discover the magic of Lairheim today!

APPENDIX

The Cast

(In Alphabetical Order)

Aistrun - (Aye-strun) Co-squad-pack Alpha with Rizelya; Strunland Keep; Rizelya's squad-pack

Ambrelya - (Am-brel-ya) Red; Haasneh Keep

Beladi - (Bell-ah-de) Double Red with Yellow; Strunlair Clan Alpha

Belistril - (Bell-ih-stil) Red and Brown; Haasneh Keep Alpha

Bestrun - (Bae-strun) Strunell Keep Alpha

Blazel - (Blay-zel) Born and raised in the Sanctuary, no clan affiliation (main character)

Bohandran - (Bo-han-dran) Strunland guard pack alpha at crater

Celedon - (Cel-eh-don) Guard at the Sanctuary; Ledonlair Keep

Chariel - (Char-ee-el) Gray, also known as the Gray Oracle; The Sanctuary

Colstrun - (Coal-strun) Horse-master of Strunland guard pack at crater

Dehali - (Dee-haa-lee) Red and Yellow; Strunland Keep; Rizelya's squad-pack

Dolhaas - (Dol-haas) Haasneh Keep

Dreana - (Dray-an-a) Young girl; Posanreande Keep

Eiden - (Eye-den) Yellow, twin to Eidstrun; Strunland Keep

Eidstrun - (Eyed-strun) Strunland Keep; twin to Eiden; Rizelya's squad-pack

Faelyn - (Fae-lyn) Brown; a healer; Strunland guard-pack at crater

Gehan - (Gay-han) Yellow and Green; Strunven Keep

Grazeen - (Gray-zeen) Green and Brown; Strunven Keep

Histrun - (His-strun) Former Strunlair Clan-pack Alpha; Strunland Keep, Rizelya's father

Jaehaas - (Jay-haas) Centaur, Haasneh Keep

Kaelhaas - (Kale-haas) Haasneh Keep

Kaieli - (Kai-ee-le) Brown and Blue; Strunland Keep; heart sister to Rizelya

Kami - (Cam-ee) Yellow and Green, identical twins to Tami; Strunell Keep

Keandran - (Kae-an-dran) Originally from Andranlair, transferred to Strunlair Keep; Rizelya's squad-pack

Kelstrun - (Kel-strun) Strunland Keep Alpha

Keshanal - (Khe-shan-al) Red and Brown; Strunell Keep Alpha

Layhalya - (Lay-hall-yah) Red and Green; Strunheim Keep Alpha

Laynal - (Lay-nal) Red and Yellow; Strunheim Keep, younger sister of Laynar

Laynar - (Lay-nar) Red; Strunheim Keep, granddaughter of Layhalya

Leistral - (Lay-ee-straal) Red and Green; Strunland Keep; Rizelya's squad-pack

Lorstal - (Lore-stal) Red; pack alpha; Haasneh Keep

Maellyn - (May-lyn) Brown with Red; Strunven Keep

Maendy - (May-en-dee) Brown and Red, with some Yellow, Helstramiester; Strunven Keep

Maheli - (Ma-he-lee) Red; Strunlair guard pack alpha at crater

Naila - (Neigh-la) Red and Yellow; Strunland Keep Alpha; Rizelya's sister

Nestrun - (Nay-strun) Strunlair Clan Alpha

Oldhaas - (Old-haas) Centaur; Haasneh Keep

Raeleen - (Ray-leen) Brown with Yellow; Strunven Keep

Rizelya - (Rha-zeel-yha) Red and Brown; Strunland Keep (main character)

Rolstrun - (Rolstrun) Strunlair guard-pack at crater

Saffren - (Saff-fren) Blue with some Green; Strunven Keep

Selestrun - (Say-les-strun) Strunheim Keep Alpha

Shandir - (Shan-deer) Legendary hero from the Great War, a White Priestess; the huge crater in the south is named after her, Shandir's Crater, also called Shandir's Misery.

Tami - (Tam-ee) Yellow, identical twin to Kami; Strunell Keep

Teledon - (Tel-eh-don) Strunland Keep

Telekhaas - (Tel-ek-haas) Haasneh Keep Alpha

The Supreme - White; the Posairs' spiritual leader; The Sanctuary

Wisah - (Wee-sah) White and Grey with some Blue; The Sanctuary; Naila's daughter, Rizelya's niece

THE GRYPHONS

Baekeek - (Bea-keek) Silent Prowlers

Broogk - (Broo-gak) Wing second to Graak; Thorn Claw

Daelaak - (Day-laak) Gold Wing; the eldest son of king Zorlaak; in line to inherit the crown

Glork - (Glor-k) Brown Feathers

Graak - (Grr-aak)Flight leader; friend of Blazel's; Thorn Claw

Keeru - (Kee-ru) Thorn Claw

Moraak - (Moor-aak) Prince; Gold Wing; in line to inherit the crown

Sheekeek - (Shee-keek) Silver Beak, a mystic

Telek - (Te-lek) Thorn Claw

Zorlaak - King of the Gryphons; Gold Wing

THE HORSES

Caela - (Say-la) Leistral's mare

Chaezreen - (Chay-zreen) Chariel's mare

Gemmy - Rizelya's pack multa

Jezhan - (Jay-zhen) Aistrun's gelding

Julay - (Ju-lay) Dehali's mare

Kressy - (Kress-ee) Rizelya's multa

Kymaya - (Kai-may-ah) Rizelya's mare

Lighzel - (Lie-zel) Blazel's mare

Luchen - (Lou-chen) Eidstrun's gelding

Tejen - (Tee-jen) Wisah's stallion

THE WORLD

The main continent is called Lairheim. The Barrens is an area of desolation, with only petrified wood and sand-glass in it. It covers a hundred-mile radius from Shandir's Crater, which is in the center of the isthmus between the main continent and the sub-continent. After the Great War, travel south of the Barrens became taboo, and so no one knows what the area is like. The sub-continent is believed to be covered by one huge swamp and is located south of the Barrens.

No one sails the oceans anymore because of the sea monsters created during the Great War. There is limited travel along the coasts.

The Provinces

There are eight provinces, each divided into eight territories. Each clan takes the name of the Province.

Strunlair

Ledonlair

Andranlair

Posanlair

Haaslair

Dehanlair

Ronanlair

Keistanlair

Days and Time

Milcron - equivalent to a minute.

Octar - roughly equals an hour. There are 16 octars in a day.

Chedan - roughly a week, consisting of eight days.

Lunadar - a month consists of eight chedans, or 64 days.

A year is eight chedans, or 512 days.

Measure - term for distance, a little less than a mile (5,000 feet).

The Months

Ahdar - Month one; Spring

Neydar - Month two; Spring

Sandar - Month three; Summer

Drudar - Month four; Summer

Godar - Month five; Autumn

Rokdar - Month six; Autumn

Eyedar - Month seven; Winter

Hondar - Month eight; Winter

The Moons

Kelar - the largest moon takes 64 days for a full cycle, measurement of a month.

Zelar - the middle-sized moon takes 32 days for a full cycle.

Chelar - the smallest moon's cycle takes 8 days, measurement for chedan, or eight-days.

Magical Abilities of the Women

There are eight types of magic, called Talents, worked by the women. Men exchanged the ability to do magic (except very basic skills) for the gift of shapeshifting into their warrior form when the Malvers' monsters appeared after the Great War. Hair and eye color indicate of the type of magic the person uses. Hair color indicates the person's major Talent and the eye color their secondary Talent. The darker the hair or eye color, the more powerful in that Talent the person is. A woman with fire magic is called a Red, one with water is called a Blue, and so on. Hair color pales with age.

The Powers

Whites - have shades of white hair. Priestesses — mind and soul workers, spiritual leaders. (Unseen in men.)

Grays - have shades of gray hair. Priestesses — also mind and soul workers but they work more with the transitions of the soul. This is a rare Talent. (Unseen in men.)

Reds - have shades of red hair — the fire workers and warriors.

Yellows - have shades of blond hair — the air workers.

Blues - have shades of blue hair — the water workers.

Greens - have shades of green hair — earth workers, plants, and are healers.

Browns - shades of brown hair — earth workers, animals and minerals/metals, and are healers.

Blacks - shades of black hair (extinct) — can work all types of magic.

Gryphons

Gryphons live in flights of several generations. Most flocks can be mixed bird-type species; except the three flights a Gryphon must be born into.

The flights are:

Gold Wings (must be born into—the royal house)

Black Feathers

White Feathers

Gray Feathers

Brown Feathers

Red Feathers

Thorn Claws

Thunder Wings

Razor Beaks

Dark Talons

Silent Prowlers (must be born into—owl types)

Silver Beaks

Green Talons (must be born into—they have poison sacks on their talons)

GLOSSARY

angulete - (an-goo-le-te) a flying serpent found in the swamps, a twisted, venomous beast

baethor - (bae-thor) a predator found in the Deep Mountains

billocks - (bill-ox) a wild, large herd beast and resists domestication

brecha - (bray-cha) one of the symbiotic pair of monsters collectively called the Malvers' monsters

ducorn - (dew-corn) a type of antelope with two twisty horns

helbraught - (hell-brac-kt) the magical halberd type blades the women use to fight the monsters; the wooden staff is the height of the woman with a 16"-24" inch blade made from helstrim attached to the end

helstrablade - (hell-stra-blade) knives made from helstrim but not keyed to any type of magic

helstramiester - (hell-sta-my-ster) masters of the helstrim alloy

helstrim - (hell-strim) a special alloy that accepts and holds magic used to make helstrablades and helbraught blades

jallopitar - (ja-lop-ih-tar) a reptilian swamp predator

janack - (jan-ack) one of the symbiotic pair of monsters collectively called the Malvers' monsters

jedash - (jay-dash) a bushy plant resistant to monster toxins and cools the area around them

jelehan - (jay-lay-han) a throwing game using sticks of varying lengths with colored bands

kehani - (kay-han-ee) the flowers of the kehani tree are sacred to The Goddess and are used by the priestesses in the temples as perfume and incense

keshe - (kay-she) a strategy board game. It can be played with as few as two players or up to ten players; the more players added, the more complicated the game becomes

lengo - (len-go) a sweet-smelling herb found in the swamps; the leaves stop bleeding and the boiled roots fight infection, especially when caused by swamp creatures and Barrens dust

marsh ragtile - a fruit tree found in the swamps where there is fresh water and no malignant pools of magic are around

mookti - (mook-tee) an early ripening spring berry that is sweet, dark purple, and grows in small clusters

multa - (mul-ta) a pack animal with cloven, platter-like feet able to carry heavy loads

narhili - (nar-hee-lee) also called narhili beasts, predators that live in the swamps during the day and hunt the surrounding area at night

oyt - a nonsensical term used to activate the fire arrows

paether - (pae-ther) a canid-like predator found in the northern part of Lairheim

sabertiger - a large white and black striped feline that lives in the Deep Mountains

sheadash - (shea-dash) a type of white stone that repels and negates any malignant magic. The Malvers' monsters can't cross it and so it is used for buildings and roads

skeaeter - (skae-ter) a large insectoid carnivorous predator

snelks - (snell-ks) a grub which eats rotten matter

taevo - (tay-vo) a stimulating drink made from the leaves and berries of the taeve bush

STAY IN TOUCH!

Sign up for Tora's newsletter to keep in touch with what's happening in the world of Tora. Receive exclusive extras, news, and discounts on my books, products, and art. I have lots of ideas and always have a project—or three—in progress.

ToraMoon.com/subscribe

Also By Tora Moon

Legends of Lairheim (Epic Science-Fantasy)

Ancient Enemies (Book 1)
Ancient Allies (Book 2)
The Scourge Incursion (Book 3)
Exile's Vengeance (Book 4)
Redemption - A Novel

The Sentinel Witches (Urban Fantasy)

Crossroads to Destiny (Book 1)
Descent Into Darkness (Book 2)
Well of Sorrows (Book 3)

Indie Author Guides

Business & Accounting for Authors
Business Plans for Authors

To get an up-to-date listing of all my books or to purchase visit:
ToraMoon.com

THANK YOU!

I hope you're enjoying discovering the world of Legends of Lairheim world and Rizelya and her team's story.

If you have a moment, please help others enjoy these books too by leaving a review on the retail site where you purchased this book, review it on a blog, share it on your social media, or even just tell your friends about it.

Reviews help other readers choose what to read and authors depend on reviews to get the word out on good books. Honest reviews and genuine word-of-mouth recommendations make all the difference.

I'm not asking for one of those awful book reports we did at school. Leaving a review will only take a minute: it doesn't have to be long or involved, just a sentence or two that tells people what you liked about the book. This will help other readers know why they might like it, too, and help me write more of what you love. But please, no spoilers!

The truth is, VERY few readers leave reviews. Please help me by being the exception.

ABOUT THE AUTHOR

Tora Moon writes Goddess fantasy and science fiction, skillfully melding different sub-genres to create unique, memorable stories. Her completed series, The Legends of Lairheim, combines elements of epic, paranormal, and science fiction into a breathtaking tale of magic, courage, and the enduring power of unity.

Her series, The Sentinel Witches, blends her love of urban/magical realism, mythology, and portal fantasy—and skates close to the edge of thriller and horror. Throughout all her works, you will find Tora's love of Goddess mythology as she weaves aspects of these into her stories.

As Tora-Iresh'nai Moon, she writes about Goddess Spirituality and shares her nearly fifty years of experience of connecting with the Goddess and the Feminine Divine.

Tora is also an artist who explores drawing and watercolor painting. Her current passion is creating and coloring mandalas inspired by the Goddess. Tora also expresses her creativity through various handcrafts.

You can find out more about Tora, her books, and her art at: ToraMoon.com

www.ingramcontent.com/pod-product-compliance
Lightning Source LLC
Chambersburg PA
CBHW061100190726
48286CB00006B/1824